THE CHANGING

There was a flurry of motion as the air itself charged, became primal, violent, laced with heat and hate and death. Vic whirled, his face going liquid and distorting, eyes burning and his lips peeling back to reveal teeth, teeth like ivory daggers that seemed to multiply in the space of an eyeblink to fill jaws suddenly too huge to believe, jaws that stretched and sprouted from a face no longer human.

Syd stumbled back in shock as something inside shrieked and shriveled, deserting him. His boot heels skidded on the loose-packed gravel, sent him tumbling back to land flat-assed on the ground. He heard Nora scream his name, smelled his death hurtling toward him, felt his eyes roll back in abject dread as the jaws clacked shut less than an inch from his face. . . .

ANIMALS

John Skipp &
Craig Spector

BANTAM BOOKS
NEW YORK TORONTO LONDON SYDNEY AUCKLAND

ANIMALS
A Bantam Book / November 1993

*Grateful acknowledgment is made for permission to reprint lyrics from
the following:*

*"EVERY NIGHT ABOUT THIS TIME" by Antoine Domino.
Copyright © 1957 Renewed 1985 c/o EMI UNART CATALOG INC.
World Print Rights Controlled and Administered by
CPP/BELWIN, INC., P.O. BOX 4340, Miami, FL 33104.
All Rights Reserved.*

*"THE DARK END OF THE STREET" by Dan Penn and
Chips Moman. © 1967 SCREEN GEMS-EMI MUSIC INC.
All Rights Reserved. International Copyright Secured.
Used by Permission.*

*"PRECIOUS PAIN" Lyrics and Music by Melissa Etheridge.
© 1987 ALMO MUSIC CORP. & MLE MUSIC (ASCAP).
All Rights Reserved. International Copyright Secured.*

ISBN 0-553-29924-7

Published simultaneously in the United States and Canada

*Bantam Books are published by Bantam Books, a division of Bantam
Doubleday Dell Publishing Group, Inc. Its trademark, consisting of the
words "Bantam Books" and the portrayal of a rooster, is Registered in
U.S. Patent and Trademark Office and In other countries. Marca Reg-
istrada. Bantam Books, 1540 Broadway, New York, New York 10036.*

PRINTED IN THE UNITED STATES OF AMERICA

RAD 0 9 8 7 6 5 4 3 2 1

For Buddy, Holly, & Damien
with love,
and thanks

ACKNOWLEDGMENTS

Vast thanks to Richard Monaco, Adele Leone, and all the folks at Acton, Dystel, Leone, & Jaffe; to Lou Aronica, Janna Silverstein, and the whole crew at Bantam; to Sandy Weinberg and Innovative Artists, Inc.; to Mike Figgis, Frank Mancuso, Jr., Josie Rosen and Gary Foster, and Annie Stewart. For keeping the wheels turning.

Love and gratitude to Matt & Alli Jorgensen; to Buddy, Holly, & Damien Martinez, and Jean Frost; to Christa Faust, for the keen eye and fearless feedback; to Richard Christian Matheson & Marie Thoin, Richard & Tara Sutphen, Jim (& Buddy!), and the Malibu Mafia; to Adam & Leslie, Linda & Kaz, Dori Miller (Yo, babe!), Gary Z., Cathy & Jesus, Cryttre, Fleener, *La Luz de Jesus*, and the greater comix underground; to Mark Williams for the cool werewolf designs; to John Vullich, Uncle Pat, Charlie, Gram, Carlo, Chris, Kathe K., Diana, Steve & Miran, Dino, Brian Emrich, Scott Wolfman & Wolfman Productions, Mary & Steve, Ervin & Elizabeth, Jim & Lois, Carl & Diane, Mike Baker, Rikki Rocket, Robert Pineda, Mike Queen, Hillbilly, Beth Gwinn, Ed Kramer, Dr. Timothy Leary, the Atlanta Center for Puppetry Arts, Craig Goden, and the World Horror Convention. And three cheers for the amazing Judy Henkel, who proved you can come back from *anything*, if your heart is strong.

Skipp would like to extend a special *thank you* and *I'm sorry* to the brilliant, breathtaking PZB. *Whatever words I say. . . .* He would also like to send great love, thanks, and apologies to Marianne, the magnificent queen of the M tribe; a great humanitarian, and a personal friend o' mine. Thanks, Mel! Thanks, Mike! Thanks, Mom!!! I owe you all the deepest debt, and the most heartfelt acknowledgment.

Craig sends thanks, and love, to Lisa W. You know why.

PART ONE

Nora

November

1

THERE WAS SOMETHING large and wet and dead in the middle of the road.

"Damn," Syd muttered, easing up on the gas, slowing to a 35-m.p.h. crawl. He just thanked God he had the road to himself, no hellbent crystal meth-crazed eighteen-wheelers on his tail. There wasn't much reaction time, coming around the bend at highway speed. Most animals learned the hard way, and this one had been no exception.

From seven yards away and closing, he tried to identify the remains. They glistened in the wash of his head-lights, mashed and splayed across the center line of the curving mountain pass. A good-sized deer? A very large dog? It was impossible to say.

He'd gotten pretty good, over the years, at playing "Name That Roadkill"; you learned to check for size and coloration, the shape of the head and tail. But the head appeared to be gone entirely, and there was nothing in the mangled mass that vaguely resembled a tail. The big rigs that rumbled through these hills at night had really out-done themselves this time, he mused. By the first light of

dawn, there was nothing left for him to go on. Just a big
fur-covered speed bump, stuffed with mashed animal pâté.

Syd grimaced, swerving mostly out of deference to the
deceased. Driving over roadkill was a little too much like
dancing on a grave. Not for the first time, he wondered
just what in the hell that thing could have been *thinking:*
what force or impulse drove it from the sanctuary of the
woods, to such a stupid and ignominious end?

His tires bit on the gravel on the narrow shoulder, and
then it was behind him, leaving Syd once again alone with
his thoughts and the slow unwind of the Mt. Haversford
Road. Soft and lonely blues on the '67 Mustang's Hitachi
stereo. Pale blue-white Camel smoke, unfiltered, curling
around the dust motes in the air. It was just another blue-
gray five forty-five in the ayem, cruising the two-lane
blacktop ribbon that gift-wrapped this stiff-backed Pennsylvania ridge, the faint thrum of a hangover dulling his
customary appreciation of the valley below.

Heat blasted out from the defroster vents; it wasn't
quite enough. These days, Syd wore a battered flight
jacket and long johns to help ward off the creeping autumn
chill. His thick dark hair was tousled, his strong, ruddy
face unshaven. He had a sleep potato nestled in the corner
of one eye, and a coffee mug wedged between his blue-
jeaned thighs. The cup said SHIT HAPPENS. He suspected
poor Bambi—or Fido, or whatever—would concur.

He had no problem with the drive itself, forty-five
minutes of clear sailing through familiar countryside. He
loved these woods, these lonely roads, this panoramic
overview. It was dragging his ass out of bed every morning that was starting to pose some difficulties for him.

Ah, life, as his pal Jules liked to say. How it do go on.

Syd felt his emotional index take a dip toward depression. "Nuh-uh," he mumbled. "Not today." He leaned forward to crank up the tunes. Queen Bee's cover of "Every
Night, About This Time" filled the car: a deep, rich, dark
chocolate voice from heaven. Her band would be playing
at Chameleon's tonight. It gave him the strength to go on.

Syd Jarrett was thirty-four years old—would be thirty-five, in less than a week—but the discontent was nothing new. He'd been born with an itch at the back of his brain that he'd never quite figured out just how to scratch. Not that he hadn't experimented around some. In fact, it was kind of a lifelong pursuit.

He remembered first cruising these same back roads as a sixteen-year-old, downing quarts of National Bohemian in the back of Jim Ilgenfritz's Pinto wagon with about eight other guys. You could barely get the bottle up to your lips in the sea of other people's lit cigarettes, bottles, faces, elbows, sweaty armpits, and backs. It was like some bizarre frathouse shenanigan—one of those old-fashioned collegiate phone booths, stuffed with old-fashioned drunken collegiate assholes—only underage, undereducated, and set on burnin' wheels. A movable feast of fragrant, jostling, bellowing buffoons.

When Fritz brought the Pinto to Dead Man's Curve at a rattling, shimmying ninety per, what with everybody screaming, that would almost scratch the itch.

But all those great teenage excuses dried up with the end of his j.d. status, and 1975 marked his personal watershed point. That was the year Marc Pankowski sent poor sweet Kimberly Myers face-first through his windshield, just three days before their graduation. From that point on, teenage drinking and driving became something of a local community crusade ... years before the advent of organizations like M.A.D.D. turned it into a national craze.

That summer was Syd's first experience with random checkpoints, spot searches, and mandatory curfews. He discovered very quickly that it was hard to scratch the itch when you were handcuffed in the backseat of a police cruiser.

(He remembered, also, the first time his old man had to come to pick him up at the township station. Chief Hoser had been frying Syd's ass for the last two hours over half an ounce of Mexican and a bottle of Bali Hai: without a doubt the worst wine in human history, the Hawaiian Punch of intoxicants. The cold blue-gray of his father's eyes had notched him like steel in that moment.

Marked him for life. "Get ready for a world of shit," his old man had said. And then taken him home . . .)

Syd sighed. That was almost half his life ago. Which, when he stopped to think about it, really kinda sucked. He didn't think he looked that old—he sure as hell didn't *feel* that old—and hoped to God he never would.

But, damn, did he ever feel tired sometimes.

As in, maybe, *tired of being alone. . . .*

And that, of course, made him think about Karen, which was no way at all to start your day. Just the thought of her now had the magic power to vacuum-pack every last speck of his joy. Like striking a match in deepest space, or picking a freshly crusted scab. Her effect on him was instantaneous. All he had to do was imagine her face.

Not that he felt the need to flagellate himself, whip up a little pity party of one. He'd had a year, since the breakup, to acquire some perspective. In his more depressive moments—which he'd learned to cope with pretty well, though they still came around with oppressive frequency—well, *sure:* it seemed like everything Syd had ever wanted out of life, or ever tried to hang on to, was either mortally wounded or already dead; and, *yeah,* now that you mentioned it, everything he'd hoped to maybe *change* in this life was hanging on emphatically, determined to outlast him. No matter how badly he wanted it.

No matter how hard he tried.

He had failed to hold his marriage together. He had failed to stave off financial disaster. Despite his deep and abiding love of music, he would never have a singing voice to rival *Jim Nabors,* much less Cab Calloway, or even Root Boy Slim. And he couldn't get out of—nor do anything to save—this nearly dead and clearly decomposing one-horse town.

Not to mention the fact that he wasn't getting any younger.

And that he was so awfully goddamned tired of being alone. . . .

"Whoa!" He caught himself, psychically teetering at the brink. "No no no *no!*" If he let himself go, it was a

long way down; that much, he knew from painful experience. The steep cliff to his right, overlooking the valley, wasn't any more precarious for all its physicality. At least it came with its own guardrail.

Depression didn't have one; and what was even *scarier,* depression came on like your best drinkin' buddy and oldest, dearest friend—the only one who *really knew you,* would tell you the honest truth about yourself. Indeed, whenever Syd got the urge to anthropomorphize, for clarity's sake, he always pictured the character of Depression as his ol' pal: the legendary Marc Pankowski.

In high school, Marc had been Mr. Popularity: handsome, glib, and well-to-do. His folks, in fact, were incredibly well-heeled: their fortunes built well before their time, in the steel industry's historical heyday. If Marc had any real disadvantages, they would have been his height (five-one), his laziness (in the upper percentiles), and his underlying conviction that other people were just plain inferior (which rated somewhere completely off the scale).

But nobody seemed to sweat much over those little details. Somehow, he always managed to swing passing grades. And making friends had never been a real problem. He had, after all, so much to offer.

So by his junior year, Marc had pretty much decided that he didn't actually *need* a personality anymore. He had a real DeLorean—fresh off the assembly line, before the cocaine scandal—to go with his brand-new driver's license. He also, ironically, had cultivated a real taste for coke and other extravagant drugs, so he always kept plenty on hand. All of which virtually guaranteed him not only a date on Saturday night, but a passel of big guys to back him up when his mouth got him in trouble.

Which began to happen with increasing frequency, yielding increasingly unpleasant results. Because the fact was that Marc's personality hadn't so much vanished as *atrophied.* It hadn't gone away. It had just gone bad.

As the sincerity vanished from his remaining social graces—and as the stories of his behavior began to spread—the nature of his popularity changed as well. Peo-

ple getting date-raped or beaten up at parties didn't sit real
well with a lot of his peer group. And the fact that he
never got nailed for any of it only heaped injustice on the
growing pile of resentment that many were feeling toward
him.

When Marc totaled his DeLorean late one night, he
had three of his buddies along for the ride. All three ended
up in the emergency room at Montgomery Hospital, although only one, Baxter Calley, actually made it onto the
critical list. Baxter had been a pretty okay fellow, when he
wasn't so coked he could barely speak; but the fucked-up,
goggle-eyed brain damage case that crutched home to the
Calley clan five months later had more stitches in him
than a major league baseball. And the headaches that came
with that plate in his head made his new personality somewhat less than okay.

Marc, of course, emerged from the wreckage utterly
unscathed. A couple of scratches. That was it. And with
his family keeping any whiff of scandal out of the papers,
it was almost as if the whole thing had never happened.

Except for the fact that *everyone knew:* at least everyone in school, and that was more than enough. The worm
had turned, as did most of his friends, including the tough
guys who had paid out his slack in the past. Suddenly,
Marc was one majorly ostracized, roundly vilified, *extremely unpopular* little high school student.

Enter poor sweet Kimberly Myers.

Nobody knew exactly what he'd said to her, or what
secret resources of guile and persuasion he'd employed on
his own behalf. But within the month, Marc Pankowski
had scored perhaps the most impressive young slice of
womanhood in the entire senior class. Kimberly wasn't the
class valedictorian, or the head of the cheerleading squad;
but she was both athletic and cerebral—was, in fact, both
a cheerleader and an honor student—in addition to being
friendly, cheerful, thrifty, brave, and genuinely drop dead
gorgeous. Syd himself had almost gone out with her
once—which was to say, he'd almost mustered up the

nerve to even ask her—and he didn't know a single guy who didn't have at least a king-sized crush on that girl.

Now, seemingly overnight, Kim Myers had become the official spokesperson for Marc Pankowski. He was totally, tragically misunderstood, she told everyone who would listen. Since the accident, he had really changed. He was *so sorry* about what had happened. And all he wanted was a chance to prove that he was really a decent person underneath.

That he was—ultimately—a victim, too.

In lesser hands, the story would have sunk like a stone. But Kimberly had the courage of her convictions. She'd fallen in love with him, after all; and she certainly was no fool. So public opinion was begrudgingly swayed; and Marc, for his part, played the role of the sad-eyed penitent for all it was worth.

That lasted for about a month. By that time, the public relations battle had been won; and with Kim still vouching for him, his old slack was back as well. It didn't take long to restore the same uneasy balance he'd held before: buying allegiance with good drugs and money, fooling most of the people at least part of the time.

Right up until that fateful night—three days before graduation—when Marc missed a critical curve on Route 79 and spun his brand-new Trans Am into a violent three-sixty, which terminated abruptly upon slamming into a utility pole at almost seventy miles per hour.

Once again, there'd been three other passengers.

Once again, Marc got away clean: a couple of bruises, a broken rib.

But this time, poor sweet Kimberly Myers had been keeping the death seat nice and warm. And when her face had exploded through the Trans Am's windshield—launching a hailstorm of glistening, red-tinged safety glass cubes and white, jagged bone—there were not enough sutures and skull-plates in the world to put it all back together.

This time, his parents couldn't keep it out of the papers. And this time, there was no one left to argue his

case. In the resulting typhoon of negative publicity, Marc
Pankowski learned what it was like for a man to be de-
spised in his own lifetime. On top of that, he was essentially disowned: cut off with nothing but a pittance, and no
real hope of coming back.

But that was not the worst of it.

The worst of it was this:

Marc Pankowski was *still around*. Not dead. Not missing. Not halfway around the world, bravely trying to start
his life over again. Sure, he'd tried to leave once, heading
out for Colorado with some vague idea of "getting into
massage"; but the sheer gravitational pull of his crime had
him back in town in less than a fortnight.

He hung out at Chameleon's now, at least three nights
a week, nodding his head in time to the music and
scrounging up drinks as best he could. His once-handsome
features were the worse for the wear, done in by hair loss,
drug use, and soul-rot. His face had grown longer, his dark
eyes more beady. All those little yellow teeth had just
completed the effect.

Syd had seen it a million times. To paraphrase ol'
Honest Abe, the Great Emancipator: once a man reaches
thirty-five, he's responsible for all of the lines on his face.
As the layers of youthful resiliency and innocence got
worn away by Time, the outer face was slowly carved into
an image that mirrored the inner life.

The older Marc got, the more he looked like a weasel.

Living proof, to Syd, that there was indeed a God.

And every so often, if you hung out in bars as much
as Syd did, Marc would try to come up and talk to you.
But only—and this was the key point—if he saw that you
were down. Like a moth to the flame of sorrow, like a bat
in a lightless cave, he could single you out from across the
room. He was tuned to the frequency.

First, he'd happen to pass you, on his way to the bathroom, and he'd ask you how you were doing. If that went
over—if you gave him anything more than an absent wave
that distinctly said *leave me alone*—he would seize the opportunity to lever a way in. His favorite jimmy was the

phrase "I know what you mean." It was a multipurpose tool.

If you said, for example, "fine"—nothing else; no "thanks" or "how 'bout yourself?"; simply "fine"—but there was the tiniest trace of sadness, or courage, or mock cheerfulness somewhere buried in your tone, Marc would stop for a second. Cock his head knowingly. Then look straight into your eyes and say, "I know what you mean."

On the way back from the bathroom, he would smile as he passed your table. That would sort of guarantee that you'd continue to be aware of him. When he got to his seat, he would look at you, to make sure that you knew where he was sitting. If you were looking, he'd nod and smile. If you weren't, he'd bide his time.

About fifteen to twenty minutes later, Marc would swing by your table again. This time, he'd employ the ever-popular "Band Gambit": a time-tested conversational ploy. If it looked like you were into the music, he'd say, "Band's really smokin' tonight!" If it looked like you really *weren't* into the music, he'd say, "Band really sucks!" If you took the bait, he was in. All he needed was one little opening.

If that didn't work, on his way *back* from the bathroom, he would ask you if you needed something from the bar. He was on his way there anyway, it wasn't a problem. Again, he would nail you with that understanding look.

And suddenly you'd realize, once and for all, that this guy was *attuned to your unhappiness*. He knew what it was like. And he was only trying to help, to help you through it, whatever gets you thru the night.

And at that point, it would dawn on you that THIS MIGHT JUST BE THE GUY to commiserate with on the nature of your immediate personal pain.

This was Marc Pankowski's hope.

It was, in fact, his one last driving ambition.

Because Marc was a psychic scavenger, and he fed off your despair. He could only get close to you when you were weak; and so he would encourage that weakness, urging you to open yourself to him under the guise of

warm supportiveness. In the process, he would naturally
pick up the first round; and if you were buying, he'd be
happy to drink with you all night. Urging you to get it all
off your chest. Unload all your secret desires and shames.
Unburden yourself of the pain of aloneness.

I know exactly what you mean.

And if you let him follow you home, either to crash on
your couch or to sleep in your bed—a mistake more than
one lonely woman had made—he would be there the next
day. And the day after that. He would hang around as long
as you let him, drop in when you least expected, call you
at work, wake you up at night, sit behind you at the movies and corral you in the bar until you finally just told him
to *GET THE FUCK OUT OF YOUR LIFE.* . . .

To Syd, depression was an awful lot like that.

There was a gust of frigid wind. It buffeted the car, bit
through the cracked window vent, sliced through the heat
blasting from his defrosters. Syd realized that he'd been
driving on automatic pilot for God only knew how long,
letting his mind wander while his body drove to work.

He checked his speed. It had dipped down to forty.

He looked at his watch. Five fifty-five.

Shit.

The road ahead curved down and to the right, as the
steep ravines gave way to a thickly wooded descent. It was
the homestretch: punch it a little, and he might still have
a job when he got there. He downshifted and pressed on
the gas, heading into the curve . . .

. . . and that was when the doe appeared, in a blur of
frenzied motion: haunches dark and glistening, eyes wild
as it closed on the side of the road. For one panicked, frozen moment, it balked at the sight of the Mustang. Syd's
foot instinctively jumped from the gas to the brakes.

Then he thought he saw something else emerge from
the woods, something huge, and the deer darted desperately into the road. Syd's heart ballooned. He tried to
swerve clear. The doe went *wump* against the passenger
side, then off. Syd ratcheted the wheel, staring into the
rearview mirror, swinging wide as he rounded the curve.

And right into the path of an oncoming truck.

"SHIT!" he barked, knuckles white against the wheel. The truck was an ancient flatbed, twenty feet away and closing on the steep upgrade. He slammed on the brakes and countersteered, seesawing the wheel to the right. *Ten feet.* The car started to fishtail. *Five feet.* His heart constricted like piano wire. And there was no time.

Four. As he veered toward the shoulder.

Three. And the guardrail loomed huge in his eyes.

Two. As his life whipped like flash cards before him.

One . . .

. . . and it was amazing, how time opened up in those very last seconds. A terrible slow-motion crawl. The old man, behind the wheel of the truck, eyes bulging in terror beneath his faded Steelers cap. Syd's own last desperate, inarticulate howl.

The truck, grinding inexorably forward . . .

. . . and then time snapped back to normal with a squealing of tires, a shower of gravel, and a great cloud of dust. Syd piloted blind for a second before bringing the Mustang to a final, grinding halt on the shoulder of the road. Inches from the guardrail, and a long hard drop.

For a minute, he just sat there, still gripping the wheel: listening to his blood pounding huge in his temples, feeling the slam of his adrenalated heart. It was a seismic sensation, like an earthquake in his chest. It hurt like a bastard, yes.

But it meant that he was still alive.

Syd threw off the seat belt, legs wobbling as he hauled himself out of the car. The truck, of course, kept right on going. Cocksucker. The coffee mug had gone flying, soaking his pants from crotch to knee and making it look like he'd peed himself. SHIT HAPPENS. That was for goddam sure.

He found himself taking a deep, halting breath, and thanked his lucky stars for the ongoing privilege.

Then he went around to the passenger side.

And got his first look at all that blood.

It started as just a little splash on the right headlight,

ballooned into a football-sized splotch on the right front
quarterpanel that gave way to a runny red smear, sliding
back across the door and away. Like an absentminded
brush stroke, or a guilt-ridden finger, pointing back at his
inadvertent handiwork.

"Oh, shit," Syd groaned. He squinted down the length
of the road and spotted it: a russet-colored heap, half-
obscured by underbrush, some thirty yards back on the flip
side of the guardrail and fifteen feet below, where the
ground sloped down to the edge of the woods. It looked
like it might be twitching a little; but between the dim
light and the distance, it was hard to be sure.

Oh, man, it's all messed up, the voice of his conscience
informed him. Judging solely by the damage to the car—a
little concave ding, at the heart of the splotch—it looked
like he had only clipped it.

But that didn't begin to explain all the blood.

When it kicked again, clearly this time, Syd knew that
he had no choice. He took a deep breath and rubbed his
eyes. His hangover throbbed behind them, dull counterpoint to the queasy oil slick in his innards. He didn't want
to do this. That wasn't the point.

Wearily, his pants legs sticking, he went back around
the front of the car, leaned in the driver's side, turned off
the engine and removed the keys. Suddenly, it was incredibly quiet. Just the jingling of the keys, the rustling of his
clothes. Off to the right, something moved very quickly
past. He looked up, saw nothing. A bird flew by. He took
the keys, still jingling, around to the back of the car and
opened the trunk, rooting around in the junk and clutter inside until his hand closed on unforgiving metal.

Then he took the tire iron, slammed the trunk shut, and
walked slowly back in the direction of the deer.

The morning breeze was chill and steady. He found it
strangely bracing. He was sweating under his thermals,
hadn't realized how much. His coffee-soaked pants were
both sticky and freezing. He tried not to think about it. As
he walked, he tried to remain focused on his stride, the
loose swing of his arms. He tried to keep his breathing

deep and even, threw his shoulders back to keep them
from tensing up around him. There were a lot of things he
didn't need to think about right now, little voices he could
not afford to let in. *But it's not my fault. But I'll be late for
work. But I didn't mean to do it.* They were chickenshit ra-
tionalizations, little Marc Pankowskis of the mind. They
were the last thing in the fucking world he needed to hear
right now.

The sun had climbed the rim of the mountain, slowly
burning off the fog as it peeled back the shadows. He took
a deep breath, exhaled slowly as he walked. The tire iron
was ice-cold and heavy in his hand. He switched it from
right to left, flexed and unflexed his stiffening fingers. The
undergrowth had grown more dense on the other side of
the guardrail. He tried to peer through it, get a glimpse of
the deer. He couldn't. Weird. He looked harder, uneasy
now, scanning for chinks in the foliage as he continued.
The deer had been laying very close to here, he knew. It
had to be right around here somewhere.

Then he saw the blood on the rail, another delicate
brush stroke of gore, a little red arrow pointing into the
thicket. He looked back over his shoulder at the empty
road. His car looked very small, and very far away. *You
don't have to do this,* said a voice in his head, as if it had
the power to absolve him.

He went over the rail, started down the steep ten-foot
embankment. The road disappeared above his head. He
skidded on his heels down the loose, rocky incline, braced
himself once with his free right hand, lost a little skin on
the heel of his palm. The undergrowth rose to meet him.
He parted it with his feet, slid farther, briefly touched off
an evergreen sapling with his left hand, the tire iron, continued to slide. Beyond the first wave of foliage, the slope
continued at a less harsh angle, carpeted in dry grass
maybe two inches tall. It felt crisp in the cold, crunching
as it buckled under the soles of his boots.

The mist was thicker down here, opaque pockets of
blue-gray shadow as yet untouched by the sun. The woods
began less than ten feet beyond. Gray light penetrated its

first line of defense in patches, was swallowed by darkness. He got his footing, took two rapid steps forward, stopped dead. Sucked his breath in sharply.

The deer was gone.

Syd exhaled, inhaled again. The deer was gone. He blinked. It didn't change a thing. Blood, a large quantity of it, lay pooled and soaking into the pine needles that carpeted the frozen ground. Syd hunkered down beside it. A few tufts of amber fur were stuck wanly to its surface.

"Oh, man . . ." His left hand throbbed. He stood, transferred the tire iron back to his right. A thick dark smear led into the trees. And the grass was bowed. As if it had crawled, or dragged itself off.

You know you don't have to do this.

He stood there, flexing and unflexing the fingers of his left hand. Trying to get sensation back. Reminding himself to breathe. *Look at all that blood. It's going to die. You're late for work. Get out of here.* Deep breaths. Steady. Counterbalancing the urge to hyperventilate, give panic an inroad. No fucking way. He tried to imagine how much this animal was suffering, took it as far as he had to. His stomach boiled and his throat constricted.

He followed the dark trail to the lip of the woods, paused, and peered inside. "Jesus," he hissed. He couldn't see anything. Faint outlines in black. The woods were filled with tiny sounds, the whistle of the wind. He took one hesitant step forward, stepped on a branch. It snapped, and his flesh constricted. His hairs prickled, stood on end. The tire iron came up, ready.

"Jesus!" There was nothing there. At least not anything he could see. He was starting to feel like an asshole in a horror movie, the kind of guy who was so stupid you just couldn't wait for the monster to kill him. The kind of guy who said shit like *I know, let's split up,* or *everybody knows there's no such thing as AIEEEE . . . !!!,* as the monster went *chomp* on their head or gizzard and everybody cheered. Like that girl in *The Evil Dead* who conveniently stripped down to her underwear before going outside to investigate those funny noises in the woods.

"Is there anybody out there?" she kept asking, over and over, till you wanted to stand up and yell at the screen, "WELL, THE NAME OF THE MOVIE IS *THE EVIL DEAD,* HONEY! WHO THE FUCK DO YOU *THINK* IS OUT THERE . . . ?"

But it was crazy to think like that, in real-life terms. He wasn't at the goddam drive-in. Syd had spent a lot of time in these woods, and as a rule, he didn't spook easily. He knew there was nothing much left in this region to be afraid of, unless you had some kind of pathological aversion to rabbits or squirrels. Just about everything that might be judged harmful to man had long since been domesticated, driven off, or destroyed.

But here he was, exactly one footstep into the woods, unsure of exactly how long he'd been standing there. Spacing out, like an asshole, with a tire iron in his hand. He found that his eyes were adjusting to the dark. He took a deep breath, unhunched his aching shoulders, took another step forward.

His foot hit something. Something moist yet solid. He stopped, looked down. Just off to the side of the trail of gore was a glistening purse-shaped mass. He touched it again with his toe, and then the wind blew the smell his way.

Suddenly, he found that he could see very well in the dark. He could see the large severed gastric organ at his feet. He could see where the trail of blackness led, and what lay at the end of it.

Suddenly, he understood why animals tried to escape the woods at night.

Twenty feet into the woods, maybe less, the carcass of the deer was splayed open, belly wet and steaming in the chill morning breeze. All of its innermost secrets lay exposed, gleaming faintly in the gray morning light. Its flanks were lacerated horribly: long razored gashes in the soft matted fur. Its eyes were blank, glazed and emptied of spark. Its tongue protruded, pinkish-gray and pallid.

But that was not the worst.

The doe's corpse rocked gently back and forth, spindly

limbs stiffly pawing the air, puppeteered in death by the great creature that now fed upon it. Long snout burrowed in the soft belly organs. Eyes closed. Ears pinned back in pleasure. Almost as though they were lovers, locked in a slow dance both intimate and timeless. Giver and receiver. Predator and prey.

There was a terrible beauty in the horror of the moment that transcended his ability to tabulate it rationally. He stared, frozen, so close he could almost taste the meat from its scent in the air.

"Oh my god," he whispered, and the wolf raised its head.

Opened its eyes.

Staring right at him.

And he didn't know if it was a trick of the light, but the face of the creature seemed to *shift:* long lupine features contracting, pulling in for a second, then spreading back out, dark fur rippling across its surface. He caught a glimmer of ivory fangs and bloodied saliva, as the lips peeled back.

But it was the force of the eyes that held him. The eyes remained unchanged. He could feel them bore into him, even through the darkness. It was that one elastic moment of truth, when a dog decides whether it smells fear on you. Whether or not to bite.

And Syd knew, in that moment, that he would not, *could* not allow himself to be afraid.

The thought was an epiphany. *I am not afraid.* He gripped the bar, still locked in his combat stance. *I am not afraid.* A little voice in his head, a distant fold in his brain, informed him that the idea of actually using it was laughable, like trying to stop a panzer tank with a toothpick. The wolf could take his arm off before he even got a chance to swing.

It didn't matter. *I am not afraid.* If death was a foregone conclusion, then fine. He accepted his death. The abandon of the damned. He accepted the fact that he was poised, now, in the heat of a lethal duet; and that, if it came, he would meet the wolf's attack.

Only the wolf was not attacking.

Just watching him.

Very closely.

And he realized that something was happening here: some kind of primal contact measured in milliseconds, in heartbeats and body English. It was imperative to make exactly the right move: no more, no less. *Show no threat. Show no fear.*

Slowly, slowly, he lowered the bar, relaxing his grip. Never changing his expression. Never taking his eyes off the beast. Not blinking. Not breathing. For one long moment's silence, nothing happened. Yes. "It's okay . . ." he began.

And suddenly stopped.

The wolf rose—slow as a striptease, gradually revealing to him its full height—and Syd felt a rush of perfect terror course through him: closing his throat, sucking the air from his lungs, undeniable and utterly outside of his control. Its eyes, when it stood, were almost level with his chest. Its body extended back into the darkness. He could not see its end.

But he could see every drop on its blood-flecked snout in astonishing detail, could hear the thunder in its lungs and smell its feral breath. For one terrible instant, the death he smelled was indistinguishable from his own.

I am not afraid, he told himself, and tried to make it true.

The wolf's eyes locked on his arm, waiting. He did not move. I am not afraid. Then it tilted its head, brought its gaze back to his, regarding him in that moment with a curious and disarmingly canine manner. I am I am. Its ears twitched, registering every molecular change in the air between them. Not afraid. And suddenly it was true.

He looked in its eyes. The wolf looked back.

For one moment, it was as if they shared a perfect understanding.

Slowly, then, it lowered its head—eyes still glued to his own—and let its jaws open wide, biting down on the breastbone of the slaughtered deer. Its jaws were enormous. Syd could hear the soft clack of teeth and wet bone.

The carcass came up in the wolf's maw easily, head lolling on its gracile neck. A moist, slender loop of intestine unfurled, dropped four feet, and dangled from the open belly. It dragged and was sullied on the bloodstained ground as the beast turned at last, heading back into the woods and the deeper darkness. Disappearing first in stages, behind the trees, then altogether. Without a trace.

Without a sound.

Leaving Syd Jarrett alone, once again, with his thoughts. Only no thoughts were forthcoming. Just the icy whisper of the wind through the trees. Just the sound of his own ragged, thunderous heart. Another sound: rising, like castanets. His own teeth, chattering. Jesus Christ. He had broken out in a full-body sweat, pasting his thermals to his skin. But the pounding in his head had mercifully vanished.

Get back to the car, the voice of reason told him, *before you freeze to death.* Good plan. His legs were shaky as he turned and started up the hill.

It took no more than a minute to climb the embankment, heading back to the road, and his car, and the world. It was all right there, where he had left it. Almost as if he had never been gone.

He wondered, picking up his pace as he walked the narrow shoulder, if any of it had been changed, or if it was him. He wondered what the upholstery would feel like. The grip of his steering wheel. The sound of the blues.

A truck rolled past, on the downhill side. He was buffeted by its shockwave, swayed slightly in its wake. He watched it rumble around the bend, then gone. A bird flew by. A sparrow this time. It had not flown south, for whatever reason. It would die if it didn't.

He wondered how he felt about that perfect understanding.

He wondered if any of it would ever feel the same again.

2

THE MEMORY OF the wolf still continued to haunt him as Syd wheeled into the hulking expanse of the Monville Mill Works: a sprawling, sagging jumble of dead furnaces and lifeless smokestacks hugging a mile-long stretch of the Monongahela River.

Once upon a time, the lifeblood of an industry coursed through there, etched in soot and sweat and molten metal. Furnaces roared twenty-four hours a day: gobbling iron ore, coke, and coal, and spewing out an endless stream of plates, pipes, and ingots to feed the world's seemingly insatiable need for steel. Some fifty thousand people had worked in the mills that lined the river, three times that many in the communities that surrounded and supplied them.

Syd had gotten his first job there in '80. The reasons seemed sound enough at the time. High pay. Benefits out the wazoo. Ironclad job security, once you got some seniority under your belt. Hell, except for the strikes, you were practically bullet-proof.

Once upon a time, that had actually been true. But for guys like Syd, it was like they'd bought into the myth just

in time to watch it belly-up and go under: jerked off by
wage cuts and givebacks and concessions, followed by
layoffs and closings and staggering unemployment.
Monville was a ghost town now: from a onetime work
force of over six thousand, less than two hundred were
scattered across its length and breadth, most of them engaged in the process of cannibalizing the great industrial
corpse.

Syd passed through the deserted Braddock St. gate,
dodging long-neglected potholes as he pulled in next to
Tommy Kramer's mud-spattered Chevy 4x4. Tommy and
Budd Ruhr were huddled in the cab, Little Feat blasting
behind the fogged-over windows. Judging from the opaque
cloud around them, Budd's last crop of homegrown was a
raging success.

Like Syd, Tommy and Budd used to be open-hearth
crew, blue-collar elite. Like Syd, they now considered
themselves fortunate to find any work at all. Syd couldn't
quite picture any of them as computer programmers, or
leaning out of a fast-food drive-through, going *you want
fries with that?*

So they worked whenever they could, wherever they
could—the last six weeks or so humping for a nonunion
contractor that was tearing the mill down, selling the
scrap, and making way for a condo development. It paid a
big six-fifty an hour, plus zero benefits. It sucked.

They were lucky to get it.

Tommy looked up as Syd got out of his car. He was a
big, bearlike man, with a craggy, bearded face and a ker-
chief obscuring his receding hairline. His eyes were red as
Bing cherries. "Drugs in the workplace," Syd clucked.
"Tsk tsk tsk."

"Can't say as I rightly give a fuck anymore," Tommy
replied, clambering out of the truck.

"D'ja hear about Bobby Carmichael?" Budd said. His
eyes were bright, morbidly gleeful. "Blew his brains out
last night."

"Say *what?*" Syd was stunned. Bobby had just returned from a five-month stint in the badass flatlands of

**PANEL
#**

2

**SEAT
#**

5

HAMPDEN COUNTY JURY POOL

RUDY LE BEL

Rudy O Bel

Arkansas, looking for work. The bank had foreclosed on their house while he was gone. His wife had packed up the kids and headed off to California. Syd had known him since high school. "Are you sure?" he asked.

"Damn straight," Budd assured him. He was a squirrelly little sonofabitch some ten years their junior, with frizzy blond hair and an enormous Metallica patch on his jeans jacket, and he thrived on disaster. "Way I heard it, finance company was gonna repo his car. He did it in the fucking driver's seat, stuck the barrel right in his *ear,* man. Brains ended up all over the dashboard, even got squished in the a.c. vents. . . ."

"Jesus."

"Way of the fuckin' world, bro'," Tommy said. "That's the ninth one this year, and we still got a month till Christmas." He clapped Syd in an embrace that smelled of stale beer and too many Marlboros, held out the stub of a joint. "Want some?"

"Nah." Syd shook his head. "Things are weird enough as it is."

Tommy nodded, gestured toward Syd's crotch. "Did you piss in your pants *again*?"

"Very funny," Syd said. He pointed to the bloodied fender. "Had a little accident with a deer, coming in."

"No shit." Budd hopped out of the truck, coming around to see. He shrugged, surveying Syd's car. "Coulda been worse. Think your insurance'll cover it?"

"Yeah, right," Syd muttered. "I'm already assigned risk. Might as well roll my policy into a tube and shove it up my ass."

"Lucky it didn't go through the windshield," Budd said, taking the joint. "Had a cousin who hit a buck up near Beaver Falls. Totaled his car." He nudged the dent absently with his work boot, smearing the blood. "D'ja kill it?"

"Not exactly," Syd said.

"Not *exactly*?" Tommy, who had hunted every single season since he was old enough to tote a gun, looked at him quizzically.

Syd explained as best as he could: about the deer and the truck, the blood-trail leading into the hollow. He meant to leave it at that, skip over the wolf part completely. But as the story unwound, he found he couldn't help himself. He needed to do a reality check.

The results, on the first round, were less than encouraging.

"That's a pretty weird story you got there, ace," Budd said. "You sure it wasn't a dog? Like a shepherd, maybe—?"

Syd shook his head. "Ever seen a German shepherd crack a deer's chest like a goddam Milk-Bone?"

"Shit," Tommy said, drawing it out to two words: *shee-it*. "You really expect us to believe you saw a wolf that big, and not ten miles out of town . . ."

"Swear to god," Syd answered, emphatic.

". . . and you actually came within spitting distance of this thing, and it just *looked* at you."

"Yep."

"And then it just up and disappeared into the woods and left you there."

"Uh-huh." Syd nodded.

Tommy looked at Syd, the car, and back. Then he took a deep breath. "I just have one question."

"Shoot."

"Did you piss yourself right when you first saw the wolf . . ."

Budd choked, almost lost it. Tommy, too, barely made it to the punch line.

". . . or did you wait till the wolf saw *you*?"

The two of them erupted into gales of laughter. Syd felt his face flush with embarrassment and anger. "Yeah, well, fuck you guys," he muttered.

"Aw, lighten up, son." Tommy threw a beefy arm around Syd's shoulder. "You wanna get insulted, check out your paycheck this week."

Syd resisted for a moment, still pissed. Then he sighed. "It really happened, man."

"Yeah, well," Tommy shrugged. "What do *I* know?

Weirder things have been known to." He gave Syd a brotherly squeeze. "C'mon, boy. Let's go see if we work today."

The three of them walked toward the gate in silence. Tommy's face had taken on a contemplative light. "This wolf of yours," he said at last. "Was it male or female?"

"I didn't ask. Why?"

Tommy shrugged. "A wolf in estrus can act pretty strange sometimes."

"What's estrus?"

"*Heat,* boy." He paused, thought about it. "November's kinda early for mating season, but you never know."

"Ooooh." Budd leered, lascivious. "Maybe it *wanted* you, Syd."

"Yeah, right." Irritated.

"Puppy love . . ."

"Put a lid on it, Budd."

"*Doggy*-style . . ." he persisted, pleased with himself.

"SHUT UP!!!" Syd and Tommy chanted in unison. Budd's grinning pie-hole dried up in a flash. Syd studied Tommy's face intently. He knew that Tommy was a whole lot smarter than his mountain-man appearance might lead one to believe. Wheels were turning in there. He wanted to know what they meant.

"So what else?"

"I dunno," Tommy shrugged. "Was it alone?"

"Why?" Budd jumped in. "You think there's more than one of 'em?"

"Beats me," the big man said. "But I'll tell ya one thing: if there *is* a wolf in these parts, I'd guess that it has a mate."

"Unless it's looking for one." Syd wasn't sure why he said it.

"Good fucking luck," Tommy snorted. "The only wolves around here anymore are the ones with suits and cellular phones."

Just then they passed a sleek black BMW parked against the warehouse wall, its polished midnight skin and hand-detailed chrome in stark contrast to the gritty ochres and browns of the yard. Tommy nodded at the little cork-screw antenna protruding from its tinted rear window. "Speak of the devil," he muttered, and nudged Syd knowingly. "Looks like Bobo's here."

Syd groaned and shook his head. A surprise appearance by Beau "Bobo" Harrell was always good for a laugh, particularly if you thought job security was funny. Harrell was scum.

More specifically, Beau Harrell was a sour, opportunistic little prick, and his contracting company was a blue-collar *gulag*. He got the contract by undercutting every other bid by thirty percent, and in so doing became one of the town's few remaining employers, last refuge for those lucky enough to get a slot and able to withstand the degradation implicit in taking it. As a boss, he was both abusive and unscrupulous; as a human being, abusiveness and unscrupulousness were his most endearing qualities.

They reached the foreman's trailer, got on the crew line. A dozen other disenfranchised souls were there, smoking and shuffling their feet. The three men joined the queue. Just then the foreman came out, a burly barrel of a man with a face like a bulldog and a fur-flapped hunting cap; the short stub of yesterday's cigar protruded from the corner of his mouth like a big tobacco tampon.

"Yessir, Mr. Harrell," he said, then turned and descended the steps. He waved his clipboard, sent groups of men this way and that. Budd went with one crew. "See ya later," he said.

The foreman checked his list, grunting. "Jarrett, Kramer, this way," he gestured. "You're tearing out the boilers in unit five."

"Lucky, lucky," Tommy muttered.

"I *love* my life," Syd added facetiously. "My life is great."

"Beats the alternative," Tommy replied.

Syd thought of Bobby Carmichael, and wondered.

3

I T WAS SIX-THIRTY when Syd finally arrived at the tiny two-story walk-up he called home, another day of gainful employment safely behind him.

He keyed open the door, pushing aside the pile of mail laying heaped on the floor. He sighed as he stooped to retrieve it; he was beat to shit, physically speaking, and the day's correspondence didn't help much on the psychological front. Bills, bills, bills, junk mail, and bills. He riffled through them absently as he crossed the room, thinking that the old saying was wrong. There was one more certainty in life, aside from death and taxes.

There were bills.

Every month, in ceaseless cycle, falling through the mail slot like some weird variation on the old Chinese water torture. The phone was overdue, the electric was overdue, his Visa card was maxxed to the point of no return. He'd long ago forgone such luxuries as cable TV, so that was mercifully absent. Ed McMahon's preening mug beckoned from a Publishers Clearing House mailer, assuring him that he *may already have won a million dollars!!!,* but Syd wasn't holding his breath.

He tossed the pile unceremoniously onto the kitchen table and headed for the bathroom, pausing en route to put on some music. The living room was tiny and run-down, but well-ordered and clean. The furnishings were strictly Salvation Army—a lamp, a seedy tweed sofa, and a Naugahyde recliner with big holes in the arms, huddled around a tacky coffee table like bums on a barrel fire.

His stereo alone was impressive—Philips power- and pre-amp, Denon tuner, Nakamichi CD and cassette deck, and an old Technics turntable for his 78s. A pair of Boston Acoustic speakers hunkered in the corners like squat sonic sentinels.

The audio system and his music collection were the only things of value he'd salvaged from his former life, and he treasured them. He scanned the rack of CDs, pulled a Melissa Etheridge disc and popped it in, hit the random search button. Syd wandered over to scarf a cold Keystone from the fridge. The player hummed for a second, then sweet sad acoustic guitar filled the air, arpeggiated cascades that transformed the cramped space of the room. The voice that followed was smoky and haunting, filled with loss:

> *"Everybody's got a hunger*
> *No matter where they are*
> *Everybody clings to their own fear*
> *Everybody hides some scar*
> *Oooooh, precious pain . . ."*

Syd grabbed a beer and popped it. The music swelled, achingly beautiful. God, Melissa could sing. He took a sip, toasting her talent. He was about to take another, when he happened to glance back at the mail, and one particular envelope caught his eye. Melissa wailed on:

> *"Empty and cold but it keeps me alive*
> *I gave it my soul so I could survive*
> *Keeping me safe in these chains*
> *Precious pain . . ."*

The envelope was postmarked Pittsburgh and addressed to
him; the handwriting was his own. The return address was
preprinted in a tiny cursive script. *Anthony P. Weisman,
attorney-at-law.* Syd felt his stomach drop like a gallows
trapdoor.

"Oh boy," he said. "Here it comes."

He sat down, readying himself. He knew in his gut
what it was. He opened the envelope; inside was a grainy
one-page photocopied letter and a very plain document
from the Court of Common Pleas, 59th Judicial District of
Pennsylvania.

Dear client, it stated bluntly. *Your divorce is final. . . .*

A few meager paragraphs followed, mostly a lot of re-
dundant legalspeak explaining why the certificate didn't
have an official colored seal but was completely legal and
authentic anyway.

Syd took a swig off his beer and flipped the page. The
attached document was just as perfunctory: *it is ordered
and decreed that on such-and-such day, blah blah blah,
Sydney C. Jarrett, plaintiff, and Karen L. Jarrett, defen-
dant, are divorced from the bonds of matrimony. Etc., etc.,
blah blah blah . . .*

Syd felt his spirit plunge, do a spastic death-jig where
his stomach had been. So much for pageantry. He held the
piece of paper up to the waning light, marveling at how
little substance there was to it. After all the pomp and cir-
cumstance surrounding the conjugal act, you'd think the
flip side would at least have some heft. Maybe be carved
in stone or something, like a memorial, or a headstone.
Here lies the marriage of Syd and Karen Jarrett.

Rest in pieces.

Syd dropped the paper and lit a cigarette. A photo
from their last summer together lay amidst the clutter of
the kitchen table. Karen was standing on the boardwalk at
Rehoboth Beach in Delaware, on a vacation he couldn't
afford that was his last desperate attempt to keep them together.

Funny, Syd thought, how pictures can lie, by the simple act of freezing time. In the photo she was smiling and

standing in the middle of the promenade: a shy and pretty woman holding one hand delicately up to her breast, one leg cocked like Venus descending from her shell. In real life the smile was a grimace, and she'd actually been backing *away,* trying to escape from Syd's intruding lens. As if she were afraid of letting him capture her like that.

As if she were afraid it might reveal something.

Syd closed his eyes and more images assembled unbidden in his brain, parading by like the Bataan Death March of love. The first time he ever saw her. The first time he asked her out. The night they first kissed. In one jarring gestalt he remembered the night she had captured his heart, and the night she had broken it.

And the ten long years that stretched in between.

> *"Everybody's got a reason*
> *to abandon their plan*
> *How can I think of tomorrow*
> *with my sorrow at hand*
> *Oooooh, precious pain . . ."*

THEY WERE YOUNG when they first met: she was twenty-two, he was twenty-five. She was lithe and willowy, with a personality so diametrically opposite his own that people sometimes wondered how they could stand each other. Where he was boisterous, she was reclusive; where he was reckless, she was reserved.

Still, they shared a connection, and it was strong. It was like they were tuned to a very intimate frequency, one that no one else could hear. And as much as their natures differed, there was a complement there, a melding of strengths. They were always honest with each other, in a way that Syd had never found with anyone else, and in the privacy of their relationship she opened up to him in ways she never had to anyone else.

He had to admit that she was a mystery to him. She had a sense of impenetrable composure, an inner serenity that intrigued him. At first it was a challenge; penetrating her veils wasn't easy. As he got to know her, he saw that

Karen had learned early in life to hide her true nature: from her parents, from her family, from the world at large. She lived in a world of unfulfilled dreams, and protected them with a veneer of innocent acquiescence. *Just tell everyone what you think they want to hear and you're safe. That's all they really want from you, anyway.* Karen spent most of her life hiding behind a mirror that reflected other people's expectations.

And then Syd came along.

He was brash and confident, with a wild streak a mile wide. He couldn't see through her mirrors, but he knew they were there. And as Syd fell deeper and deeper in love, he longed to find the person hidden behind the looking glass, and let her out at last.

Easier said than done. It took trust, and trust like that was hard to come by. They were together for years before getting married. Syd was marriage-shy, not because he was afraid of commitment but because he had seen too many people who did it and then let the spark go out, only to end up trapped in loveless frustration, dead inside. He never wanted to be like that.

And then one day, some seven years into their relationship, it struck him: here is a woman who truly loves you and wants you and you love her and just how many times do you think that *happens* in a lifetime?

When they tied the knot they literally got a standing ovation as they walked away from the altar: family and friends cheering them on, the organ music swelling, the autumn sunset ablaze as if God himself were on hand to personally wish them well.

And Syd found, much to his amazement, that he loved being married almost as much as he loved her. It wasn't a trap at all. To the contrary, it was liberating; there was a power in the knowledge that he had a partner, someone with whom he was mated for life. Someone to watch over, even as she watched over him. Syd was amazed at how he could look at Karen and feel the same exhilaration as the first night they'd kissed. And when they made love he felt time melt away, as if the joining would last forever.

It blew him away. He wanted to give her everything, be everything for her, fulfill her heart's every desire. And bit by bit, he began to truly believe that he could. No matter what happened, they had each other. They had the rest of their lives. They could beat the odds and build something that would really last a lifetime.

For a while it looked like they actually might.

And then everything started to go wrong.

Maybe it was a long-buried fault line in their dynamic. Maybe just a series of random events, connecting with one another in near-lethal precision. The recession hit. The bills started to pile up. Karen got pregnant, only to have it end in a sudden and ugly miscarriage that sent her pinwheeling off into her own private hell.

Little by little, they started to drift apart.

For a long time, Syd blamed himself. He had failed to provide for them. He had failed to make the dream come true. He blamed her, too; for not trying, for rolling over and giving up in the face of hard times. He got scared, and the fear got him angry, and he pushed himself that much harder, doing anything and everything in a grimly determined attempt to keep it all together.

Eventually the sheer stress of it all just ground all the sweetness out of him. His sense of humor curdled, turned caustic; his hope became desperation; his desperation soured into bitterness.

Meanwhile, Karen drifted. Months went by. Years. He pressured her to take control of her life, get a grip, do something to help. She responded by drifting from one low-paying dead-end job to another, ended up making a halfhearted stab at real estate. The first thing she did was find a big old house, which she brought Syd to see. He saw the spark light in Karen's eyes for the first time in what felt like forever. And that was all it took.

They managed to buy the place, and Syd set to restoring it with a fervor; sanding floors, painting, ripping out fixtures, making it theirs. To him it was way more than material, worlds beyond simply improving the resale value of an investment. He was trying to build a repository for their dreams, make physical his hope for their continued future together. It was home. It mattered. He poured his heart into it, as if by sheer dint of will he could transform it into a fortress strong enough to deflect the forces that threatened to overwhelm them.

All the while, the wheels kept turning. The economy worsened. The bills kept coming. Syd managed to keep them alive, but the uncertainty was wearing on him. The real estate market went quagmire-soft in the face of more layoffs, more closings. Karen's career didn't earn a dime, but it got her into the bars a lot, where she began to quietly drown in her own insecurities and depression.

The gulf between them grew colder and colder by degrees.

Until the inevitable happened.

> *"Each road I walk down*
> *reminds me of you*
> *This whole town is haunted*
> *There'll never be anything new ..."*

ONE NIGHT KAREN happened into the sights of a yuppie lounge-lizard party animal named Vaughn Restal. Vaughn was a fixture on the local singles scene: boyishly charming, with curly black hair and a cheesy, easy grin. His special gift was helping women in trouble—especially married ones. He listened to their problems: with their husbands, with their jobs, with their lives. He tapped into their deepest longings. He liked to make them feel special.

And he had a special way of making them feel it.

Vaughn befriended Karen: running into her casually, encouraging her to share her feelings. He was always there with a smile and a hug and a sympathetic shoulder to cry on. He was a nice guy. He was concerned for her. He bought her lots and lots of drinks.

On the home front, things were growing increasingly distant. Karen had become a virtual shadow in the hallways. And Syd was no fun at all anymore. When they

spoke at all, their conversations revolved around a seemingly never-ending parade of problems; and as Syd became single-minded in his determination to get them out
of the hole they were in, Karen felt increasingly lost and
powerless in the face of it. They became estranged, each
lost in their own inability to cope.

It wasn't long before Karen's nights out making business contacts started to run later and later. And it wasn't
much past that before her shmoozing became a nightly
thing. It was all just part of the business, after all. And if
Syd didn't like it, well, he was the one who'd been pressing her to go out and hustle in the first place, now wasn't
he?

But by then Syd had begun to pull out of his anger. He
felt like a man trapped in a rubber monster suit, a life-
sized replica of himself, fashioned entirely of bile and bad
feelings. It had taken him a long time to recognize that
fact, even longer to find the zipper and finally set himself
free.

As he did, the anger sloughed off of him. Syd began
making overtures, trying to heal the damage, to rekindle
the fire they'd let go out. Karen responded with indifference and suspicion. Why was he being nice all of a sudden? He was up to something, no doubt, trying to
manipulate her somehow. She went out every night, stayed
out till the bars closed. She shared nothing, told him exactly what she thought he wanted to hear.

Something was going on. He could feel it in his gut.
The certainty of it uncoiled every night as she walked out
the door, slithered through their daily silences, tightened
round his throat as he watched her sleeping face. Finally,
when he could stand it no longer, he asked her. And she
turned that perfectly innocent face to him, looked him
straight in the eye, and told him. Nothing was happening.
She was out with friends. It was all in his head.

End of conversation.

Honesty was implicit in their relationship; Syd literally
didn't know how *not* to trust her. He asked her a question;

she gave him an answer. He had to believe her. He knew she was lying. It drove him mad.

Bit by bit, the mirror began to crack.

One day Karen stopped wearing her wedding rings. Vaughn had told her it made him uncomfortable to be seen in public with a married woman. He told her to take them off.

That night, in bed, Vaughn told her that he loved her. He told her that Syd was an uncaring bastard who could never make her happy. He fed her insecurities carefully, nurturing the hurts with hugs and smiles and his throbbing, burning love until at last they blossomed and ripened.

Until at last, it was harvest time.

It was a sticky-hot August night, and Syd had been up for hours: staring down the darkened street, waiting for the swell of headlights that would herald her homecoming. He felt time slow to a crawl, then stop altogether, the excruciating drag of one second into the next advancing nothing. Each tick was punctuated by the same nagging litany: where was she? Was she dead in a dumpster somewhere, was she wrecked and bleeding in a ditch? Was she okay? Why was she doing this?

It drove him crazy. He resented the inconsideration, dreaded the implications, felt hijacked by his own concern. Worry was not optional. She was a part of him. She was out there somewhere. She was lying.

Through the night, he paced: a caged animal, trapped within the boundaries of civility, suffering the crimes of the polite. It was an unwritten law of the domesticated: wreak whatever emotional havoc thou wilt, but never, ever make a scene. Any violation was acceptable, so long as you did it neatly. As long as you didn't make a mess.

He felt an urge rise up from somewhere deep within. It was a living thing: bestial in its simplicity, unfettered by caution or reason. It made him want to howl and scream and rip through the lies, feel them kick and squirm as he tore them to bloody shreds. Feel them hurt, like he hurt. Feel them shudder. Feel them die.

It was a good feeling. It was clean. Strong. Real. It

gnawed clear through to the core of his being. Taunting.
Torturing. Beckoning to him, over and over and over.

Release me.

Syd wrestled with it all night. And when Karen saun-
tered in sometime the next morning, he was waiting:
sunken-eyed and unshaven in the darkened living room.
Steeped in shadow, eyes ablaze, he looked up from his lair.
His voice croaked one question. One word.

Why?

She looked at him, innocence incarnate. Whatever did
he mean? Syd's reply came on a leash pulled tight. Was
she genuinely stupid, or just incredibly cruel?

Still feigning that perfect blankness, she faced him.
Are you saying you don't want me to go out? she asked.

No, he said quietly, looking across the miles-wide
chasm between them. *I want you to leave.*

Karen couldn't believe her ears. Syd said it again. He
told her, in that dreadful, constricted whisper, that this was
no longer her home. He told her if she ever wanted to figure out what went wrong, to let him know. But until that
day came, if ever, she was not welcome here.

And she had to leave. Now.

There was danger in his voice. She left, that very day.

Two days later, she returned. Her world had begun to
crumble. She confessed her sins reluctantly. She confused. There was someone else.

Syd felt his world come unglued. He needed the truth,
in all its ugly grandeur. He needed to know it for what it
was. Slowly, he pulled it out of her. Yes, she was involved.
Yes, it was an affair. Yes, she had feelings for him.

The words punctured Syd. Breaking up he could deal
with. A random fuck was not fatal, either. But this . . .

This was different. He knew by the tone of it, her eu-
phemistic phraseology delicate as a dull knife to the windpipe. *Involved. Feelings.*

This was more than a sleazy little series of one-nighters.
This was betrayal.

Syd reeled, his guts twisting into tiny inextricable
knots. He asked her what his name was. She wouldn't tell

him. He asked her again. She fought to hide it. He asked her again and again: doggedly pursuing, cornering her. Until she broke down and told him.

Syd heard the name.

And he went berserk.

He could feel his soul split, torn between the horror of it all and the animal writhing inside him, snapping at its chains. *Something must pay.* Not like this. *Something must die.* He told her Vaughn was scum. She said nothing, shielding him with her silence. Vaughn was good. Vaughn's heart was pure. The thing inside him howled. He told her that Vaughn was a legend in slime. She defended his honor. Vaughn loved her, she said. Syd told her she had to choose. She said she couldn't hurt him.

What about me, he asked.

She said nothing at all. Karen stood frozen: unable to turn back. Unable to go forward. Unable to move.

Syd turned, heading for the door. She watched, eyes glazed with fear.

Please don't kill him, she said.

Please don't kill him.

It was a hard request to honor. Killing him was a palpable option. To feel his flesh rend, to hold his bruised and bleeding face, drinking in his destruction as the light guttered, winked out. It would be perfection. It would be sublime.

But he looked at her shivering, terrified. And he still loved her.

And he said that he wouldn't.

On the way out a voice popped into his head, clear as you please. *Take your gun,* it said. Syd had to stop and think about that one for a moment, as the whole scenario sprang full-blown into his mind. *He would bring the gun. He would pull the gun. Vaughn would feign toughness, say something stupid like* what are you gonna do, shoot me? *And then he would.*

And that would be that.

No, he decided. Not like that. The act was too easy, the repercussions too messy. He called Jules, screaming for a reality-check. Jules concurred: guns were a bad idea. He proceeded to trot out a host of sound, rational reasons why Syd didn't want to waste his life on behalf of these people. Syd heard them all, understood them implicitly. Yes, violence was not an answer. No, he didn't want to go to jail. None of it meant anything to the part of him that was in pain. The part that lusted for blood, and death, and destruction.

Jules ended up urging Syd not to do anything stupid, held him on the line until he promised he wouldn't. Eventually, Syd relented.

Besides, he knew: if it came to that, he wanted to do it with his bare hands.

Vaughn was drunk by the time Syd got to the refurbished yuppie love-nest he called home. For all of his great undying devotion, Vaughn was quick to deny everything. First he told Syd that nothing had happened. Syd called him a liar.

Then he said it was just a joke. Syd said it wasn't funny. He said that it was nothing personal. Syd told him he took it kind of personal when someone fucked his wife. Vaughn said he didn't want to get physical. Syd told Vaughn he'd *already* gotten physical, the moment he'd fucked his wife. Vaughn cracked, blurted out that it was all Syd's fault: if Syd had been doing his job, this never would have happened. . . .

And that was when Syd hit him.

And it was wonderful, it was bliss, the dull crunch of broken bone like sweet music as the thing inside him uncoiled and rose, lusting for the clarity of chaos, begging for more. Syd felt alive, unbound: every cell awake, aware, as if he were smashing through the lies while he pounded Vaughn's face into pulp, wanting nothing more than to keep right on going, to rip his smug and preening face off, to hack through flesh to bone and beyond, to tear him down to essence, to fundament, to miserable withered soul-shrieking bits. . . .

It was an epiphany rendered in blood; and like all

epiphanies, it was fleeting. A police cruiser came and hovered on the periphery, restoring order by proximity. Syd's rational mind regained dominion, reining the other side in. Don't ruin your life. Don't go to jail for this. It's not worth it.

The police car sat, not moving, not reacting.

Waiting.

Reason won, but barely. Syd backed off just enough to permit Vaughn to slither away, the better to lick his wounds. Syd allowed him to, tethering the murderous urge, aware of how tenuous his grip on it was. Knowing how easily it could get loose again. Knowing what it wanted.

Liking what it wanted.

Vaughn resurfaced days later, mumbling into his beer about having walked into a door. It didn't matter. Vile as he was, Vaughn was but a symptom. The disease lay elsewhere. The damage was already done.

And if there was any hope of survival, there was healing to be done.

Syd tried. Whatever else might be said, no one could take that from him. He tried. For the better part of the next year Syd limped in and out of counseling; crutching like a zombie, trying to piece the shattered fragments together. Trying to undo the thing that could not be undone.

It was no use. The trust was gone. As Karen's secret world shattered into a million glittering fragments she retreated, the better to protect herself from the truth she could no longer bear to face. She found out through the grapevine that Vaughn Restal had been fucking three other women the whole time he was helping himself to her, and that each and every one of them got his special slime-coated vow of true love and deep, caring commitment as well. It only drove her deeper and deeper inside.

For months Syd played cheerleader to the faltering cause: buying her flowers, courting her constantly,

apologizing for his part in their undoing. Trying to make
her feel his love. Trying to ignore the fact that he was
dying inside. Hoping that she would return to him before
he could go no further.

She never said she was sorry, or that it would never
happen again, or any of a hundred other things that could
have eased the pain, helped to heal their suffering.

Worst of all, she could never bring herself to tell him
the one thing that could have restored him, the one thing
that might have helped to wipe the slate clean. The thing
he needed most to hear, more than anything in the world.

I love you.

One day he realized that he just couldn't do it anymore. There was no blank check he could write her from
his bottomless emotional reserves. He'd given her every
chance he had to give, and quite a few that he hadn't. He
was all used up.

Syd packed his things, filed the papers, and walked
away; trading his home for a skeevy little two-room
walk-up in another part of town, the woman he loved for
an empty bed, and a pocketful of dreams for what was
left of his pride. That was a year ago. In the process
he got his life back, such as it was. And with it, his
integrity.

All it cost him was his past and present, and the only
future he knew.

The one with Karen.

The one that officially ended, today.

SYD LOOKED UP. It was dark outside. The CD had long
since played out, wrapping him in silence. The cigarette
was a three-inch-long ash, poised between his fingers. The
decree lay on the table, where it had fallen from his grasp.
Droplets spattered its surface; it took Syd a moment to realize that they were his own tears.

"God," he whispered. *"I gotta get out of here."*

He looked at the papers with disdain, then crumpled
them into a tiny little ball. Keeping it around was like

hanging on to a severed limb. Syd had tried to hold on to the good that he could still feel, only to have it slip away—wraithlike, ephemeral.

The bad was much more durable. It was as though the trauma of the breakup had all but blotted out his ability to connect with anything but the pain.

But he had loved her; of that, he was certain. He had the scars to prove it. The memory of his love was seared into his soul and etched into the marrow of his bones. Ten years took up a substantial piece of your heart; it left a big hole when you finally cut it out.

He was tired of whipping himself with her memory. He had stitched up the hole, spent months waiting for the scars to scab over. He'd heard his friends' polite inquiries a hundred times; felt innocence turn suddenly awkward as they asked *how's Karen, oh really, gee, I'm so sorry to hear that.* Then, silence.

His responses had winnowed down, too—the heart-wrenching outpourings of the first few months gradually giving way to fewer and fewer details, like colors fading from a painting, or a vital sign slowly going flatline. Until finally people stopped asking altogether, grateful to be relieved of the burden.

Until finally, it was reduced to its lowest common denominator of truth. *Things just didn't work out.*

It's in the past, he told himself, choking back a wrecking-ball-sized lump in his throat. It's behind me now. Just let it go.

Syd grabbed another cigarette, picked up his lighter. He flicked it on, listened to the tiny hissing flame.

Just let it all go. . . .

The balled-up wad of paper blossomed into flame as he placed it in the ashtray. Syd picked up the photo. He hadn't seen her in over six months. He doubted that he would ever see her again.

"Good-bye," he said. Then consigned her to the pyre as well.

Karen's face turned black as the emulsion bubbled and crisped. The fire flared bright for an instant, then receded, leaving only ash. Syd stood, looked at his watch. Seven-fifty. Jesus. If he hurried, he'd have just enough time to change and get the hell over to Chameleon's before either Queen Bee started or he blew his brains out.

Whichever came first.

4

CHAMELEON'S WAS A creaky little roadhouse dive
that specialized in cheap drinks, so-so pizza, and su-
perlative rhythm and blues. Its capacious gravel parking
lot gobbled a sizable chunk of turf at the foot of Mt. Royle
and Dirks Mill Pike, well on the outskirts of town. At
night, you could see the lights of the city splayed out before you, from miles away. It underscored how far out in
the boonies you were. How far removed from, quote, CIV-
ILIZATION. Unquote.

The music always hit you first. It was loud, even during the daytime, banging out through the double doors and
into the lot; and it was always, always good. One thing
you had to give the owners: they didn't skimp when it
came down to the tunes. Though the kitchen, lighting and
overall decor were decidedly low-tech, they had popped
some serious bucks on the house sound system, and it
wailed.

They also had a new-fangled CD jukebox, which Jules
had crammed to the hilt with coolness: little independent-
label reissues of vintage, seminal recordings rammed right
up against the latest in showy big-budget technique. So

you got Johnny Winter's mid-'60s album "Progressive Blues Experiment" back to back with Albert King and Gary Moore's British 1990 duet. Prehistoric T-Bone Walker. Posthistoric Robben Ford. Johnny "Guitar" Watson and Roy Buchanan. Jimi Hendrix and Buddy Boy Hawkins. Muddy Waters and Stevie Ray Vaughan.

Jules liked all kinds of down 'n' dirty music, but his love was the blues. Jules was the most authoritative and genuinely passionate lover of the blues that Syd had ever met. He had tintypes from the Mississippi Delta to go with his old 78 rpm's, musty hardbound volumes on the music's history that he'd picked up over the years at all those book fairs and flea markets he loved to attend.

What's more, Jules had actually spent a big chunk of his youth wandering the country, by his own telling "searching for the heart of the blues." It was something Syd had always admired him for. And in working Chameleon's for the last decade, he'd managed to book—then meet and, in many cases, befriend—more than half the living legends still at large. From there, he'd become both a walking encyclopedia and self-styled curator, playing steward to every shred of data or memorabilia he picked up along the way. Not bad for a big ugly inbred bastard from the white-trash backwaters of Washington, Pa.

And that was the most amazing thing about Jules. He moved at what might look like a leisurely pace, but he always followed through. When he examined an issue, he tended to examine it thoroughly; if he let a person or thing get close enough to nestle its hooks in him, he was in for the duration. Jules would not volunteer an uninformed opinion; and he wouldn't volunteer an opinion *at all* until he felt he had earned the right. These were issues of trust, and of adequate information. Issues he took very seriously indeed.

Jules had been there for Syd, all through the divorce and the whole painful sequence of events leading up to, around, and through it. He had been Syd's sounding board, till the wee hours of the morning, on more occasions than Syd frankly cared to admit. He had offered encourage-

ment, support, friendship, and—when it came down to it—
some painfully honest criticism.

Which was why Syd felt the need to talk with him tonight. He needed a little comprehensive perspective. On
his encounter with the wolf. On those papers in the mail.
And on what weird tenuous connection, if any, there might
possibly be between them.

Syd rolled in at eight forty-nine. Red was stationed just
inside the double doors, as usual, collecting the five-dollar
cover charge. Red was there mostly to inspire awe and
dread, help deter excessive rowdiness and the criminal element. He was ugly and large and he excelled at his job.
Fights didn't tend to last long at Chameleon's. He gave a
poker-faced nod of recognition as Syd ambled up, then let
him slip in ahead of the throng without paying. Privilege
of the insider.

Syd continued on. He knew maybe a third of the people there by name, two-thirds of them by sight; but he
could deduce what ninety-eight percent of them were
drinking, all the way from the door. Tommy was there,
with a couple other guys from work. Their pitchers were
loaded with Genuine Draft: too pale to be Bass, too rich to
be Schaefer or Rolling Rock. Budd and his main squeeze
Holly huddled by the popcorn machine, smooching over
strong Cuba Libres with extra lime. Trent, the second-
string bartender, was whipping up what appeared to be a
Slippery Nipple for Tammy Eberhardt. And the Knuckle-
head Brothers, Gary and Steve, were getting ready to perform some serious Jaegermeister damage; they took their
liquid hallucinations very seriously.

Jane the barmaid smiled at him as she approached, tray
of drinks in hand. She was a mischievous spirit, on the
lean side of twenty-something, with a presence that belied
her age and her petite stature. She always seemed to have
energy and enthusiasm to spare. Syd liked the way her
dark hair spilled over her shoulders, the way her face was
shaped: angular cheekbones framing a thin-lipped, intelligent smile, a slightly crooked nose, and wise, dark eyes

that picked up on everything and seemed to constantly sparkle with secret amusement.

She also had a kickass sense of humor, and a habit of not taking a scrap of shit off of anyone. Syd also greatly appreciated the fact that she hated Vaughn Restal. In fact, at that moment he wondered why he hadn't ever thought to marry her, instead . . . or virtually anyone else, for that matter.

"Hi," he said, perking up a little in her presence.

"Nice to see you changed your pants," she said.

"Oh, god." Mortified. "Does *everybody* know about this now?"

Jane just smiled and sashayed past. His spirits both rose and fell, pleased by the strokes but completely embarrassed. Did *she* think he'd peed himself? And where the hell had she seen him? He eyed the crotch of his pants unconsciously, just making sure it hadn't happened again.

There were a pair of big-haired women at the bar, flanking a small hairy man. Before them, Jules stood, smiling indulgently. Syd guessed that they were trying to play "Stump the Bartender." Syd was sympathetic. He'd been trying to stump Jules since they first met, fifteen years ago. He'd pretty much resigned himself to the fact that it would never happen.

"Okay, okay," the small hairy man said, as Syd came within earshot. "Set me up with a couple of Prairie Fires, then." He looked incredibly smug, glancing from the breasts on his left to the breasts on his right and back again. Syd stopped and watched, curious. This was one he didn't know.

But Jules just plucked two shot glasses off the shelf and the Cuervo Gold off the speed rack before him. His oversized body's movements were surprisingly graceful, fluid, and precise. He poured a shot of tequila into each, replaced the bottle, and scooped the Tabasco from the condiments shelf, measuring out five scrupulous drops per shot and then sliding them over to Monkey Boy. The thrill of victory, the agony of defeat.

"And what will you ladies have?" Jules inquired, expression professionally neutral. It wouldn't do for the bartender to gloat.

"I wanna Tootsie Roll," said the one on the left, snapping her gum.

"I'd like a Screaming Orgasm, please," said the one on the right, looking bold and embarrassed all at once.

"And I," Syd volunteered, bellying up beside the Tootsie Roll queen, "would like a Hemorrhaging Brain."

"Right you are," Jules said, lobbing a sidearm grin at Syd. Then he filled a pair of fancy highball glasses with crushed ice. Into the first he poured one ounce of Creme de Cacao, then topped it off with orange juice and shook it vigorously. Into the second he emptied half-ounce increments of amaretto, Kahlúa, and Absolut (for the Screaming part). Cream polished off the rest of the Orgasm. Again, he shook, then slid them over to the ladies. The hairy man paid in full. Jules turned to ring it up.

When he turned back, his wily gaze was trained on Syd. A longneck Rolling Rock appeared in his hand. He cracked it open and set it down. "Thanks," said Syd. Jules nodded his head. His eyes, deep-set beneath their steep cro-magnon brow, had the warm glow of the genuine wild inside. There was something entirely primitive about his features, placing him somewhere between Tom Waits, Ron Perlman, and Andre the Giant on the evolutionary scale: a rough-hewn quality to the long, horsey face, with its coarse black crop of hair, thick eyebrows to match, squat, prominent nose and sly, expansive deadpan grin full of slightly overlarge teeth.

It was a great face, all in all, and it suited Jules perfectly: full of character, full of surprises. It was a face that people were predestined to underestimate. Jules liked that, and used it constantly. You had to be paying attention if you wanted more than a fleeting glimpse of how quick he actually was.

"So how goes it this evening?" Jules automatically washed up behind the bar as he spoke, running the tools of his trade from left to right through the hot sudsy water, the warm rinse, the cool rinse, then onto the drain boards, without once looking down.

"Kinda weird, actually," Syd replied. The words *I'm divorced. I almost got ate by a wolf* hung back for the moment, reined in by propriety and his own innate sense of comic timing.

"Ah-hah." A scrutinous Mona Gorilla smile. "So were you serious about that Brain?"

"Well . . ." Syd stopped and thought about it for a second. "Actually, I just kinda said it to be funny. But . . ."

Jules wiped down the bar, set the rag down, waited.

"They *are* really good," Syd acknowledged, musing.

Jules nodded sagely. "Delicious."

"And they do look disgusting."

"There's always that."

"But I don't usually drink anything but beer."

Frowning. "You're right."

Syd grinned. "And you're just agreeing with everything I say."

"One hundred percent."

Syd laughed, shook his world-weary head. "Now *that's* a professional," he said, and finally got a laugh out of Jules as well. "What the hell. Let's do one up."

By that time, a few more people had poured in the door, were making their way to the bar. Syd turned to watch them come as Jules turned for the peach schnapps and Baileys Irish Cream. A handsome young black couple, maybe slightly overdressed. A peck of essentially harmless good ol' boys. A lonely, dark-haired, fiercely-bulimic woman in her forties, whose name Syd could never remember. Behind her, a dark figure in the doorway, its identity as yet unclear.

When he turned back, Jules was pouring the schnapps into a five-ounce rock glass set out before him. "I love this part," the bartender said, then opened the Baileys and meticulously dribbled it into the glass.

The result was sheerest magic, purest mixological alchemy. No matter how many times he saw it, Syd never ceased to be amazed. It was way better than sea monkeys, cheaper than Claymation, tons more fun than an EPT. The second the Irish Cream hit the schnapps, it began to congeal into a brown, brainlike, undulating mass that floated in the clear liquor like an ugly fetus in amniotic fluid. Little fissures erupted across its surface, increasing in complexity as it grew. By the time Jules was finished, it even had a little brain stem. Such was his consummate skill.

Syd stared at the tiny shriveled thing in the glass, felt something oily respond deep in his bowels. Suddenly the wide-open deer, in all its glory, was back in his mind's eye. Jesus, he thought. What the hell was I thinking?

He didn't know why he'd failed to put it together before, what perverse side of him thought this would be a good idea. But the fact was that he didn't *need,* just now, to see something that looked so much like his own internal organs. Much less to strain such a thing through his teeth as it tipped back down his throat.

Then Jules applied the grenadine Hemorrhage, letting thick red fluid drift down to fill the brain grooves and make them gleam. Syd cross-indexed the visual reference against his gag reflex, found himself provoked but holding steady.

He turned away, for a breath of fresh air.

And that was when he saw her.

5

THE DARK SHAPE in the doorway had paid its cover, was descending the steps toward him. That *it* was a *she*, he could clearly see.

And, dear god, what a she it was.

Syd felt suddenly like Glenn Ford in *Gilda*, watching Rita Hayworth for the very first time. The same stunned disbelief: closing his throat as she riveted his attention, rendering him incapable of either speaking or looking away. The same cruel certainty that he would *never again*—no matter how long he lived—be this close to a woman so utterly, unequivocally compelling.

She moved closer, charging the very air around her as she parted the crowd. Syd literally *felt* her before he saw her clearly, sensed the power implicit in her presence. Strips of light and shadow illuminated and concealed her in stages as she came. The flashes were revelations, each more startling than the last.

First, her body, emerging from silhouette: a black leather biker's jacket draped over a body-hugging minidress, concealing her tight, excruciating curves even as it revealed just enough to stoke his imagination to flame. Her legs were black-stockinged, breathtakingly long, immaculately sculpted, altogether painful to behold. Long cascades of hair the color of blood and cinnamon caressed square and elegant shoulders, flowed past the delicate expanse of her throat. Her eyes were brilliant, backlit emeralds, burning with a feral green light; her lips were wet plush beestung dreams of glory, bite-red against her fine pale skin. Her mouth was wide and sly, the corners turned slightly downward in a naturally sardonic, inward grin. Once again, like the rest of her, so intensely intoxicating that it hurt to directly address them with his eyes.

As she turned Syd caught a glint of silver; it took him another second to register the tiny, delicate circle that pierced the rim of her left nostril. A nose ring. Jesus. It only served to underscore her aura of mystery, an exotic addition to her already overwhelming mystique.

Syd tore his gaze away and turned to Jules. Jules looked like Syd felt: slack-jawed, bug-eyed with shock. All he needed was a spittle-cup. Syd looked around the room, saw the exact same expression on every guy in the place.

And the other women . . .

The heat of every male glance was offset a dozenfold by the arctic glare of their companions. Singly or in pairs, alone or mated, contempt and competition slam-danced in her wake as the mystery woman polarized and galvanized the room. Heads turned, eyes averted, elbows jammed ribs even as sneers fought to mask freshly torpedoed egos.

For her part, the stranger seemed to acknowledge their defeat even as she negated them. The message was clear, with every step she took. She was more than the most beautiful woman in the room.

She was the *only* woman in the room.

It was sexual Darwinism at its finest, and the facts spoke for themselves. This woman was no mere cycle slut, no brainless black-leather bimbo on the prowl for cock. She was a goddess in motion, a pheromonal cyclone of sexual heat. The most spectacular female, without a doubt, ever to set *foot* in this dive.

And she was coming closer.

Oh god. Syd gulped, watching her move. Feeling his flesh constrict around him. *Oh god.* Feeling completely unworthy in her presence. His gaze dropped down to his lap, which began to stir with a life of its own. Given his own snowball's chance in hell, he couldn't imagine a more irrelevant sensation.

Suddenly, he didn't want to see the lucky sonofabitch who had come with her, or whom she had come to meet. He knew that he would hate the miserable prick, purely as a matter of principle. No matter *how* cool that prick might turn out to be. . . .

And that was when the loneliness kicked in; worse yet, the futility of even being smitten with the urge. Because, yes, he had lusted out of his league before. And, yes, it was always a painful thing, the perfect complement to that I-am-a-piece-of-shit feeling. To crave the unattainable was to court disaster, the total destruction of his hard-won self-esteem. He didn't need, right now, to feel any worse about himself.

Any more than she needed to be stared at by *him,* he realized, and felt even more like a fool. It was entirely possible that she'd come all the way out here in the hope of *not* getting stared at by every unemployed steelworker in the state of Pennsylvania. Already, the smoky air was filled with apelike hoots and whistles and hollers. It made him, as always, deeply embarrassed for his gender. He wondered if she knew what she was getting herself into.

In that moment, he resolved to break the chain. Stop staring. Help turn the tide back to its own damn business. He had a few things to discuss with Jules, anyway. Like his sanity, for instance. Now was as good a time as any to stop torturing himself.

Having resolved all that, he turned around to look at her again.

Only to discover that *she* was now looking at *him.*

FOR A SECOND, his mind totally emptied of thought: like a flashpot had gone off between his ears, blinding his inner eye. Then thought and sight returned as one, and he was watching her scrutinize him from ten feet away: head cocked slightly to one side, one long finger absently tracing her lower lip. Her nostrils flared, just the tiniest bit, as if she were tracking on the basis of some all-but-imperceptible scent. The nose ring gleamed and sparkled in the dim light.

Then she started to smile—with her eyes locked on his—and he got the very strange feeling that she'd somehow found what she was looking for. And he realized that he'd been mistaken about at least one other thing.

She knew *exactly* what she was doing.

He, on the other hand, didn't have a goddam clue. "Whoa," he muttered under his breath as she took one step toward him. The word didn't begin to sum up how he felt. Panicked. Amped. Exhilarated. Confused. "Um," he said, and then she was another step closer.

He looked abruptly away, stared hard at his lap, his knees, his boots, the floorboards beneath. He could feel her eyes upon him still. It brought sweat prickling to the surface of his skin.

Look at her, he told himself, and found that he could not. He shot another quick glance at Jules, found that Jules was staring back at him, no help at all. Suddenly, he knew that the heat on his skin was not her eyes alone.

All eyes were upon him.

Upon them both.

And then he felt her proximity, the heat of *her* skin, as she took that final step. He could smell her: a steamy, luxuriant musk that unraveled what little remained of his composure. He could feel his pulse thud through his borning erection, a terse yet jubilant echo of his own hammering heart.

When at last he looked up, she was already beside him, leaning into the bar. She smiled at him, nailed his gaze once and for all. Her voice, when she spoke, was silken, lethal.

"Hi," she said. "Is that your brain?"

"What?"

She pointed to his drink. It took a second to track. "Ah ..." he said, and numbly nodded yes.

Again, she smiled. "May I ...?"

And before he could answer, she reached across to take the glass and raise it, ever so slowly, to those lips.

But when her tongue snaked out—glistening, frighteningly long—to scoop the lump of congealed and bleeding Baileys from the glass, he could stand it no longer.

He started to laugh.

Amusement gleamed in her emerald eyes as she swallowed. "Now," she said, "you'll have to tell me why you're laughing."

"Umm ..." Laughing some more, slowly shaking his head. "I guess it's maybe because I'm in shock."

"Ah." Waiting for him to elaborate.

"Because ... umm ... I don't understand what's going on?" He hoped that, by his phrasing it as a question, she might show him some mercy.

No dice. "And what *is* going on?"

He laughed again, harder this time. "You're not gonna give me a fucking ounce of slack, are ya?"

At last, she laughed as well. "Well ... *no*." Her eyes positively danced. Her laugh was deep and rich and dirty. What a surprise.

"Okay." The simple act of making her laugh broke the tension at some subtle but critical level. "Maybe it's because you just swallowed my brain, and I don't even know who you are."

"Ah." She took the bait, proffered her hand. "My name is Nora."

And Syd didn't know what else to do, so he took her hand into his own. And the rush of that first contact sent a physical shudder through the muscles of his back, made the filament nerves running down his spine glow green with the light from her eyes. He looked into those eyes, searching for some clue as to her intentions, saw only wry amusement and the purest molten fire.

And he wanted to say *my divorce is final. The wreck-*

age of my life has begun to settle, and I think I might be ready to try and live again.

And he wanted to say *I almost died today. Twice. Maybe three times, if you count that letter. And I am such a mass of scar tissue and damage that it's a miracle I can feel you at all.*

And he wanted to say *just don't lie to me. Please. That's the only thing I ask.*

Because it's the one thing I don't think I could survive.

But he couldn't. And because he couldn't bring himself to find or speak the words, couldn't cough them up from the depths of his soul and hack them out into the world, he found himself at a crossroads. What he feared—more than anything—was that this would all vaporize should he try to hold on to it. What he wanted—more than anything—was to believe that a moment such as this could actually *be* this direct and real.

As real as the hand he now held in his own.

That hand was warm and slender, surprisingly calloused and strong. It hovered expectantly, neither giving nor taking, but simply awaiting his next move. Syd didn't know what else to do, so he brought it slowly to his lips, kissing the web of flesh that joined finger to finger to hand.

It was clear, from her eyes, that she approved.

"Nora," he said, her name thick and powerful in his throat. "So what are we doing?"

"That remains to be seen," she told him, smiling. "But I think we're off to an excellent start."

6

IT DIDN'T TAKE long, in the grand scheme of things, to move from point A to point B.

Nora was nothing if not direct. She had no interest in small talk, past the barest fundamentals: his name, his beverage of choice, did he live alone. Syd found that this was not a problem, so long as she kept touching him like that. Thus far, she had displayed no inclination to stop.

It started with the barest of fingertip contact as he handed her her drink. Nora drank Southern Comfort, neat. As he raised the glass to her grasp Nora's little finger curled into the palm of his hand, the nail grazing the calloused skin there, then raking outward as she withdrew. Her fingernail was long and sharp, and the resulting sensation set off a chain reaction in Syd's nervous system that left him visibly shaking.

He sloshed the shot glass as she took it, spilling a dollop of sweet liquor on his fingers. Nora took his hand in hers, brought it to her lips. He watched her tongue emerge, soft and pink and darting, to lick them clean.

When Syd could see straight again, he looked at her. Nora was smiling.

By the time the band took the stage at a quarter past ten, it had started to get truly disgusting, so they moved from the bar to a booth near the back. It was dark and warm, semiprivate and cozy; and from there, things heated up with mind-bending speed.

The first kiss, for example. From the moment they sat her lips were upon his, bluntly bypassing all pretense of seduction, the better to get to the heart of the act itself. There was no mickeymouse subterfuge, no jockeying for position or storming of the psychosexual ramparts; just a straightforward escalation of intensity that left Syd simultaneously unnerved and elated.

Nora was the kind of kisser for whom the act commanded total concentration, and absolute devotion. He could feel her soul moving through the delicate interplay of lips, the perpetual subtle shift and glide of her head: nuzzling sideways and leaning in to deliver one liquid punchline after another; then drawing back, to taunt and tease, to let her teeth and the soft pointed tip of her tongue provoke him to passionate attack.

She was aggressive, but she knew when to relent, in fact had an exquisite sense of give-and-take. She liked to have her mouth invaded. She liked to let her mouth invade. Her kisses consisted of peaks and valleys and long slipsliding continuums, wherein nothing existed but his mouth and hers and the hot swirling dance in which they were entangled.

And then she would start to move her hands, ever-so-slowly; and it was as if time had shifted gears and he could glimpse all the subtle mechanisms at play. Suddenly, time was measured in the long, slow seconds it took for her graceful fingertips to glide through his hair, luxuriantly trace the outer whorls of his ear, then slide back to settle on the nape of his neck, where they would inscribe intricate little patterns at the base of his skull.

It was at that moment that the world went spinning away, only to return a microsecond later, strangely amplified. It was as if all of his senses had expanded a bit beyond their normal boundaries, rendering his impressions of

the woman before him and the room around him in over-
saturated clarity.

And then he would remember that *he* had hands, too,
and the universe would instantly expand to contain the multiple dimensions of the game: one hand cupping the back of
her head, basking in the richness of her hair; the other ex-
ploring the strong muscles of her back, the delicate ridge of
her spine, the long graceful slope to her ass.

And all the while, their mouths would be moving:
breathlessly working in tandem, wordlessly communicat-
ing their intention. And when her other hand came up to
stroke his chest, squeeze one nipple erect inside his shirt,
he would run his hand along the firm high crest of her hip,
and her fervent mouth would grind into him hard as her
body pressed flush against him.

And then he would submerge again, coaxing a moan
from deep inside her, fingers circling and probing the secret
space inside her jacket in the seconds before she peeled out
of it. Occasionally they would break for a moment, come up
for air and each other's eyes.

They had just done both when the bass drum thudded,
and the voice boomed out from the p.a.'s speakers:

"LADIES AND GENTLEMEN, PLEASE WELCOME
THE FINEST BLUES SINGER THIS SIDE OF THE
MISSISSIPPI! LET'S HEAR IT FOR *QUEEN BEE AND
THE BLUE HORNET BAND!!!*"

The applause that followed was thunderous. Queen
Bee was a house favorite, and the place was packed. But
Syd was more than a little surprised to see Nora pull back
and break the spell. She let out a war whoop, joining in
the general clamor. She beamed at him.

"Wow," he began. He stared at her, slowly regaining
his senses. "You know . . . ?"

And then his voice was lost as the band kicked in, a
full-tilt boogie that walloped against the walls. There were
dozens of folks who had come for one reason. They took
over the dance floor and made it their own. The tune was
a smokin' instrumental: no Queen Bee as yet, just the Hornet Band a-buzzin'. Guitar Mark's gray fedora was pulled

down over his eyes as he dug down deep into the evening's first solo. He had a face like Satch from the Bowery Boys, but *damn* that boy could wail.

"YOU KNOW THIS BAND?" Syd hollered out. He had no other choice.

She nodded with vigor. "I *LOVE* QUEEN BEE!"

He grinned, shook his head. "I *KNEW* THERE WAS A REASON I LIKED YOU!"

She laughed and snuggled in close, brought her lips to his ear. *"We need another drink,"* she said, just barely loud enough to be heard. *"And then you need to dance with me."*

He drew back for a second, made a broad comic grimace, then shook his head sadly and mouthed the words *I don't dance.*

She drew him back. *"You do now,"* she whispered.

At that moment, her hand landed on his thigh and squeezed, thumb sliding up the inseam. Syd sucked in breath, shut his eyes, let them open. It was definitely time for a drink. He found his gaze casting around for the waitress. Jane was at the next table; he brought a hand up and waved. When she looked at him, he saw her eyes were dark with disapproval. Then she nodded, finished up her business, collected her tip and headed toward them. Nora turned just as Jane drew near.

Abruptly, Nora rose.

Syd looked up, startled. Her hand left his crotch, took hold of his as she stood. He could feel the tension coursing through her. She pulled, and he rose as well, confused. He looked at Jane.

Jane had stopped dead in her tracks.

And though Syd couldn't see Nora's face, Jane visibly *stiffened,* then averted her eyes. Was it fear that he saw there? He wasn't sure. Without another word, Nora brushed past her, heading for the dance floor with Syd in tow. He tried to meet Jane's gaze as he passed, could not. Nora was leading him too quickly away.

And then he was weaving through the crowd, following her, in awe of the swath that she cut through the masses as he trailed in her wake. The back of her dress was deep-cut and laced, scooping down the exquisite expanse of flesh clear to her sacral dimples. As he moved he found himself torn between the contours of her ass and the sight of all those eyes upon him: familiar faces, transformed by surprise and naked envy, viewing him in an entirely new light. The light her proximity cast upon him.

And he suddenly remembered not wanting to see the prick she'd come with, or come to see. Remembered what an automatic response that was, how deep it ran, and how ashamed it made him feel. *Now* somehow, in the course of the evening, he had *become* that prick. For all of its perks, it was not an entirely pleasant place to be.

He could see it in the eyes of the good ol' boys, clustered around the bar. He could see it in the eyes of the small hairy man, his shapely companions for the moment all-but-forgotten. He could even see it in his good pal Tommy's eyes: a cold spark of jealousy and pain, beneath the plastic smile and supportive thumbs-up gesture.

He wondered, for a moment, what it was that Jane had seen.

Then Nora was bellying up to the bar, the crowd magically evaporating before her, re-forming at her periphery. He sidled up beside her, and looked in her eyes for the first time since they'd left the table. They sparkled with mischief, only barely contained. At least *one* significant factor hadn't changed. But there was something else there, too: something hard, and harder to place. It was the knife-edged glint of experience, and it summed up her feelings for the whole room and everyone in it, save himself.

"TWO DOUBLE SHOTS OF COMFORT!" she called across the bar to Jules. He nodded, shot a quick glance at Syd. Syd looked at Nora. *"For us,"* she said.

He hesitated a second, then leaned close to her ear. *"I don't do shots,"* he said. *"They make me go away."*

"Relax," she assured him. *"You ain't goin' nowhere."*

Then Jules was there, with his customary flourish, dispensing the rich red liquor. Nora carried no purse or wallet, save a little woven drawstring bag she dangled from one wrist. From this she withdrew a ten-spot, then slapped it on the bar just as the Hornets brought their jam to a close. By the time they all finished applauding, the ten was gone, and her change had replaced it. She left it where it lay, turned back to Syd.

"To us," she said softly, in the pocket of silence.

And raised her glass to his.

The sweet whiskey burned a track down his gullet, made a beeline for his medulla oblongata. Shots always went straight to his head, and this one was no exception. He could hear the applause well up again, Guitar Mark's voice shouting something over it. Over the heads of the crowd, he saw the Queen Bee herself take the stage. *"Come on!"* Nora said, taking his hand once more.

And then they were wending once again through the crowd—up onto the dance floor, toward the front of the stage—just as the band broke into its slow shuffling four-bar intro. Queen Bee positioned herself behind the mic stand: a big wide powerful-looking angelfaced black woman, beautiful and gifted and strong. Her face and voice had the kind of character that takes lifetimes to accumulate. When she sang, all the world's sweet sorrow, heartbreak and pain found embodiment in that voice, that soul.

She was singing now. His favorite Queen Bee tune. The one that he connected with best. He had listened to it just this morning. Before the deer.

Before the wolf . . .

> *"Every night, about this time*
> *I go to sleep, to keep from cryin' . . ."*

. . . and Syd found himself thrown back to those moments, that sensation of hollow dread that began in his marrow and emanated outward, felt it well up and nearly subsume him in the moment before Nora stopped and turned and drew him close . . .

> *"Every night, about this time*
> *I go to sleep, to keep from cryin' . . ."*

. . . and then he thought about Karen, and all the years he'd already pissed away on her behalf: operating under the sway of her illusions, suckered in by his own need. Desperately trying to resuscitate an already-butchered thing. Trying to rebuild a relationship that was rotten to its foundations . . .

> *" 'Cause my baby, yes my baby*
> *Always runnin' 'round . . ."*

. . . and the thought of it—the thought of *her*—was so utterly toxic to his soul that he flinched from it, constricted against it, tried to drive it shrieking from his heart and mind. Its poison sank deep into everything it touched: the beautiful music in his ears, the incredible woman in his arms.

And then Nora kissed him again: twirling gracefully with him, in time with the music. And it was so altogether absolutely fine that it resisted and transcended the poison, overran the tiny voice in the back of his mind that said *what if she's cheating on some husband somewhere? What if she's lying, too?*

But the reality of this woman, this stranger, this mysterious Nora who had blown so overwhelmingly into his life was like an island of salvation in a vast and brutal sea. There was substance in her presence. There was power in her touch. It made him feel strong, to be kissing this woman. It made him feel almost immortal.

As her body pressed against him, the alcohol caressed his brain. And all of it conspired to free him from his pain. Her kiss contained more than a whiff of liberation. Her saliva felt alive in his mouth. Every single cell of his being bore testimony to that truth.

Syd kissed back hard, felt something long sleeping begin to stir within him.

He stopped and looked at her. Her eyes flashed in anticipation.

"Let's get out of here," she said at last.

7

THE BONNEVILLE MOVED through the night like a
shark through dark waters, following the scent of
blood. It was a late-model beast: its hide spattered and
gravel-scarred from too many back roads and unpaved
parking lots, the paint-job stippled with road salt and rust
until it faded to a bruised brownish-red, the color of scabs.
The license plate was mud-caked to the point of illegibil-
ity.

Like the car, it was stolen. It was not a problem; the
owner would not be looking for it anytime soon.

The driver pressed on the gas, nudging the big car up
to a stately seventy-per. The engine roared to life, hurtling
into blackness as the road opened up before him. The sky
above was crystal clear, alight with stars. The headlights
and dashboard illumination were off, the better to blend
with the night.

The driver didn't need them; he could see just fine.

Up ahead a sign proclaimed YOU'VE GOT A FRIEND IN
PENNSYLVANIA. The driver chuckled as it disappeared behind him. He was a hulking shadow behind the wheel, one
hand steering languidly while the other draped over the

empty passenger seat. He was completely underdressed for
the cold, clad only in battered leather duster, black T-shirt,
and jeans. A tiny chain of skulls dangled from his right
ear, jiggling from the wind and road. A scar bisected his
left cheek, a thin seam that arced from the corner of his
mouth to the outside edge of his eye socket. It was the
sole imperfection in his otherwise killer good looks, and
even at that gave him a dangerous smirk, as if he was possessed of some secret, lethal knowledge.

A tiny silver bracelet dangled from his grasp. An uncapped bottle of Wild Turkey was nestled between his
thighs. He reached for it, took a long sweet pull, felt it
burn through his bloodstream. It put a nice edge on things,
sharpened him up for the hunt.

The road was a secondary highway, utterly deserted
but for the big rigs that periodically rumbled past. Utility
poles and power lines whipped by like ghosts, punctuated
by the occasional darkened house. Cold breeze blasted
through the open window, rustling the papers scattered
across the floor. Road maps and local music mags from a
half-dozen backwater burgs littered the interior like a tell-
tale trail of bread crumbs, offering leads.

The driver sniffed the air, testing it. He could smell the
locals, tucked in for the night in their little crackerbox
cages, all snug and safe in their beds. No cages for him;
not now, not ever. He sneered at their smug assignations,
reveled in the uneasy glances he inspired. It amused him,
filled him with contempt just as surely as he filled them
with dread, the shapeless fear of the herd. He could feel
their brows tensing in slumber as he passed, a fleeting
shiver like a bad dream flitting across unconscious
mindscapes, then gone.

He was a predator, cruising through a land fat with
prey. There was danger in his gaze, death in his kiss. But
not for them. Not tonight.

Tonight he had other plans.

The radio burbled under the roar of the wind: a smoky,
sinister groove snaking out of the speakers. The driver
smiled, thumbed it up a notch. Bass and drums conspired

with lonely guitar to pump out an insidious backbeat; the singer's voice was husky, ripe with threat.

> *"Last call for whiskey, baby*
> *It's time to drive you home*
> *Let's pray it's not too far from here ..."*

The driver fingered the bracelet. His hands were big, prominently veined, strong yet strangely delicate. The bracelet was a pretty little thing, a dainty chain with charms hanging from it. Long fingers pinched each one in turn, like a string of rosary beads, reading them by shape. *Heart ... bell ... flower ...*

His fingertips were smooth, the skin tough as glove leather and pebbled like a dog's paw, utterly devoid of fingerprints. His touch, like all of his senses, was keenly attenuated, highly tuned.

The bracelet was a souvenir from a sweet young thing he'd scarfed in a dive two nights ago, just outside of Morgantown. The memory of her still lingered on his tongue: soft and pink and tight, sweet young meat in fishnets and boots and a black leather bustier.

peace symbol ... guitar ... a tiny silver skull ...

He hadn't even been interested at first, so caught up was he in the hunt. But then their eyes had met, and she smiled, and the spark had lit inside him. And it dawned on him that it had been a while, really, far too long in fact.

Her breasts were small but very firm, like the rest of her. *A spinner.* Her hair was a dark cascade of curls against milk-white skin. He liked the way her hips cocked when she danced, a grinding circular motion.

dagger ... crucifix ... devil ...

He took her down the road a piece, then he took her right there in the backseat, her legs hiked up over the headrests and spread wide to receive him. He liked the noise she made when he slid inside her, full of hunger.

He gave her what she wanted. Then he took what he wanted. She fought him, at first. He liked that even better.

On the radio, the music played.

" 'Cause the road is rotten, honey
You know the road is long
A lot of things can happen
in the time that you'll be gone, gone ..."

The driver grinned. How true. Her name escaped him—Karen? Sharon? No matter. They all tended to blend together after a while, just faces and bodies and legs and asses, all meat for his table. And aside from the thrill of the chase, not one of them ever meant a damned thing to him.

She had to understand that, he told himself. It was all about the joy of the hunt. Sure, you might focus on 'em in the heat of the moment—what good hunter wouldn't? Let 'em know your eye was on them, and they would never, ever get away. That was half the fun. But still, in the end it was just meat.

Like Karen-Sharon. Whatever. He was hell with names, but he never forgot a face.

And even if he did, hers was still in the trunk.

Up ahead, the trees gave way to a clearing; he could make out the winking red glow of a Stroh's sign. He tossed the bracelet out the window and eased off the gas, scanned the tree line as the needle dipped to sixty, fifty, forty, thirty ...

He slid past, scoping the terrain. It was a low-slung building, set back into a carved-out niche in the woods. Classic roadhouse configuration. The place was packed; a good three dozen cars and half again as many vans and four-by-fours were scattered across the parking lot. A porta-sign at the driveway read *live music ... wed wet T-shirt nite ... drinks 1/2 price ...*

The muted thud of a band filled the niche, underscored by the distant pulsing of a hundred beating hearts. Off to one side of the building, he spotted a huddle of people sneaking a quick joint in the cold. Another car pulled up and parked, its occupants piling out and pushing into the front door of the bar. Easy to lose yourself in such a place, he thought. Easier still to lose someone else.

But not for long, he added. Not for long . . .

The driver sniffed, sifting the many heady scents. The stale reek of tobacco and whiskey and beer. The tang of sweating flesh. The sweet hot funk of lust and hunger and naked human desire.

And, underpinning and permeating everything, *her* smell. Undeniable. Unmistakable. She'd been here recently, immersing herself in the crowd, trying to throw him off. But she was in heat, and she was cruising. Might as well spray it on the door, babe, he thought. You're so fucking easy. . . .

The scent was strong. The thought occurred to him that she might be here still, off in the bushes somewhere, or in somebody's bed. Getting off. Getting *fed*. The thought maddened him: a spike of jealousy jammed through the center of his skull, crowding out every other impulse. Dredging up things that snapped at his soul like a dog on a chain.

He touched the accelerator; the Bonneville rumbled and slithered by. He waited until the woods resumed before pulling onto the shoulder, some two hundred yards down.

He shut the engine off and sat very still, contemplating the darkness. The moon was there, in many ways his best and truest love: the only woman who'd always stood by him, and never let him down. Which was more than he could say for *some* people he knew.

But he didn't want to think about that right now.

There was a rumbling in the driver's belly: the hunger for meat, and the hunger for payback. The deeper hunger, beneath it all. Eating was the least of his worries: hell, he could scrounge a snack from just the leftovers in the trunk. As for payback . . . well, maybe tonight he'd get lucky. He sure as hell hoped so. For his sake, *and* hers.

But the *other* hunger, the one only she could fill . . . well, that was a problem. That gnawed at him mercilessly, sent spasms up his spine and made his brain itch in a place he just couldn't scratch. The more he thought about it, the crazier he felt. She was off somewhere, giving it up to some unsuspecting shmuck. And if he didn't get there in time . . .

And suddenly the chain snapped, and the beast was loose in his brain. The balance in him shifted, his man-mind taking a backseat to his other nature, skittering off like a lantern tossed down a well. Suddenly the car felt too confining, boxy metal bearing down on him when the stars alone were all he wanted over his head. He reached up, raking his fingers across the ceiling liner, prying out huge divots, pressing his bulk against the seat until the seat supports groaned and buckled from the stress.

He had to get out. Wrenching the handle, he pushed open the door, stepped into the night, kicked it shut. The wind was wild, and fiercely cold; with that, he could relate. His clothes were too constricting to suffer for another second; his skin itched madly, hotter than a hundred sunburns. He peeled off the duster, tossed it into the open window. His black cowboy boots followed, then his T-shirt and jeans.

Finally he stood, naked to the night. His body was wiry-muscular, his arms cabled and covered with tattoos, each a different likeness of the woman he sought. The inkings shifted with each subtle play of ligament and sinew, until she appeared alive, rippling beneath the surface.

The night bathed him, felt alive on his skin. The roadhouse lights twinkled through the trees. His nipples hardened in the chill air; a tiny silver ring dangled from one, glimmering in the moonlight. The wind shifted and a backbeat came to him, faint as a pulse. The ghost of the snaky melody still echoed in his head, a lunar love song if ever there was one. He began to hum along.

"Last call for whis-key, baby . . ." he sang, "it's time to drive you home . . ."

His voice doubled and deepened in mid-croon, like a man teaching a dog to sing. The thought tickled him royally.

He glanced back at the interior of the car, the pile of clothes laying there. His belt buckle dangled gleaming on the seat: a stainless-steel rectangle, big blocky letters spelling *V* ... *I* ... *C* ...

That's my name, he thought, wildly amused at the thought of his totality being so neatly contained in a word. Vic smiled as he went around to the back of the car, chuckled as he reached into the trunk, laughed out loud as he stepped away.

By the time he reached the tree line his jaws had elongated, the better to accommodate the depth of his mirth, and his grin had blossomed with many, many sharp and shiny teeth.

Vic ran his tongue across them, conspicuously pleased, as the moon conferred her blessing, racing through the midnight sky.

It was all he could do to resist the urge to bay.

8

T HE WEIRDNESS DIDN'T hit him until they were almost out the door. But when it came, it came down hard.

One second, Syd was escorting this devastating woman to his car. The next thing he knew, there was an icy tapeworm of dread unfurling in his gut.

It started when Nora informed him that they needed a bottle for the road. Not at all an unreasonable request, but there was one tiny problem. In the commonwealth of Pennsylvania, the only place you could legally buy takeout wine or booze by the bottle was a State Store. These altogether joyless institutions were, of course, a public service of the Liquor Control Board: the same bunch of spoilsports who shut down bars for serving drinks to minors. This helped explain why shopping there felt so much like filing with the I.R.S.

Among their many customer-pleasing qualities, State Stores promptly shut down by nine, even on Friday and Saturday nights. Which, he emphasized, made it kinda tricky for them to pick up a fifth of Southern Comfort on the way back from the bar.

This, however, was not the answer Nora wanted to hear. And his assurance that he had half a case of Keystones in the fridge did nothing to assuage her concern. They needed hard liquor, she insisted. They needed Comfort. Simple as that.

Syd considered the problem logistically for a minute. Breaking into a State Store wasn't such a hot idea, though they both agreed it would probably be fun. Fortunately, they were at a bar; and though bars were only allowed to sell carry-out *beer* in the state of Pennsylvania, there was always a chance that the rules might be bent, this being kind of a special occasion and all. Chameleon's usually had plenty of backstock, and Nora seemed to have plenty of cash on hand. Syd had neither, but said he would be happy to play liaison, see what he could do. It was good, at such times, to have friends in high places.

So Syd asked Jules, and Jules said sure, which meant that everything was fine and dandy. Right up until the point that they arranged to meet around back for the actual handoff.

Nora didn't like that idea at all. She said she didn't see the point; and Syd was surprised to see that the notion actually seemed to make her nervous.

Jules explained that this wasn't the kind of transaction you did in full view of the general public. Not only would *everyone* start sidling up and begging him to slip them bottles of Cuervo on the sly, but you never knew *where* those fun-loving guys from the L.C.B. might be lurking: they looked so much like real humans sometimes, it was almost frightening.

So rather than risk jeopardizing the club's license, not to mention his own livelihood, Jules would just go down to the basement, grab a bottle off the rack, pop it in a paper bag, and meet them in five minutes by the rear kitchen entrance. They could just drive by the back of the building on their way out of Dodge. No muss, no fuss.

That seemed simple enough—to Syd, anyway—but that was when Nora started getting a little twitchy. She just wouldn't let it go. She asked Jules why he couldn't just

hand them the paper bag *here*. He said that, well, technically, he *could;* it would just be a lot cooler the other way.
She said that she didn't understand what the big deal was,
if it was in a closed-up grocery bag. He could be handing
over a bunch of clothes, or a handful of sandwiches. He
could be handing over anything.

By this point, thirsty customers were starting to stack
up around them. Jules took a deep breath and looked at
Syd. Syd picked up his cue at that point, saying yeah,
man, we understand your position, thanks a lot, it's not a
problem. Then he turned to Nora and told her not to
worry. He would get it.

That was when Nora stared him dead in the eye and
said, "I can't believe you guys are such a couple of
chickenshits."

And the thing was, it wasn't just the words. It was entirely the way that she said them. These were not words
that were intended to tease, or josh, or otherwise cheer-
fully cajole; they drew blood, and had been whipped out
for precisely that reason. The quiet ferocity of it stunned
him. It wasn't just uncalled-for; it was goddam spooky.

That was when the tapeworm first began to uncoil.

Oh fuck, Syd thought, looking from Nora to Jules and
back again. Jules was the most level-headed person Syd
had ever met—the man had trained himself to deflect almost anything—but it was impossible to miss the flinch
that rode the moment of impact on this one. It was, of
course, because he had not been expecting it. The shift
from yellow to full red alert had gone down in the space
of a second; there just wasn't enough time to get the
shields up.

Syd knew exactly how he felt. In a word: bush-
whacked. But when he looked back at Nora, the one thing
he saw no trace of was sympathy. What he saw was smug
self-righteousness, a defiance totally unmitigated by apol-
ogy. What he also saw was someone who was starting to
show the effects of all those double shots. One look in
those eyes and it was definitely time to look back at Jules
again.

When you knew someone really well, it was amazing how precisely you could read the fine print of their faces. What X amount of raised eyebrow means, in an otherwise impassive countenance. Syd knew that Jules's expression could be broadly interpreted to mean either *this woman is an asshole* or *your call, man. It's up to you.*

But the most literal interpretation would have to be *are you sure that you know what you're doing?*

And the answer to that was: no, he wasn't. All of a sudden, he wasn't sure at all. He was drunk, too—there was no two ways about it—and up until about a minute ago, he'd been well on his way to *falling* for this woman. But he'd been around enough mean drunks in his day to develop a pointed aversion response. It was, at the least, a major turnoff; at worst, a deal-breaker. And it pissed him off besides.

When he looked back at Nora, it must have been in his eyes, because her own eyes flared over a nasty little smile. It was the kind of smile you only see on people who adore a bloodbath. "Let me know what you decide," Jules said, then went off to tend his clientele. Which left Syd and Nora alone together, locked in a war of the wills.

"You want to tell me what this is about?" he inquired.

Her eyes squinted suspiciously. "You want to tell me what you mean?"

"Aw, c'mon, Nora. Don't be coy with me. You're the last person in the world I wanna fight with right now." He looked at her as he spoke. "We were having *so much fun*. . . ." He let the words trail off and smiled a little, ruefully, because it was so utterly true.

Her features softened momentarily, though her eyes stayed flint-hard. "Maybe we still *are* having fun," she said.

"Yeah, well." Syd dropped the eyeball war for a moment, sighed long and deep, brought his gaze back to hers. "I gotta admit, darlin': it kinda rains on my parade a little when I ask a friend for a favor . . ."

"Ah." The hackles were back up, as quick as they'd fallen.

"... and he winds up getting kinda pissed-on for it,"
Syd continued. He could feel himself step over the line of
romantic propriety and instantly regretted the inelegance
of the phrase.

"Ooh, *baby!*" she said, and her eyes were like fireballs
of raging emerald glee. "Believe me: you haven't seen me
take a piss on someone yet. When I do, you'll know it."

"Oh." Snide. "Well, *that* sounds promising. . . ."

"You don't seem to know what's going on here," she
cut in, wild and fiercely grinning. "I don't think you even
know what you're made of. You're a pretty cool guy, Syd.
But you're kind of a dink, if you know what I'm saying."

The words stung. "No, I don't. What the hell *are* you
saying?"

"What I'm *saying*," and for this she leaned in close,
"is that I don't fuck domesticated animals. I eat them."

He laughed. So did she. She leaned in, until her nose
was nuzzling up against his ear. "And I think you should
know what you're rubbing up against," she murmured,
"'cause if you haven't figured out by now that there's an
element of *risk* involved here . . . then, baby, you'd better
wake up, 'cause you're in for an awful shock."

She pulled back, hovered inches from his face, eyes
blazing, imperious. It was a withering look, to be sure.
And it probably would have shriveled ninety-nine percent
of the men she met. But the combination of liquor, lust,
and just plain stubbornness had ignited something belliger-
ent in Syd. He met her stare head-on, faced her down.

"So what the *fuck*," he said flatly, "has that got to do
with whether I score you a bottle out the back door or over
the counter? Can you explain that to me, please?"

And because he was staring into her eyes—and because he was doing it so intently—he could see the fear
resurface, flicker across them before she had a chance to
raise the screens. It sent up an urgent warning flag, its
double-edged message exceedingly clear. *She is not about
to go out back. And she is not about to tell me why.*

It was the moment of truth and decision.

And that was when she kissed him.

And once again, he found himself sucked in and swal-
lowed, drowned and intoxicated by her presence. The feel
of her flesh. The taste of her lips. The unmistakable heat
of her passion. There was something so utterly real *about*
her—so fundamental and pure—that it made him question
every objection he posed, made him doubt every appeal to
caution.

He gave himself over to the kiss.

And, in doing so, sealed his fate.

9

VIC HUNKERED IN the choke of woods just beyond the roadhouse parking lot: long teeth sawing strips from a thin severed limb, cold blue eyes locked on the bright neon light in the clearing. Cars pulled in and out, loading and dispensing chattering bundles of humanity; the woods a safe distance away from him rustled with life. But the space immediately surrounding him was deathly still, a pocket of silence in a bustling netherworld. Other night creatures gave him wide berth, sensing it was for the best. He didn't blame them a bit.

Vic chewed contentedly. It wasn't yet time to scatter the bones, leave them out for scavengers to disperse. There was still a lot left on those bones, even if it *was* two days old. Vic preferred fresh meat, but he had to admit that the aging gave it a gaminess he rather enjoyed. And it was only right that you ate what you killed.

The chewy hollow at the crook of the elbow was surprisingly rewarding: not a whole lot of flesh there, but the texture was superb. And he liked the fact that you could make the fingers waggle if you gnawed on the tendons just right. He braced the arm with one huge misshapen paw, made toothy puppet magic. Wave bye-bye to all the nice people, Karen-Sharon-whatever.

C'mon and wave hi to my baby for me.

The dead fingers twitched feebly, just above the frozen grass: less waving, it seemed, than desperately clutching after life. Oh, well. Vic had hoped it might be good for a laugh, but it was actually kind of depressing. He cracked the arm like a crab's leg in his jaws, and the fingers just stopped.

So much for playing with your food.

This was the downside of the stalking process. Killing time. Keeping his man-mind both amused and in check. His animal nature was pure, unadulterated physical focus: ears cocked, eyes locked on target, massive body poised and alert, every nerve tuned to the tiniest motion around him.

But his man-mind was a capering monkey, and it loved to swing from limb to limb: restless and chattering, easily bored, far more a creature of the trees than the ground below. It had a way of racing away with him, even as the nervous system remained locked in the thrall of the beast: sometimes dragging his emotions along with it, making soul-art with handfuls of flinging shit.

Which was maybe why he found himself crouched here in the dark: way the hell out in the middle of Bumfuck, Pa., just upwind from some cheesy little r&b dump, with his animal nature wholly driven by the memory of Nora's scent while his man-mind went crazy for something to do. If he could just stroll in there and shoot a game of pool, have a drink, maybe KILL somebody, this wouldn't be a problem. It was the *restraint* that was driving him mad.

The moonlight tugged, her cold light balming his core. He took a moment to savor her glow, was struck once more by how totally misunderstood was the relationship between her and his kind. He loved the moon—was crazy about her in fact—but he certainly didn't *need* her to turn. For that, he needed no one's help. He was fully the agent of his own Change.

So why, then, did he love her so much, spend so much time in her company? He might as well ask, *why love women at all?* He loved the moon because she spoke to him, was fluent in all his tongues. When his blood howled, she whispered encouragement in his veins, smiling down from the blackened sky as he roamed the darkened earth. She understood his desires and hungers. She questioned nothing, yet understood everything.

He loved her because she was beautiful, and mysterious, and powerful, and remote; because she was perpetually both there for him and simultaneously, maddeningly out of reach.

Most of all, he loved her because she touched a deep and secret place within him that mortal meat only dreamed of. The vibrations that steered the ocean's tides clearly exerted their pull upon him as well. He was in love with the way she yanked his chains.

It was a quality that only the finest lovers shared.

And so, each night, he sang to her, laid sacrifices on her altar. And each night, she returned to him, no questions asked. In many ways, the moon *was* the ultimate mistress: she never got jealous, never threatened him, never tried to have him killed; and she never made him chase her halfway around the goddam country, either. She was always just *there*. He wondered why more women couldn't be like that. It sure as hell would make his life a little easier. . . .

And such were his thoughts in the moment before the front door of the roadhouse opened. Vic leaned back on his haunches, grinning horribly through his rows of teeth. *Is this him?* he asked himself. *Is this the miserable fuck that I'm gonna have to kill tonight?*

The door hung open for a moment, as if in shock.

And then out he came.

"Son of a *BITCH!!!*"

Syd stepped outside and got power-slammed by a faceful of wind. The night had turned unexpectedly savage in the couple of hours since they'd come together: temperature plummeting into the twenties, with a windchill factor that dropped it into the single digits. The blast that whooshed up to greet him was a serious, sobering smack in the face; it pulled his flesh taut as a snare drum head, made his corpuscles cringe underneath the skin.

"SYD! SHUT THE DAMN DOOR!" Red hollered over the din inside.

"SORRY!" Syd yelled back, as a gaggle of latecomers crowded past him and pushed up to pay the cover. He stepped out of their way, let the door shut behind them. The wind gave it a boost on the back half, and it slammed home with a mute finality.

Leaving him out in the cold.

And all by himself.

"Damn," Syd hissed, and turned to face his mission. Nora had remained adamant about slipping out the back door; finally in exasperation Syd had said that *he* would get the car, swing around to meet Jules, then come back around front to pick her up. It appeased her only a little.

"Hurry up," she'd said, then kissed him again. The kiss was hot, hungry, almost desperate. As if she was afraid she would never see him again.

Syd stuffed his hands in his pockets and started across toward his car, feet crunching on hard-packed stone. As he walked he realized that he was seriously buzzed; Nora was definitely not the only one feeling the effects of so many double shots. Correction, he thought, as he pitched and weaved around a pickup truck: he was higher than a fucking kite. The sights and sounds of the night seemed razor-sharp, incredibly clear; frosted windshields sparkled in the arc-light glow, flickered from the multicolored neon beer signs in the windows; the crackle of boots on gravel echoed in his bones.

Beyond the parking lot, naked trees and lush evergreens swayed together in the pale moonlight: great gangly skeletons, huge hulking leviathans, dancing with the whistling wind. The moon was nearly full, completely unsullied by clouds. The cold made everything crisp, beautifully severe; the wind in his eyes made the lights beam like

stars; the alcohol underpinned it all with the detached sur-
realism of a dream. His brain felt loosely moored inside
his skull, as if any minute now it would disengage, go spiraling off.

Syd shook his head, trying to clear it. It had been ages
since he'd gotten high, easily a decade or more since he'd
dosed or done mushrooms, but the feeling threw him back.
It was the preternatural feeling of *something coming,* the
high-voltage subterranean hum of doors about to be blown
open. It was a feeling that had been growing all night, one
that started the moment her tongue first slid between his
lips. . . .

Syd shivered, his lips still electric from her touch. Behind him, Queen Bee's rhythm section receded to an urgent thud as her voice wailed over the top of it. *"Harder
than a Freight Train."* Yee-hah.

His car was just ahead, at the far end of the lot. He
could see it glistening faintly in the distance as he jogged
between a Volvo and a battered Plymouth Fury. As he
made his way through the rows of neatly parked cars, he
didn't see anything that jumped up and screamed "Nora!":
no sleek black Porsches with zebra-striped seats, no
cherry-red Alfa-Romeos. He could always be wrong, but
he seriously doubted that she drove a Yugo.

*Funny she didn't say anything about having to leave
her car here,* he noted. Then again, not funny. Or particularly surprising. Syd got the feeling there were *a lot* of
things she wasn't telling him. It made him uneasy, thinking of the unknown baggage that could be coming along
on this particular ride. It reminded him why he was so bad
with one-night stands, why he had so few of them to his
credit. There was always a life, just past the fantasy. And
life could get messy.

As he reached his car, a thought struck him. *You could
just leave.* It was completely ridiculous, strangely appealing. Syd considered what it would be like: actually getting
in, starting up, and driving away without her. He pictured
Nora: sitting at the bar, growing increasingly impatient, in-

creasingly pissed, until she eventually got the hint and left, cursing him for his gutlessness.

. . . you're a nice guy, Syd, but you're a bit of a dink . . .

Syd winced, her words stinging at his memory. At the edge of the lot the Mt. Haversford Road beckoned, a black macadam ribbon ready to carry him back. But to what? Syd felt more keenly than ever how empty his life had become: wandering shell-shocked through his private wreckage like a bomb-blast survivor, neatly stacking the shrapnel, making piles of nothing.

Still, Nora had spooked him, back in the bar. Worse yet, there was genuine fear beneath all that attitude. *But what was she so damned scared of? A jealous ex-boyfriend?* That would certainly suck. *A pissed-off current boyfriend?* The tiny voice nattered in his head again, painting ugly pictures he didn't want to see. Begging other questions he wasn't sure he wanted the answers to.

Then again, he told himself, he could be way off-base. Maybe she'd had some kind of horrible experience in a parking lot at night. Some kind of assault. Maybe rape. Or a loved one killed.

Maybe even a loved one killed by the maniac who was *EVEN NOW LURKING IN THE SHADOWS . . . !!!*

"Aieee," he said out loud. "You bet." Yep, nothing like irrational terror to get the blood going. It was also distinctly possible that she'd come from outer space, and now was afraid that a tractor beam was gonna yank her back up to the mothership. Or that she was really a murderous fugitive from justice: Jessica Rabbit meets Boxcar Bertha.

Or maybe that the wolf was out here somewhere, waiting for them. . . .

Syd stopped, felt a shiver run through him that had nothing to do with the cold. Why did he suddenly think of that? His skin prickled and his ears perked up, suddenly tuned to the sounds of the night. For a moment he thought he could feel it *out there* somewhere: lurking in the darkness beyond the trees, shadowing him, tracking his every move.

Suddenly, the music from inside the bar felt as far away as his car had seemed, by the side of the road in the

first light of dawn. He blinked and the morning's tableau
returned: belly organs gaping, splayed out in his mind.

"This is stupid," he told himself. It didn't help. He
picked up his pace, scanning the parking lot for big hairy
monsters and scary ex-boyfriends.

Nope. Nothing. Not even an engine running. The parking lot was full of cars, but utterly devoid of souls.

Then why can't I shake this feeling?

He reached the Mustang, unlocked the door, and slid
inside. The interior was freezing—even without the wind,
it was like sitting in a meat locker. His breath fogged the
windows into an opaque translucence as he fumbled with
his key, fingers numb and tingling as he jammed it into the
ignition. The engine cranked and shuddered. The dash
lights winked and glowed; the defrosters erupted with
more cold. Syd pressed the gas a few times, coaxed it to
roaring life.

As the car idled his hands came up to grip the wheel,
seesawing it back and forth as he weighed his options.
This woman was trouble; he'd seen it already, could feel
more coming. More than that, even: this woman was *dangerous*. Her voice came pinwheeling back. *I don't fuck domesticated animals.*

I eat them.

Yeah, right. He could use a little of her kind of danger
right about now. She was also, he reminded himself, the
most real, vital, utterly *alive* thing he had felt in years.
Maybe ever. It felt as though his whole life was leading up
to this, his fate riding on it like a high-stakes gambler, bet-
ting the house on a single roll of the dice.

The engine idled down, ready to roll. The air from the
vents began to warm, blowing off the condensation that
clung to the windows. Chameleon's lay directly before
him. To one side, the safe road beckoned. To the other . . .

Syd reached down, put the car into gear.

And started to move.

VIC SKIRTED THE perimeter of the parking lot, tracking the
slow-moving car. His prey was oblivious, as usual. Ani-

mals were different; they never questioned their instincts. It was nature's way of compensating them for their lack of reasoning power, and it made sneaking up on them a real challenge.

People, on the other hand, reasoned instinct away, and almost always chalked it up to superstition until it was too late to do anything about it but scream.

It was what made them so easy to hunt: they simply couldn't believe that it was happening. In the heat of the moment they invariably disassociated, thinking *wow, just like on TV!* As if life were a cop show, or a movie they once saw. And before there were movies, a book they'd once read. Or a story, told round the campfire. Or anything that served to lift experience into the province of legend. Render it larger than life, and thus beyond them. It was ironic; their power to imagine was their greatest source of strength, as well as their most fatal flaw. It made anything possible for them, even as it kept them forever out of the moment.

Vic knew, from experience, that the moment was all there ever was.

The human side of his mind flashed suddenly on an old Gary Larson cartoon: two leopards up in a tree, about to pounce on an unsuspecting explorer as one of them whispers to the other, *"Watch this! These things make the greatest expressions!"*

Vic's man-mind laughed and laughed; the sound that came out was a bestial grunt. His eyes sparkled gleefully, feeling the bloodlust start to flow as his body moved through the underbrush. His limbs were well-muscled, powerful: they worked in perfect harmony, covering distance in virtual silence. The car's brake lights came on, as the big metal box slowed and rolled around the side of the bar.

Around the back! Vic smiled; his flat tongue lapped over razored teeth in anticipation.

This was *more* than perfect.

This was gonna be *fun. . . .*

•   •   •

THE ALLEY WAS dark and foreboding, maybe fifteen feet from the cinder-block backside of the building to the ditch that marked the property line beyond. A big metal dumpster hunkered by the side wall just before the turn, further obstructing his view and pinching his access until there was barely enough space on either side to squeeze through.

The woods behind the bar were thick and oppressive: overhanging branches from some of the smaller trees towered above him like big bony hands, waiting to snatch the unwary patron who occasionally ambled back to smoke a joint, take a leak, or hurl. It was a great place for an ambush, but until tonight it had never occurred to Syd exactly how creepy it was.

Syd's side windows were still fogged; he rolled them down, the better to see as he angled his car into the alley and slowed to a crawl, trying not to scrape the paint job or go into the ditch. Just past the ravine the ground rose, putting it almost level with the passenger side window; as he turned his hi-beams raked it like searchlights, casting harsh shadows in their passing.

Something moved: scuttling through the bushes, just outside the periphery of his vision. Syd tensed, thought he caught a flat glowing flash of nocturnal eyes. He looked again, but his headlights were pointed the wrong way now, restoring the woods to shadow. He peered through the passenger window, searching . . .

. . . and that was when the door boomed: swinging out toward his car, blasting him with light and the dull rhythmic roar of the band.

Syd gasped, jolting in his seat.

Jules stood in the crack of light from the kitchen, a paper bag in his hand.

"Took you long enough," Jules said. "I was beginning to think da boogeyman got ya." He saw Syd's obvious palpitations, and one eyebrow went up. "You okay?"

"Yeah." Syd lit a cigarette, took a calming drag. Jules watched him, then leaned in surreptitiously.

"Here," he said, slipping him the bottle. "You never got this here. Don't drink it all in one place."

"Thanks," Syd replied, taking the bag and stashing it. "And, um, sorry about the scene in there." He gestured toward the bar, and Nora.

"S'okay," Jules patted his arm. He paused for a moment, looked off. "Janey says she got a bad vibe off her." Then back to Syd. "You sure you're okay to drive? You were slammin' 'em down pretty hard in there."

"Yeah, I'm cool. Thanks, man."

Jules looked at him a moment, then nodded. There was a pregnant pause, as he weighed his next words carefully. "So," he said, "you sure you know what you're doing?"

Syd met the gaze, laughed nervously. "No," he said, shaking his head.

"But I'm doing it anyway."

"Yeah, well." Jules nodded, leaned in the window. "Just remember, man: dogs that show their teeth are usually the ones that bite."

Syd took that bit of wisdom with an uneasy grin. "I'll be okay," he said. "Really."

Jules shrugged. "Well, I'm freezin' my nuts off," he said. "Take care of yourself."

Syd nodded. "Later."

Jules leaned back into the kitchen, let the big metal door hiss home. As it clicked shut, it took the light with it; the darkness that remained seemed even deeper for its absence. Syd felt an anxious tremor rumble through him, as he eased off the brake. . . .

. . . AND VIC HOVERED: body crouched and twitching at the edge of the trees. He had held off, bargaining with the beast inside: not taking the man as he made the first corner, waiting to see his purpose.

He was glad he had the moment the back door opened and the cook stepped out to make their little clandestine transaction. He watched them talk, saw the bag change hands. Numbers didn't frighten Vic, but witnesses could be troublesome where time was a concern. So many victims, so little time . . .

But now the shithead was alone again, and that was very good. The car was nearing its prime kill point, where the driver had to negotiate the second turn. As he angled out the driver's attention would be on the forward motion; as the car pulled away it would leave Vic in a picture-perfect blind spot.

The moment was at hand. Vic stood, giving himself over to it entirely. His man-mind rolled back like a shark's eye in the seconds before it bites, giving the beast inside him full sway . . .

. . . and the creature began to trot, then run, body building momentum as its blood raced and its wild heart sang the song of the kill. . . .

. . . AND IN the moment before he pulled away, Syd thought he saw something in the rearview mirror. Something dark. Something moving. That was all that it took. It put the lead in his boot as he tromped on the gas; and by the time he looked back through the dust, it was gone.

But he couldn't shake the feeling that something was coming. Its pull was strong, deep, inexorable as a river moving under the earth. It felt like *destiny:* waiting to blindside him as he rounded the next bend.

So when he pulled around front to find Nora waiting just inside the door, part of him was not entirely surprised. She stepped out and stiffened, as the wind shifted into her. Then she was moving toward the car with surprising speed: throwing open the passenger door and jumping in before he even had time to stop.

"Go!" she told him. *"Now . . . !"*

Syd didn't need to be told twice. He punched it, the Mustang's tires biting hard into gravel and catching, rocketing them out of the lot in a hot-rubbered hail of flying stone. . . .

10

Just as, sixty miles away, a low-rent dope dealer
··· named Billy Hessler looked up from his latest transaction. He wasn't sure exactly why. There wasn't time for
it to matter. There was barely time, in fact, for him to see
the snarling, hurtling mass come crashing through the passenger side window of his Trans Am. He winced from the
impact, brought one arm up to shield his face. Two seconds later it fell to the floor, sheared off at mid-bicep.

His face followed a few seconds later, hitting the car-
pet with a thick splutting sound. Blood sprayed the inside
of the windshield as the body kicked and flailed. Vic
crouched atop him and reared his massive head back, then
brought it down savagely, his snout cracking the breastbone like a pickax, plunging deep until he found the succulent, still-beating heart. He seized upon it and shook: the
body spasmed and sagged.

Vic sheared off and swallowed a great steaming hunk,
tasting the terror and the panic. He could feel his victim's
screaming lifeforce enter him even as the flesh slid down
his throat, the stolen spark merging with his own, becoming part of him. Amping his power.

Making him stronger.

It was a high to end all highs, the consummate rush. Naked energy surged and crackled through his nervous system, overloading his senses. Vic growled and thrashed, ripping deeper into the steaming pile of human meat ...

... and then the buzz receded, ebbing off to a low thrumming rumble. His man-mind glitched back into focus a heartbeat later, and as it did his rational side returned. Vic sniffed the corpse: surveying his grisly handiwork. Searching for clues.

Shit! he realized. *Wrong guy.* He sniffed some more, grimacing. *But he's seen her, and lately. Haven't you, buddy?* Bill Hessler's head was pitched forward, dripping. Vic grabbed the skull, jerked it up and down, nodding. *Sure you have.*

He released the head, let it flop to the side. She was close. He knew that much. The scent was faint, maybe a day old. Poor ol' Bill couldn't give him much more in the way of information, but he did have some cash and a valid Visa card. Vic also found a regular pharmaceutical warehouse stashed under Bill's front seat—percodans and black beauties and honest-to-god quaaludes, not to mention a half-ounce of crank, which was a real plus.

Vic reached down, and pushed the body aside. As he slid into the driver's seat he looked at the face lying in the seat well. Still upon it was an expression of utter disbelief: as if he never even knew what hit him.

Vic licked blood from his lips, and laughed.

They never did.

11

NORA WAS A cool one, Syd had to give her that. Even whipping out of the parking lot at a psychotic sixty-mile-per-hour climb, she managed to keep her expression essentially neutral. Only problem was, she kept looking back over her shoulder, and it kind of ruined the effect. Syd, for his part, kept one eye glued to the rearview mirror as they hit the road, watching for the headlights she seemed to be anticipating.

When they came, a moment later, his heart jumped and skipped a beat.

"*Fuck,*" Nora hissed. She was riding sidesaddle in the bucket seat, her knees toward Syd; but when she saw the lights appear in Chameleon's driveway, her body tensed and drew in tight: head down, legs up in an almost fetal crouch, as if she were trying to provide the tiniest possible target.

Syd leaned hard on the gas, felt his adrenaline surge in tandem with the Mustang's rising roar. The poor old 289 under the hood was too cold to be pushing this hard; it clattered and groaned, rising valiantly to the occasion. As they hit eighty Syd leveled off, the blinking neon Chameleon's sign diminishing behind them as they blasted down the road.

But it wasn't until the mystery car pulled out, heading in the opposite direction, that Nora actually dared to breathe again. She exhaled deeply, then turned and settled into her seat, rummaging through his cassettes as if nothing had happened.

Syd took a deep breath, waited. A sign to the right warned of sharp, winding curves for the next seven miles. He eased off on the gas, coming into the first turn, brought it back down to sixty-five. She stiffened a little as they slowed, but said nothing.

"So," he said. "You wanna tell me about it?"

Nora sighed deeply, abruptly gave up the search for tunes, stared dead ahead. He waited, negotiating the turn. To their right, the mountain sloped nearly straight down, the valley sprawling beyond. Her hand reached down between her knees, came up with the brown-bagged bottle. He watched her peel back the seal, twist the gold cap loose. The smell was medicinal, sweet, like cough syrup. She took a long pull, tilting her head to let it slide down her throat. Then she offered it to him.

"No, thanks," he said. She shrugged, contemplating the mouth of the bottle without drinking.

"I love Southern Comfort," she said. "It's like a bourbon liqueur."

"Nora . . ."

"A friend of mine said that to me once. Michael. I always thought it was a very elegant description." Her voice turned wistful. "A bourbon liqueur." She seemed to savor the words, and the memory they framed. Then she took another swig, much smaller this time, and turned to look at him.

Now it was Syd's turn to cringe a little. He was amazed by how quickly jealousy bloomed, embarrassed by his own presumption. Her eyes upon him were unnervingly frank. They had not missed a thing.

"So," he said, keeping his voice as level as possible, "was that your friend Michael back there?"

"No." She didn't flinch, did not look away.

"Okay. Then, if you don't mind me asking . . . who *was* that back there?"

"Did you actually see anybody?" She was watching him, if anything, even more closely than before.

"No. But I had a really strong sense of being *shadowed,* if you know what I mean." She nodded, said nothing. "And I'll tell you real honestly, as straight as I can, so there's no misunderstanding later: I just went through an incredibly ugly and painful divorce . . ."

"Ah." At last, her eyes averted.

". . . so there are certain things I'm very sensitive about right now." He glanced at her in the pale light of the dashboard and moon. She took another healthy pull, then lowered the bottle and stared at her knees.

"Did you love her?" she asked. It was hard to be sure, but he thought he saw a flicker of jealousy play across that face. It was weirdly gratifying.

"Yeah, I did," he said, smiling a little. "But, in retrospect, it probably wasn't a very good idea." She let out a rueful little laugh of her own. "The point is that I spent a lot of nights wondering where the hell my wife was until six o'clock in the morning. And when I finally *found out* where she was, my nights got even worse. I hate the idea of anyone spending their nights like that. Especially on my behalf.

"Which is why, if you've got a boyfriend, or a husband . . ." He paused for a reaction; her face gave away nothing. ". . . this is something I really need to know about. Now. Before we go any further. Okay?"

"God, this is so awkward," she said.

He nodded, thinking *oh fuck, here it comes.*

"No no no." Obviously, his poker face wasn't as good as hers. "It's not like that. What it *is,* is . . ." She groped for the words. "Okay. I guess I just sorta went through a divorce, too. Even though we were never really married. A guy I was involved with for a very long time before I realized that—how did you put it?—loving him wasn't such a hot idea."

The road swept wide to the left. Syd concentrated on his driving, felt rather than saw Nora's eyes upon him as she continued. "The only problem was, he had a hard time with the idea of losing me. He didn't want me when I was *around*, mind you—when I was around, he couldn't keep his hands off every bitch in a ten-mile radius—but the second I was gone, well, suddenly I was the only thing he *could* think about. If you know what I mean."

He did. Just before he left Karen, in fact. For some strange reason, the sight of all those boxes packed up made her realize what she was losing. At about half past the twelfth and final hour, she had finally begun to make all the noises he'd been waiting to hear. *I'm sorry. I DO love you.* All of which boiled down to one simple message.

" 'But what'll I do *without* you'?" he said.

She nodded. "Exactly. Too little, too late. So now what happens is, every couple of months or so, he'll get tired of chasing bar bitches around and decide to see what ol' Nora is up to. Remind me of his undying love."

"Lucky you."

"Lucky me." She took a small hit off the bottle, again offered it to him. This time, he thought about it a second before declining.

"Aw, c'mon," she persisted. A hint of the old deviltry was back in her eyes. "Now that we know all about each other, you've got some catching up to do."

"We're almost home," he said, and the last word audibly caught in his throat; it had a barb of unexpected sadness on its tail that took him completely by surprise. *Home.* What a fucking joke. He thought about the dinky little rattrap he was dragging her back to, felt suddenly ashamed.

He heard her breath catch and hold as she tracked his emotion. Shit. He tried to think of some kind of clean segue to safer ground: a self-effacing quip, a droll observation, anything. Nope. His cupboard was bare. The silence ballooned between them. He could feel the heat of Nora's gaze, or maybe it was just the flush of his cheeks. He wished he could bring himself to look at her, but he couldn't just yet.

"So this guy," he said, almost defensively. "I get the impression he makes you nervous."

"Don't worry about it," she said flatly. "I can take care of Vic."

The silence welled back up, oppressive.

And that was when she broke the barrier between them. The barrier of distance. The barrier of flesh. She made a tiny animal noise that went right through him—a kind of sympathetic, nuzzling trill—and then her left hand came up to touch his hair, just his hair, tracing the curve of the back of his skull on the way back down his neck. The sensation was subtly yet potently electric, less like a vibrator than a Van de Graaff generator. It awakened a tickle at the base of his brain. A very deep itch.

A very very deep itch.

Then she leaned across the space between them, and he could practically feel the air molecules part as her exquisite face made its way to his throat, lightly kissed the pulse point just below the jawline. He felt his blood respond to the kiss, the proximity of her body, the touch of her hands as the first firmly cradled the back of his head and the second began moving softly across his chest.

Then her tongue slid up and around the bend of his jaw, flicked the lobe, softly entered his ear. He moaned as she leaned into it, body-press in hot conjunction with her tongue's wet, probing tip. His flesh began to stir. He shifted in his seat uncomfortably. She nuzzled him, withdrawing the tongue. With her right hand, she snaked inside the buttons of his shirt.

The road began to swim before him.

Nora grabbed the bottle in her right hand, took a deep pull of Comfort, swallowed hard, then tilted her mouth up into his. He tried to keep his eye on the road, but the pull of her kiss was too intense. He had to yank himself back just in time to catch the westward leaning of the mountain pass they drove.

She pulled away from his lips. Her breath was sweet.

He somehow negotiated the curve. Outside, the wind whistled and howled. She brought the bottle to her mouth again, came back up to kiss him.

When he opened his mouth to her, Southern Comfort and alchemy flowed from her lips. She had warmed and brewed it, imbued it with some of her magic. He could not help but swallow.

From then on, there was no turning back.

The first rush hit him like a velvet sledgehammer, knocking him back in his seat as his hands fought to grip the wheel. It became very hard to concentrate. The road before him wound wide to the left, then right, then back; it had become an endless wiggling string of convolutions, with steep cliffs that yawned panoramically at every twist and turn.

He felt suddenly like he was gliding on one of those Disneyland bumper cars that ran on a jetstream of compressed air, floating almost magically above the world. It was hard to believe that there were actually tires under his car, making contact with an actual world that would open up dramatically for him if he missteered, careening off into a worst-case scenario that he could picture only too clearly. The car, firing off the edge of the cliff. The first full somersaulting scream. The moment of truth, as the roof caved in and the whole thing erupted in flames, rolling down and down and down in a consummate mangled meatgristle epiphany of screams. . . .

No no no, *he heard her say, as if she were in his head.* No no no. *His vision swam back in focus, and he recognized the topography ahead. He was driving just fine. He was driving just fine. He had driven this road a million times. It occurred to him that he had been drugged somehow, but he failed to see how the information helped. Then her tongue was back in his ear again, and he gave in to the sensation.*

When it was time to turn, she helped him believe it could be done.

You're okay. *She whispered the words in his ear. He was astounded by how powerful they sounded.* You're doing fine. *He saw the mountains give way, settle into flat-lands and streetlights, the tight clusters of buildings and driveways and stoplights that signaled civilization. He turned the car right, went straight, turned right again. Lights streamed past, their colors glaring overhead: reds and yellows, lurid greens and ghostly blue-white hues, all garishly bright.*

Somehow he found his building, pulled to a stop, parked. He practically had to crawl to the door, but it was okay; she took the keys and she let him in. And it was so great to be inside, surrounded by familiar smells as he as-cended the stairs, made his way to sanctuary. At last the front door opened, closed magically behind him. He was home. He knew where everything was.

But his clothes were making him crazy. He just didn't understand how they worked anymore. He was so grateful when she helped him peel them off, litter them across the floor. Sometime between a second and a century later he collapsed onto the floor, writhing, unable to tell which were arms and which were legs, and how his limbs coor-dinated.

And Nora was there, sweet centering guiding force. When she ran her hands down his chest he felt the skit-tering universe suddenly calm, become manageable. She touched him again and his cock swelled and slapped his belly impatiently. She kissed him, ran her tongue and teeth down the length of his torso, found his erection, and took it into her mouth.

He began to growl.

Not only because it felt so incredible, but because he could smell *her now, and it was the most amazing, most ab-solutely all-encompassing scent he'd ever known. She changed positions, straddling him and lowering her hips to his face. She was hot, astonishing, dripping with life. He snuffled at her as she started to moan, a deep guttural rut-ting cry. Her hands gripped his hips, dug in, pulling him closer. His hands came up to peel her panties down . . .*

. . . and then he was burying his tongue inside her, feel-ing it strain as he lapped at the folds, aching to reach

deeper within. Her body lost control. He could feel it move around him, pressing down until the world disappeared and only her pussy remained, wet dark triangle framing the axis around which the universe madly swirled.

And her pussy unfolded, her pussy revealed, her pussy was the gateway to the center of the earth. It was like giving head to all creation. It made him feel like a god. She made noises he couldn't believe; he answered with a voice he'd never heard before.

Syd lost himself in worship, gave himself over to her power.

And it went on all night long.

12

SYD AWOKE FROM a dream of dying, to the sound of the front door's slam. No segue. No newsreel. No Warner Bros. cartoon. One second, he was screaming as he watched his slick red abdomen unzip and disgorge; the next, he was staring at the pool of warm drool collecting on his pillow.

"Hrnngg," he intoned, wiping a stringer of saliva from his lips. He rubbed his eyes and tried to focus. The light in the room felt all wrong: the sky outside was slate-gray, its sombre hue draping the walls and the sheets with long shadows that crawled.

He groaned. It was warm in the room; he was sweating under the covers. He stirred, stretched, and instantly regretted the move; it felt like every muscle and ligament in his body had been wrenched in the wrong direction. The smell of sex was everywhere: in his nostrils, in his hair, all over the bedding. He was naked and caked with pasty, half-dried secretions. He was also more than a little disoriented; his brain felt spongy, sodden in his skull. Syd squinted at the clock. It read ten to six. Too early to be awake, that was for sure.

Then he heard the footsteps in the living room, coming toward him; and in the moment before she opened the door, it came back to him.

Nora . . .

"Hey," she said, breezing into the room. "Move over, you nasty man." Winking as the door creaked shut behind her. She had changed clothes since last he'd seen her, but he barely had time to register the fact, because she started peeling them off upon walking in.

Peeling was something that she did extremely well. She was certainly built for it. Her body was both lean and deliciously curved, with a narrow waist and round, inviting hips; her breasts were small but full, with high dark nipples and just the right amount of sag. As she slid out of her jeans, it struck him with a kind of stunned remorse that this was the first time he remembered seeing her naked, despite all the obvious physical evidence to the contrary.

What the hell had happened? He barely remembered driving home. He wasn't accustomed to blackouts, and it kind of flipped him out. On the other hand, he wasn't accustomed to doing shots, either, or getting his brains fucked out by beautiful and mysterious strangers. He guessed it was possible that the two were connected somehow.

Then Nora was upon him, slithering up the length of the bed, wrapping herself tight around him. Any regrets or reservations wilted in the heat of her embrace, were completely vaporized by the long, penetrating kiss she pinned him with, the sultry spiced scent of her skin. The kiss was at once deep and urgent, timelessly luxurious: as her tongue went wild inside his mouth it sparked a fire in his brain that spread down his spine, sent shock waves of ecstasy reverberating through to his toes.

All in all, it was a great way to start off the morning.

The only problem was, by the time they came up for air Syd realized they had been utterly swallowed by darkness. The dawn should long since have burned off the shadows. This had him confused, until Nora pointed out the moon rising outside the window. He looked at her, shocked.

"You let me sleep *all day*?"

"Well, we were up pretty late last night," she countered, "and besides, you were crashed." Syd had to admit that that was true: the second part, at any rate. Nora cuddled into him, slid her hand down to wake his rousing cock. "Plus it gave me a chance to go get some things," she added. "I hope you don't mind."

Syd nodded, not quite sure what that meant. "Yeah, it's fine," he said. "I just . . ."

"Oh, shit," she said suddenly, cutting him off. "Before I forget . . ."

She let go of his penis and jumped up, exiting the bedroom. Syd watched for a moment, perplexed. When she didn't come back he pulled himself creaking from the bed, followed on unsteady legs.

In the living room was a battered suitcase, plunked down in the middle of the floor; from the kitchen came the clinking and rattling of bags being unloaded. Syd rounded the corner to find Nora lit from the open refrigerator, a package wrapped in bloody butcher's paper still in hand. Eggs and fresh produce graced the interior shelves; on the kitchen counter were two more bottles of Southern Comfort, plus some tequila and a couple of bottles of wine. From the looks of it, she'd taken the State Store and the farmer's market by storm.

Syd watched her work, his tracking still a little sluggish.

He asked how she'd gotten around. Nora gestured to the window. Syd peeked outside; there was a frisky-looking little Camaro with Louisiana plates parked out front. He nodded, then asked how she'd gotten out to pick it up. She said it wasn't real hard to get people to take you where you want to go, if you just knew how to ask.

Nora went back to unloading groceries and Syd watched her, not knowing exactly how he felt. On the one hand, there was a *Play Misty for Me* kind of presumptuousness to her sudden domesticity that took him more than a little off-guard. On the other hand, there was the sight of her naked backside as she leaned into his fridge. He thought about it, tried to phrase the next question as neutrally as possible.

"So are you just passing through, then," he said, "or will you be hanging around for a while?"

"I'm gonna have to keep moving," she said over her shoulder, "sometime in the next couple of days or so."

"Oh," he said, instantly disappointed. It was not the answer he wanted to hear; he wondered what was. Syd moved over to the kitchen table, picked up his cigarettes.

Nora stood and closed the door; suddenly they were illuminated only by the streetlight's blue-white glow. As she turned, her eyes locked on his, and Syd felt his heart begin to free-fall. He lit a smoke and leaned against the table, trying to keep his voice steady, feigning nonchalance, failing utterly.

"So, um," he began. "So while you're in town . . ."

". . . I'd like to stay here with you," she finished the thought for him. "If that's okay."

"Not a problem," he said. Nora closed the refrigerator door and stood. She was naked and magnificent and two feet away. That was two feet too many. Nora beamed, looking quite pleased, if not entirely surprised. She closed the narrowing distance between them, enfolded Syd in a steamy embrace. They kissed again, long and sweet, tapping very deliberately into each other's soul-fire.

"You know," he said, when the kiss finally broke, "you're welcome to stay a little longer. If you like."

"Mmmm," she murmured. "On the other hand, you could come with me."

Syd just stood there for a second, waiting for the other shoe to drop. Nora's gaze upon him remained fixed and steady. His heart's free-fall lurched to a shuddering halt, hovered uneasily in midair.

"Yeah, right," he said.

"Yeah," she said. "Right."

There was a pause. "You're serious," he said. She nodded her head. Either it was true, or that shoe was taking an incredibly long time.

"I couldn't do that—"

"Why not?"

"Well, for one thing . . ." he began. And then he stopped.

And it dawned on Syd that he couldn't think of a single good reason. And that surprised the hell out of him. It was as though his entire internal map had spun one hundred and eighty degrees in a heartbeat, showed him a possibility he'd never really considered before.

"I just couldn't," he reiterated.

"Why couldn't you?"

"Well," he said, turning away from her, starting to pace now. She watched him. "Umm." Running this new equation through his head. "Well, let me see." Still wary. "Are you going anywhere in particular?" She shook her head. "But you've got to get there right away." She nodded, emphatic. "Right. So I guess we're talking a Jack Kerouac, *Easy Rider*-kinda thing."

Nora let a cryptic little half-smile slip out, gave a little hand-wiggling gesture. *Sorta kinda.* Close enough.

"I don't know," he said, slipping into his best young Jack Nicholson, "I was never really a drop-out-and-find-America kinda guy." He laughed. She smiled. "I mean, I read *Zen and the Art of Motorcycle Maintenance* when I was fourteen, but that's about the extent of it."

She watched, said nothing.

"I've kinda got roots here."

"I noticed."

"And, to be real honest, we barely even know each other."

"This is true."

"And I've got some questions about how you live without a steady job . . ."

"You mean how *I* live?" The invisible walls came up, for the first time since the bar.

"No, no. I mean how a *person* lives." It was amazing

how quickly the sweat glands responded to tension. "Like how anyone lives. Like how I would, for instance."

He realized that he had stepped near a tripwire, logged it, couldn't help but wonder what it meant. She just stared at him, abruptly intense, her vulnerability a thing of the past. Suddenly, his own extreme nakedness disturbed him; he realized it was because it no longer felt safe. He'd gone straight from *relaxed* to *extremely uncomfortable* in the time it took to generate a bead of sweat.

"I don't know ..." Trying to talk his way through it. "... I've always had kind of a wild streak. But it always comes slamming back into my practical side. The part that wants to know how everything works, and needs to know that everything's taken care of." He looked at her again. Her face remained unchanged, but her body untensed minutely.

"You still haven't answered my question," she said.

Syd paused, laughed nervously. "This is crazy ..." he said.

She nodded, said nothing.

"I mean, I just met you. We don't even know each other. You know what I'm saying?"

"What *are* you saying?"

She was still looking at him, unraveling his defenses with the directness of her gaze. He was beginning to feel a little like something in a petri dish. "What *am* I saying? I don't know! I mean, I hate my job—fuck, I *have* no job, when you get right down to it. And I really have no home, either. But I'm kinda settled in *anyway* ..." She just looked at him, giving away nothing. "... and this is where I am.

"At least until I go somewhere else."

He finished up, waited for her reaction shot. She was cool, no doubt about it, but there were a few chinks in her ego armor. When her eyes flashed at the word *home,* Syd caught a glimpse of her need.

It was every bit as great as his own.

He could tell that she knew that he knew. He could also tell that she hated having slipped, even a little.

"I guess I'm gonna have to think about it," he said. "I gotta admit, though, you kinda caught me by surprise."

"Get used to it." She smiled ruefully. The walls inched down.

"Believe me . . ." Taking a step toward her. ". . . there are a couple of things around here that I'd *very* much like to get used to."

"Ah." Again, the dirty laugh. They were back, at last, on familiar ground. He took another step toward her, weighed the space between them for evil vibes. They had been dispersed. Hallelujah, amen. Nora stood before him, defiantly inviting, with her high breasts and tight belly, long legs and extravagant hips. The streetlight transformed her, made her pale flesh seem to glow, rendering her a hungry spirit in human form, come to claim and be claimed by him.

He pulled her close, felt her body press into his. She was cold fire; Syd, a moth to her flame.

And all, for the moment, was right with the world.

13

THE MOMENT WAS perfection; one might even go so far as to use the word *blessed*. The kind of moment that you could spend a lifetime searching for, and once experienced, spend the rest of your life trying vainly to equal. It was wonderful, magical, absolutely unprecedented.

And, like all perfect moments, it was utterly doomed.

In Syd's case, it lasted long enough to get them from the kitchen to the bedroom. He paused just long enough to let her grab one of the bottles of Comfort, then scooped her up in his arms and carried her through the living room, his cock bobbing like a divining rod.

The bed appeared before them like some mythical island paradise. Syd laid her down across its white expanse, slid his right hand between her thighs. She was incredibly, gratifyingly wet: his fingers dipped and figure-skated along her slippery length, teasing her to frenzy before burying themselves in her depths. Her reaction was overwhelming, his every tiny motion provoking an avalanche of response. He used his hands and mouth to send her over

the brink and back a half-dozen times before they could
stand it no longer.

But when Nora went to pull him up and astride her,
Syd's brain suddenly kicked in.

"Hang on a sec," he mumbled, then reached over to
the nightstand and began fumbling with the drawer. Just as
he opened it Nora pulled his hand back, placed it on her
breast, and thrust her tongue deep into his mouth. Syd lost
himself in the onslaught; it was with great effort that he
tore his hand away, resumed his search.

Nora squirmed in protest, grinding her hips into him.
The resulting wave of ecstasy threatened to submerge him
completely, and it was all he could do to speak, no less remain even marginally rational. With his last ounce of will
he broke the spell.

"Wait," he said, as he reached into the drawer, ex-
tracted a little foil packet, started to tear it open. When she
saw what he was doing she pulled back and looked at him
like he was out of his mind.

"What are you doing?"

"What do you think? I'm gonna use a condom."

"Not with me, you're not." She plucked the packet
from his hand, tossed it across the room.

"Very funny," he said, and reached for another one.
Nora leaned forward and nipped him on the arm. *"Ow!"*
he yelped. "Cut it out!"

When he went for the drawer again, Nora grabbed his
hand. Syd twisted out of her grasp. She wrapped her legs
around his waist. "Nora, stop it," Syd said, trying like hell
to outmaneuver her. "C'mon, baby, I'm serious. . . ."

"So am I," she replied, a fiercely wicked grin on her
face. She squeezed her thighs together, locking him in a
fleshy vice-grip: Syd squirmed, surprised both at her
strength and the relentless quality of her resistance. As
he struggled the horseplay burgeoned into an impromptu
erotic wrestling match.

They whipped back and forth on the mattress, a manic
tangle of limbs: her legs squeezing his midsection, his
hands scrabbling to pin down her arms. As she reached for

him again Syd grabbed her left hand, pinned it to her right. Leaning into her with all his weight, he twisted toward the nightstand, managed to snatch another rubber from the drawer . . .

. . . and that's when it began to turn: the thrashing becoming less like loveplay and more like a genuine battle of wills. Nora's left hand broke free, made a grab for the packet a split second after Syd closed his fist around it.

"Gimme that," she demanded.

"No way. It's the last one."

"Good," she replied. She tried to peel his fingers open, couldn't; as he resisted he felt her movements become frenetic, almost ugly in their intensity.

"Shit, Nora . . ." She continued to struggle, started wrenching his fingers painfully apart. A sudden wave of anger roiled up inside him.

"Goddammit, I said *cut it out!*"

He yanked his hand back and away, fist raised up and out of her reach. For a moment it hovered there, looking almost as if he were ready to slug her. Nora's eyes flashed, brightly expectant; as he lowered his hand the light faded, and she pushed him away.

Syd slid off of her and to the side, where they lay panting and staring at the ceiling, as the heat of the encounter ebbed away, left a frigid vacuum in its wake. Syd was monumentally pissed, and more than a little confused. He lay in stilted silence, listening to the sound of their breathing and wondering if she was actually going to say anything, explain the sudden lunge into irrationality. Apparently not. The air space between them remained charged, awkward, tense.

Finally, he could take it no longer. "So," he said, as gently as he could manage, "you wanna tell me what this is all about?"

"Nothing," she said flatly. There was a cryptic pause, then more softly: "I hate those fucking things."

"Well, I'm not wild about 'em myself," Syd offered, trying to ameliorate the weirdness. "But they *are* kind of a necessary evil."

"You didn't need one last night."

"Yeah, well, I was blasted out of my skull last night."

"But you still didn't use one."

"Yeah, I guess," he said warily, again wishing he could remember more than shreds and fragments.

"So what do you suddenly need one for?" she asked, her tone interrogatory, bristling. Syd looked at her as if she were joking, saw only deadly earnest intent.

"Oh, gee, I don't know, lemme see . . ." he replied, rolling his eyes, ". . . there's accidental pregnancies, incurable diseases . . ."

"So you think I'm *diseased*?"

"*No!* Jesus, Nora, I'm just—"

"I don't have time for this shit," she spat, sitting up and sliding to the edge of the bed. Syd groaned; this was getting way out of hand. Nora began rooting through the clothing on the floor, found her T-shirt, pulled it on.

"Nora, c'mon," Syd said, trying to end-run the escalating weirdness. "Don't be like that. . . ." He reached out to her; as he touched her back Nora whirled and slapped his hand away.

"Get the fuck away from me," she growled. She glared at him, furious . . .

. . . and for the second time in as many days, Syd got a whiff of genuine *threat* off of her. As if things could tip at any moment, veer clear from *uncomfortable* into *downright dangerous*. He flashed back to last night, the incident with the bottle, Jules's low-key backdoor interrogation. *Are you sure you know what you're doing? If you haven't figured out that there's an element of* risk *here* . . .

"Whoa," he said. His hand froze in space, backed off very, very slowly. Nora found her panties, angrily slipped into them. He closed his eyes and slumped back on the bed, horrified, the countdown to meltdown already ticking off in his head. *Next would come the jeans, then the boots, one by one. Then an angry stalk across the room as she grabbed her jacket, perhaps punctuated by a choice last taunt or two. Then into the living room. Out the front door.*

And out of his life.

Forever . . .

As visions went, it was incredibly clear, like fast-forwarding reality. The resulting depression blew through him like a pre-flash of impending disaster, setting off all his internal damage-control alarms. Syd was already bracing himself emotionally by the time the words even left his lips.

"I'm sorry," he murmured, the ache in his voice heartfelt, genuine. "I just don't understand . . ."

His words trailed off. The room went still. Syd opened his eyes. Nora was sitting on the edge of the bed, staring into the shadows. Her hair obscured her profile; she shuddered, and in the dim light it looked as though she might be crying. She took a deep, halting breath.

"I can't *get* pregnant," she said bitterly, still staring straight ahead. "Okay? So you can relax. You don't have anything to worry about." Her voice was hoarse, laced with the pain of confession. She brought one hand up to wipe away an unseen tear, then shook her head.

"I'm sorry," she murmured. "I shouldn't have said that. . . ."

Syd sat up, moved toward her. As he got close she held perfectly still, quite literally ready for anything. Syd went to take her in his arms and she started to pull away. But when he persisted, she suddenly gave in.

And that was when the walls came tumbling down.

Nora turned, embracing him with a quiet fury, burying her face in the crook of his shoulder and hugging him fiercely.

"I'm sorry," he whispered, as one hand came up to stroke her hair. He kissed the crown of her head and a little sound escaped her, the merest wisp of despair welling up from some desperately lonely place. She curled deeper into him, clinging to him like a rock in a raging current. The gesture struck a deeply protective chord in his soul, something beyond the simple understanding that he had found someone with damage greater even than his own.

He felt torn: one side of him saying *run away, this woman has too many problems, she's emotionally unsta-*

ble . . . , the other saying *she's hurting, she needs you, she's the most passionate, intense creature you've ever met in your life, and you're* crazy *if you let her walk out that door.* . . .

Syd held out a heartbeat longer, weighing his conflicting emotions. Then Nora spoke again: her voice achingly vulnerable, filled with longing.

"I just wanted to feel you inside me," she said. "I didn't want anything between us."

She took another halting breath, and Syd's heart started to glow like a roadside flare as the balance of his inner scales tipped at last. *"I know,"* he whispered. *"It's okay."*

And it was true. He knew when it came right down to it, he wasn't really worried about catching something from her, and in the heat of the moment all the safe-sex lectures in the world were completely overridden by the fact that *he* wanted to feel *her,* too: unobstructed or unhindered in any way, and as intensely as possible. Maybe it was stupid: a foolish, even life-threatening risk. He didn't care.

All he cared about was her.

It was a revelation, a pure flash of emotion as yet unbound by the complications of relationship or the fact that she was still mostly a mystery, and it frankly surprised the hell out of him. *You can't fix her problems,* a voice in his head warned. *You can't even fix your own.*

It was the voice of experience. It didn't matter. She was here in his arms, and she was in pain. He wanted to make the pain go away. She was here in his arms, and she felt alone. He wanted to show her that she wasn't. She was here in his arms, and she was afraid.

He wanted to make her feel safe.

And that was perhaps the most amazing thing: that simply by being this close to her, he felt like he could. She made him feel strong. She made him feel like he could do anything.

He gave her a reassuring squeeze. She nuzzled him in response, her head resting on his breast. Her lips found his left nipple, began to kiss it. As her tongue grazed its surface—a completely sensual yet strangely nonsexual gesture, more the way a child suckles for comfort—it awakened within Syd a powerful, almost *maternal* impulse.

Then her teeth came into play, and his arousal returned a thousandfold. And this time, the lovemaking was slow and sweet and tender, an act more of profound healing than animal abandon. As he slipped naked inside her, Syd's last rational thought was that he had never felt this close to another living being.

Nora began to move, setting the rhythm of their union. Syd responded in kind. He felt their flesh merge, as they fed each other's need.

And he was not afraid.

14

AFTERWARD THEY NAPPED, awoke ravenous. When Nora decided to make food, Syd was happy to let her. He was amazed at her energy reserves, that she seemed to be unstoppable, immune from fatigue; if anything, she was even *more* vibrant than before.

It was more than he could say for himself. Syd was spent; it was all he could do to load a CD into the player and then drag himself to the table. Robert Johnson's "Come Into My Kitchen" seemed only too appropriate. Music filled the air, mingling with the cooking smells.

Syd watched her work, fascinated. Nora prepared food with a fluid, offhand grace: a choatic culinary whirlwind creating an incredible mess, from which emerged a truly splendid meal. She had gone out of her way to get the freshest possible cuts of meat: and though she cooked them far rarer than Syd was accustomed to, he had to admit that she was a phenomenal chef.

The steaks were heavily marinated; the greens strangely spiced, slightly bitter. When Syd wrinkled his nose she insisted that it wouldn't kill him, playfully promised him gross bodily injury if he didn't eat. Syd shrugged and drowned the salad in dressing, ultimately wolfing his portion down with a vigor that belied his misgivings.

They dined by candlelight, huddled around the tiny kitchen table. As they ate, they drank. Nora had already started the first bottle of burgundy while she was cooking, cracked the second before they were halfway done. Syd opted for beer, pulling a cold can from his dwindling stock in the fridge.

And as they ate and drank, they talked. Or more, *he* talked. Nora, it turned out, was a lot more interested in knowing about him than in revealing much of her own intimate history.

Her listening skills, on the other hand, were extraordinary: her attention rapt, her questions thoughtful and penetrating. She had that rare talent to make him feel that he was genuinely fascinating, the most interesting person she'd ever met. She could hang on every word without seeming to fawn, laugh without appearing facile. By the end of the meal she had inspired him to disgorge great hunks of the story of his life: his childhood and the lost years of his youth, the symbolic significance of his upcoming birthday, his feelings of frustration at how life never seemed to work out the way it should.

The death of his marriage fascinated her; the sordid saga of Vaughn Restal, in particular. Indeed, Nora resisted his every impulse to short-form the events, pressing him to recount every gory blow-by-blow, in near-forensic detail. It felt odd, at first; it had been a while since Syd had felt comfortable talking with others about his past, even longer since he'd found a sympathetic ear not already deafened by repeated exposure.

But as he finally reached the end of the meal and the story, replete with the obligatory shrug and sigh and lighting of cigarette, her eyes were brightly attentive: taking in every nuance of feeling, searching his every expression for hidden meaning.

"So why didn't you do it?" she asked.

"Do what?"

"Kill him," she replied.

Syd looked at her, surprised. She said it as if it were the most natural thought in the world, as if *questioning* it were crazy. It was a first. "Well . . ." he began, then stopped.

She looked at him; he took a drag off his cigarette, shrugged. "I don't know. It wasn't worth ruining my life over, I guess."

"But your life was already ruined."

"Yeah," he agreed. "But he was just an asshole, and if she was dumb enough to go with him, then fuck her, too." He said the last part with as much conviction as he could muster, hoped like hell it would fly.

One glance at her told him it didn't. Nora's gaze went right through him, pinning his soul like a searchlight on an escaping convict. "That's bullshit," she said, "and it's not the point."

"Yeah? Well, exactly what *is* the point? I mean, *he* wasn't the problem," Syd argued. "He was a symptom—"

"He was an *intruder*," she interrupted. "He snuck in and stole something that was yours, and you let him get away with it."

"Karen wasn't *mine*," he objected. "Christ, you talk about her like she was my property or something."

"Not property," Nora corrected, "but yours, nonetheless. Just like *you* were *hers*. You made a deal, you *gave* yourselves to each other . . ." She paused, added softly, ". . . it was a covenant."

"And *she* broke it. . . ."

"Yeah, she did. And what did *you* do?"

Syd opened his mouth, stopped short again. Nora's eyes were bright and searching. "I don't think . . ."

"*Don't* think. *Feel.*

I wanna know how you felt that night," she said. "I wanna know what you wanted to *do* about it."

Syd looked at her, looked away. "I wanted to kill him," he said at last. "I wanted to tear his stupid fucking face off."

"Better," she said. "At least that's honest." She leaned across the table.

"So why didn't you?"

The question hung in the air like an indictment. Syd took a swig off his beer. Nora watched him intently. Her eyes were inescapable; in the soft glow of the candles they looked hypnotic, otherworldly.

"I don't know," he said. "The cops came, and it felt like the moment had come and gone. I missed the window." He sighed resignedly.

"After that, I would periodically get this feeling, like I wanted to go hurt him again. Like beating him up just wasn't enough. It was like, he hadn't suffered enough yet; *I* was still hurting, *my* life was still fucked, but *he* just got to skate away as if nothing ever happened. But whenever I talked about it, everyone would tell me how wrong they thought that was, like I was some kind of psycho or something. . . ."

"And how did that make you feel?"

"I thought—" He stopped, corrected himself. "It *felt* like it was the only right thing in the whole sick fucking situation. Like if I *didn't* stop him—even if I had to kill him to do it—then nothing else in the rest of my life would ever mean a goddam thing."

He paused; Nora nodded thoughtfully. "There's a word to describe the reaction of everybody you talked to," she said. "It's called *theriophobia*."

"Come again?"

"Theriophobia. It means *fear of the beast*. It's like a projection, a kind of self-hatred. Fear of the violent, irrational side of your nature. Most people are scared to death of it."

For the first time in the conversation, her eyes looked away, out the window to the street below, as though searching the shadows. "They spend their whole lives running away from it, and punishing anyone who doesn't. They tell you it's crazy to feel things like that, like you're a monster for even having such thoughts, much less doing something about it."

"Yeah, but it's funny," he said, almost wistfully, "while it was happening, it was the cleanest feeling I'd ever known. It wasn't so much irrational as something that *transcended* reason. There was no doubt, or guilt, or second-guessing myself. I had no idea what was going to happen next, or how things would play out, and it didn't even matter. I just knew what I had to do. . . ."

"But in the end, you weren't true to it," she said. "I mean, he's still alive, right? He still slinks among us." Syd looked down, nodded.

"Yeah, he hangs out down at Fifty-Five South and all the local yuppie watering holes. But at least he pisses himself at the mention of my name."

"Uh-huh."

She didn't say anything else, just *uh-huh*. She didn't have to. It was uncanny, her knack for nailing him: in the space of a second she had reduced the wild, bestial side of Syd that had so terrified his friends and acquaintances to a toothless, yapping lapdog. Her tone of voice was neutral, utterly without malice or judgment, but no less deadly for it.

Syd swished his beer, drained the dregs. It was the last one in the house. He glanced at the little pile of cans before him, checked his watch. Twelve-fifteen.

"Helluva time to run out of beer," he sighed.

Nora watched him a moment longer, then stood, blew out the candles, crossed around to his side of the table.

"So c'mon," she said.

"Where are we going?"

She leaned over and kissed him on the forehead, then whispered in his ear.

"Out," she said.

15

T HEY WERE HALFWAY to Chameleon's when Nora
had a change of heart.

They were high up on the Mt. Haversford Road, Tom
Waits's moody "Bone Machine" playing low on the stereo.
For the last twenty minutes Nora had been lost in thought,
preoccupied: she stared out the window, watching the
shifting shapes just outside the headlights' glare. When
they passed a sign that read REST AREA 1 MILE, Nora
turned.

"Pull over up there," she said.

Syd looked at where she was pointing, shook his head.
He was feeling kind of weird, and he wanted a beer to
calm his nerves. "I don't know," he protested. "It's gettin'
kinda late. . . ."

"Just for a minute," Nora said. "Please . . ."

She placed her hand on his thigh, squeezed. Syd
sighed and slowed, wheeling the car off the road and into
the parking area. It was dark, utterly deserted, just a wide
barren strip of asphalt, butt up against the rim of the forest. A few picnic tables dotted its perimeter, empty and

forlorn. Syd pulled into a slot, left the engine running, the lights on.

"Okay," he said. "Now what."

Nora reached over and shut the engine off, then sat back, admiring the night.

"Beautiful, isn't it?" she sighed. "I love it up here."

"Yeah, me, too," Syd said. He looked around, distracted, then checked his watch. Twelve forty-five. "We should really go," he warned. "The bar's gonna close soon."

"Mmmm." She paused, nodded thoughtfully. "I've got a better idea."

Nora leaned over and kissed him, and as she pulled away Syd heard a *click* . . .

. . . and then she was throwing the door open, stepping outside. Syd looked first at Nora, then at the ignition.

The keys were gone.

"Aw, shit," he groaned, annoyed. "Nora!"

But Nora just ignored him, moving away from the car and into the trees, the headlights casting giant shadow-puppets before her.

"Nora!" Syd shouted. Nora kept moving. Syd threw open the door, climbed out after her. He called to her again. Nora disappeared, laughing. He called to her again.

Nothing.

Syd cursed and considered his options. Not many. She was playing games with him. He was stranded. He was starting to get pissed.

"NORA!!"

From the trees, her echoing mirth. There was nothing else to do. Syd cursed again, and followed.

The woods were still and silent as he picked his way through the underbrush, the only sounds around him his own clumsy fumbling and the subtle rush of breeze through branches. The weather was a little warmer than yesterday, but not by much: he could still see his breath, felt the damp night chill on his skin. A gentle breeze wafted around him, hissing through the trees. Syd had left the Mustang's headlights on, the better to see her with;

they tossed garish monster-movie shadows before being utterly absorbed by dense growth. Twenty yards in and he was steeped in darkness, without a clue as to how he was going to find her.

Then, without warning, the headlights shut off.

And the real blackness settled in.

Syd whirled, caught the last faint glow of dying light. His pupils dilated, desperately trying to capture every stray bit of luminescence. Then it faded, withdrew.

And Syd was screwed.

Because the night that descended upon him then was not city-night, not twinkly-lights-in-the-distance night or even creepy-don't-go-down-that-back-alley night, where the shadows skulked and huddled in corners and between street lamps.

This was nature's own mother night, and her dominion was complete. Syd couldn't see his hand in front of his face, his feet on the ground, or the way back to the car. He felt suddenly helpless, trapped. He probed around with his left foot, took a testing baby step forward. His leg snagged a fallen branch, then bumped painfully against a rotten stump. His eyes bugged wide, cones and rods screaming.

He stopped, let his sight adjust until he could make out shapes, vague silhouettes. It was still horrible. He blundered forth, hands clutching blindly, calling out her name.

"Nora!" he whispered. *"Nora, dammit, where are you?"*

"I'm right beside you."

Syd spun; squinting, surprised. One of the shadows moved, and Nora's form became faintly visible: leaning against a pine, an arm's length away.

"Jesus!" he hissed. *"Don't do that!"*

"Why are you whispering?"

"What? Oh . . ." He caught himself. "Nora, quit fucking around. The lights just went out on the car."

"I know," she said. "I turned them off."

"You did what . . . ?" Syd stopped, stymied, wondering how she had doubled back and then found him again so quickly. He couldn't see her face, but there was no mistaking the amusement in her voice. He reached out to her, a blind man reading flesh braille. "Let's just get out of here. . . ."

"Why?" she replied. "What's the rush?"

He started to say something else, but she just kissed him again, effectively silencing his objections. Her mouth was a warm sanctuary; Syd felt his senses unconsciously focus around it. He touched her face, then slid down her neck to her shoulders. When he felt the bare skin of her back, Syd stopped, shocked. She was topless.

"Jesus!" he gasped. "What the fuck are you doing?"

Nora just laughed, pulled him close. As she did he realized that she was not just topless, she was completely stripped, bare-ass naked in the middle of the pitch-black woods. Her flesh was taut; her nipples stiff, yearning. She nuzzled him; as she did her fingers snaked inside his jacket, began unbuttoning his shirt. Industrious little creatures, working overtime.

"Take this off," she ordered.

"I don't want to," he said, pulling her fingers away. She kissed him again, and Syd felt his resistance crumble. Nora pressed against the rising bulge in his pants, squeezed. The thought of one more beer seemed suddenly irrelevant, unnecessary.

"You don't need another beer," she whispered, as if reading his mind. She kissed him again. "I know what you need."

"What," he countered sarcastically, "to screw out in the woods?"

"Maybe," she said, meeting him, attitude for attitude. "If you wanna be with me you better learn to expect the unexpected. Know what I mean?" Syd paused, then nodded.

"Good."

Nora started to peel his jacket off; Syd hovered on the threshold of abandon, then shrugged, let her. "Anybody ever tell you you're out of your mind?" he said.

"All the time." She peeled his shirt off, let it drop. "Constantly." She dropped down, pulled his boots and

socks off, then unhitched his jeans and tugged them down.
As he stepped out of them she came up, grabbed his wrist
and unsnapped his watch, tossing it on the pile.

At last Syd stood before her, utterly naked. "That's
more like it," she said. "Now, relax. Breathe. Feel the
night."

Nora wrapped her arms around him, hugging him tight.
Her body was a furnace, radiating heat and passion; her
hair was wild and tangled, smoke-scented. Syd began to
shiver, as much from excitement as from the frigid air. His
teeth chattered. Nora began to massage him, her fingers
tracing patterns across the surface of his skin.

"You've got so much bound up inside," she said softly.
"It's keeping you trapped. There's a whole world around
you that you're not even seeing, Syd," she said softly.

"You *need* to see it."

She kissed him again, punctuating the message. Nora
reached down, came up with a small glass vial.

"What's that?" he asked.

"Trust me," she said.

She uncapped it, poured a dollop of dark liquid onto
his chest. Syd was instantly struck by the thick, sharp
aroma of scented oil. It was at once bittersweet, earthy and
biting, like chlorophyll with teeth. "This'll warm you up,"
she said.

She was right about that: as it touched him, Syd felt his
skin flush, tingling. She chased the rivulets down his belly
with her fingers, smearing it on his torso, across his throat,
down to his groin. It burned there, in glaring contrast to the
night air. Syd gasped, felt his penis burgeon, throbbing. She
poured some onto the crown of his head, and his brain
started broadcasting test patterns.

She dropped the vial then and began rubbing against
him, and Syd felt their flesh merge, her heat transferring to
him. The smell of Nora mingled with the oil, became one
swirling sensation. It filled his nostrils, dizzying. His head
felt feather-light, his inner ear rumbling with the sound of
his own roaring blood . . .

. . . and for the second time in as many nights he felt

that sudden rush of acute *clarity:* a fierce, almost cellular awareness of her presence, the astonishing sensitivity she aroused in him. The awareness extended to his surroundings: as he gazed out into the night the forest took on added dimensions, his vision perceiving newly-visible layers upon layers of shadow, etched in purple and blue-gray and black. The cold felt suddenly bracing, exciting.

Nora stopped then, looked off into the foliage. "C'mon," she whispered. She took his hand, started to move away from the tree. Syd stiffened, suddenly reluctant. Sex was one thing; naked with her like this, he could be anywhere, they could be humping on the White House lawn and he wouldn't care. But wandering through the woods . . .

"Where are we going?" he asked, tightening up again.

"Out there," she said simply.

"What about our clothes?"

"What about 'em?" she replied. "They ain't going anywhere."

"But we can't just run around naked."

"Yeah?" she said. "Why not?"

"What if someone comes?"

"Yeah, boy, that would be terrible," she chided, then clucked her tongue reprovingly. "That's some wild streak you got there, Syd."

Nora broke contact then, stepped away; as Syd watched she melded into the shadows, her silhouette blue-lit, ethereal. His clothing lay heaped beside him, a freshly shed skin. He looked at her, playful and wanton, and more than anything in the world he wanted to have her, right there, on the ground, now.

"You'll have to catch me first," she said, reading his mind.

Syd pushed off from the tree, moving toward her. Nora darted out of reach, surprisingly nimble and quick. Syd took two steps forward, immediately landed his bare foot on a bramble.

"Shit!" he yelped. He stumbled back, hopping, and his other foot stomped on a small round stone. "Ow! Fuck!"

He lurched to the side, impaled his ass on a sharp stick and toppled backward, landing flat on his can in the dirt.

"GodDAMMIT!"

Laughter rang out from the darkness.

"Oh, very funny!" he called out. He stood, brushing dirt and pine needles off his butt. Syd looked over to his clothes, thought about getting dressed, or at least putting his boots on.

That's some wild streak you got. . . .

Her words echoed back, caustically precise. She knew how to push his buttons, all right. Even when he knew she was pushing them. It awakened a competitive impulse in him in spite of himself, made Syd want to play this game on *her* terms, and win. To prove something to her, and to himself in the bargain.

Just off to his left the bushes rustled, and Syd caught a fleeting glimpse of flesh. By the time he turned, she was gone. Syd grew quiet, began moving very carefully: toes digging into the moist earth, trying to anticipate his every next move.

He took three steps, harpooned himself again.

"Ow!" Syd leapt back, lost his balance and banged his knee on a rock. "Ow! Ow!" The resulting bumbling tap dance landed him facedown in the dirt, picking leaves from his teeth. As he sat up, something whizzed through the air, struck him in the back of the head. Syd yelped, whirled, looked.

A pine cone.

Somewhere off to his right, Nora snickered.

"You bitch," he grumbled.

Syd picked more brambles from his heels, then hunkered down and rethought his strategy. He was going about this all wrong, trying to *think* his way through the woods. He took a deep breath, exhaled slowly, taking in the night.

The wind shifted, brought with it dozens of subtle gradations of scent, sweet pine and ripe mulch and rich earth. Syd began moving intuitively, relying more on inner sense to guide him. As he did he realized that every molecule of his body felt energized, alive, a billion tiny sensors embedded in his exposed skin.

Something small stirred and skittered in the underbrush. A twig snapped, some thirty feet dead ahead. He stopped, waiting. Another crackle, maybe three yards farther to the left. Something was moving; it was larger, Nora-sized. Syd crouched, began tracking with it, no longer thinking in terms of point A to point B, but instead seeking the natural trails that abounded. As he did the environment seemed to transform around him, become less hostile. There was no path to speak of, yet one revealed itself with every step, his mind and body focusing down, becoming attuned to the sound of her movement and the flow of the land.

He paced her for several minutes, moving silently, weaving closer. And as he hunted her Syd was amazed at how good it felt, how liberating it was to roam free through this natural world. His mind felt clear for the first time in ages, unburdened by the baggage of his life, and he marveled that he'd never thought to do it before.

She was just ahead of him. Twenty feet now, maybe less. Up ahead there came a soft burbling sound, richly musical in timbre, suddenly audible under the riffling wind. He hadn't noticed it before, recognized it instantly: the sound of a running stream, trickling down the mountain. Nora was making her way toward it. Syd moved off to the side, flanking her. He would sneak up, catch her at the water's edge, make love to her there.

A dozen paces farther he caught his first shimmering glimpse of the stream. It was shallow and rocky, the stars overhead refracting across its rippling surface; he looked up and saw the sky ablaze through the trees, a billion pulsing diamonds set in satin oblivion, presided over by the radiant moon.

Something moved, not ten feet to his left. Syd froze in his tracks. She was trying to sneak up on him. He crouched down, ducking behind some brittle weeds, readied himself to pounce . . .

. . . and then stopped, suddenly wary. As his hackles raised, set off a thousand tiny alarms. . . .

Because something was wrong, completely wrong. In the way the tall grass crackled and parted around it; the way the woods went deathly silent in its wake.

In the way it moved, on two feet too many.

He listened, confused. And then his heart squeezed tight, a bloody fist in his chest, as the realization blossomed klieg light-bright in his skull. Every hair on his body went rigid, erect.

Something was lumbering through the brush. Something huge, hulking. He heard its breath, ragged and panting, as it broke through to the water's edge, began lapping thirstily. The wind shifted, and Syd caught a whiff of dank, matted fur.

Oh god. Images of the wolf came crashing back, flooding his senses. *Oh god.* He backed up, almost stumbled, catching himself. Syd could not see it from where he stood. He prayed it could not see him.

The creature stopped drinking, shook massive jowls, stood dripping and silent, the image horribly clear in his mind's eye. Syd unconsciously synced his breathing with its own, trying to mask the sound of his life. Terror blossomed and grew, billowing through his soul. He realized that he had no idea where she was, no way to warn her. He had to get away undetected, find her somehow. . . .

The wind died down, shifted, came back at Syd's back. As it gusted he felt his sweat go chill, making his teeth chatter again. The wind blew on, oblivious, carrying particles of his scent with it.

Blowing toward the stream. Toward the beast.

Oh shit, Syd thought. *Oh shit oh shit oh shit* . . .

Ten feet away, a low growl sounded.

And that was it; Syd's sudden oneness with nature went flying out the proverbial window as he took off, desperately trying to escape.

The woods reverted instantly: turning on him in the blink of an eye, becoming an endless implacable barrier. Roots and rocks rose up to trip him; branches clawed at his flesh; trees loomed and threw themselves in his path. Syd glanced back, caught a flash of feral eyes, heard the sound of massive limbs, tracking him off to the right.

He could feel it bearing down on him, thought crazily of the tire iron in the trunk of his car, his car that was parked in a distant galaxy, the car he'd never see again. *I'm not afraid,* he tried to tell himself, fooling no one. He was scared out of his mind, a mind that was already filled to brimming with grisly images: the shock of its stinking bulk slamming into his back, the hideous razored rending as its murderous teeth closed on his throat. Syd scrambled, veering off the path, plowing through a thicket, adrenaline obliterating the pain.

It was almost upon him. Syd vaulted over a fallen tree, landed badly, his left foot striking a root and throwing him off-balance. Syd screeched and toppled, landing painfully on his shoulder.

And he knew in that instant that there was no way to escape, nothing to do but die, or die fighting. His mind shrieked and spun. Syd scrabbled to his feet, grabbed a chunk of branch the size of his forearm from the ground. It was solid enough, with a three-inch spike of jagged limb protruding from one end, a primitive war club. Syd raised it high as he braced himself, then turned to face his attacker: the fear focused to one point, let loose in a wild, primal cry. . . .

Nothing happened.

There was no moment of sickening impact. No flash of slavering jaws. No Wild Kingdom battle-to-the-death. There was just an elongated nightmare moment as Syd stood, trembling, locked in a lethal last-stand stance. Ready to kill the next thing that moved.

But there was nothing chasing him.

Nothing chasing him at all.

"SYD?" Nora's voice, calling from the darkness. "SYD!"

"NORA! GET AWAY!!"

Something cracked behind him; Syd screeched and did a frantic pirouette.

It was Nora, stepping from the darkness. She approached, her voice tense, wary. "Syd, are you okay?"

"There's something out there," he said, searching the shadows, the club still tight in his hand. "Something was after me."

She peered in the direction he pointed. "Well," she said. "Whatever it was, it's gone now."

Again, that unmistakable amusement. It poured fuel on his flayed and burning nerves, left him agitated, incensed. There was nowhere to focus the anger, no one to train it on but her.

"What's the matter with you?" he cried, pulling away, glaring. "Are you fucking deaf? Didn't you *hear* it??"

Nora remained unfazed. "All I heard was you, running around and screaming like a maniac."

"IT WAS OUT THERE!!"

Nora said nothing, let the evidence speak for itself. Syd stood panting for a few moments more, before it became clear that she was right. It was gone now. His adrenaline eased off by degrees, leaving a profound exhaustion in its wake.

Nora stepped closer, put her hand on his shoulder. He flinched. "Shit, Syd, you're bleeding," she said. "Here, put that thing down and let's get out of here." She went to take the club, found Syd would not release it, his hand still humming with unspent survival instinct.

It took her almost a minute to get him to drop it; the moment he did, it was as though the remainder of his strength leeched away. Syd deflated into her, suddenly woozy, hollow, fragile as a reed.

"It was out there," he insisted. "It was right behind me."

Nora nodded, neither believing nor disbelieving, but merely accepting his experience. She slipped a supportive arm around him, buoying his sagging bulk.

"C'mon," she said. "Let's get you home."

16

*H*E REMEMBERED VERY little of what followed next:
fragmented images, bits of experience.

They arrived back at his place sometime around three
A.M. Nora had driven, Syd being in no condition. He remembered being helped up the stairs; led to the bathroom.
He remembered the shower, mud and blood swirling together, brown spirals curling down the drain. He remembered her warm hands helping him into the bed, tucking
him in tight because he honest to god didn't have the
strength to pull the blanket up himself.

He remembered asking if she was coming to bed with
him, her replying that she'd be there soon.

And then he was gone, descending into a bright wash
of dream-river current, where a million flickering images
of crazy dream-logic rushed over him, like rainbow fish in
an endless succession.

It was there that Syd first began to perceive how
deeply his world was changing. How the freight train of
destiny he'd sensed last night was already mowing him
down. Unconscious, barraged by images he kept secret

even from himself, Syd absorbed the colors of understand-
ing, uninterrupted by the tyranny of the mundane.

While in the living room, Nora stepped into another
world entirely.

THERE IS THAT one amazing second, when you watch a
thing spin out of control, and you know exactly what is
going to happen. You can calculate where it is going to hit,
how fast and how hard, and you can even begin to visual-
ize the extent of the damage. The only thing you *can't* do,
in fact, is stop the collision from happening.

The most amazing second was the one in which you
knew it was too late.

Nora watched the bottle drop, and got that old familiar
shiver. Like liquor, death, and orgasm, it was a feeling she
never got used to, no matter how many times it happened:
a sensation so potent it obliterated all prior experience of
it, coming each time fresh and new. From the moment the
bottle slipped between her fingers, she could feel the
voidrush in her spine, whirling vertiginously in her throat
and her bowels.

"Fuck!" she spat, weaving slightly as she danced out
of shrapnel range. The bottle exploded, in terrible confir-
mation of her fear. She watched the liquid plume, the glass
shards disassemble and soar. Half-empty, half-full, it
clearly no longer mattered. What it was, was all over the
place.

"Shit!" she hissed, her eyes on the shards and the
spreading stain. She didn't know if she was more angry
with the bottle for breaking, herself for dropping it, or the
floor for being so goddam hard. She was simply, suddenly
infuriated; her anger flaring like a pyromaniac's wet
dream, squirting colorful light and dangerous fire in every
direction.

Then it dissipated: an emotional impulse with the life
span of a glorious one-shot firework display. And when
the last sparks had fallen to earth, she was left with nothing but the emotion that preceded, and that emotion was

inescapably *dread:* a vast and all-encompassing fear, huge as the universe itself, dark and exquisite and born of experience. It was the backdrop for everything she knew, and everything she felt. It was her emotional bottom line.

By the time the red mist and green dust had settled, Nora was crying again.

Of course, this was nothing new. Crying was something Nora did quite a bit of lately. She'd been fighting the impulse practically from the moment Syd had crashed, telling herself everything is fine, he's doing great, it's going to work this time. But being left alone with her thoughts and his things was probably not the greatest idea; she'd learned enough about his history to infuse them with meaning, and meaning inevitably equaled pain.

But that was the way it always went, as much a part of the pattern as the need to feed. It was emotional damage that made the nightmare come alive: emotional damage, and the scars that it left behind. And Syd's spartan waystation at the crossroads of life was crawling with artifacts, regardless of how stripped-down he believed his world to be. The evidence was everywhere. She'd smelled it from the second she walked in the door.

Like his music collection, for example. It was the one thing he claimed was completely his own; but, of course, he was completely mistaken, because Karen had sprayed all up and down those old vintage LPs, left her scent on every CD case and speaker cone. Every time he listened to any of the music he'd picked up in the last ten years, it would throw him right back on the time they'd spent together: the fighting, the fucking, the moments of peace, and all the passion he'd ever invested in their love. That bitch had left her mark on them as surely as if she'd scratched her initials directly into those black vinyl grooves and iridescent discs.

And the same went for everything else in his life, from the clothes he wore to the car he drove to the comforter on his bed. Even tonight's dinner dishes, which still sprawled across the kitchen table. Even after flavoring them with the herbs necessary for Syd's awakening—yohimbe and kava kava, cannabis indica and damiana—Nora could still smell Karen in every hand-me-down plate and utensil. Did he have any idea how hard it was for her to eat under those circumstances? Much less make love on those sheets?

She felt the anger flicker back, but it was quickly subsumed by sadness. She picked an album blind, going more on smell than on musical taste, not even caring what it was, just needing to hear something that was post-Karen, something they'd never listened to together. It wasn't easy.

She got a grip on herself, began cleaning up the mess, her hands trembling as she handled every jagged piece. The fact was, she wasn't mad at Syd at all. And today had been nothing if not hopeful. Her instincts were right about him; she could feel it. And *Christ,* his potential notwithstanding, Syd was the first guy she'd found that she actually *liked* since . . .

Since Michael. The words came up unbidden. *Since Michael.* Up from the nowhere place that she tried so hard to bury. Even now, as the tears burned her eyes, and the sorrow welled up in her so huge that she thought she would surely burst, there was no stopping the voice when it came.

Since Michael died.

And that was when the music came up to smack her, with a gentle wash of tremolo guitar. It was an old blues tune, something off a soundtrack to a movie she'd never even seen. It was amazing how cruel background music could be, how brutally ironic and synchronistically apropos.

The name of the song was "The Dark End of the Street," a tune that she'd heard a million times or so. She didn't know who was singing this time, and didn't care. The voice was rich and raw and soulful, and it collided perfectly with the pictures that had crept back into her mind, sent her reeling down her own private memory lane. . . .

> *"At the dark end of the street*
> *That is where we always meet*

Hiding in shadows, where we don't belong
Living in darkness, to hide a wrong
You and me, at the dark end of the street.
You and me."

She had met Michael on an Amtrak luxury liner, heading from Albuquerque, New Mexico, to succulent, intoxicating New Orleans. Grabbing the train was a sudden stroke of inspiration, at a time when she'd desperately needed one; after that fucking incident in Las Vegas, with the imitation redheaded strippers and the leaking generic garbage bags, it had been time to put some serious distance between herself and Vic. Besides, she loved Amtrak; it was a great way to see the country, the only form of long-distance transit other than driving that let her feel somehow connected with the earth.

Michael was a handsome Italian drifter and ne'er-do-well, long ago of Brooklyn spawned and never quite released from the bounds of that distinctive macho stance. Forty years old and displaying it proudly, very definitely holding on to his looks, he was far and away the pick of the Amtrak litter that weekend. He had been traveling since Seattle, spending almost all of his time in the bar car on the downstairs level of the double-decker train.

From the moment their eyes met, she knew he was special. Everything about him gave off that instinctive alpha male pheromone rush: his amused confidence, his complete sense of self-possession, his innate ability to intimidate lesser males simply by ordering a beer or strolling through the car. She'd noticed it instantly; the fact that the furtive leers and pickup vibes evaporated around her the minute she started talking to him told her everyone else knew it, too.

Nora was charmed by the fact that he *didn't* hit on her, even though his attraction to her was crystal clear. Hell, he could even admire her strategic flashes of thigh and cleavage and not lose his train of thought as they talked.

And talk they did: for hours upon hours, long after the

sun had set and on, as the train rolled through miles of
endless black night. Getting to know each other. Revealing
themselves by degrees. By the time she dragged him back
to her sleeper, she had all but decided.

The first night confirmed it. Michael was an astonishing lover, devout and confident, with great strong hands
and a passionate mouth and an artist's appreciation of what
made her erotic mechanism tick. Better than Syd. Maybe
better than Vic. Certainly better than the Vic she'd fled.

It was hard *not* to succumb and give herself over to the
Change, in those first few nights—his dense and knowing
cock drove her crawling mad—but the hurtling metal walls
were close, and she knew that if she let herself go there'd
be no stopping it, and she'd have to kill just to cover her
tracks. There were two hundred and thirty-seven passengers on board. It was easier to just rein in the beast. But
God did he make it hard. . . .

> *"I know that time is gonna take its toll*
> *We have to pay for all the love we stole*
> *It's a sin, and we know it's wrong*
> *But our love keeps comin' on strong*
> *Steal away to the dark end of the street*
> *You and me."*

The beautiful thing was, he was already a small-time
grifter and criminal; there was no need to soft-pedal the
seamier aspects of the life. He'd done time, so the realities
of the cage didn't need to be spelled out for him. By the
time they landed in New Orleans, she believed that she had
finally found the man of her dreams. All she had to do was
take his monster out for a little run in the dark.

St. Louis Number 1 was a huge old standing cemetery
on Rampart Street, on the border of the French Quarter.
There, against a tableau of whitewashed marble and burnt
red mausoleum brick, she set Michael's animal spirit free.
They fed that night on thugs and vagabonds, gloriously
rampaging amongst the dead.

Michael was a natural, and his gratitude knew no

bounds. Together, they spent two glorious months on the run, conquering each hurdle in his evolution with savage grace and surprising ease. She cultivated and nurtured his bestial side, trained him in the ways of the hunt. His killer instincts, never buried far beneath the surface, emerged full-blown and formidable. When Vic came—and it was only a matter of time, she knew—Michael would be ready. There was no doubt in her mind.

And he, in turn, was good to her: treating her the way she'd always wanted to be treated, the way she'd always wished Vic would have known enough to treat her. He didn't go chasing after every little bitch he saw. He knew that he would never find another Nora. He loved her totally, worshipped her without kissing her ass, and she had never felt more happy or alive.

But, of course, it was too good to last. . . .

> *"They're gonna find us*
> *They're gonna find us*
> *They're gonna find us, love, someday*
> *You and me*
> *At the dark end of the street."*

Vic finally caught up with them in Mississippi, on a night so swollen and miserable with heat that the sweat beaded thicker than blood on your skin. He ambushed them out back of a zydeco shack, upwind and completely off-guard. They were drunk on bourbon, Cajun stomp, and each other. Michael fought like hell, but in truth he never even had a chance. She blamed herself; there just wasn't enough time before he had to put it to the test. The look in his eyes when Vic's jaws closed on his throat would haunt her for as long as she lived: not so much one of pain as a terrible, infinite regret.

She had slashed Vic then, with murderous intent: a razored divoting rake across *his* face, showering Michael's agonized countenance with a red rain not his own. It was the first time she'd ever taken a real shot at Vic, for all their years of fighting; and it was very nearly the last thing she ever did. Only Michael's last dying efforts saved her, keeping Vic busy disemboweling him just long enough for Nora to get away.

And even now, when she closed her eyes, she could see that road stretching out before her. A road made bleary by a river of tears and the terrible fear that there was no hope at its end. She could remember it all as if it were yesterday.

She could still hear Michael's screams.

> *"And when the daylight hour rolls around*
> *And by chance we'll go down the town*
> *If we should meet, just walk, walk on by*
> *Oh darling, please don't you cry*
> *Tonight we meet*
> *At the dark end of the street."*

Nora leaned hard against the sink, bracing herself against the sorrow, the wracking sobs that would not stop no matter how hard she tried. There was no defense against the sadness when it came, no way to fend off or reason with the pain. And not enough booze in the world to drown it in.

Her throat felt dry and rank with phlegm. Cotton-mouth, on top of everything else. She groped out blindly through her tears for the bottle, then remembered it was shrapnel in a pool on the floor.

"FUCK!" she yelled, purely reactive now: no longer Nora, but a hysterical re-creation, a creature made entirely of red wine and grief.

The terrible truth was, *there was no hope.* She'd feared it then, and she feared it now. She was as doomed as a lobster in a restaurant aquarium, as doomed as doomed can be. Vic would never die, and he would never stop coming, and nothing she could do or say would make a goddam bit of difference.

And here she was, in the middle of as grim a nowhere town as she'd ever found, in the apartment of a guy she had met just last night, contemplating a happily-ever-after life of monogamous downwardly-mobile domesticity. As if such a thing were even possible, not to mention desirable; as if it were even an option at all.

But the fact was that part of it was *incredibly attractive;* she was surprised by how strongly the feeling surged. As much as she loved the night and the roaming and thrill of the kill, she was—dare she admit it?—tired. Tired of the road and the running, the relentless shadowy trail. Too many miles. Too many faceless strangers in nameless bars, snuffling after her like a bitch in heat and paying for it with their lives. It used to be fun; now it was just stale. Spent. Old.

Then again, what wasn't? She certainly was not getting any younger; quite the opposite, in fact. Even given the obvious perks of her turbocharged metabolism—she was eighty-eight years old and didn't look a day over thirty-five—she was still a long way from immortal.

Worse still, lately it seemed she was feeding more and getting less for it; the glistening predatory rush she used to get from swallowing another's life essence was receding to a dull, throbbing buzz. She wasn't bouncing back like she used to, either. Indeed, not a day went by that she didn't check her face for lines, her tits for sag, her ass for loss of definition. It was age as gravity, and more: it was youth as a fading window of opportunity.

And that made her think about the *other* urge; the one she measured by the ticking clock that thundered ever louder inside her. The need to love and be loved by someone who saw her as the center of all creation, someone who would be there long after her strength and beauty had faded. Someone whose love would never leave her, who would never let her die alone.

She longed to feel the life growing inside her, to cradle her baby's tiny, helpless form in her arms, to feel its mouth pressed to her nurturing breast. It was a naked desire, one that sprang from her deepest self, and it transcended all logic or politics or reason. It was both incredibly human and utterly animal, the one point where her warring natures inexorably met.

And no amount of running could put it behind her. Or the fear that snapped at its heels.

She thought about the little white lie she'd told Syd this evening, the one about not being able to conceive. *Not a lie,* she instantly amended. *Not exactly.* It was very true that she hadn't been able to carry a young one to term. And she feared whether she could ever get pregnant again, especially after Vic . . .

Nora stopped in mid-thought, unable to face the memory of the last time she'd tried, and what Vic had done. It was his fault, the shit. It had to be. *He* was the one who was corrupted: he'd been at it too long, far longer than she. Yes, they both fed against nature: perverting the instinct even as they strengthened it; she knew it in her bones as every new theft coursed through her veins. It was cannibal karma, a shortcut to power. And it was an abomination.

But *she* could turn it around, and he never would. He was a dead end; *she* wasn't. It was what she told herself, what she needed to believe. She had the power, she was an experienced and seasoned survivor, she held the future in her belly and between her legs. All she needed was a fresh chance. Vic just couldn't give her that.

The question was, could Syd?

Could *anyone*?

And that was when the fear caught up to her, in all its rabid, snarling glory: slashing at her flanks, bringing her tumbling down. The idea that she had inadvertently polluted herself beyond repair. Feeding on the forbidden spark until she was a barren and empty vessel. Unable to hold, let alone give forth life. It was simply too much to bear.

It was just another one of the little things Vic hadn't told her about, way back when he'd first seduced her from the mortal normalcy of her girlhood in the mountains of Montana. She flashed back to that long-ago time—the memory distant, faded, worn with time—when she was still nothing more than a good girl with a bad streak, and he

*was the deadly handsome stranger that drove her daddy
crazy.*

*Nora was all of fifteen when Vic blew into town and
blew her neat little world apart: promising her the passion
and danger she'd always dreamed about, the kind she
knew she would never find as the precious only daughter
of a successful, upright Christian cattle rancher. Vic offered her the moon, and everything under its cold blue
light. Nora was only too happy to accept.*

*So he stole her away one night, running south all the
way to Mexico. Along the way he also stole her heart and
her virginity, though not in that order and with not much
of a fight. He showed her how to Change, how to hunt and
feed and roam the night, how to live wild in a world full
of human cattle ripe for slaughter.*

*He showed her the ways of the wolf inside, and in the
process made her over in his own image.*

But he never told her the price she'd pay. . . .

Nora stopped, realized that she was crying again.
"No," she hissed, then reined it in tight, forced herself to
take a minute, reassess her situation. True, looking at this
squalid Pennsylvania ghost town didn't exactly inspire her.

But Syd was another matter entirely. Yes indeed. He
had passed the first test: he had the wild seed inside him,
and was stable enough for it to take root. He was instinctively protective. And he was a good lover: enthusiastic,
empathetic. Eager. Maybe not as good as Michael, at least
not yet. But not a combination you found every day, nonetheless.

Vic had never been able to walk that line; even if he
had been able to get her pregnant, he would have made the
worst father in the world. Abusive, selfish, drunken, and
cruel. God help them if they were girls.

Syd, on the other hand, would never rape his own
daughters. This much she could tell, and that in itself
made him stand out from the crowd. She could tell that he
really liked her, on top of his obvious hard-on and in spite
of his anger tonight. And there was something so enor-
mously satisfying and rewarding about being genuinely

cared for, appreciated for who you really were, instead of just being craved as a fuck machine.

But what was she going to do? Set up shop and play house, hanging around town until she got herself mired in this decaying postindustrial tar pit? Was she insane? In the same amount of time, Vic could find them, kill them, travel the world, and write a book about it.

Which meant that, if she wanted Syd, she'd have to defer his nesting impulse somehow. Get him to go on the road with her. And train him like a sonofabitch. Maybe by the time they were in a position to tear Vic limb from limb, they'd also be in a position to settle down somewhere. Start a little pack of their own.

But how would she talk him into it? She hadn't a clue in the world. She'd never been so intensely focused on such a regular Safety-First Clyde, such a do-goody waste of talent. Tonight was important; at least, he had proven that he had some fight in him. But would he survive the Change, when it came, or would he fry in the transition? She had no way of knowing. He was more concerned that the cable bill be paid wherever they landed. He was soft. That was all there was to it.

But he's good. She paused to reflect on the thought. *And he loves me. Or at least he will.*

And when he gets in touch with his nature, he will be the one I need. I know he will. All he has to do is let go of his bullshit: all those things that he thinks he needs to have.

Then he will be perfect, she thought.

Then he will be mine.

And suddenly the smell of Karen was everywhere in the apartment: that drip-dry vegetarian cooze, with her chlorophyll cunt. Nora couldn't blank it out, couldn't make it go away. She was tasting blood, and it wasn't her own. Her cottonmouth was intense, utterly untenable; she pulled a glass off the counter, filled it with water from the tap.

When she brought it to her lips, she smelled essence of Karen.

And something snapped.

"Fuck!" She flung the glass down, smashed it into the sink. "Fuck you!" And it was too much, just all too much, the pain and the memories and the desperation, the fear that relentlessly hounded her like a ravening pack. "FUCK YOU!" Not knowing exactly who it was she cursed, not even caring, as the tears came back with a vengeance: a raw, wracking sob erupting up and out of her like a poisonous black wave. She was drunk, she was wired, she was cursed and running on fumes. Something had to give.

There was a plate by her hand, stacked ever so tidily in the drying rack. She wrenched it loose, let it fly. By the time it blew up, she already had another in hand. Another plate. Another stupid stinking plate.

She felt the Change start uncoiling in her guts, straining at its tether. *Now*, it screamed. The plate exploded with a bright brittle crack, loud as a gunshot. *Not now*, she thought, beating it back. A glass came up, came down again, sending sharp shiny fragments up to dance before her eyes. *Now*. Her head pounded and she slammed the counter. *Not now*. This wasn't the right time. Her mind was spinning. These were not Syd's things. They were Karen's things. They had to die. He had to understand.

She smashed another plate. It was not enough. She smashed another one. Syd's voice called out from the bedroom. *Not now*, she thought, growling. It wasn't time.

She was running out of time. . . .

And that was when the hands grabbed her from behind. Nora let out a mournful low, like an animal embracing its doom. The arms were strong, and she buckled and sagged within them. The Change subsided: kept down, if barely. He was talking to her, but she could only hear jangling, jumbled noise. She had to get him ready. She had to tell him soon.

"I'm sorry," she managed, and then once again started to cry.

The song had changed. It was obscenely upbeat, straight out of Motown in its perverse jauntiness. She vaguely recognized the melody. "Destination Anywhere." Background music could be so cruel.

"I'm sorry," she repeated, and then he turned her around and kissed her. "I'm sorry." Pulling her mouth away. The room was spinning. The world was spinning. When Syd spoke again the words spun in her mind.

"It's all right," he said, and she wanted to believe it. Only she knew it wasn't true.

17

*I*N THE DREAM, *he was home again.*

Syd ran through his house, frantically calling his wife's name. A terrible storm lashed the windows, echoed off the roof. Something was pounding on the front door, demanding entrance. They had to get out of there. Something was coming, something horrible. He had to find her.

Just then Karen's voice rang out somewhere behind him, and Syd turned in time to catch a fleeting glimpse of her moving up the stairs. He chased after her, but as fast as he ran he could not catch up; the house itself conspired against him, the floor sagging beneath his feet as the stairs stretched and corkscrewed like an Escher print.

He fought his way to the hallway, found door upon door before him, each one revealing more ruined and desecrated space: a gutted bedroom, a trashed nursery, the crib shattered, the plush toys lining the walls ripped to pieces and scattered, their bright plastic eyes blindly gleaming.

The storm crashed and boomed outside. The pounding redoubled with a vengeance, the door groaning from the

*impact of the blows. He could hear the wood bow and
crack, start to give way. Syd turned . . .*

*. . . and that's when he saw Karen, standing at the
head of the stairs: her face an empty mask, devoid of reaction. He could hear the front door crashing inward, feel
the wind that rushed through the house as the lightning
flashed and blistered the sky. Karen stared at him, blankly
uncomprehending, as something huge and made entirely of
shadow ascended the stairs, rose up behind her.*

*Syd tried to move: the floor held his feet, trapping him.
He tried to scream, anger fueling his fear. Can't you see
it? Can't you feel it?? What's wrong with you?? He tried
to warn her, but when he opened his mouth no sound
would come out.*

*Karen watched his desperate pantomime, her eyes
blank as mirrors. He watched in horror as the shadow descended, completely engulfing her. There was a terrible
rending sound. He could not watch. As he looked away
something soft and moist hit his leg, slid to the floor. Syd
looked down.*

*Just in time to see that perfect mask land wetly at his
feet. . . .*

Syd jolted awake, completely disoriented. The dream
fled in the cold light of consciousness, retreating from his
grasp even as he tried to chase it. Karen's face fragmented,
wraithlike.

And then it was gone.

Leaving Syd panting, afraid to move, unable to clearly
remember why. He lay like that until his heartbeat slowed
to somewhere near normal, then let his head sag back into
the pillow. He looked at the clock. One-thirty. Jesus.

Nora murmured and curled into him, warm and serene.
In sleep there were no traces of her previous emotional
holocaust; indeed, the Nora who nestled so peacefully into
the crook of his arm was so far from the hysterical creature smashing dishes in the kitchen as to be another spe-
cies entirely.

He had to admit her behavior had spooked him: he'd
never been close—emotionally *or* physically—to someone

who was so prone to violent mood swings. Nora's explosion had yanked him out of a dead-black slumber, sent him lurching into the kitchen to quell her private rampage. She had wanted only to be fucked once he'd finally eased her back to bed. This they had done, despite his fatigue: Nora pinning him to the bed and grinding with such unhinged abandon that he thought he would pass out. It was fast and furious and over almost before it started, the carnal equivalent of beating drums to ward off evil spirits, an act of desperate intensity.

She punctuated her climax by raking her nails across his chest so hard that she actually drew blood, effectively obliterating Syd's orgasm in mid-squirt. Then she collapsed, still clinging to him, and fell almost instantly asleep.

Leaving Syd to wonder what the hell had just happened.

It was clear that whatever baggage she was carrying around was heavy and full of God only knew what kinds of secret pain and punishment. It was also clear that hand in hand with her passion came the full-blown mother of all tempers. It was bad enough sneaking up on it from behind, dodging shrapnel and carrying a heartful of devotion; he shuddered at the thought of ever facing such anger head-on. He had the feeling that going up against Nora would not be fun.

Oh, well. She was here, she was with him, and he didn't want her to go. Weird as it all was, he could not imagine kicking her out of his bed. What had she said about risk? He decided he'd take his chances.

As Syd turned toward her his stomach suddenly flipped, did a curdling somersault into his bowels. A yawning emptiness opened like a trapdoor inside him, and he felt as though he had been scraped hollow. *Damn,* he realized. *I'm starving.*

It came as a shock, not just the immediacy of it but the depth. It was as though he had never felt this level of pure unadulterated *craving* before, as far removed from ordinary appetite as a paper cut was from a traumatic amputation. And though he was so hungry that it had come full circle, until the mere *thought* of food now made him queasy, Syd realized he'd better eat something soon, or suffer the consequences.

He disengaged from Nora, started to get up. His gorge ballooned menacingly. Not good. He sat back down, took a deep breath, thinking *not puke I will not puke I will not* until it actually seemed to work.

He tried again. Better this time. Nora stirred beside him and slumbered on, oblivious. Pulling on sweatpants, Syd made his way out of the bedroom. His legs were quivering, unsteady as he moved. Syd felt loosely held together, as if any moment he might rattle apart and fly all over the room. He did a quick internal gauge as he reached the midway point between the bathroom and the kitchen, decided that no, he really wasn't about to hurl, but yes, he was incredibly dehydrated.

The kitchen won. Syd groaned and stumbled forth, careful to watch for any stray frags of glass. The fridge was just inside the door, and that was good. Hands shaking, he grabbed a half-gallon bottle of water off the shelf, brought it to his lips. A flood of icy liquid sluiced down his gullet, diluting his roiling gastric stew. He kept on drinking until he had drained fully half of it. By the time he was finished he actually felt a little better.

Syd surveyed the refrigerator's contents. Eggs sounded okay; hell, maybe he'd even whip up a little breakfast-in-bed action, surprise her with it.

The first order of business was clearing away the debris. The sink and counter were littered with stray shards and slivers of ceramic and glass, and some had flown clear across the room. It took a good twenty minutes and a great deal of care to clean them all up; the whole time his thoughts jogged between worrying about what was bothering her and imagining what one of the plates would look like sailing at his head.

Once finished, he got the ingredients out and piled them on the counter. His kitchen setup was spartan, consisting of leftover items Karen hadn't recquisitioned for her own needs. There was a big black cast-iron frying pan hanging on a hook over the stove; he took it down, plopped it on the front burner and fired it up.

Next he began chopping veggies, using the big chef's knife that he'd insisted upon taking. As he worked, the frying pan started to smoke on the stove; Syd pinned back the heat, then carved off a hunk of butter and tossed it in. It sizzled and liquefied as he lifted the pan and rolled it, coating the surface.

Setting it down, he pulled a stainless-steel mixing bowl from the cupboard and opened the egg carton. There were six to the count, a neat three-egg omelet each—but then he saw that one sported a gummy-looking crack across its surface.

"Ugh," he grimaced and set it aside, began cracking its siblings into the bowl with a fluid one-hand motion. Yolks swirled and ran, making a miniature cholesterol whirlpool. He tipped them into the heated pan.

The eggs bubbled and spread, browning at the edges; Syd waited a moment, then folded in half of the cheese and veggies. As they melded together in the pan he got down two plates, quartered an orange, put two slices on each one.

The kitchen filled with cooking smells; as he worked Syd began to realize that his appetite wasn't responding the way it should. Though he was enjoying the process, and the hunger still raged inside him, everything he was making seemed strangely unappealing. It wasn't that the food wasn't good: the eggs and cheese were okay, and the vegetables were perfectly fine. He sniffed the butter to see if it was rancid; it was fine.

Too much excitement on not enough fuel, he figured, shrugging it off. He'd feel better when he got something into his system.

The smells mingled in the air oppressively. His belly burbled and gnawed at him. As he flipped the omelet he actually began to feel dizzy. He leaned over and cracked the door leading to the porch, took a deep lungful of air. Just then a voice sounded behind him.

"Hi."

Syd turned and saw Nora standing by the doorway, wearing nothing but one of his flannel shirts. Her hair was sleep-tossed and wild; the shirt itself was unbuttoned, held closed only by her folded arms. She was bleary-eyed, more than a bit embarrassed.

"Hi," he said. Silence.

"Whatcha makin'?"

Syd smiled wanly, pushing his hair back. "Breakfast," he replied. "Well, more like brunch, actually. I was gonna surprise you."

"Mmm," she murmured, leaning against the fridge. "Ain't you sweet."

Syd moved back to the stove, and as he did she scooted over and slid her arms around him from behind. "Sorry about last night," she said.

"S'okay." Syd shrugged, kept cooking.

"I've just got some shit to deal with. . . ."

"S'okay," he repeated. She paused, gauging the vibe. "You're not mad?" she asked.

"I wouldn't go that far," he said. "I mean, I don't like seeing you hurting like that. Not to mention it's really hard on the dishes. . . ." He flashed a smile; she didn't return it.

"Anyway," he added, "your past is your business, not mine. You want to talk, I'm here to listen. Otherwise . . ." he shrugged, let it go at that.

Nora hugged him. "You know, you're pretty swell," she said.

"Well, I'm swollen."

She snickered then. A good sign. "I noticed," she said, burying her face between his shoulder blades as her hands slid down his stomach and into his sweats. Her shirt fell open, and Syd could feel her breasts press against his naked back. His beleaguered cock began to respond in kind.

"Keep this up and you'll never eat," he scolded.

"Maybe," she replied. "Maybe I don't *need* food." She bit him on the shoulder. "Maybe I'll just eat you."

"Suit yourself," he said. "I, on the other hand, will die."

"Aw, poor baby." She released him, leaned back against the counter. He finished the first omelet, scooped it onto the plate.

"Here you go," he said. "Bargain-basement cuisine from Chez Syd." He passed her the plate.

"You first. You're the starving one."

"Nah," he replied. "This'll only take a second."

He grabbed another egg. She spotted the defective one, picked it up.

"That one's bad," he warned.

"You sure?" Nora turned it in her fingers, sniffed it. "Smells okay to me."

Before he could reply, Nora cracked it on the counter's edge, brought it to her lips, and tipped it back down her throat. She gulped it down, then wiped her mouth.

"Yum," she said. She picked up an orange slice, peeling the pulp away with her teeth. Syd made a persimmon face. "Jesus," he grimaced. "And I actually *kissed* those lips?"

"What?" Nora said, nonchalant. "They're good this way."

"Uh-huh," Syd said skeptically. "This is all a cheap ploy to avoid my cooking." He cracked the egg he was holding, poured it into the bowl, and picked up the fork.

"Oh, shit," he groaned, stepping back.

"What?" she asked. He gestured queasily. Then she looked in the bowl, and all the color drained from her face. Nora gasped.

Floating in the bowl was a gelatinous, malformed mass: tiny body soft as a Dali-clock, little stringers of blood curling around it, threading through the clear amniotic fluid. It was a chicken fetus, right down to the beak and bulging eye sockets. A grinning little rictus was frozen on its dead, gooey face.

Syd dropped the fork and stepped back, his head suddenly reeling. He looked around wildly, then turned toward the back door: wrenching it open, pushing through the screen, and falling out onto the porch.

He was leaning against the rail—coughing and sputtering, a thin rope of spittle trailing from his lips—when Nora appeared in the doorway. "Syd, are you okay?" she asked, her voice tense and choked. She reached out to touch him.

He pulled away, leaned his head against his arms. Then the sickness took precedence, and he visibly slumped. A high-pitched buzzing trilled in his ears. "I think—" The buzzing got louder. He shook his head, trying to clear it. "I think maybe I . . ."

He took a step away from the railing, and his legs folded under him.

"Syd!" Nora cried. She lurched forward, caught him by the waist. "Syd, what is it?"

"I . . . feel sick," he mumbled.

"You're okay," she urged, an undercurrent of panic swelling in her voice. "You're just having a bad reaction. . . ."

Reaction to what? he thought to ask, but the words wouldn't come out of his mouth. "Nee'ta . . . laydow . . ." he slurred.

Steadying him, Nora helped Syd off the porch and into the kitchen. The food smells assaulted him again and he doubled over, body spasming.

"Hang on, baby," she said. "Hang on."

Nora steered him back out of the kitchen, heading for the bedroom. By the time they were halfway there he had broken into a full-body sweat, his skin going hot then cold then both at once. His consciousness dislodged and descended, spiraling in his skull.

When Nora next spoke her voice seemed distorted, a million miles away. His brain couldn't quite make out the words she said.

But he could've sworn they were *oh god, here it comes. . . .*

18

NORA AND SYD huddled on the bed like a macabre Madonna and child, as the first tremors wracked his flesh.

Nora cradled his head to her breast: fighting down her panic, rocking him like a baby. In the last half hour his body temperature had plummeted to near hypothermia, then rocketed clear into fever-dream territory. She had scoured the apartment, gathering every sheet and blanket and towel, which were now arranged into a heaping semi-circular cocoon on the bed, forming a makeshift sweat lodge. A bucket was positioned within easy reach. A washrag soaked in ice water sat ready and waiting on the bedside table; the bottle of Comfort was uncapped an arm's length away.

Nora took a slug off the bottle and braced herself, beating back her own fear in the process. The mixing bowl still sat on the kitchen counter, taunting her. She didn't know what to make of the omen, was afraid to even look at it as she broke open the ice trays, raced through the rooms ...

   ... but when she closed her eyes she could see herself:

*huge with child but not ready yet, screaming at Vic as
they pulled away from the parking lot of the shithole Texas
dive where she'd caught him again, his nose already halfway up some beehive-headed bimbo's crack. She could see
herself, screaming at Vic as they roared down the highway, his face contorted with anger and resentment and
rage.*

*She could hear herself, the horrible dull-knife agony
twisting in her guts as the contractions hit, sent her reeling and clutching at the dashboard. She could hear Vic's
screams, mingling with her own, as he rocketed off the
highway and onto a pitch-black back road.*

*She remembered the moon, looming over her through
the rear window. As full and cold as she felt, as she
pushed and pushed and pushed through a blinding veil of
pain. She remembered Vic's halting liquor breath as he
cradled her head, remembered the smell of her own sour
outpouring, a gushing torrent threaded with red, as she
ushered forth the wrongness.*

The wrongness that slid from between her legs.

*Most of all, she remembered the silence. Like a shroud
that descended to engulf them, as Vic lifted the tiny misshapen body to the sky. To the night. To distant mother
moon.*

A silence broken only by her own wretched sobbing.

And the feeding sounds that followed. . . .

Nora stopped: blocking the memories, forbidding any
further thought on the subject. That was a long time ago,
she told herself. Ancient history, to be forgotten at all
costs.

This was now. And she had work to do.

Nora took another swig. She was as ready as she'd
ever be. And it wasn't like she hadn't done this before.
Initiation was one thing: just about anyone with the spark
in them could be jump-started, tapping into the root of the
beast through the combination of intoxication and manic
sex-magick. And she knew how to pick 'em—weeding out
the dweebs and lost causes almost at a glance—so it was

rare that she didn't get her pick through the first set of hurdles.

But *mastering* it . . .

That was the hard part. There were so many ways to fumble, so many things that could go wrong. The kinds of walls they had built-in to shield them from their nature. The strength and resiliency of their human mind relative to the ferocity of their animal instincts. The sheer *force* of their imagination . . .

In the end, there were an infinite number of worst-case variations on blowing it. But only one real way of getting it right. First you had to free the beast. Then you had to learn to *ride* the fucker. Primal essence was soul nitro, explosively unstable, and tapping into it always meant working without a safety net.

The price of failure, plain and simple, was death.

Sometimes they got unruly and she did it in self-defense; sometimes they just couldn't get it up, in which case they were meat. Worse yet were the doomed ones who couldn't weather the inner storm that awakening invariably aroused. And while it was a certainty that life without tapping their true nature meant consignment to the hollow strictures of man-meat, freeing the beast without the necessary mental power to harness it was tantamount to turning a starving tiger loose on a sleeping keeper. Unchained after years, sometimes decades of repression, rabid with appetite, the animal side would literally eat its host alive. It was not pretty.

"*Uh-nuh* . . ." Syd twitched and shivered, a clammy chill seeping across his skin. He could barely speak. "*N-Nora* . . ."

"I'm here," she whispered, feeling his forehead. He was burning up. His breathing was alternately shallow and gasping; his heart jackhammered inside his rib cage.

Nora wrung out the cold rag, sponging his brow. She cursed herself for not having seen this coming. He'd breezed past the first hurdles as if he'd been greased, and tricked her into thinking he could take awakening in stride.

But he was so bound up, and she had so much riding on this, and there wasn't enough time, and . . .

Stop it, she thought. She reminded herself that she'd *expected* him to crash hard: men inevitably took it harder. Every man she'd ever met was ultimately a child, and any kind of sickness reduced them to infants.

But this . . .

She couldn't kid herself. Syd had not only unlocked the cage, he'd blown it clear off the hinges. There was no way of knowing what he'd do.

"What's happening to me?" he asked, his hands clutching at her, weak as twigs. His eyes were closed, his whole being seized in the grip of raw mortal terror. Nora gripped his hand, felt him vibrate like a bowstring.

"You're fine, baby, you're doing fine," she whispered. "Just tell me what you see."

"N-nothing . . ." he stammered, his teeth chattering like porcelain castanets. *". . . c-c-can't s-see . . ."*

"Yes you can," she told him, trying to guide him. "You've just got to *concentrate.* Focus your will, look around you, and tell me where you are."

"L-lost," he murmured, *". . . it's dark . . . I'm s-scared."*

"Don't be, baby, I'm here. . . ."

"S-so scared . . ."

Another seizure hit; Syd started to thrash. Nora grabbed the bottle. Liquor lowered the inhibitions, loosened the mortar holding the inner walls together. She took another hit for herself, then fed him some.

"Here," she whispered.

"I . . . I . . ." he stuttered. *"I c-cannh . . ."*

His eyes were rolling back and forth in their sockets, unable to fix or focus. She chased his mouth with the bottle, made contact, tipped it back until amber rivulets trickled down his chin.

"Achh," he sputtered, coughing out at least as much as he managed to swallow. He held it down, then suddenly doubled over.

"Ahuuagh!"

"Shit!" Nora pressed him toward the bucket as Syd pitched forward and heaved up a quantity of fragrant bile. "It's okay, get it out. Get it all out." She rubbed his back, let him void until she was sure he was empty, then pulled him back into the cocoon and pressed his face to her breast.

"Here. Suck." Nora offered her nipple to him. Syd's mouth found it and locked on hungrily: drawing it in, filling the vacuum. The contact completed a circuit between them; she took another hit off the bottle, felt her nipple burn as it stiffened in his mouth. As he suckled she began to secrete: transfusing energy. Feeding him.

Syd sucked hungrily. His cries subsided, as an eerie quiet fell upon the room. Nora kissed his hair, felt the storm inside him stirring in her core as well, connecting them like a thunderhead moving across some vast inner plane.

Nora closed her eyes, reached out with her mind. She could see the tiny latticework of veins in her eyelids grow distant as a blood-red sunset, ephemeral as heat lightning, as she descended into blackness. Searching for the plane where all consciousness meets.

Searching for him.

"I'm here, baby," she whispered. "Can you feel me?" Syd mumbled, nearly comatose.

"Can you?" she urged.

He fought for control. A moment later, thought came back to him, echoing through her mind.

Yes . . .

Black static suffused her inner vision, wrapped her in its inky embrace. She delved into the darkness, trying to pierce the veil between them.

"What are we doing?"

Rruhn . . . running . . .

"Where are we running?"

She hovered over him: listening to his breathing, waiting for his reply. A rumbling started deep in his chest, resonated through his torso, as the blackness gave way.

And he was in the woods again.

He was running, a fierce wind raging around him: trees groaning under its sway, vaulted limbs knitting patterns like shattered glass over his head . . .

Syd fought to hold on to the question, felt his mind fragment into a billion glittering bits of thought. Nora held him, his muscles rippling and writhing, his entire body a disjointed confederation of flesh, cells quivering in sympathetic vibration . . .

. . . as he tore through night and storm, running from the beast at his back, his feet punctured by jagged stones. Ragged underbrush snagged his flesh, ripping hunks from him that flapped like streamers, as the beast bore down upon him. . . .

Syd's heart was an out-of-control pile driver in his chest, slamming him mercilessly. His body rocked with spasms, every vein and artery suddenly straining to the bursting point, racing down his arms and across his chest, slithering like angry serpents up his temples. The sound coming out of him mounted in intensity . . .

. . . as the animal's howl wound around and through him: merging with the storm as it blotted out all thought, all sensation save his awareness that he was there, *hurtling inexorably forward, unable to stop as more and more pieces of him stripped off, reducing him to meat to bone to bloody writhing essence. His feet became entangled in clinging vines, his legs unable to keep up with the pace.*

Syd tripped, lost his balance, fell screaming in blackness . . .

. . . and the scream became a raw keening cadence that went on and on and on, long after his vocal cords had shredded and his lung capacity exhausted itself. It was the sound of revolution: his mind divided, his cells at war, his DNA splintering at the seams.

Syd's spine went rigid. Nora braced herself.

And emergence was upon them.

"AHHHHHHHNAHNAHHHURTS IT HURTS IT HURTSSS . . .!!!"

He broke contact, howling in agony, every muscle and sinew and ligament wrenched to the breaking point. A blood vessel popped in his temple, sent a thin spritz arcing out to spatter the sheets. His limbs stiffened under the covers; his lungs took in one final heaving gasp of air.

And then—just when it seemed it could go no further, that he would simply explode in a bright red spray of flesh-and-bone confetti—he stopped.

For Nora it was like watching a burning fuse disappear into a keg of dynamite and *not* blow up. Moving quickly, she stripped the blankets back to reveal his naked torso, gleaming with sweat and flush with struggle.

"C'mon, baby," she pleaded, and began massaging his chest. "C'mon . . ."

His engorged veins receded, like ripples on the surface of a pond. His breathing resumed, shallow and halting. . . .

He was at the heart of the forest, the eye of the storm twirling madly above. His body was gone: his essence distilled to a Syd/not-Syd awareness that hovered in the air, permeated the space. A preternatural calm enveloped him.

And the sound of feeding came.

The great wolf stood in the clearing, its maw buried in the chest of its freshly fallen prey. He watched in horror as its head dipped down, disappeared completely into the glistening breach . . .

. . . while in the room Syd shuddered, as the plane of flesh just under his rib cage suddenly distorted and ballooned outward . . .

. . . and as the carcass shifted Syd suddenly realized that it wasn't a deer at all, it was human, *naked and gutted and gleaming on the forest floor. The beast dug deeper, jostling the corpse. Its head flopped and tilted toward him, revealing its face.*

"NO!!!" Syd's eyes opened wide, staring blindly up. Nora snapped out of her trance, was back in the room again. She took hold of his face, brought hers close.

"Oh god," she cried. "Syd!"

"NO!!!" he screamed.

"Syd, listen to me!"

Syd's consciousness reeled as his own eyes stared back at him, dead and caked and opaque. The wolf wrenched

*and tore a new hunk free, making the cadaver's head bob
and nod as if in recognition. . . .*

"OH GOD STOP IT!!" His voice boomed off the bedroom walls, his arms and legs curling inward, going fetal.
"MAKE IT STOP!!"

"Look at it!" Nora told him. "Look in its *eyes!*"

"I CAN'T . . . I . . . STOP IT!"

"Concentrate, Syd! Make it *see* you!"

*Her voice echoed back to him like a lifeline as the
great wolf stopped and withdrew, its snout red and dripping. It turned, revealing a face gone monstrous, distorted:
human features stretched over canine skull, a grinning
abomination rendered in obscene lupine parody. The wolf
licked its chops, and Syd's soul shrieked as he realized . . .*

. . . the beast *had his face, too.*

*It stood, regarding him with eyes utterly devoid of con-
science or pity. They were predator's eyes, and they fixed
him mercilessly as the beast started toward him, growing
with every step until all he saw were eyes and teeth and
eyes and jaws and bright shiny eyes. . . .*

*He could hear its breath, smell the fetid stink of it, feel
the deep rumbling in its chest as it advanced. And he
found himself drowning in those twin shimmering pools of
light.*

As the wolf took another step.

And was upon him.

SYD CAME TO: his head nestled in Nora's lap, his mouth
loosely gaping. He was staring at the ceiling. A track of
dried saliva graced his cheek. Nora was stroking the spot
just between his eyes, making tiny little circles. Over and
over, over and over. Calming. Centering him. Syd gazed at
her with infant eyes, his mind filled with questions he
didn't even know how to ask.

"Now you know," she said.

His eyes stared a moment longer before fluttering shut.
Nora laid his head to her breast, and his mouth found her
nipple, settled there. She slumped back, exhausted and
drained.

Syd drifted off, leaving Nora to watch over him. Listening to him breathe. Tracing tiny little circles.

Over and over. Over and over.

Until, together, they fell into a dark and dreamless sleep.

19

<u> </u>

$\mathbf{H}$E AWOKE HOURS later, with her nipple still in his mouth.

The first stirrings were uncolored by words, or names, or memory, as he emerged from the oblivion that had claimed him. The sky outside was dark, the room steeped in shadow. The moon shone pale and high through the windows. The clock said eleven-eleven. He could not remember quite who he was or even what he was, or what had happened. There was only his need and her presence, quietly entwined.

Syd's lips encircled the swollen rim of the areola, feeling the ripe fullness of her breast. As his tongue touched her nipple, she stirred as well, unconsciously responding.

And every point of contact expanded his map, sent another sensation to remind him that yes, there was that, too, as her belly pressed into his chest and her hands found his back, traced lazy patterns across its breadth. Their bodies shifted position; she drew him closer and he felt his entire nervous system light up, transmitting desire at the speed of thought.

And that was when she moaned, a husky rumble that

started in her chest, filling his ears with exquisite sound, sending energy pulsing through his body, recharging and revitalizing him. His hands found her hips and her hips were glorious, her hips were the cradle of all creation, her hips held the heart of the mystery.

And that was when she turned and tipped him on his back, straddling him; as he slipped inside her she leaned forward so that her breasts dangled before his lips.

"Bite," she whispered.

Her nipple grazed his lips, raked across his incisors. She moaned, picking up the tempo.

"Do it harder," she told him.

Syd obliged, his teeth pulling at the erect flesh. He sucked the point of her breast deep into his mouth; Nora's hair cascaded around his face as her head began to shake from side to side, rocking in counterpoint to her undulating hips.

"Harder," she urged. He did, felt something stirring at the base of his spine. Her head was whipping wildly back and forth now, as she urged him on.

Syd bit her harder, until he felt like any second he would saw it off and swallow it. A distant part of his mind told him this wasn't right, this must hurt like hell. But Nora wasn't complaining. Far from it: her rhythm was ecstatic, frenzied, verging on violence. She rode him furiously, impaling herself again and again as he gnawed her breast, felt unyielding incisor meet resilient tissue and strain it to the breaking point. He loved it. Wanted it.

Wanted *more*.

Nora cried out. The feeling inside him began to rise: he rose with it, half-sitting now, lunging and snapping, leaving crescent-shaped welts on her chest. A high whining sound came up and out of her, the sound of a psychic fuse being lit. He answered with a fiercely guttural growl, a voice that came wholly of its own volition.

Nora flipped her hair back and away from her face. Her eyes rolled up, showing white. Her lips skinned back. She sucked air and hissed, snapping her pelvis in visceral punctuation, each thrust sending another spike of pleasure into and through him.

He was going to explode. Her torso arched and writhed. She tipped her head back, and Syd saw the open expanse of her throat pulsing inches from his face . . .

. . . and at that moment he wanted nothing more than to tear into her windpipe and taste the steaming copper spray. It would be so good. It would be the best. Syd rose, his jaws opening wide. . . .

And that was when he hit the wall.

"No," he gasped, and immediately felt something snap inside him. It was like dropping a lug nut onto a buzz saw blade; there was a ping and a chug and suddenly the balance was off, the whole mechanism spinning dangerously out of control.

"No!" Nora cried, her body suddenly out of sync with his. Syd tried to hang on, to keep from being pummeled to death by the wave he'd moments ago ridden the crest of. *"Don't stop. . . ."*

But the moment was gone; there was no longer any pleasure in the pain. The crescendo faltered, fizzled; her motion turned savage, radically overcompensating. The more she advanced, the more he withdrew. He didn't want to, hated that he couldn't control it.

And Nora . . .

Nora was all over him, crazy with need; Syd withered in response. She kissed and bit and slammed with the desperation of the damned. *"Don't stop,"* she whispered, *"don't . . ."*

Vainly he rallied, brought his teeth to her neck, torn between lust and revulsion. He bit her as hard as he could, but it was feeble now, a toothless imitation. And that just made her crazier, like tossing a rabid dog a rubber bone. He tried again and she twisted away from his mouth, glaring at him. A naked fire burned in her gaze.

"God*dammit*!!" she hissed. "*Not* like that!

"Like *this!*"

She fell upon him: her hands grabbing his arms and

pinning them as her hips hammered his loins and her mouth found his neck and locked on.

Syd heard a snarl and felt a hot slash of pain. He writhed and tried to get out from under her, discovered that he could not, that he was trapped, she was much stronger than she looked, and all the strength he could muster was not enough to pry her off.

The lovemaking turned ugly, as she raced to a climax that he had no part of except as meat. He wondered if this was what it was like to be raped and realized no, this was even *more* fundamental. This was what it was like to be *taken*, like a predator takes its prey: helpless, in pain, to be used and consumed. . . .

The thought shriveled him instantly. He deflated, slipped out of her.

And Nora lost her mind.

"GOD *DAMN*!!" she bellowed. She rolled off of him and stood, panting, crackling like a downed power line. Syd grabbed his throat instinctively, half-expecting to feel the gush of his own blood cascading through some great ragged fissure.

"SHIT!" Nora turned, punched the wall. "Why did you *stop*?" she demanded. "Goddammit, Syd, we were *so* fucking *close*! Couldn't you *feel* it?"

Syd stared at her, aghast. There was no blood. His throat was still intact. "What are you talking about?" he croaked.

"Why did you stop?"

"I don't know," he blurted. "I . . .

"You *what*?"

"I thought I was going to hurt you!"

"HA!" she scoffed. "You couldn't hurt me if your *life* depended on it!" She began pacing back and forth. "I can't *believe* what a fucking pussy you are sometimes," she muttered.

"Hey, fuck you—"

"Oh, great, *now* you're tough," she ripped into him. "*Now* you can get it up. So where were all those balls five minutes ago, when they could've done some good?"

Syd's mouth opened, closed again. That one scored a direct hit, kicked his legs right out from under him. "I'm sorry," he said, looking away. His head wanged, a knot of tension blossoming behind his eye sockets. "Everything just got weird all of a sudden. . . ."

"Says *who*?" she countered. "Did you see me complaining? I *wanted* you to bite me, Syd. I *needed* you to."

"You don't understand. . . ." he began.

"What's to understand?" she spat.

"I wanted to kill you!" he exploded. "I swear to God, Nora, for a second there I was gonna seriously hurt you."

"Good!" she said. "That's what I wanted you to feel."

"What the hell for?" Syd was stymied. "I don't want to hurt you, Nora. I don't want to hurt *anybody*."

"Oh, yeah? What about Karen?"

The remark came from out of nowhere, took him totally off-guard. "What the fuck are you talking about?!" Syd said defensively. "I don't want to hurt Karen. . . ."

"Yeah, right," Nora gave him a deadly look. "Tell me you don't dream about ripping her smug, lying little face off." She watched his reaction, knew she'd hit a nerve. "And what about whatshisname—" Nora smiled viciously, drew the name out for maximum sarcasm, "—*Vauuuughn*."

"Shut up."

But Nora wouldn't shut up, and Nora wouldn't back off. "Tell me you don't lay awake nights thinking about him," she continued. "Tell me you don't think about your wife lying there with her legs spread, about the look on her face when he slid his dick inside her. . . ."

Syd closed his eyes, trying to contain his mounting rage as Nora methodically twisted the knife. "The one she put in her mouth . . ." She leaned in close, practically whispering in his ear. ". . . the mouth she *kissed* you with—"

"WHY ARE YOU DOING THIS?" he shouted in her face. "WHAT DO YOU *WANT* FROM ME??"

"I want to know if you've got what it takes," she said flatly. "And I want to know," she said, "can you let it *out*?"

"Let *what* out?" he asked, incredulous.

"Don't be stupid," she answered. "What do you think is going on here, Syd? What do you think happened last night? Do you think this is all an accident?"

"I don't know what you're talking about. . . ." Syd muttered. His head was throbbing now, as if his brain had just grown too big for his skull. He brought a hand to his temples, massaged them gingerly.

"It's not chance that we met, Syd," she said. "It's fate. I *chose* you. You've got it *in* you.

"But you've got to let it out."

"LET *WHAT* OUT?!"

"Your strength," she said. "Your power. The thing you've kept strapped down your whole goddam life.

"I want it, Syd. I *need* it. And if you can't give it to me, then you're no fucking good to me at all."

The last line hit him like a roundhouse punch; Syd glared at her through the pain. "So what," he muttered sarcastically, "you want me to bite chunks out of you and beat the shit out of people on your behalf? Anything *else*? Do you want me to *kill* for you, too?"

"If need be," Nora replied. She was dead serious. "I at least want to know that you *can*." A rueful light shone in her eyes. "I need somebody who can take *care* of me, Syd, somebody who'll be there when I need him with more than just the best of intentions, not just another well-meaning wimp who can't get it up in the clinches."

The insult was targeted, absolutely intentional. Syd sulked and smoked as she threw on her jeans, then her shirt, then her sweater. Every article of clothing she donned put another layer between them, until finally Syd was alone in his nakedness.

"Well," he said at last, "I guess maybe you need someone else."

"I guess I do," she replied. Her tone was both caustically brutal and threaded with regret. "I guess I do."

Nora's boots were at the foot of the bed; she stepped into them in silence, then turned and scooped her jacket off the chair by the door.

She paused on her way out, and they regarded each other defiantly. Syd stubbornly met her gaze, refusing to give an inch. The look on her face as she turned her back on him was at once haughty and contemptuous and incredibly sad. He listened to the clack of her boot heels and the jingle of keys as she moved across the living room.

There was a moment of silence after she rounded the corner, and his heart leapt, thinking *she's coming back!* Then he heard the sound of the front door opening and closing behind her.

And she was gone.

"FUCK!!!" he roared, vaulting off the bed. The ashtray tumbled off, spilling its smoldering contents onto the floor as he grabbed his jeans, fumbled into them.

"NORA!!"

Syd ran out into the living room, saw in a glance that her bags were gone. A car engine cranked outside; Syd raced to the window, saw her headlights come on.

He banged on the ancient frame, trying to pry it free. The moldings seized up and held and he punched it, fist smashing the wood so hard that the pane cracked, sending a tinkling shower of glass raining down to the street.

Nora's car started to back out of the space.

"NORA, DON'T GO!"

Syd spun, dashed for the door: throwing it open, taking the stairs two at a time. Halfway down he stumbled and pitched forward, slamming into the banister and whacking his knee on the heavy wood. "SHIT!" he screamed, kept running as he hit the first-floor landing, threw the outer door open.

He made it to the street just in time to see her taillights wink and disappear around the corner.

"NORA!" he screamed. "NORA, I'M SORRY!! COME BACK!!"

Lights came on in the houses across the street, as lumpy profiles peered out at his distress. *"WHAT'RE YOU LOOKING AT?!!!"* he shrieked. The lights blinked out again. Syd looked back, saw the last of her exhaust dissipate into the night.

He stood there, shirtless and shivering. Nora was gone. He was in shock. The throbbing in his knee came to him, registered as pain. Nora was gone. He wiped his hand across his face, felt something sticky, looked at his hand. A gash glistened where he'd torn it open.

Breathless and bleeding, Syd hobbled back to his apartment. As he limped up the stairs a part of his mind vaguely wondered where his cigarette had landed, if it was even now smoldering, turning to a fire that would burn the whole goddamned building down, and him along with it.

He should be so lucky.

20

I T WAS TWENTY till two when Vaughn Restal finally decided to call it a night.

Up until that point, he had to admit, the evening had
frankly sucked. Trish Reinhardt had informed him, not two
hours before, that it was over between them. Ray had
found out about them, and they'd gotten all weepy on each
other, and damned if they hadn't decided to try and work
things out. He was gonna help her start her own *business*,
fer chrissakes. Go figure.

Vaughn was vexed. Trish had broken the news to him
in mid-nightcap; ensconced in a cozy little corner at Fifty-
Five South, his hands tracing the inside of her thighs under
the table, contemplating the way her ass would look bent
over his breakfast nook once they got back to his place.

Vaughn liked variety. He also liked Trish's ass, which
was nice and creamy and tight. The two went hand in
hand, so to speak; and Vaughn had handled Trish
Reinhardt's sweet backside at every available opportunity
over the last three months. In his apartment. In *her* apartment, while Ray was doing the swing shift at Caterpillar.

On his balcony. In the park. In the car on the way to the bar.

He had big plans for that ass, not to mention every other part of her. Which was one reason why he'd been so upset when she fessed up as to her intentions. Marriage counseling; yeah, right. Go for it, baby. Ray was a jerk, and he didn't understand her: Trish had made that real clear the first night they'd hooked up. He certainly didn't know the first thing about making her happy, and Vaughn doubted that he ever would. "But he *really loves me*." Uh-huh. If he did, why did she hook up with ol' Vaughn in the first place?

Because Vaughn had made her *happy*, that's why— probably for the first time in her whole miserable life. He genuinely *cared* about her, goddammit, and she cared about him—or so she said. So now she was gonna go back to some numbnuts workaholic who ignored her? He needs me, she said. Yeah, well, what about *me*? he thought bitterly. What about *my* feelings?

It wasn't fair. Vaughn drained his beer, lit a cigarette and poured himself another from the pitcher of Killian's on the table before him. He was hurt. The least she could have done was give him one last pop for the road, maybe blow him in the parking lot. At the *very* least, she could have given him some advance notice; save him shelling out for one more romantic dinner, maybe give him a chance to line up some other plans for the evening.

Plus, they'd come in *her* car, on account of someone having spiked Vaughn's gas tank with a pound and a half of Domino's last weekend. Fortunately he only lived a few blocks away, but that was hardly the point. It was cold outside. It was all just damned inconsiderate, was what it was.

Vaughn sipped his beer and stewed. He felt victimized. He didn't really *like* messing around with married women; deep down he really considered himself to be a pretty okay guy. He just had a thing about women-in-need; he was attracted to them, to the point of being driven. They came into the bar, looking all lost and lonely in that way Vaughn could never resist. Could he help it if so many of them happened to be trapped in archaic, decaying relationships?

If he could find any personal fault at all, it was that he was just too damned sensitive. He felt too much, cared too much, wanted too much for them. It was like a chemical thing. So they opened themselves up to him, and he liked to make them feel good. Past that, he just couldn't help himself. He was only human.

Besides, was *he* to blame if these guys couldn't hold on to their women? If they'd been doing their jobs right, it never would have happened.

Vaughn sighed. When he stopped to think about it, it had really been kind of a lousy year. Tonight's letdown with Trish was nothing new; in fact, it was practically becoming a *déjà vu* experience. Before her, there'd been a string of similarly short-lived relationships: with Darlene, and Melissa, and Laurie, and Marcia . . .

And Karen, a voice in his head piped in. *Let's not forget Karen.*

Vaughn winced. Come to think of it, that's where this whole downhill slide had started. Her and her fucking psycho of a husband. Correction: *ex*-husband. Like that was really his fault. His hand came up instinctively to touch the crooked hump on his nose, the one that blew his profile and made him feel insecure, and he wished he'd never even seen the bitch. It seemed as though his luck had soured in the aftermath of that experience, like their bad karma had rubbed off on him somehow. He was sorry and all, but *really*. Like they wouldn't have flamed out anyway? It was ridiculous.

The whole thing just undermined his confidence, he realized. And he got really tired of watching his back. Like the gas tank thing, for instance; it almost ruined his fucking engine, and was gonna set him back almost four hundred bucks, to boot. And what about the time he got his tires slashed outside Mr. Bill's Crab Shack, and he wasn't even *with* anybody. Did anyone ever think about that? No, it was just Dump-on-Vaughn Day. It wasn't fair.

Oh, well, he thought, *what are you gonna do? There's*

all kinds of assholes in the world. He finished his beer and turned his attention to salvaging the rest of the evening.

It didn't look too promising. He scanned the room; there were maybe thirty people scattered across the bar. Fifty-Five South was large and dark and spacious, with high ceilings and a long brass-railed bar perpendicular to the row of big picture windows that looked out onto Front Street. The walls were covered with funky photos and counterculture gewgaws in a homegrown Hard Rock Café kind of effect. It was a cross-cultural hangout, and it tended to attract a mix of college kids, working people, and young professionals.

Although not, he amended, at the moment. At this late hour the pickings were pretty slim: everyone was either already hooked up for the night, or not worth the bother. A trio of sloppy-drunk coeds were getting scoped by a quartet of equally sloppy jocks. He half-wondered which of them would end up being odd man out.

A cluster of lonely-looking middle-aged guys lined the bar, nursing beers and bleak futures. A half-dozen couples conversed, oblivious to everyone and everything else. Vaughn sighed; at least *someone* was having a good time. There was a blonde down on the far end who looked like she could use some company, but she was a little shopworn and twenty pounds too heavy to register on Vaughn's empathy scale.

Oh, well. Vaughn checked his funds. The dinner tonight had tapped him; he had exactly ten bucks left with which to get lucky or cab it home. He was just about to abandon all hope when the door swung wide, accompanied by a blast of head-clearingly-cold air. Vaughn looked up, and suddenly he was trying to scrape his jaw up off his knees.

Oh my god, he thought, astonished. *Who is THAT?*

She was gorgeous, and she was wasted: two qualities he deeply admired in a woman. Her hair was long and tousled, her jacket unbuttoned in spite of the cold; and when she slid out of it, Vaughn just about slid right out of his

boxer shorts. Even in a sweater and jeans she bypassed
babe, went clear to *goddess*.

Better yet, she looked like a kindred spirit, which was
to say she looked like she'd just been through some shit.
Her eyes were red-rimmed and positively aglow with turbocharged emotion. His senses were keenly tuned through
years of practice, and he recognized the look instantly: she
was in *breakup mode*.

Vaughn smiled. She hit the bar and kicked back a
Cuervo shooter like it was a Dixie cup of Kool-Aid, did
another one in the time it took for him to bring his own
glass to his lips.

He couldn't take his eyes off her; she was clearly a
woman after his own heart. Vaughn liked the way she
moved, simultaneously deliberate and over-the-top. She
flipped her hair back and away from her face; Vaughn found
himself staring at the muscles in her neck. They looked
chewable in the extreme. And as for the rest of her . . .

Trish Reinhardt's ass was a sack of wet cottage cheese
by comparison. Correction: there *was* no comparison. This
woman was in a class all by herself. Vaughn watched,
waiting. No date showed up, no pissed-off hubby or beefy
beau. By all outward appearances, she was alone.

Maybe the night wasn't a complete whack, after all.

He thought about it for a moment, weighing his previously sagging spirits against the lateness of the hour. Not
a lot of time to get to know each other. Still, he thought,
nothing to lose by trying. Besides, she really looked like
she could use a friend right now.

He signaled the waitress on her way back to the bar,
slipped her the sawbuck, and asked her to do him a big big
favor. She nodded and hustled off; Vaughn put his feet up
and struck a decidedly casual pose, the better to watch as
the line played out. If she didn't take the bait, no biggie.
He was just a nice guy, buying a cute girl a drink.

But if, on the other hand, she did . . .

Please, he thought. *Oh please* . . .

The bartender appeared in front of her, placed a fresh

shot on the bar. She fingered the glass, as if searching it for clues. The bartender gestured toward Vaughn. She turned and scanned the room, stopped when she came to his shady little corner. Her eyes flared.

Gotcha.

Vaughn tipped his drink to her and smiled, gave her just the tiniest wink. Nice-guy shy. Her eyes flashed, and she smiled what he thought was a sly and very wicked smile. *Yes,* Vaughn thought. *Please come over oh please please please . . .*

But instead of coming over to his table, or even inviting him to sidle up beside her, the woman drained the glass in a single gulp.

Then set it back on the bar. Grabbed her jacket.

And left.

Vaughn was flabbergasted. He watched her disappear through the door, caught the most fleeting of glimpses of her as she headed down Front Street. How could she *do* that? It was so *rude*. The very least she could have done was say thank you, maybe come over and have another. Maybe even—God forbid—buy *him* one.

"Well, fuck you very much," he sighed. He reached for his cigarettes, discovered he was down to his last two. "Great," he muttered. There was no doubt about it. He was in hell.

The waitress came back around, dropped him his change. He counted it out, tipped her two. "Thanks," he said dolefully. There wasn't even enough left for more smokes, no less cab fare. He wondered for a moment if he might not be cursed.

"Can I get you anything?" the waitress asked as she scooped up the empty pitcher and glasses.

"Yeah." Smiling wanly. "A new lease on life."

"Sorry. Fresh out." She swabbed the table. "But seriously, folks. It's last call."

"Okay. How 'bout a shooter?" he asked. "And maybe a smile? I could use one of each right about now." The waitress smiled. She was cute, he realized now; her short black hair and green eyes gave her a punky, gamine quality. Her legs were a little thicker than Vaughn liked, but nothing he would kick out of bed. "So what's your name?" he pressed, his interest piqued.

"Karla. With a K."

"Ah-hah." He pretended to be amused. "So, Karla-with-a-K. What are you doing after you get off?"

'Going home with my boyfriend," she said, deflecting him.

"Oh," Vaughn said. "Lucky guy."

It was the waitress's turn to feign amusement. She rolled her eyes and returned to the bar. He watched her ass sadly as she departed. It wasn't one he'd be getting to know.

Sure enough, when Karla came back, she was all business. "Thanks," she said, taking the last of his cash. "Have a good one." She headed off without another glance back.

Yeah, sure. You bet, he thought morosely. He couldn't imagine how it could get any worse.

It was just past two by the time Vaughn hit the street.

The wind had picked up considerably, bitter and biting. In fact, the weather forecast had underscored his day just perfectly: *warm and sunny early in the day, turning much colder as the night wears on.* You could say that again. It rustled through the trash in the gutter, sent cigarette butts and old dead leaves pinwheeling end over end, chasing each other down the empty sidewalks. Front Street was desolate, the last vestiges of nightlife having already packed off to the sanctuary of warm bodies and beds.

Up ahead, a lone taxicab prowled, slicing across the intersection at the end of the block. It slowed when it saw him. He shook his head. *Damn.* The cab gunned its engine and sped away; an old newspaper danced like a dervish in its wake. Vaughn watched it spin, felt his head echo the motion.

The wind gusted again, knocking him off-balance. This utterly sucked. The air cleared his head somewhat, but the ground still felt rubbery beneath his feet: that last shot had snuck up on him, left him with a beer-and-tequila cocktail sloshing in his guts. Killian's alone was bad enough: it always gave him a vaguely reamed-out feeling, as though his bowels had been freshly Roto-Rootered. The Cuervo had capped it like a shooter of mucus and grease.

A nagging little voice in his head lectured him on the perils of mixing liquor, warned him that he'd pay in the morning. He tried hard to ignore it, though he knew it was certainly right. The thing to do right now was keep moving. Take deep breaths, get his blood circulating. Get home.

Vaughn stuffed his hands in his pockets and hugged the wall, stumbling past the darkened shops and stores, hiding from the wind. Somewhere, a trash can tipped into the gutter with a hollow metal clang. He started at the sound, felt the hairs on the back of his neck stiffen and tingle, kept walking.

It was less than two blocks later that he started to get that old familiar feeling: like a hair-triggered silent alarm that tingled down the length of his spine. *Watch your back,* it told him. *Watch your back.* It was a reflex action, a survival skill, born of too much time spent dodging drunken boyfriends or vengeance-crazed mates. It was wrong roughly three-quarters of the time, but it had saved his white ass more than once.

Vaughn cast a nervous glance over his shoulder, searching the shadows. Nothing but wind, whipping down the empty street. A dog loped across an intersection a few blocks back. There were a lot of strays in town these days, he remembered, courtesy of jobless families picking up and moving on, in the process leaving ol' Fido to fend for himself. They lived in abandoned buildings and empty lots, eventually turned feral and ran in packs, ripping into trash and feeding on rats, or the odd luckless cat. He stared for a moment longer, just to be sure. Nothing. *Just paranoid,* he told himself, and continued on his way.

But a dozen steps later, he felt it again. Substantially stronger. Frighteningly so.

Vaughn looked back, caught a fleeting glimpse of furtive movement some twenty yards behind him. Someone was moving in the shadows, hugging the wall and pacing him. It occurred to him that he was about to get jumped. His system began to brace itself. He took another peek: something was definitely back there. *Just my fucking luck. Thanks, Trish.*

And that started the wheels turning in his head: thinking *Ray, oh shit, what if it's Ray?* That put a real blush of reality on it. He wondered just what the fuck she'd told him, in the heat of the confessional crunch. Had she spilled the beans on their sexual positions? Had she told him little details that drove him nuts? There was no telling what a guy might do—even a doughy little putz like Ray—if you gave him an image vivid enough, goaded him over the line.

Vaughn was moving just as fast as he could without breaking into a run. He was trying his best not to show it; but he, himself, would not have been fooled. His stomach burbled and churned. His temples thudded with adrenalated blood. His bladder ballooned in his jeans. He had to piss like a fire hydrant. Great.

The good news was that he did not have that far to go: another three blocks and he was home free. The bad news was that he had to turn onto Beaver Street at the next corner to do it. Vaughn's apartment was a loft in the warehouse district, and the homestretch was not nearly so well-lit.

The other bad news was that, whoever it was, *it* was getting closer. Ten yards now, and closing. Still hugging the shadows. It was definitely a setup. *But not a mugger,* he thought. They would usually stalk more openly, approach under the pretense of asking directions or bumming a smoke—at least until he was within striking range.

Shit. It's Ray. It's gotta be. His mind raced in drunken overdrive: plotting panic vectors, weighing his options. Running was out of the question: he was already a heartbeat away from heaving, and his bladder felt like it was going to explode.

But there was something else about it that didn't sit well, especially since his run-in with Syd. Vaughn's pride still stung at the memory; it shouldn't have gone down that way. Syd had just gotten lucky, on account of how distraught Vaughn was over Karen. He also fought dirty, the sonofabitch. He hit him when he wasn't expecting it. The guy was a fucking animal.

Ray, on the other hand, was not a big man: five-five, tops, and not much known for his machismo. Vaughn was six feet, one-eighty, and a pretty fair hunka manhood, if he did say so himself. If push came to shove, Vaughn knew he could take him.

His spirits lifted as he sized up his odds. The more he thought about it, the more the whole thing pissed him off. He was cold and tired and he felt like shit, and now some asshole was gonna jack him up just 'cause he couldn't keep his woman home? Honest to god, enough was enough.

There was one more street lamp before the corner, casting a wan circle of light on the darkened sidewalk. It was maybe ten yards away when the glimmer of a strategy formed in his mind. Vaughn smiled, moved away from the wall, steering ever so casually toward the light.

And he began to rehearse a speech in his head, the speech he would make when he hit the spotlight. He'd starred as Conrad Birdie in the Central High School production of *Bye Bye Birdie* oh those many years ago; so he knew a thing or two about stage presence, not to mention projecting his voice.

Okay, fucko! he planned to say. *I see you slinking around in the dark! Let's see what kind of man you are in the light!* Or something hard-hitting and edgy like that. Ever since Syd, he'd paid particular attention to the tough-guy dialogue in action films; he'd learned firsthand, when it came down to fighting, the withering power of a good one-liner.

He could picture Ray now, stepping into the spotlight: be he pudgily defiant or suddenly embarrassed, realizing too late what a fool of himself he'd made. No matter how it played, Vaughn saw himself coming out on top. He couldn't picture it any other way.

Unless, of course, it wasn't *Ray . . .*

And that was when all his alarms went off, less than twenty feet from the edge of the light. That was when he began to turn, just in time to see the darkness descend upon him. A flash of teeth, so many teeth, moving toward him at such an incredible speed, closing the distance in seconds that vanished before he could even scream . . .

. . . and he started to run, legs desperately pumping under him, fleeing for dear life as he realized *christ it's a dog a fucking feral dog.* And he didn't get a clear look at it but he could hear the ragged chug of its breath and the slap of its feet as it closed the distance, and he knew it was huge, a shepherd or wolfhound but wrong, it was much bigger, it was built like a refrigerator like a car like a motherfucking *truck. . . .*

Vaughn ran like a bastard, boots clomping wildly on the pavement, his all-state track star days way too many tar and nicotine years behind him as he tried to make the corner, slipped, recovered . . .

. . . and then came the moment of impact, as the animal hit him three quarters from behind and slammed him sideways, like being run over by a truck with a great slavering mouth bearing dozens of chrome incisors. He felt fangs like roofing nails punch into his midsection even as his head cracked the pavement, was dragged forward by the sheer momentum of the attack. Vaughn tried to scream but the jaws clamped down, got a deathgrip on his midsection, squeezing the air out of his lungs in mid-shriek as they tumbled into the street lamp's glare.

Then the light struck his eyes, half-blinding him, making ugly dots swim in the frozen air. His mind raced madly, thinking *it's gonna kill me someone save me please jesus help!* as he scrabbled and fought to escape. His left arm was free, and he flailed out with it, desperately twisting in the animal's jaws. He aimed for the snout and missed, struck a glancing blow over its eye. The beast released him just enough to turn.

And Vaughn got his first good look at his destroyer.

not a dog not a dog at all oh jesus

And Vaughn got religion in that instant, oh yes he did, pissing himself and praying to his maker as the horrible maw clamped down harder this time, piercing his jacket and sweater, cracking his chest like a walnut. He felt something go *pop* and squirt stale rank mist, as twenty years' worth of pent-up tobacco smoke vented from his punctured right lung . . .

oh god oh god help me

. . . and then he was out of the light, removed from the light forever: the monster lifting him in its jaws, carrying him helplessly farther into the warehouse dark. He smelled himself, borne on the beast's hot breath, got a vivid flash of his future at the pay end of the food chain. The animal started to run and his mind blacked out, snapped back again: awash with agony, denied the luxury of oblivion. There was no escape, save death. And death was still minutes away.

Vaughn spontaneously voided, almost as a courtesy, loading his pants and throwing up the last meal of his life. Chunks and stomach acid wrapped around his face, lay scalding in his eyes as the monster loped across the broken rubble of a back-alley lot.

Then suddenly he was falling, the agonizing pressure on his torso released. There was no mercy in the movement, just a sickening plummet and the brittle crack of his skull fracturing as his face smacked a ragged outcrop of cinder block and *slid*. His cheek came away like cheese through a grater. His head filled with billions of stars.

The seeing part was over now, and shock was setting in. The noises he made were not human at all. Blindly, he shivered as the thing flipped him over onto his back. He heard panting, felt the tug of something working at his belt, then the front of his jeans.

Dim confusion flickered in his muddled trauma-mind. Buried memories wrenched themselves free, floated to the surface as raw experience. Was he having his diaper changed? It seemed like it, yes. But there was blood in his mouth. His vision whirled and blurred. His mind skittered and split in half, trying to make it make sense: part regressing to infancy, part fast-forwarding to death.

A giant loomed over him. A hairy mountain with hands. Its breath was a swampland of hot damp rot and something else that he recognized. It took him all of one infinite second to place; and, once known, it was too late to forget. It was a smell that yanked him unpleasantly back to the present.

The smell of tequila.

oh god.

Then his sodden pants were shredding and sliding down his legs, bunching in tatters at his ankles as his bare ass slapped the icy ground. *Oh god,* he thought, his mind at once totally, terribly clear. His scrotum retracted into a shriveled pouch, his penis turning thimble-sized as it shrunk like a turtle's head ducking into its shell. Vaughn went fetal, felt his sanity smack against reality like a bird hitting a plate-glass window as the beast hunkered over him, its monstrous hands gripping his knees. He fought to keep his legs closed. It spread its arms wide. Vaughn heard two wet *pops.*

The world went hot and white.

He came to less than three seconds later: his pelvis cracked like a sloppy-wet wishbone, his hips dislocated, his thighs mashed into the ground on either side. The monster hovered at the shattered juncture as its great snout descended, buried itself in his all-too-exposed crotch. His mind bargained madly through the pain, going *sorry I'm so sorry I'll never fuck again oh please jesus . . .*

The monster sniffed him a moment, reading his scent. Then the corners of its ghastly mouth curled upward, became something that very much resembled a sly and wicked smile.

And then the jaws snapped and closed, sawing through strips of omentum and coils of colon, coming up from below to latch hold of his spine and shake it like a dog with a rag. He shrieked and wheezed, shrieked again. His bowels tore loose as his spine went *snap* and the world went red and numb and dead, as the great chomping maw came away with a mouthful, leaving him a huge raw jigsaw-puzzle gap where his groin used to be.

OH GOD OH GOD OH GOD OH

At that moment, Vaughn merged with the scream, became that wild and dying sound, his soul spinning out and out of his throat like a slowly unwinding thread. His eyes attempted one final focus, saw only eyes and fur and blood-covered snout. It hovered inches above him, brimming.

And then, horribly, opened wide.

Vaughn Restal's mouth was open, too, caught in the act of his last dying gasp. It left him no defense against the sudden gushing torrent of his own masticated organs, a steaming mouthful of entrails spilling into his face. His mangled penis slapped his cheek like a gory coda: a pallid slug, skidding down its own slime trail.

Vaughn Restal died, choking on his own shit and viscera.

Nora felt certain that Syd would be pleased.

21

IN THE HOURS that followed her departure, Syd had way
too much time to drink and think: pacing the too-small
confines of his apartment, alternately damning her and
cursing himself for being such a fool. He'd actually gotten
dressed to go chasing after her, got all the way down to his
car before he realized he didn't have a clue where she'd
gone, if she was still even in the town. Or the state, for
that matter.

And that thought had made him crazy, sent him careening back to hit the bottle and bounce off the walls.
And even though three days ago he would have laughed
out loud if someone had suggested that he would ever let
himself get so totally flummoxed over a complete stranger,
he could not deny it: she was *in* him now, under his skin
and in his blood, completely invalidating his previously
sacrosanct autonomy.

The phrase *rebound relationship* sprang to mind. Syd
laughed until he cried. This was not about "healing" and
"feeling good about yourself" or any other psychobabble
bullshit; this was something he'd hungered for his whole

life long. The simple truth was he needed Nora, needed her desperately in his life.

And now she was gone.

He stumbled into the kitchen, found the bottle of tequila, downed a double shot, looked around. Detritus from their lost weekend lay scattered across every available surface. He began to clean: muttering to himself as he sorted through the wreckage, tried to put his life back in order. Dirty plates and crusted cookware, empty bottles and full ashtrays were everywhere. He found a broken wine bottle in the living room; as he washed the dishes he found the little-chicken-that-wasn't, still congealing in the bowl.

What the hell was that all about? He tried to remember and the pain between his eyes returned, a dullbright throbbing ball of misery deadbang in the center of his skull. The only way he could make it go away was to *not* think about it, concentrate instead on the mundane.

Syd thought of Karen, for some strange reason. As he cleaned he flipped the stove light on, spotlighting the little figurines perched atop the range hood. They were the figures from their wedding cake: little wind-up Godzilla and King Kong toys, custom-altered into a tiny monstrous bride and groom. King Kong sported a little top hat above his nasty simian scowl; Godzilla had a veil, and clutched a tiny bouquet to her scaly reptilian breast. When you wound them up, they whined and wobbled mechanically forth, and sparks shot out of their mouths.

Syd looked at them, began to giggle.

Just like real life, he thought.

And that started him to laughing, a manic Renfield cackle that continued as he wandered from room to room to room, for the first time realizing that what he had was not a home but a shrine, an altar to a dead past upon which to sacrifice his hope for the future.

Whatever else Nora had done, she had also—in the space of a few short days—blown holes in every weak-kneed rationalization he had for continuing to piss his life away: letting it slip past him one second, one month, one decade at a time, until one day there would be nothing left but bitter regrets and recriminations; miserably staring back down the wrecking-ball trail of all his missed and blown opportunities.

For the first time in years, he'd actually felt like it was good to be alive. Like it was worth any price to stay alive, so long as it was lived on these terms and no others. By comparison, nothing else mattered: not his job, not his friends, not the place where he grew up or the existence that had evaporated out from under him. It was all completely worthless without her.

He wandered into the bedroom then, collapsed into a fugue-state of physical and mental exhaustion. As he drifted off the events of the last several days blurred and ran in his mind until he didn't know what was real and what was a dream anymore, or exactly where the line was drawn.

He only knew that since he'd met Nora the life he'd been living made no sense at all.

If it ever had.

SYD AWOKE TO strange sounds from the kitchen. But this time, he didn't wake up confused. From the moment his eyes opened, there was only one thought in his head: the sum total of all his obsessional focus. His only prayer, answered.

She's here. She actually came back.

There was no way to overstate the magnitude of his relief. It was like getting the Governor's phone call, two seconds before they threw the lever and the trapdoor dropped. To downplay his relief would be to minimize his panic, and his panic had been nothing short of epochal.

But at the same time, there was no peace in the revelation, no automatic reprieve from the killing tension. Her return did not imply a full pardon. It might merely be a stay of execution: a way of dragging out the torture for another day or two.

I gotta go out there, he told himself. *And then we've got to have a little talk.*

He had blacked out on the bed with all his clothes on.

His body, upon waking, was exactly where he'd left it. He pulled his face from the pillow, looked up at the clock. It said five thirty-six. He heard the clank of plate on plate, unconsciously braced himself for the *déjà vu* sound of destruction. When it didn't come, the psychic noose eased off a notch: not enough to free him or anything, just enough to keep him from choking on the stress.

His footing was a little unsteady as he hoisted himself up. He braced himself on the bedside table, instantly flinched as he remembered the cut on his hand. He looked at his palm.

The gash was gone.

Had he really cut himself? He couldn't clearly recall. All this drinking had screwed with his memory as well as his equilibrium. Syd had some very uneasy associations with alcoholism, and the psychology of blackouts frankly terrified him, with their tacit self-exonerating clause of *oh, I must have been drunk, I didn't know what I was doing*. Lurking way in the back of his head was the understanding that they'd have to discuss this aspect of their relationship someday. But not yet. Certainly not now. There was plenty of time to work those kinds of problems out later.

The main thing was, Nora was back; and there wasn't a thing in the world that couldn't be worked out from there.

Syd opened the bedroom door and the smell hit him: rich and heady, overpoweringly compelling. It was the smell of meat, receiving the kiss of flame. She was cooking again.

He vaguely remembered something about yesterday morning—was it yesterday?—and feeling ill from the odor of food cooking. He felt no such illness now. He tried to lock on the memory, felt it skitter from his grasp, usurped by the staggering aroma.

Then he rounded the corner, and Nora was there: barefoot and freshly showered, wearing nothing but one of his shirts. Her magnificent hair was damp, swept back. A skillet was sizzling on the front burner of the stove.

She looked up, saw him. The space between them began to hum, as if someone somewhere had thrown a switch, charging the air with nervous energy.

Then the next thing he knew, she was crossing the kitchen: wrapping her arms around him, burying her face in his neck. Her embrace was more than strong; it was ferocious in its intensity. Syd felt a rush run through him. Every place where their bodies connected pulsed with energy. She kissed his neck, and his knees went weak.

"I am so sorry," she whispered at last.

"Me, too," he said. He felt his throat tighten, forced his words through the gap. "I was afraid I'd never see you again."

"I couldn't stay away," she said, then added almost in a whisper, "especially not today."

It took a second for that to sink in; then suddenly it dawned on him that he'd *utterly forgotten:* in all the excitement and insanity of the last few days, it had totally slipped his mind. "Oh my god, you're right." He shook his head and laughed out loud. "Thirty-five. I can't fuckin' believe it."

"Believe it, Grampa." She grinned and licked his nose. "Happy birthday."

He laughed again, and then they kissed: a soul-searching plunge into each other's depths. When they came up for air he said to her, "I can't believe you actually remembered."

"Hard to forget the birthday of someone you love so much," she replied.

Syd did a double take. "Excuse me?"

"I said, I love you."

Syd heard the words and felt something give inside him, like a floodwall collapsing. The words were like a force of nature that swept away every stick and shred of resistance. And it felt so good to hear those words again, to know down to his bones that they were true, that this was really happening. His mind sped back to the day he was married: to the feeling of standing in a chapel as a robed and rambling priest prayed to some distant, cloud-bound deity.

And all those words were fine and dandy—they'd assuaged the flock in their search for meaning—but Syd himself in that moment had taken an alternate route: reaching inside, to make a very personal covenant. *This is the one I've chosen. This is the one I want.*

Then he flashed forward, back to the wild and wonderful creature in his arms. And suddenly it was all very clear.

"I love you, too," he said, losing himself in her eyes.

And because he was inside those eyes—because they were virtually touching souls—he knew that she knew the utter depths of his conviction. Knew that he would do anything for her: drop everything he'd ever owned, dump everyone he'd ever known, chase down the shadows in the darkest corners of the world. And even *kill:* yes, without a doubt. He would even kill for her.

Nora saw it very clearly, in that moment. Slowly, she nodded her head. Her eyes had never been more intense.

"You must be starved," she said. He nodded. Nora gestured toward the kitchen table. A place setting was lovingly laid out. "Have a seat," she said, and he gladly complied.

Then she went to the stove, returned with a heaped and steaming plate. Syd looked in amazement at a huge curving slab of meat, two fried eggs sidling up to it like a pair of bulging eyes.

"Jesus," he softly exclaimed. "Is that steak?"

"It's a special cut," Nora explained.

"Mmmmm." Inhaling deeply. "Where did you find this in the middle of the night?"

Nora smiled. "Oh, I had to hunt around a bit. But I finally found a place that had what I was looking for." She took a seat across from him, her eyes bright and attentive. "Dig in."

Syd smiled, picking up his knife and fork. The meat

was red and thick and rich, barely singed by the grid-
dle. Drops of juice squeezed from the striations as he
sliced it, dripped from a lone protrusive vein. Nora
watched attentively as he brought a forkful to his mouth,
popped it in, began to chew. His eyes went wide. His
smile expanded.

"Well?" she asked, grinning. "Do you like it?"

"It's ... *great*. Jesus!" There was reverence in his
tone. Nora beamed. Syd chewed and swallowed. "I've
never tasted anything like it." He took another bite,
chewed thoughtfully. "How'd you make it?"

"Secret recipe," she teased, and it was clear that her
delight was enormous. She watched as Syd chowed down,
cutting another hunk off the slab and scooping up a forkful
of eggs.

"I can't believe how hungry I am," he said, champing
happily. "Aren't you gonna have any?"

"I already ate."

Syd nodded and dug in. As he ate, he felt a strength
and a clarity return to him. There was something in the
bloody taste and buttery texture—in the experience of the
meat itself, dancing around his teeth and tongue—that
grounded and centered him in his body. It was the most
deeply satisfying meal he'd ever had.

Syd took one last look around his kitchenful of ancient
relics; and in that moment, it was over. The withered um-
bilical cord that had held him to this dying place was severed; the cut was surgical and clean.

"Darlin'?" he said. There was food in his mouth. He
talked around it. "I've been thinking about everything you
said."

"Uh-huh."

"And I decided you're totally right. There's nothing to
hold me here." He sawed off another hunk and shoveled it
in, then waved his fork at the room. "A couple of days to
get it together, and"—he stopped in mid-thought, picked a
piece of gristle from between his teeth—"I could probably
be ready by the end of the week."

Nora grimaced slightly. "Why so long?" she said. "I don't understand."

"Well," Syd countered, "basically, I'm ready when *you* are. . . ."

"And what if I'm ready today?"

It was Syd's turn to grimace. "I still need a couple days," he said. "Till Friday, at least. . . ."

"No," she said.

"Nora . . ."

"I'm not staying around here that long."

Getting frustrated now. "Baby, I've got a lot of shit to take care of. There's loose ends to tie up, people to say good-bye to, I've got to pick up my paycheck from work . . ." He tore off a hunk of bread, began sopping up the blood and yolk that intermingled on his plate. "Plus I wanna see if I can unload my stereo. . . ."

Nora stood then, began pacing the cramped confines of the kitchen. "Waitaminute, waitaminute," she said, suddenly annoyed. "Are you saying we've got to hang around here for the rest of the week so you can sell a goddamned *stereo*?"

Syd looked at her, surprised. "Well, shit, between that and my CD collection I can probably get close to a grand. . . ."

"Who *cares*?"

"What do you mean, 'Who cares?' *I* care!" This was starting to piss him off. "I mean, leaving's one thing, but I can't just cut and run without a dime in my pocket! How are we gonna pay for gas? Hotel? *Meals*?" He speared the last of the meat off his plate, scarfed it down. "I mean, we *do* plan on eating, right?"

Nora bristled with tension. "Why do you worry about shit like that?" she asked. "Money's never been a problem for me—"

"Yeah, well, money's *always* been a problem for me!" Syd cut in, definitely annoyed himself now. "I've had to work for every fucking cent I ever got! And I think about things like that because it's my *nature* to think about things like that!"

There was an electric beat of silence as they faced off. Syd made a conscious effort to pin back the tension in his voice, the sudden flaring rage he felt.

But the fact of the matter was that he was pissed. And he was *not* gonna be whipped into submission by this woman, no matter how much he loved her. She could see it in his eyes. She could hear it in his voice. But rather than flipping her out, it was visibly getting her off. There was a carnivore's curl to her fierce little smile, and he had her complete attention.

And Syd realized that this was a woman who liked to play hardball; *that* was what made her such a contrary bitch. She was no fawning little batty-eyed baby girl, waiting for daddy to spank her when she was bad. He got the feeling, in that moment, that he was finally earning her respect.

Syd stood abruptly, moved toward her. Nora held her ground. Her eyes never left his. He caught her by the sink, wrapped his arms around her.

"Listen," he said. "Last night you said you wanted my *strength*. You wanted someone to take care of you." He pulled her close, drew her tight. "Well, this is part of my strength. I gotta take care of myself. If I can't do that, then I can't take care of you.

"And then I'm no fucking good to either one of us."

He held her, leveling her with his gaze. Nora met it with equal fervor. There was one long elastic moment, where everything hung in the balance.

Then she embraced him, and he felt a wave of raw emotion pour out of her as a low, throaty moan escaped her lips.

"On the table. *Now*."

And he gave himself over to the urge, the insatiable sensation, picking her up and spinning her around in his arms, then lifting her up to set her on the table. Her hands swept back as her legs wrapped around him, drawing him in. This time, the sound of breaking dishes didn't bother him a bit. Her hands found his zipper and tugged it down to free him even as his hands unbuttoned her shirt, exposed her nakedness.

They made love savagely, the table bucking and groaning beneath them.

And this time, when she told him to bite her, he did.

It was the best.

22

BY THE TIME Syd arrived at the mill, it was ten twenty-six. Not so great from a job-security standpoint, but he was no longer thinking longevity. He parked and shagged it up to the foreman's trailer, taking his sweet time to do so.

There was no line, of course, and hadn't been for four hours; the distant sound of clanging echoed through the plant, bespeaking men already well into doing their job. He got a weird pang of nostalgia, listening to it: the kind of feeling you get when you know you're doing something for what is probably the very last time. Even the dust kicking up around his heels had a flavor that he found himself noting and filing: an experience captured, a memory preserved.

Beau Harrell, on the other hand, was not a nostalgia-inducing experience. Syd could smell him from twenty feet outside the door, and one thing was for certain: the sooner their lives were no longer intertwined, the better.

He was seated, squat and sweating, behind his desk when Syd walked in. In person, Beau was even less impressive than he was in theory: an ugly little toad-man,

Horatio Alger gone horribly wrong. He was a self-styled wheeler-dealer and post-Reagan robber baron; but despite his fancy German car and Armani suit, he still managed to carry his success with the cheesy élan of a trailer park tyrant, a big mean fish in a small and stagnant pond.

His bald head caught the reflection of the bare light bulb in the center of the ceiling. He had put on weight, squeezing his seams like an overripe kielbasa. Looking at him, Syd couldn't help thinking of Jon Polito in *Miller's Crossing,* minus the ethnic slant and esoteric ethical contemplations: running tings, ya gotta know, it's a lot tougher den you'd tink. He had a ton of paperwork spread out before him, as usual—the man was nothing if not ambitious—and as he looked up, his expression shifted abruptly from apelike grin to rabid foam-at-the-mouth exasperation. He tended to stammer when upset.

"Jarrett!" Harrell bellowed. "You're four fuckin' hours late! You better have one huh-*hell* of an explanation, I can tell you that!"

Syd noted the drying-up of neanderthal laughter, cast a glance off to the little sofa to his right. It was Beany and Cecil, Bobo's toady and pit bull, respectively. Beany was Bennie Holtzapple, a wormy little pissant in a black leather Members Only jacket and a turtleneck, and he was blessed with a knack for agreeing with whatever Bobo said. Cecil was Cecil Karwicki, and he was built like an industrial freezer. He wore a navy cashmere overcoat over jeans and a snow-white designer sweatshirt, and his feet sported pointy black sharkskin boots that looked made for kicking. His feet, like his hands and every other part of him, were enormous. He had the total mental wattage of a refrigerator bulb, and he did exactly as he was told.

Cecil held, in his beefy mitts, a dog-eared copy of *Big Butt* magazine. Suddenly, Syd understood completely: it wasn't just that he was late, but that he'd interrupted something important. An honest-to-god enormous mudflap stared at him from the glossy back cover, beneath the slogan *MORE BUTTS FOR YOUR BUCKS!!!* Syd couldn't help but crack a smile of his own.

"What's so, what's so fuckin' *funny?*" Beau demanded to know.

"Umm ..." Syd shrugged, grinning. "*Big Butt* magazine, I guess."

"Don't get fuckin' suh-smart with me!" Bobo was practically apoplectic. "You, you got some explainin' to do!"

Syd tried to wipe the smile off his face, couldn't quite bring himself to. The reek of Brut and pheromones was unpleasantly thick in the room. He was not a welcome addition to their sweaty, leering inner circle. They wanted their *Big Butt* all to themselves.

Jesus. Syd started to laugh. He got a sudden vivid flash of Nora, juxtaposed it against the fumes off this squalid cro-mag boner session. He could practically taste the rancid low-rent locker-room tang, cheap and stomach-churning, redolent of the fragrance of heedless jiz and macho posturing.

"JARRETT!" Bobo was standing semi-upright now, leaning hard into his desk, asserting his authority. He looked like a flabby, shaved baboon. His face was red. His jowls jiggled over his too-tight collar. He had the kind of washed-out pale blue eyes that come from thirty years of Johnny Walker on the rocks. "WHAT'S SO FUCKIN' FUNNY?!"

And there was something in the way he did it—some trigger buried in the tone of his voice, the smell of his sweat, the look on his face—that reached out and spoke directly to the new Syd: the one now awakening under his skin. It was like opening a single can of Alpo in a kennel full of starving dogs. It was like giving him Vaughn Restal to tear through all over again. Suddenly, everything *about* Beau Harrell consumed him with the urge to kill.

And it was all he could do to restrain himself.

Because as he looked in those eyes, all he could think was this man is a joke. *He didn't deserve the power he had over other people's lives. He didn't deserve to live at all. In a sane universe, miserable creatures like him would be lucky to make it through the day without being dragged down, torn apart, and eaten alive. They would live in holes and count their blessings, afraid to go out by day or night.*

It would be—by any standard—a substantially better world.

Part of him felt obliged to act on that understanding. Or maybe he was overexplaining it to himself. Maybe it was more a matter of imagining how enjoyable it would be to watch Bobo's throat peel open, the esophagus bared, then enjoy the whistling windpipe spritz as his trachea shredded.

Either way, suddenly Bobo's face didn't radiate quite the same level of self-righteous psychopathology. The eyes were still bulging, but their motivation had changed. Fear had replaced the bullying bluster.

There was a noise, very faint, off to his right. Syd turned. Cecil had closed the magazine. It lay very flat and still in his hands. It was clear that he was following all the changes in the room as well. At the next whiff of escalation, Cecil would stand. And then there would be violence. It was as simple as that.

Syd could feel his hackles rise. Cecil was easily six-four, two hundred and twenty pounds. His approach was purely business. He was rumored to have killed. Syd looked at him now, knew it to be true. But he also knew something else.

You're scared. It was a gut knowledge, an animal certainty. He stared calmly into Cecil's eyes, waited for the information to impact. It only took a second. They widened, then narrowed to slits. It was fear, alright, but mixed with an underlying thread of confusion. Like he didn't quite know *why.* Syd shifted his weight forward, ever so slightly. Cecil shifted back in his chair, maintaining the distance between them.

In that moment, all four of them were stripped to their primal essence: four mammals in a box too small, poised on the brink of primacy war. Even Beany had tuned in to the bestial frequency. It was a moment of astounding clarity. Syd savored it—the power and strangeness—holding his gaze hard on Cecil's for one more second.

And then, all at once, he let it drop.

And it was like throttling down on an industrial turbine, pulling back the reins on a runaway horse: not so much a loss of power as a conscious suspension of its exercise. It would be back, anytime he wanted. It would be there forever.

Syd looked back at Beau Harrell, who evidently was seeing him now in a whole new light: not so much with respect as with *dread*. It was, to Syd's mind, a substantial improvement. He smiled.

"I just came in to say I quit," he said at last, surprising everyone, himself included. "And I'd like my paycheck.

"Now."

His tone was perfectly level, menacingly matter-of-fact. It was not phrased as a request, nor was it received as one. Bobo looked like someone had just dropped an anvil on his head.

"Payday's not until Friday," he said. "You know that."

"I know," Syd said pleasantly. "Make an exception."

Bobo's glance flickered from Syd to Cecil to Beany and back. Syd's eyes remained on Bobo. Bobo looked like he was going to blow a hose. "Ch-checks aren't cut yet," he stammered.

"I know," Syd said. "Write one."

Syd leaned forward. Bobo's head retracted into his shoulders, like a turtle flinching into its shell. There was a tense pause, punctuated only by the sound of sweat popping on Bobo's pate. Then Bobo leaned over, mumbled something, and pulled his ledger out of the desk. Beany and Cecil exchanged nervous, furtive glances, as if witnessing a miracle. Syd smiled as Bobo pulled out a pen, began to write. He waited patiently. Doing nothing. Ready for anything.

"Huh-here," he mumbled. "Duh-don't come back."

"Don't worry," Syd said. "I won't."

Bobo finished scribbling, tore the check free, and held it out. Syd plucked it from his grasp and Bobo flinched again, as if he feared Syd might take his hand with it, as a souvenir.

"Thanks," Syd said, smiling pleasantly. He glanced at Bobo's henchmen. "Take care, fellas. It's been a slice."

He turned, the trio of eyes following his every move. As he did he made a special point of acknowledging Cecil, whose hands still clutched the magazine. "Y'all take good care of those massive fannies now, y'hear?"

Then he was out the door and gone, laughing to himself from the moment it shut. A wave of giddy exhilaration rolled over him. *Damn,* but that was fun! *Damn,* but those guys were stupid! If he'd known that quitting could be this much of a rush, he'd have done it a long time ago.

The forty-degree morning was warm on his skin. It made him feel comfortable, confident and strong. He felt like he could handle anything.

He felt like he could take on the world.

23

THE MOON WAS innocent tonight. For this cycle at least, its power had peaked, was already on the wane. It could no longer be held responsible for anything that happened, not even in theory.

Nora watched it through the windshield, and wondered just who she *was* supposed to blame.

Because Syd was in the driver's seat, blissfully oblivious, blasting them down the winding road to the bar where they'd first met. *It's the only other thing I have to do,* he'd told her. *But it's very important to me, okay?*

Of course, it was not okay; and she tried to tell him so. But her best arguments were utterly in vain. He just needed to say good-bye to Jules and a couple of the others, needed to say his good-byes to the place. Chameleon's was the only thing left in this town that meant a thing to him.

This had put Nora in a position both awkward and extremely delicate. From a relationship standpoint, it was really not a good night to push too hard. The rest of the day had been absolutely revelatory; they'd been drinking and celebrating since roughly noon, when Syd had returned

home early from work. He was full of himself, full of his
power as he relayed the story of Bobo and his sudden
"change of heart." He told her they could leave as early as
tomorrow. He was even selling his precious stereo to some
guy at work for five hundred bucks, which she had to admit would keep the wheels greased until he was up and
running.

So what was not to like? All in all, Syd was in too fine
a mood, playing too smoothly into her hands. So when he
suggested they go out, it was hard to say no. But there was
no getting around the very real dangers implicit in the
move. She had lost a couple days of lead time, after all; it
was entirely possible that Vic could just show up at any
moment.

Nora quashed the thought and the shudder it rode in
on, took a deep swig off the Southern Comfort bottle, then
turned to take a long hard look at the man beside her. His
profile glowed in the dashboard light. She couldn't get
over how fired up he was. It was a mixed blessing in the
purest sense, both wonderful and terrifying; she didn't
know whether to be more thrilled by his ardor or frightened by his newfound assertion of will.

Because Syd had eaten of the flesh, and now he was
feeling it: revealing aspects of himself that had never before seen the light of day. Nora could never predict what
would come roaring out; what secret scar tissue and raw
potential; what deeply repressed desires and rages. And
though Vaughn was a weasel, his lifeforce was strong, his
predatory instincts unquestionable; even regurgitated, it
was enough to propel Syd to the next level.

The question was, what next?

So far—with her, at least—Syd was remaining a
slightly feistier version of his own sweet self. But she
would be watching closely to see where and how his newfound fire expressed itself.

And on whom it would be unleashed . . .

Syd grinned as he negotiated a winding turn, then
punched the Mustang up to eighty-five. Right now, from
the looks of it, rage was the furthest thing from his mind.

He flicked his smoke out the open window, grabbed the bottle of Bud from between his knees, took a healthy swig, and grinned some more. His driving hand drummed on the steering wheel, in time with the raucous tunes. He looked like he was maybe sixteen years old.

And again she felt the pang. The one she'd been feeling, more and more, ever since the little speech he'd made over this morning's breakfast of Vaughn and eggs. It wasn't just love that she was feeling now. It was the first stirrings of *trust:* an altogether rarer and more dangerous commodity.

Because she could picture the home Syd would build her, the promise he held. The images were like snapshots in a scrapbook, keepsakes of an impossible future. They were there, oh yes indeed, as inevitable a projection as the baby faces she imagined when she cross-referenced her looks with her chosen man's and did the genetic math.

And that was at the heart of it, wasn't it? She was *certain* she was pregnant; she could feel it. Her breasts were tender to the touch; her belly felt full and sensitive. As they drove Nora found herself touching her abdomen, surreptitiously probing for life. She was already doing her DNA homework: grafting Syd's chin onto her cheekbones, divining the compromise position between his eyes and hers.

If it was a boy, would he be slender and wiry like her, concealing his strength behind a streamlined, deceptive grace? And if it was a girl, would she inherit his dark eyes and stocky peasant build, translate it into the kind of pale and black-haired *zaftig* abundance that Nora found attractive in women?

Would the child be beautiful? There was no doubt in her mind. She had already fallen in love with the planes and angles of Syd's face. He had beautiful, arresting eyes. And very good teeth.

Plus he's strong. She smiled, just thinking about it. *Getting stronger by the second.* There was little question in her mind that he could deliver on his promise, given the proper circumstances and a little bit of luck . . .

. . . and no Vic waiting in the parking lot, with fangs bared and murder in his eyes . . .

. . . and that was when the second set of pictures emerged, and they were not pretty at all. In her mind's eye, she watched Syd's profile peel off in a clean red sweep. She had seen Vic kill enough times to know what it would be like. It had never been enough for Vic to simply kill, that sick motherfucker; he needed trophies to cart around, like merit badges of courage, for bravery under fire.

Once upon a time—way back, before the deterioration, before Texas and the point of no return—she had conjured baby faces with Vic, as well; and yes, of course, they were beautiful, too. She had carried those pictures around with her for years and years, before she finally realized that they would never come to pass.

And it was only once she had given up—torn Vic utterly out of her heart—that she had become his lifelong, tireless obsession. That was when the tattoos began to appear, like hashmarks denoting time served. As if he could hold on to her somehow by capturing her likeness in his flesh. That was when the chase began, in earnest.

And that was the most infuriating, horrifying part: it wasn't until he understood that he really, truly could not have her that he seriously began to want her. And in so doing, to seriously make her life a living hell.

Now he wouldn't rest until she was back in his clutches again. Or dead. Maybe both.

Her dread increased in intensity, the closer to Chameleon's they drew. At the same time, there were a few mental bones she could throw herself. Better to get this over with. It would get them out of town that much sooner, and anything that accelerated the process of putting this place far behind them was fine with her.

They rounded the last bend, came into the homestretch. She saw the little red and yellow lights. There really was

no choice but to try and enjoy herself, hope for the best.
Hoping against hope.

Nora swigged hard off the bottle of Comfort. And
abandoned herself to her fate.

SYD'S GOOD MOOD was already beginning to sour, practically from the second they rolled onto the lot. In reality, it
was just a series of diddly little nonevents; but taken together, they spelled erosion, and the beginnings of a night
steering steeply toward the downhill side.

It started when Syd went to park the car, only to be reminded that Nora insisted upon being dropped by the door.
Not a big deal, right? But it reminded him unpleasantly of
the other night. He had managed to keep Nora's crazy ex-
boyfriend out of his thoughts—she didn't talk about her
past, and he'd pretty much left it alone—but there was
something about being made to feel paranoid on your own
stomping grounds that made Syd's blood boil. So that was
enough to start it.

He'd dropped her at the door, then gone back to his favorite spot and parked. Getting out of the car, he found
himself acutely aware of his surroundings. He looked
around, searching the shadows as he sniffed the woods for
danger. There was nothing out there, as best as he could
tell. He realized, for the first time in ages, how much he
responded to the smell of the woods at night, and paused
to savor the crisp autumn scents: pine, rot, animal spoor,
the actual smell of the cold itself.

His spirits had dropped a little more as he walked back
across the lot. It was the same weird nostalgia he'd experienced this morning at the plant, only magnified to the fif-
tieth power: this was a place he actually loved, not a place
he'd simply endured. This was gonna hurt, he realized.
This would not be an easy good-bye.

At that moment, Syd had felt a strange sense of *clo-
sure:* the end of an era upon him. He wasn't sure if it was
just saying good-bye to Jules, ushering in the post-Karen
epoch, or if it was the entire first half of his life wrapping

up. In the final analysis, it hardly mattered. *It is what it is,* he told himself.

And right now, it is time to move on.

The feelings didn't diminish as he walked in the door. The achingly familiar smells: wood, smoke and beer, the fragrant perfume and funky sweat moved him to his core. Someone had slapped "The Alabama Song" on the juke-box; somehow Jim Morrison singing about finding the next whiskey bar made the moment perversely complete.

Chameleon's on a Monday night wasn't nearly as packed as the weekend shows—there was no band and no cover charge, no Red standing watch at the door, no Jane on hand with a smile or a sly observation to share—but they still had a sizable crowd. Very few people he knew, but that was okay, too. Fewer speeches to make.

Jules was already motioning him forward with a wiggle of one finger. Nora was sitting near him at the bar; she turned at Syd's approach. He sensed a weird competition between them, as he ambled up.

The long-necked Rolling Rock appeared in Syd's hand before he even took his seat. "Happy birthday, man," Jules said. He raised his iced tea in toast. Syd said thanks and clinked his bottle with Jules's glass, then turned to Nora. She had two double shots set up. When she slid one over to him, he toasted with her as well, then engaged her in a quick sloppy soul-kiss that tasted of caramel and bourbon.

Then she asked him if he was going to tell Jules. Of course, Jules said, "Tell me what?" Which put Syd in the awkward position of having to leap right into his explanation, without any setup or anything. Which kind of pissed him off.

It didn't help that Jules wasn't exactly supportive, either. It was like trying to tell Tommy and Budd about the wolf, only a hundred times worse; like showing someone the most beautiful work of art you could possibly create, only to have him ask you if you'd ever *really* considered that career in locksmithing.

Jules had a million irritating questions: irritating mostly because Syd didn't have any solid answers. *Do you know where you're going?* No. *Do you know what you're going to do with your shit?* No. *Do you have any money saved up?* No. *Do you have any idea how you're going to survive on the road?* Well, no. *Did you already quit your job?* Well, yes! And, hey, so long as you're at it, why not just ask if I still remember the difference between my ass, my elbow, and a hole in the ground?

Nora interrupted to order another round. There were a couple of other customers queueing up for the firewater of their choice. Jules excused himself for a minute, leaving Syd's little outburst to dangle in midair.

"This is what you can expect," Nora said under her breath, "from people who just don't fucking get it." And Syd, pissed as he was, was inclined to agree.

So by the time Jules got back with their drinks, Syd had built up a considerable head of steam. He didn't even wait for the next interrogatory round; he just launched into a little preemptive strike of his own. He had some questions *he* wanted to ask, if Jules didn't mind horribly.

Like, for example, hadn't Jules done the very same thing at one point in his life? *Yes, sort of.* And didn't he now spend many a night waxing nostalgic about those very same bygone days? *Yes, but* . . . Syd interrupted then, asked so exactly what in hell *did* Jules have against people taking a little calculated risk with their lives. *Not a thing,* Jules said, *as long as it looks like they know what they're doing.* Syd's anger spiked and redlined. Was he implying that Syd didn't know what he was doing?

I don't know, said Jules. *Do you think you know what you're doing?*

And that was when Syd lost it.

"You know what I think?" he spat, sneering, "I think you're jealous!" The anger was as irrational as it was all-encompassing: a lifetime of frustration, lubed by alcohol, unstoppable in its fury. "I think you went out and *tried* to stake your claim in the world, and it just chewed you up and spat you back. I think you shot *your* wad, and now you don't want anyone else to even get a chance.

"I *think*," he hissed, "that if anything this intense ever

happened in the whole of your measly, pathetic life, you'd know what the fuck you were talking about.

"But it hasn't, and you don't, and that's about all there is *to* it."

The space around them went dead silent, save for the white-noise wash of dead air. Syd's anger retracted as quickly as it had come on, leaving him embarrassed and weirdly defiant in its wake. His brain went condo to accommodate the multiple voices in his skull, slamming up against the wall of attitude he'd just thrown up: screaming *are you out of your fucking MIND?*; mumbling *I can't believe I just said that;* peripherally aware that others had begun to stare or back away, catching the emotional gist, if not the actual riff he'd just unleashed. He felt a dozen pairs of prying eyes upon him, heard a dozen whispers slither like snakes down his spine. Nora, too, was watching him: her gaze alert, alarmed.

And as for Jules . . .

Jules never took his eyes off Syd. And Syd could tell from the look in those eyes that he'd hit some genuine tender spots, the kind only old friends can ever really touch. Syd and Jules had logged a lot of time together, confessed their fears and dreams and a multitude of sins in the privacy of friendship. Syd had just taken aim from that privileged position and emptied both barrels point-blank in his best friend's face. The past regrets. The futures that never panned out. The hopes abandoned in the wake of a youth that was gone forever.

He'd nailed it all.

But instead of decking him or inviting him to take a fucking hike, Jules just shook his head. And when he spoke, his voice was low and soft, gently lethal. He spoke to Syd alone.

"Man, when you wake up from this—and you *will* wake up—you're gonna remember this conversation. And it's gonna make you feel real stupid.

"But that's life," he concluded. "You do what you gotta do."

Syd desperately wanted to say he was sorry, that he

took it all back, he didn't mean to hurt him, that this was an important move and it would mean a lot to have Jules's blessing.

What came out instead was, "If you were a real friend, you'd back me on this."

"If I backed you on this," Jules sighed, "I wouldn't be a real friend."

At which point, Nora scooped up Syd's hand before he could even begin to respond, saying *come with me* and dragging him off through the crowd. Her manner was urgent, uncompromising. Syd looked back at Jules as they went. The big man's eyes stayed on him until the crowd closed ranks, severing the connection.

As they hit the dance floor, Syd was still reeling. The pain was back, wanging through his brain. Were they gonna dance now? He didn't really feel like dancing.

But instead she led him down the hallway to the bathrooms. Or was it the back door she was leading him to? No, the women's room, its door banging open as she entered, pulling him in behind her. He asked her what she thought she was doing. She told him to shut up.

There was no one else in the bathroom. The stall in the back was empty. She threw the door open, pushed Syd in. His mouth opened with a question. She filled it with her tongue, and her hands went down quickly to undo his belt.

No one else can do this, she whispered, jerking his pants down. *No one else understands.* Taking him in hand. *It doesn't matter what anyone else thinks.* She squeezed him for emphasis, kissed his neck. *There's only one thing that matters.*

Then she was moving, down and down and down, to take him into her mouth. He leaned back against the wall, the reek of air fresheners and raw lust intermingling with the spinning in his head and the burning in his loins.

You and I, she said.

And then sucked his vessel dry.

VIC KNEW IT the second he pulled onto the Mt. Haversford Road.

Up to that point he'd been starting to get a little annoyed. He'd tracked Nora all the way into Pittsburgh, where he'd scored a copy of *Pennsylvania Musician,* found the names of the local clubs. Vic hated cities; *way* too easy to mask her trail in the swarming concrete jungles. Sure enough, he'd lost it altogether sometime late Saturday, which forced him into the aggravating position of spending all of Sunday covering the same ground over and over, just hoping to get lucky.

And then just today as he was heading out of town and flipping across the radio dial, searching for tunes, he caught the tail end of a late news wrap-up. He missed the first part, but that didn't matter: the little bit that he caught was more than enough. The part that talked about the *mutilated remains of an unidentified adult white male found this morning in the warehouse district of Monville* . . .

Vic cackled. Gee, he thought, wonder who did *that*? He checked his map, found Monville, and realized that the bitch had actually *tricked* him: kept him thinking she was heading east, when in reality she'd doubled back to the west.

An *official access only* crossover appeared before him and he whipped across it in a cloud of dust, nudging up to ninety as his anger stoked to a fine burn. *Tricked* him. How could it be? Either she was getting smarter, or he was slipping.

Vic thought about it, ultimately rejected both possibilities. This was just a new wrinkle in the game, is all. Fine. Great, actually: it upped the ante, put a keener edge on the hunt.

Besides, he thought, Nora wasn't the only dog that could learn new tricks.

He chilled out a bit once he got south of the city, resisted the urge to just burn up the highway all the way to Monville. No sense in getting sloppy, especially if she was getting cagey on him. He spent the next few hours checking out the dozens of dives that dotted the western Pennsylvania outback.

And then about forty-five minutes ago, he hit on a

twisty little two-lane blacktop snaking through the mountains, and there it was: after days of sniffing cold leads, that unmistakable scent. She'd been here, all right, and recently. She was lubed. And something else, too.

She had *company....*

Vic came upon the little blinking neon sign at nine forty-five, and smiled. It was secluded, tucked up in boonies, with woods and mountains all around. Even the name was perfect.

He wheeled into the big gravel lot, took stock of the number of cars, noted that it was pretty crowded. That was not so good. But there was a nice inconspicuous spot on the far end that had a clear sight line to the front door. Vic pulled in and shut the engine off, then reached under the seat and pulled out Billy Hessler's long-lost bag of crank.

Two king-sized lines later, he threw the door open, stuck one long black-booted leg out into the night.

Her scent was heavy in the air as he made his way to the entrance. It mingled with the drugs in his system, made the bloodlust rise and burble inside.

By the time he entered, he felt ready for anything.

IT STARTED JUST after she'd finished with Syd, booted him out of the bathroom, made him wait in the hall. "I have to pee," she told him. "Alone." It was all she had to say. The sex had rendered him malleable, so much Play-Doh with a boner. She shut the door behind him, turned back toward the stall.

And that was when it hit her. Hard.

There was no spotting to warn of its onslaught. There was only *pain:* sudden and shocking, excruciating enough to double her over before she could reach the toilet.

Oh no, she thought. *Oh god no ...*

By the time she got her skirt up and her panties down, she was already spattering the cold, grimy tile.

NO! her mind shrieked, as if she could *will* herself to turn back the tide. She thrust her hands between her legs, trying to block the flow. *NO NO NO ...!!!*

But there was no stopping it, and no denying the implications. Even before the first red drops gave way to the flood, the fear grew huge inside her. Tearing straight through doubt to certainty. Erasing any question, and every last speck of hope.

There was no life taking shape in there: no baby in the making, no little recombinant Syd-and-Nora Jr. knitting itself into substance within her. Not now. Perhaps not ever.

At least not anymore.

And then the deluge came: thick rivulets of defeat, flooding her with pain and loss as they sputtered and sluiced from her inner workings. Nora began to mewl, then moan, then sob, as her last chance and worst nightmare lay spinning on the surface of the rippling pool. It formed a little curlicue, like a question mark.

Nora caught a glimpse. That was all that it took. She cried and cried for a full five minutes, careening through anguish and grief to hysteria and back. Until there were no tears left, nor any point to them.

Then the first wave subsided, and the numbness set in: cloaking her in a smothering black veil of grief. The pain became a dull, cramping pulse.

This doesn't mean anything, she told herself desperately, the words a tiny floodwall of hope against a tidal wave of madness. *This doesn't mean shit. We've got plenty of time to try again. Plenty of time.*

Just as soon as we get out of here . . .

She coughed, forcing out one last thickening freshet, and realized in that second that she didn't even have any goddamned tampons—she hadn't thought to bring any, hadn't thought she'd *need* any. It was the capping absurdity. Nora wound up stuffing a wad of toilet tissue in her panties to stanch the flow, then stood and flushed on her way out of the stall. Her failure swished down the pipes and away, never to be seen again.

Syd was right there when she emerged, of course: sucking emphatically at his unfiltered smoke, kicking up a little nimbus that encircled his head as he waited in the hallway. Doing just as he was told.

Good boy, she was tempted to say. *Good doggy . . .*

But then her knees began to buckle, and her head began to spin, and before she could catch herself he was there: holding her close as she fought down the darkness, the second wave of sorrow crashing over her now, threatening to unleash the tears and the terror that she couldn't allow him to see.

"We gotta get out of here. . . ." she whimpered at last, appalled by the weakness in her voice.

"*Shhhh,*" he whispered, smoothing her hair with one strong and gentle hand. "*Shhhhh . . .*"

And she allowed herself to be comforted, while she waited for her strength to return. It would only be a minute. Just a minute. That's all. Then they could be on their way, kissing this pisshole dive and this pisshole town one last good-bye.

Just another minute, she told herself. *And then I'll be just fine. . . .*

HIGHER EDUCATION HAD never been a priority for Jules O'Donnell. He'd never gone to college—barely made it through high school, in fact—and his bartending certificate was the fanciest piece of paper he'd ever aspired to own.

But if the school of hard knocks gave out degrees, Jules was a certified master. Twenty years behind a bar was nothing if not educational, an in-depth field study of the lexicon of human moves. In the wanderlust of his misspent youth he'd swabbed counters and tended taps in everything from the poshest Frisco fern-bar to the skeeviest Long Island titty-joint, even tried his hand at the cruise-ship circuit for a year or two in his late twenties before returning home to these peaceful green hills.

His major, without a doubt, was in animal politics. Mating rituals were a specialty: Jules could lay winning odds on the success or failure of a proposed coupling before the ice melted or the head was off the first draft. He'd heard every pickup line and snappy comeback a million times; his big toothy grin had presided over the shots that launched a thousand bachelor parties, and his sympathetic nods had accompanied the beers that drowned ten thousand sorrow-drenched separations. Jules had been the impartial observer of hirings and firings, of births and deaths, of pickups and breakups from coast to coast to coast, and his knowledge was immense.

But of all his time-tested and finely honed skills, the one he counted on the most was the one that whispered *trouble coming.* Which was why his eyes instinctively went to the door a split second before it creaked open.

And the dark man came in.

It wasn't just his physical presence, which wasn't so much massive as *radiating* mass: like a psychic projection of size beyond his form. It wasn't the macho body english or the earring or the black-leather badass biker accoutrements: all were standard issue in these parts. Nor was it the fiercely smirking slash that lined one side of his face: Jules had seen good-looking guys with scars before.

No, it was the way the testosterone count seemed to go up the second the stronger crossed the threshold: air molecules charging like iron filings in a magnetic field, polarizing the gender lines across the room. It was the fact that every male that came within range looked, then *looked away*—instantly and unconsciously intimidated into a big-dog-meets-little-dog territorial imperative—while every female the stranger passed looked, then *looked again:* a purely instinctual attraction-reaction that did split-second biological end runs around the higher concepts of love and loyalty and fidelity.

It was the realization that the stranger not only seemed to expect the reaction, he *enjoyed* it.

And most disturbing of all, it was the creeping sense of *déjà vu:* the gut knowledge that he'd only ever seen one other person who could so polarize a room just by walking into it, and she was even now making a very good friend behave in some very strange ways. Jules wished Janey were here to provide him with a reality-check, or Red were on hand, should his instincts prove accurate.

But alas, Janey was off tonight, and Red only worked the weekends. That left Jules, two waitresses and the night cook, holding the line against an uncharacteristically heavy

Monday night. The business was like that: sometimes you saw the crowd coming—on a weekend or St. Paddy's Day or a Super Bowl Sunday—and you were ready for them; sometimes you counted on them and they *didn't* show, lured elsewhere by the promise of two-for-one drinks or a wet T-shirt contest.

And sometimes—like tonight, for instance—they just appeared, completely unexpected and in droves, presumably driven by the same forces that sent lemmings careening off cliffs.

As for what drove the dark man . . .

Jules rinsed and racked glasses, sixth-sense alarms clanging at the back of his skull, as the stranger stopped and sniffed the air like he was sifting it for clues. Everything about him conveyed a sense of malign *purpose*, like some renegade ambassador of bad will on a merciless mission. They made the most fleeting of eye contact, just enough for each to register the other, and then Jules looked away: began wiping the counter as the stranger moved through the crowd, parting the throng like Moses on a Red Sea stroll. The wiping motion brought Jules to the center of the bar, within easy reach of the Mossberg Persuader twelve-gauge he kept stashed behind the ice chest.

And then, in a move both completely calculated and utterly natural, the dark man *turned*, sidling up to the shadowy far end of the bar, to take the proverbial catbird seat: his back to the wall, his eyes commanding virtually the whole of the room at a glance. Jules watched without watching, instantly understood the subtle dynamics of the play. To serve him, Jules would have to step out of reach of the gun.

The dark man smiled as Jules looked up, and Jules knew that *he knew*. And that it amused him.

Jules sighed. There was no other way to play it. He moved down the bar, shifted into his most accommodating demeanor. His smile, when it came, was all business. Only the twinkle in his eyes conveyed the underlying message. *My bar. My rules.*

Don't fuck with me.

"Howdy," he said. "What'll ya have?" Bringing the rag up to swab within an inch of the dark man's elbows. As the stranger's eyes dropped to register the intrusion, the rag disappeared and a fresh napkin took its place. *We live to serve. Be nice.*

The dark man looked up, smiled. His eyes projected a practiced indifference, but his pupils were huge, the light that shone behind them like black fire. "Double shot of tequila," he said, leaning on one palm. "If you don't mind."

"You got it," Jules answered, laying down a glass and grabbing a bottle from the speed rack. He poured expertly, filling the glass to the marker line with one hand while scooping up a slice of lime from the garnish bin with the other. He replaced the bottle and came back up with a salt shaker, set it by the glass. "New in town?" he asked, meaning *when are you leaving?*

"Oh, just passin' through," the stranger replied, meaning *none of your fucking business.* He tipped the shaker, made a little mound of salt appear on the crook of his thumb and forefinger. Then he downed the shot in a gulp, licked the salt, and bit the pulp clear from the rind.

He had no sooner dropped the rind to the napkin than Jules had cleared it away, erasing all traces of the transaction. "Enjoy your stay," he said, meaning *leaving so soon?* "That'll be four bucks."

"Why don't you go ahead and set me up again," Vic said, meaning *why don't you blow me.* He fished a twenty out of his pocket. "And, uh, keep the change."

Vic smiled at the ox serving him, kept right on smiling as the big dumb bastard did as he was told. Son of a bitch had gotten on his nerves practically from the minute he walked in the door, the way he eyeball-fucked him and all. Like Vic gave two shits and a squirt about his dinky little dump, or any of its grazing herd. He flipped him a five-spot just to get him to back off, show him that Vic was nice, Vic meant no harm, Vic was a regular friend to the animals.

The bartender returned with a fresh setup and a hard look, and Vic thanked him just as sweet as you please. He was just starting to fantasize what that big moon face would look like coming off in his hands when a giggling bevy of 4-H queens bellied up to the other end of the bar. The ox looked over.

"Duty calls," Vic said, and gave another big smile. All the while thinking *some other time, pal. Some other time*.

The ox hovered a moment before lumbering reluctantly off, pausing every so often to flip him the baleful sidelong glance. Vic ignored him, happy to be free of the distraction. The smile evaporated from his face, as his attention turned to the darker matter at hand.

She was here somewhere. The fact that he had not spotted her yet was of little consequence; to the contrary, the simple certainty of her proximity calmed and centered him. The chasing part was over.

All he had to do now was sit back and wait.

Vic sipped his shooter and thought of punishments, the appropriate payback for all his trouble. Disfigurement was appealing on a certain brute level, but ultimately out of the question. He fingered his own scar absently, reminded himself that Nora could be her own kind of dangerous; and besides, he *liked* the way she looked. Marring her beauty would truly be like cutting off her nose to spite his face. There was just no percentage in it.

There were, however, alternatives.

Like her *pick*, for instance.

His grin magically rematerialized. Taking out her luckless little runt of the moment was a given, but doing it in some suitably spectacular fashion might impress upon her the error of her ways. Maybe not stop with his face this time, but peel the little bastard from head to toe like a grape: reduce him to raw, writhing shreds, *then* rip out his fucking heart and eat it still-steaming before her eyes. Maybe even give him a peek at it before the linkage between flesh and spirit ruptured and the light winked out, so the fucker would know exactly where his soul was going.

Or, rethinking the equation, perhaps it would be pleasant to crack his head like a walnut, scoop out great spongy hunks and munch munch munch until he reached the cerebral cortex, and then holler down his brain stem.

That would be a hoot. Little fuck was probably thanking his lucky stars this very moment, his nose half-buried in Nora's fragrant tail. Or vice versa, maybe.

That was okay. Vic downed his shooter and twirled the glass on the bar, felt the bloodlust go from boil to simmer. That was just fine. Right about now, he realized, that poor sucker must think he's just about the luckiest guy alive.

Ah, well, Vic thought. *Didn't they always.*

Uncle Vic would teach him different. And then, when he was done, he'd make *her* clean up the mess.

His imagination sated, Vic gestured to the ox for yet another round. As he did his gaze strayed to the dance floor, the loose crowd of gyrating humanity tuned into some vintage Blind Blake. As the bartender brought him his drink the sea of bodies momentarily parted, allowing Vic a clear sight line to the back of the room.

And that's when he spotted her.

"Nora," he said.

OH, SHIT, JULES thought with dawning horror, as the dark man stood and stepped away from the bar. *He knows her. He said her fucking name.* He looked back to the dance floor, saw one silhouette moving against the current, a second in close pursuit. He wanted to call out to them, sound some kind of warning.

But he could see the dark man already in motion, beelining toward the dance floor.

And he knew it was already too late.

NORA SMELLED HIM a second before she saw him coming.

Oh no. Freezing her in her tracks. *Oh no.* Feeling the void billow up in her soul. There was that one amazing second, when you watched a thing spin out of control. That second was happening now, and her only emotions were panic and horror.

Then the moment snapped, and instinct took over.

The first thing she did was let go of Syd's hand. There

was a crowd, thank god there was a crowd, it was a simple matter of moving fast and keeping her head down. Syd said something. Music swallowed the sound, even as it receded. She picked up her pace. It occurred to her that she had not even said good-bye. The thought was a dangerous distraction. She kept going, parting the human cornfield with scarcely a ripple, heading for the door. She prayed to God that he hadn't actually seen her.

But of course she knew he had.

AT FIRST SYD couldn't make heads or tails of it. One minute all was right with the world: Nora's palm locked in his as they emerged from the hallway.

Then in the space of a second it *changed:* flesh going taut and cold, her fingers tensing and snatching away. Syd started tracking from the second she detached, going *what the fuck?* as she darted and weaved, cutting a zigzag swath through the room. Syd followed, jostling dancers and sploshing drinks as he plowed through the pie-eyed obstacle course.

He called her name; she ignored him. He saw the back of her head, lost it behind a potato-shaped couple. They parted as he plowed through, doggedly in pursuit: leaving a trail of irate curiosity, picking up gawkers in his slipstream.

"NORA!!" he called out. "WAIT!!"

She was past the fringe of the dance floor now, heading for the door. He could feel her desperation through the heat of the crowd. He tried to track her movements, the absence of logic behind them.

Then Syd hit the outer perimeter of the crowd, and saw the man-shaped shadow bearing down on her. He was moving fast, on a collision course. His body shifted in the light, revealed a face Syd instantly hated, its features forever burned into his DNA. His fists clenched and as his adrenaline kicked in, riding the shockwave screaming through his guts.

And he *knew:* that was the strangest part. Syd knew before his brain even had a chance to register the escape

vector and intercept course, before his memory had time to
regurgitate the stories and process them into fact. The
knowledge was instant, undeniable. The name, when it
came, was bitter on his breath.

"Vic," he hissed . . .

. . . AND THERE WAS nothing like the feeling of those last
few steps, when he knew for a fact she had nowhere to
run. It was that one instant, at the end of the hunt, when
the hunted finally grasped its fate, understood that it was
going down. Total satisfaction, in that moment of truth.
Such a feeling of completion, of absolute mastery.

For a moment they froze, with six feet of distance between them: Vic wallowing in predatory glory, Nora swimming in stark terror. He'd never thought of her as a timid
soul, but there she was: for once utterly speechless, like a
big-eyed bunny rabbit.

It was not a good look for her. It only lasted a second.
Then she began to back up, and he paced her, making an
exaggerated show of how leisurely he could be.

"Well, hell, Nora," he said, smiling wide. "Long time
no see."

Nora snarled and showed teeth, but she wasn't fooling
anybody. If she'd been wearing her ears, they'd be pasted
back so flat on her head they'd look like she'd ironed 'em
down. She took another step backward. He continued to
pace her.

"You just stay away from me, Vic."

"Oh, princess . . ." He shook his head wearily, but his
grin was enormous. "You know I can't do that."

Suddenly, her pick of the week appeared alongside her,
wired extraordinarily tight. It poked a hole in Vic's smile.
He had the kind of crazy look about him that said he was
about to go badly savage. Vic sized him up in a glance.

Nora'd been working her mojo, all right: sonofabitch
was primed, and coming on strong. In a couple of months,
he might have actually turned into a problem, instead of
the dogmeat he was about to become.

But he was green, not attuned to his nature. He had no

idea what he was up against; he'd probably never even turned. In an open encounter, he'd be dead in seconds. That alone was enough to incur Vic's contempt.

Worst of all, though, Vic could smell Nora all *over* that unworthy piece of shit. And vice versa. All the way down to his cum on her breath. All pretense of magnanimity went out the window as the pictures that it posed made Vic berserk.

The urge to kill them both was very nearly more than he could bear.

SYD, FOR HIS part, was completely unintimidated: too crazy with his own bloodhunger to register Vic's danger level, too concerned about Nora to care. They were about the same size, that was all he knew. Cecil had fifty pounds on him, easy.

"Hey!" Syd hollered, stepping into the free-fire zone between Nora and Vic. "Hey, *shithead!"* They stopped, and Syd squared off, four feet from where Vic held his ground.

"Back off, little dog," Vic said. His voice was infuriatingly condescending. "I'll eat your fucking brain."

"Vic!" Nora cried, calling out his name. It barely registered on their map.

"Yeah?" Syd took another step forward. "We'll see who eats *what,* motherfucker!"

"SYD!" Nora, beside him. "NO!" There was genuine terror in her voice.

Vic's lips peeled back in a leering, lethal grin.

And a shadow seemed to pass over his face . . .

. . . AND THEN VIC stopped, as the cold, blunt business end of a shotgun barrel connected with the soft hollow behind his left ear. Vic stiffened. The barrel nudged him twice, for emphasis.

Sonofabitch. The ox was right behind him. Cocksucker had snuck up on him in all the excitement. Vic began to turn, and the gun stayed with him, maintaining that delicate, deadly contact. He stopped, noted that the fucker had

placed himself well, in a blind spot and well out of reach.
Slick. Dude had even taken care to make sure that, should
he choose to pull the trigger, the only thing Vic's brains
would hit on the way out would be the wall.

It chilled him out, right then and there. He really had
no choice. For all of his power, there was nothing in Vic's
repertoire that worked against a skullful of buckshot at
close range. He felt the power of the Change ease out of
him, exhaled slowly through his teeth. Then he smiled,
tried to keep it breezy.

"Problem, officer?" Raising his hands palms-out and
waist-high.

"Not anymore," Jules replied, meaning *blink and I'll
blow your brains out.* "But I believe it's time for you to
go." His tone was measured and neutral; the shotgun's
mouth gave one more kiss, then withdrew. Meaning *now.*

The jukebox finished playing, wrapping the room in silence. Vic looked around; all eyes were upon them, the entire bar's collective breath held in anticipation of his next
move. Vic's gaze took in the entire room at a glance,
skipped Syd entirely, shifted back to Nora.

"Well, darlin'," he said. "You heard the man. You
know the deal.

"So what's it gonna be?"

NORA FELT THE question land in her lap, felt the attendant
surge of imminent doom envelop her. It was like playing
hot potato with a hand grenade. Vic and Syd had already
pulled the pin, started tossing it back and forth, creating a
deadly situation that could blow at any second. Jules and
his gun had put an end to that volley, but it hadn't done a
thing to defuse the potential explosion.

So Vic, in his wisdom, had tossed it to her at the very
last moment. That ruthless, murdering sonofabitch. He
knew her options, could guess how she'd play them.

And the game was over, no question about it. All she
had to do was read the look on his face. Every thought in
his head was now etched on those features, emblazoned in

his knowing gaze. He held nothing back. He was reading her, too.

The moment of truth had finally arrived.

The fact was that he would never stop coming. He would never ever stop. He would follow her wherever she ran, ambush her whenever she rested, dog her tracks every step of the way for the rest of her miserable life.

She looked in his eyes, and they told her that, yes, this was destiny unfolding: the once and future pattern of her life, immutably fixed for all eternity. She would never escape the bond they'd forged, the hideous tie that bound them still. There was no one to turn to, and no force short of death that could keep them apart.

And if, by chance, she should meet someone—and for a moment, dare imagine some other, *happier* twist of fate—Vic would kill him. It was really as simple as that. She understood now, with a terrible finality, that there would *never* be enough time to get one up and running. Vic would always arrive too soon. Without mercy, and without fail.

Nora watched the last remnants of her dreams collapse, her plans vaporize, her strategies turn to dust. All of the endless running—every desperate attempt to rebuild her life—had been a cruel joke. A charade of astonishing depth and malice. The ache in her belly only served to confirm that she had pulled the wool over her own eyes, and in the process, chewed up dozens of lovers over thousands of miles. And for what?

For nothing.

For nothing at all.

She couldn't bring herself to look at Syd, though his eyes were hot upon her. She was already trying to forget what he looked like, erase from her mind all painful delusions of the things that might have been. And Vic's gloating countenance was far too much to bear. He'd known her decision, almost before she did. He knew her all too well.

But there *was* one last card she could play; a single

move left to her before she conceded defeat. She could not save herself; that was a given.

But as for Syd . . .

"I'll go with you," she said to Vic at last, her burning eyes averted. "If you swear—you *swear*—that you won't hurt him."

"WHAT?"

Syd looked as if he'd been shot, as all the color drained from his face. "WHAT?"

"Syd, shut up," Nora snapped. "It's over." Then she turned to Vic, and Jules saw her terrible resignation. "Swear to me," she reiterated.

And Jules realized in that moment that she really *did* love Syd: twisted as she was, her feelings were genuine. Then he looked back to the dark man, to the smile on his face, and was more than half-tempted to blow it right off, blow him right the hell out of their misery. Vic was just looking for the right way to cunningly phrase his end of the bargain. There wasn't a genuine fucking bone in his body.

"I swear to Christ," Vic said, "I won't even lay a finger on him."

Nora stared at him hard. "You won't *hurt* him," she insisted.

Vic looked from Nora to Syd, and back again. "Like I said," he said flatly, "I won't touch him." He looked over his shoulder to Jules. "You, I can't make any promises about. But as for *him* . . ." He gestured to Syd dismissively, as if it scarcely even mattered.

Then he turned his attention solely to Nora.

"So," he said, "shall we?"

A long silver chain appeared in Vic's hand, like a magician pulling flowers out of his sleeve. It was fine-tooled and delicate, easily five feet long, with a tiny silver clasp on the end. He extended his hand, offered it to her.

"Nora," Syd implored her. "Nora, you can't—"

Nora shook her head and stopped him.

"Good-bye, Syd," she said.

And now, at last, she met his gaze, her tears welling up defiantly. Her eyes never left his as she took the chain, its silver clasp gleaming in the light. And before God and everybody, fastened the clasp to the ring in her nose.

"C'mon," Vic gave the chain a playful tug. She flinched minutely, stoic in her submission.

All the struts went out from beneath Syd's conviction. It was amazing how fast, and how complete the devastation. Jules could do nothing but helplessly watch him sag, visibly *deflate,* from all the holes that had been punched in his core.

"Nora," he said, but there was no steam left in it. His eyes, like hers, were brimming with tears. The despair in them was beyond measure.

Then she turned and, with Vic leading the way, walked out of the door.

And out of Syd's life.

THE DOOR EASED shut again—slowly, slowly—and for Syd Jarrett, there was a fifteen-second slice of infinity when all Creation was reduced to that narrowing gap. Watching the darkness as it winnowed down to nothing. Then gone.

Then gone.

As if from a distance, he felt the world start up again without him: disaster averted, and on with the show. Somebody laughed, too loud; it was almost like a signal. All at once, the muted buzz gave way, the party resuming in earnest.

Syd just stood there. Silent. Thrumming. Paralytic with shock and pain. The jukebox came on, abrupt and startling. Billie Holiday. "Tain't Nobody's Business If I Do." Underneath the boisterous relief of the crowd, the clinking glass and chinkling change, Syd felt his nerve endings begin to unravel, his heart crisp and shrivel inside his chest.

"Syd." Voice first, then the hand on his shoulder. Syd recoiled from the touch, his eyes aflame.

He began to shake his head.

"C'mon, man." He felt Jules behind him, trying to steer him back to the bar. "You gotta let it go. . . ."

"No." Syd growled, wrenching suddenly free. There was violence in the gesture. It was barely restrained. Jules stepped back, staring into those burning eyes.

And for the first time in ten years of friendship, Jules was afraid of him.

Syd smelled the fear, found it strangely exhilarating. The killing rage hurtled forth like a living force, a separate entity with a mind and a will all its own. *Yes,* it said. *You SHOULD be afraid. You should ALL be afraid . . .*

. . . and then it struck him that no: not *them.* There was only *one* who should have such reason to fear . . .

. . . and then he was moving, hitting the door with both hands, sending it slamming back to crash against the wall as his feet smacked gravel and his eyes scanned the biting black air. Thinking *sonofabitch, I'm gonna rip right through you. I'm gonna tear you to fucking shreds . . .*

. . . and then he spotted them, at the far end of the parking lot: Vic, closing the passenger side door of a battered sedan; Nora inside, head down, shoulders slumped. They were maybe sixty feet away. Vic looked up, saw Syd coming, ignored him.

"HEY!" Syd called out, moving faster now, the killing rage singing in his blood as he crossed the parking lot. "HEY, YOU!"

Vic waltzed around the front of the car, heading for the driver's side. The thought that Nora was afraid made him crazy; the idea that she was scared *for* him sent Syd clear over the top. Syd himself felt no fear, only a terrible clarity of purpose.

"HEY!!!"

Twenty feet now, and Vic still showed no sign of response. Adrenaline surged through Syd's system: every cell humming in anticipation, restless for impact.

Ten feet, five. He could practically taste his blood "MOTHERFUCKER, *I'M TALKIN' TO YOU!!"*

He got there just as Vic reached the driver's door. Nora called out Syd's name; it was lost beneath the roaring in his ears as his left hand snaked out, grabbed Vic's shoulder, spun him around . . .

. . . *and then the air itself changed, became violent, as Vic whirled, face gone liquid and wickedly distorting, mad eyes alight with a ravening flame as the mouth grew wide and kept on growing, lips blackening and peeling back to reveal so many many teeth . . .*

. . . *and the teeth, like ivory stilettos, flicking up to fill jaws far too huge to believe. Jaws that stretched and sprouted from the terrible no-longer-human face: long snout long jaws long gleaming spikes that snarled and snapped like a beartrap full of bayonets.*

Syd stumbled back, his bootheels skidding on the loose-packed gravel, his tumbling ass-backwards on the stony ground. Nora screamed. Syd's eyes rolled back, as the dark shape descended . . .

. . . and then Syd felt the teeth graze the soft skin of his cheek: light enough to tickle the stubble there, sharp enough to break the skin. Just a nip. A warning.

And then they stopped.

Syd's blood thudded painfully in his temples, as his eyes refocused, fixed on the figure before him. There was a disorienting moment as the form seemed to glitch and shift in the darkness, like a rippling man-sized hole in the night.

Then Vic was standing by the car door again: his features his own, recognizably human. There was no mistaking the smile on his face.

"You may not believe it, punk, but this is your lucky night.

"You get to live."

Vic hopped into the car, started it up. Syd tried to stand, couldn't. The sedan wheeled around, spun out, took off, sending back a shower of gravel and grit.

Syd coughed and sputtered as the big car pulled away, his vision blurred and blinded. He couldn't read the license or make or model, couldn't even see the back of Nora's head through the frost-encrusted window.

By the time he could see or breathe again, the sedan

was but a glowing blur on the crest of the hill. And by the time he stood, it was gone completely: swallowed by the night, and the road, and the cold. Taking Nora with it.

And leaving Syd shaken. Defeated.

Alone.

24

THE NEXT SEVERAL hours were a groggy, broken man's descent: a drunken tumble down the well of madness and despair.

Syd sat near the end of the bar, his eyes staring at some distant receding horizon while his sight turned wholly inward. There was no shortage of torturous images there, no dearth of painful memories and excruciating might-have-beens. They collided in his head with a shower of sparks where his dreams of the future used to be.

And—indestructibly burning at the center of it all— was the prismatic, multifaceted image of Nora. An image that radically shifted from one moment to the next, depending on exactly where he stood. As the hours passed his mind moved constantly, viewing her from every conceivable direction. Trying to get a fix on who she actually was, the better to grasp the parameters of the vacuum she'd left behind.

There was Nora the catalytic agent and life-changing force: sweeping out the dead wood of his shipwrecked life, urging him to rebuild and set back out to sea. There was Nora the party animal *cum* fertility goddess: reawakening in him a boundless, transcendent appetite for life. There was Nora the vulnerable and tragic enigma, caught mysteriously weeping in the middle of the night. There was the dominant Nora, built of thunder and flame. The submissive Nora, led away on a chain.

And then there was the new face he had only seen tonight. The secretive face.

Of the Nora who lied.

And that was the bottom line here, wasn't it? That she had fucking *lied* to him: about her supposedly broken-up relationship with Vic, and God only knew what else. That Syd was ultimately nothing more than a pit stop on a long and twisted road that those two would probably be traveling forever.

The wounded part of him desperately needed to believe that was true. To think anything else was entirely too painful, pointed far too many fingers back in his direction. How could he have been so stupid, so utterly suckered by his own desperate hunger? Against his better judgment, against all sense or reason, she had breached the defenses of his little fortress of one. He had let her *in*.

And she, in turn, had released something within him.

And that was the point where his sanity threatened to skid completely out of control, go careening off into the uncharted abyss. Because something very weird had happened in the parking lot, and in one incandescent nightmare flash Syd had borne witness to something that he could neither accept nor deny. Acceptance was tantamount to deciding that yes, the world really was flat, after all, and there really were monsters waiting just over the edge, ready to eat you up. It was stupid. It was impossible. It was simply too much.

And if anyone had told him that three days ago, he would have laughed.

But he had *seen* it, and the certainty of the vision was a red-hot poker thrust into the deepest folds of his brain, igniting that long-hidden itch. Missing pieces of the lost weekend suddenly jigsaw-clicked into place. And Syd's reality, already frayed at the edges, began to unravel entirely.

As he recognized the face Vic had revealed.

The face so much like the creature in his dreams . . .

"No," he said quietly, feeling a lid of denial slam down in his head, sealing off the knowledge. "No," he repeated, fighting his way back to the room in which he sat. He reached for his bottle, trying to insulate himself from himself with alcohol. His hand trembled as he brought it to his lips.

He looked around the room. The rest of the patrons at the bar kept a respectable distance; whatever they were saying about him, they were keeping it amongst themselves. And Jules was simply Jules: a silent, beneficent presence behind the bar. He didn't hover nearby, didn't say a word; but every time Syd's bottle emptied, a full one mysteriously appeared in its place.

There were some critical things to be said between them: explanations and, even more important, *apologies*. But it was tough for Syd to even think about Jules, and way too soon for them to talk. The fact that Jules understood this—that Jules was so fundamentally cool—only made it that much harder. It underscored what an asshole Syd had been, how completely undeserving of such consideration.

So when it came down to last call, and Jules suggested that Syd stick around for a couple, the offer was gratefully accepted.

It was twenty minutes to two.

THE YELLOW SHUTTER Inn was a low-slung cinder-block structure rimming the tarmac of Route 18 just north of Atlasburg. It advertised both half- and full-night rates, with a mid-afternoon "executive special" for the lunch-hour quickie; its rooms boasted water beds, mirrored ceilings and in-room porn, and reeked of industrial-strength disinfectant and spent lust; its parking was discreetly situated away from prying eyes, around the back.

All in all it was a sleazy little affair, and its stock-in-trade was sleazy little affairs: marital infidelities and workplace flings, with the odd pickup or truckstop trick filling out its nightly roster of seamy couplings and low-rent fantasies. The clientele as a rule wanted two things: to get kinky, and to not get caught. As such, they tended to assiduously ignore both the faces of those who shacked up next door to them and the noises they made from behind those closed doors.

Which was exactly why Vic had chosen it.

It was one forty-five when he sat down on the edge of the bed to pull his boots back on. He was mindful to keep the sloshing to a minimum, not that it really made much difference. Nora was deep in Noraland: her body gone fetal on the bed, her brain blasted into oblivion.

They'd been there a little over two hours: long enough to complete the preliminaries of round one, namely *reestablishing dominance*.

The no-tell motel had been part inspiration, part calculation: under other circumstances he would have killed Nora's little hero on the spot and hiked it over the nearest state line, then dealt with her mood in due time. But the bitch had gone and made her little power play, and that had complicated matters. For one thing, Vic knew that she wasn't kidding. Worse yet, she'd dissed him in front of the whole bar: daring him to show his true self, just begging him to make a mess. As if she was just itching to blow their cover, bring things crashing down around them. As if he would ever actually let her get away with it.

No, no, he thought. Not like that. Granted, he was pissed enough to consider it as they pulled out of the lot, what with that little dipshit following them out and all. And Nora's attitude as they hightailed it down the highway made it even harder: she sulked and drank and stared out the window so sullenly that it was all he could do to keep from yanking her chain clean out.

He diddled with it absently as the miles unwound before them, one long arm slung over the seat back, inches away but not touching her. Not yet. They drove on in silence for a while, covering distance, merging with the night. When he offered her the bag of pharmaceuticals she absently grabbed a handful, washed them down with a long pull off the bottle he conveniently provided.

He told her he'd missed her. She said nothing. He joked that fun was fun, and she'd given him a good run this time. His voice was all honey and ground glass. He laughed, made a crack about the look on Syd's face at the moment of the Change, wondered absently if he'd loaded his pants in the aftermath. Her silence was deafening.

Little by little, Vic began to burn.

By now they should be at each other's throats: Vic egging her on and fending her off, Nora lashing and snapping to beat the band. It was foreplay, the fight before the fuck. It got their juices running. It was simply the way it was. Or at least the way it used to be, back in the good old days.

But this . . .

At least the last time, she'd taken a chunk out of him by way of payback. Vic could respect that. But now she just sat, staring and stewing, lost in her own private Idaho. And it was starting to bother him.

"Hey," he said softly. Nora did not look, did not turn. *"Hey!"* Louder this time.

He gave the chain a perfunctory little jerk; her head whip-cracked around to pin him with eyes at once steely and bright with tears. "Aw, c'mon, baby," he said. "Be nice."

And though his tone went suddenly silken, the words came out laced more with threat than entreaty. Nora looked away, took another drink. Vic shook his head. "Baby, when you gonna learn?" he said.

"You and I *belong* together."

With that his fingers snaked along the seat back, started working their way through her hair. She bristled, stiffened, staring dead ahead. "There's nobody else in the world for me," he said. His fingers probed the wild cascade of hair, found the spot at the base of her skull. Her eyes closed, her whole body tightened like a guitar string being tuned. Gently, with surprising tenderness, he began to massage: tracing sensual little hieroglyphs. Nora began to vibrate, in spite of herself.

"And there's no one else for you but me," he said. "You *know* it's true."

Nora's eyes stayed closed, as a solitary tear stole out and rolled down her cheek. Vic's fingers kept moving, playing her strings. A low moan welled up, halfway between desire and lament. Vic smiled to himself, unseen in the darkness.

And then the Yellow Shutter had appeared like a beacon in the night, and suddenly Vic knew just what to do. Nora waited in the car as he checked them in, and by the time he got her to the room she was resigned enough to accept her discipline, and just wasted enough to want it.

The room was small and tacky, fake pine scent clinging to the fake-leopard wallpaper. Vic ushered Nora in, tossed their bags in behind her. Nora was pliant by then, shell-shocked and damned near comatose. As Vic peeled her clothes off he caught the first whiff of discharge; the wad of sodden tissue confirmed it.

"*Whew,* you're ripe," Vic scolded, unable to keep from smiling as he stripped her bare. Nora shuddered, and Vic instantly picked up on it, read her perfectly. "You really think he could do it for you? Huh?" Unclipping the chain, letting it slip to the floor. "Think *anybody* can?"

He threw her belly-down onto the bed, proceeded to pull the rope from his ditty bag. *"Bitch,"* he hissed. *"So you're gonna blame me for your problems?"* Nora moaned as Vic yanked her legs apart, began to tie her off.

Her arms came next; she offered no resistance as he hoisted them over her head. Vic was thrilled to note that the management had conveniently provided eye-hooks, thick steel anchor points bolted deep into the four corners of the bed frame.

I love this place, Vic thought. He finished her off, making sure the knots were nice and tight.

Nora lay bare-assed and spread-eagled. Her hair hid her face. That was okay. That wasn't the part of her he was primarily talking to. Vic grabbed a pillow and shoved it under her belly, to improve the elevation. The milk-white half-moon hemispheres of her ass rose invitingly before him. Vic beamed. So she wanted him to make a mess; well, okay. The ropes weren't the only things that were nice and tight.

Vic stood and stripped, his erection fiercely throbbing. He crawled back onto the bed, let his face slip down into the dark folds between her legs. Her blood was thick, like honey on his tongue.

He licked one long finger by way of foreplay, wormed it into her ass. Her back door was irised shut, the only part of her that still offered him resistance. Vic withdrew his finger, then spread her creamy cheeks. "It's good to have you back," he said.

Then fucked her ass until she bled.

And though at first she tried to hide it, to bury herself in her shadowland and deny him even the tiniest of cries, he could feel her starting to yield. He could feel it in the tremors that rumbled through her flesh, like the shockwaves following an earthquake. He could feel it in the way her sphincter quivered with each successive thrust. As he moved he spoke to her, his mouth close in her ear, invading her mind as he violated her body.

"No one else can do this." He pressed deeper, tearing through her walls. *"And nothing else matters."* She clenched that much tighter, tried to shut him out. *"There's only one thing that matters. . . ."*

Fresh blood flowed, easing his passage. He could feel it coming, building to a head. Vic wound up, pelvis arching as he leaned in close, his voice as soft as thought. *"You belong to me,"* he told her.

Then rammed the message home.

There was that one final moment of resistance, and then Nora groaned and opened wide to receive him. *You belong to me.* Her ass bucked and writhed, fighting him even as she surrendered. *You belong to me.* The last shred of fight was swept away like a sapling in a floodpath as

Vic hammered at her, kept hammering until she could resist no more.

Her screams, when he came, were music to his ears.

HE LAY THERE afterward, listening to her breath. He was happy, sated. The satisfaction went worlds beyond mere sex. In the end, he knew, it was not about getting off. It was about *giving in.*

He waited until he was sure she had passed out before getting up and cleaning himself off.

As he dressed and sat to pull his boots on Vic reached back, patted her naked backside. Nora was definitely down for the count. Good girl. Her flesh glistened in the dim light from the bathroom; her sweat smelled of pain and resignation, the sweet funk of defeat. One whiff made him hard all over again.

And just in time, too, he thought. After all, it was just about time for round two.

And his other unfinished business of the night.

25

B Y TWO TWENTY-FIVE the last of the stragglers had cleared out, leaving Jules to finish closing up for the night. The front door was locked. The speed racks were stocked and racked and ready, the ashtrays and trash cans emptied, the sinks and bar all wiped till they gleamed. Bonnie and Heather, the night waitresses, had barely cashed out and split their tips when Jules looked up from doing the books, told them to go ahead and leave. On the way out the door they each stole a quick sidelong glance at the lone figure huddled at the end of the bar. Jules smiled and nodded as they waved good-bye, told them each to have a good one.

Then the door clicked shut behind them, locking Jules and Syd in.

And Jules breathed a hefty sigh.

Now for the real work, he thought. He put away the ledgers, locked out the register, cued up some Buddy Guy tunes and pulled two icy longnecks out of the cold chest. He ambled down to the far end of the bar and set one in front of his friend.

"Cheers," he said, clinked Syd's bottle with his own.

Syd lifted out of his trance, nodded glumly. Jules took a long pull off his beer, set it back on the bar, waited. Patience was a virtue. There were a million things to be said, but if experience were any guide, they might be a while in coming.

To his surprise, Syd cut to the chase fairly quickly. He picked up his beer, took a gulp. "Thanks," he said. His voice quavered, raw with anguish.

"Anytime," Jules replied, took another sip of his own. "You okay?"

The laugh that came had not a trace of humor in it. "Oh, yeah, never better," he said, then stopped to swallow the fist-sized knot in his throat. "Shit," he mumbled. "I'm such an asshole."

"Sometimes," Jules concurred. "But I don't know many people who aren't."

"I can't believe it," Syd continued, shaking his head, almost as if he were talking to himself. "How could I be so fucking *blind*?"

Jules paused, shrugged. "Love," he said. "Fucks with your reflexes."

"Yeah, well," Syd countered, "never again." He drained his beer, set it down with a hollow *thunk*.

It was Jules's turn to be cynical. "Uh-huh," he muttered. He finished his beer, scooped up Syd's bottle. "There's three things that I'm sure of," he said. "One is that you've had a very shitty night. The second is that there's no way in hell that you are in any shape to drive."

"What's the third thing?" Syd asked.

"I'll tell you when we get home," Jules said.

Syd shook his head grimly. "I don't think I can go home right now."

"I meant *my* home." Jules turned and tossed the empties. Syd looked at him as he grabbed his jacket and came around the bar, as if he didn't quite get it. Jules smiled, laid a big hand on Syd's shoulder.

"I got two cold sixes of Sam Smith's Pale Ale and the new Sarabande digital remasters of Muddy Waters' lost sessions," he explained. "Now you tell me, who *else* is going to properly appreciate that?"

For the first time in hours, Syd managed a smile. It was weary, halfhearted, clouded with emotion. But it was a start. He nodded, rose from his stool. He wobbled slightly, adjusting to the change in altitude.

"Whoa." He groaned as his bladder woke up and sent urgent telegrams to his brain. "I think maybe I better take a leak first."

Jules nodded back. "I'll go warm up the car," he replied.

They split off, each heading in their respective directions. Syd weaved across the dance floor, alcohol and exhaustion making his brain bob like a Ping-Pong ball in an oil slick. As he reached the mouth of the hallway he turned, suddenly hit with the urge to thank Jules again. For being there. For being a friend.

"Hey, Jules . . ." he began.

But Jules was already gone.

JULES'S TEETH WERE chattering by the time he reached his car, a big black Chrysler New Yorker parked nose-in near the southeast corner of the building. Syd had once remarked that riding with Jules could turn a trip to the 7-Eleven into a near-religious experience; it was like floating down the road with your favorite band wailing in the back.

And it was true: while Jules was nothing if not iconoclastic in his tastes—living very simply on the spartan first floor of a converted Victorian manse on the outskirts of town—his road tastes were nothing short of regal. The Chrysler was big and square and imposing, a rolling slab of unabashed gas-guzzling Detroit iron, fifteen years old, immaculately maintained.

The interior was a Ricardo Montalban wet dream of rich caramel-colored leather, overstuffed and opulent. The sound system was an Alpine custom installation—complete with a remote-controlled multidisc CD changer, bi-amped crossovers, and subwoofers under the seats—and it had set him back over two grand.

Money well spent, Jules always thought. He didn't care a hell of a lot about real estate or furniture or the other anchoring accoutrements of civilization. His home was clean, and comfortable, but apart from his music collection it was clear that it was but a stopover point on the way to something better. Once upon a time he'd actually made an overture to permanence, had some posters from the Monterey Jazz Festival mounted in matte black frames. They were still leaning against the dining room wall, awaiting a decision as to where to drive the nails. Such was his nesting instinct.

The road was another story. He'd bought the car some five years ago, as a reminder to himself that one day he would hit it again, just take off for parts unknown, carrying nothing more than the song in his heart and his love of the blues, and whatever worldly goods would neatly pack into the Chrysler's cavernous trunk. The car itself became a kind of rolling icon to his freedom, and the mere sight of it never failed to cheer him.

One day, he thought. *One day I will.*

Provided, of course, I don't freeze to death tonight, he amended. It was fucking cold out here, the temperature easily in the twenties. He fished his keys out of his pocket, grappled with the little black remote dangling off the key ring. He punched the disarm button, waited for the chirp.

Nothing happened.

What? he thought, his hackles instantly up as his eyes searched for broken glass or gutted dash. Everything was intact. He remembered the cardinal rule of troubleshooting, which he'd come up with after watching two guitar players stall a gig for twenty minutes and drive the roadies crazy because they weren't getting power to their amps, only to discover that they'd unwittingly plugged into each other's access jacks.

Always check the stupid shit first.

Jules flipped the remote over. The battery had fallen out.

"*Shit,*" he sighed. He reached into his jacket pocket. The battery was there, along with the little plastic cover panel. Shivering, he fumbled the pieces together, pushed the button. The disarm signal chirped obediently, automatically unlocking the doors in the process.

Jules jumped in and cranked it up; the big V-8 rumbled to life. He flipped on the defrosters, waited for it to start warming before stepping out again. He stood, turned to shut the door . . .

. . . and that was when he saw the reflection in the driver's side window, coming up from behind so fast that he barely had time to turn before it slammed him into the door panel, breaking his arm and three ribs just from the force of impact. Jules thought to cry out to Syd, but there was no time, no time at all. Slavering jaws fastened on his throat, cutting off his screams before he had a chance: severing his larynx even as they slashed his jugular and carotids, sending hot red rain to paint the side of the car.

The rest was over in a matter of seconds.

But it seemed to take forever.

SYD FELT SICK as he flushed the urinal: a queasy-hot churning in the pit of his stomach that spread through his chest to his limbs, started his extremities to tingling. Vertigo spiked him in the temples, sent a dull clang echoing through his brain, and as he leaned forward till his forehead grazed the cool, graffiti-laden tile, he felt like he might just pass out.

"Whoa," Syd mumbled, fought to remain lucid and standing. He pulled back, forced himself to focus on the wall, the jittery scribblings that graced its surface. Some disgruntled customer had done a little magic marker mayhem, a crude hairy phallus plunging toward a garish caricature that looked like an Easter Island icon with teeth. The words stopped moving, registered in his brain.

THIS PLACE SUCKS. BITE ME WHERE I PEE.

"Asshole," he grumbled, turned away. Who wrote that? Behind him, water swooshed and gurgled, releasing the medicinal waft of urinal cakes and recycled beer. The plumbing burbled and belched obscenely as he moaned and reached for the door.

His head cleared somewhat as he escaped the claustrophobic confines of the bathroom. He took a few steps, felt the buzz recede into the background. Still drunker than shit, but at least he wasn't gonna fall over. *I'll be okay,* he thought. *I'll be fine.*

Let's just get the fuck out of here.

"Hey, Jules," he started as he entered the dance floor, "did you see what some asshole wrote—"

He stopped, looked around. The bar was empty.

Strange, he thought. He could make out the faint subsonic rumble of a motor running outside, wondered why Jules hadn't come back in to shut things down. Syd crossed the room, heading for the front door. As he did he realized that the place felt suddenly ominous around him, as if he were somehow attuned to the residual vibe of everyone who had ever been there. It felt like everything else in his life: weirdly alien, suddenly soured. As Syd laid his hands on the door handle he wondered what was happening to him, and if he would ever feel the same about any of it again.

Syd pushed the door open.

And stepped outside.

THE DOOR SHUT behind him, locking him out. Syd squinted, scanned the lot. It was desolate, devoid of life. Two cars were left, demarcating an area that could hold two hundred. Syd's Mustang was off to the right, some three rows back. The departure of the other vehicles had left it alone, giving it a strangely abandoned quality. Jules's big boat was to the left, toward the far end of the building. As Syd veered toward it he could see wisps of exhaust curling from the tailpipe. But no Jules.

So where the hell did he go?

Syd cursed himself for not thinking about the door, propping it ajar. There was nothing else to do now.

"Jules?" he half-whispered, immediately thought *why are you keeping your voice down, stupid?*

"YO, JULES!"

No answer. His cry was swallowed up by the empty lot.

As he moved closer to Jules's car he saw that there was a patch of gravel steaming by the driver's door. It looked like Jules had spilled some coffee, or taken a leak. Neither theory made any sense. Another smear graced the door panel, thick as paint. Syd reached out, touched a finger to it.

And his heart froze.

"Oh, fuck," he gasped. "Oh, fuck." The world went fun-house wobbly around him. From the darkness there came a moist cracking noise. Syd looked up with eyes wide as pie plates.

Something was moving in the shadows on the other side of the car. His head spun, consciousness pinwheeling across the inside of his skull, and for one brief disorienting moment he thought it was a very large dog hunkered over a ripped-open garbage bag. Then the thing in the shadows reared up and he saw that it wasn't a dog at all.

And the garbage bag had *legs*. . . .

Oh god. Syd doubled over, puked right there on the spot: hacking and retching up a vile spew of bile. It splattered on the ground, mixed with the blood pooling there. When he opened his eyes again he saw that the creature had risen, was standing crookedly. It was a huge malformed silhouette, easily seven feet tall. Its eyes burned like molten slag. It looked at him and made a very bad animal sound: low and menacing, strangely pleased. Its lips curled back, flashes of light glinting off its teeth.

And suddenly everything Syd knew about keeping cool and not showing fear was bullshit, rendered worse than useless as his legs started moving all by themselves. Running. Running.

Behind him, a fearsome howl rose up.

Syd ran, the beast hot behind him, its loping stride overtaking his own desperate retreat. His car was thirty million miles away, his car was parked in a distant galaxy. And the thing behind him was gaining. Syd's survival instinct kicked in, hurtling him forward . . .

. . . and then he was there, slamming into the passenger side of his car a heartbeat before the shadow-thing caught up to him. Somehow his keys found the lock, his hands

pried open the door. He dove across the interior and pulled
the door shut a split second before the beast smacked into
the side. The passenger side window cracked and starred.
Syd jammed his key into the ignition. The engine shuddered and groaned.

"MOTHERFUCKER!!" he shouted. "GO GO GO!!"

A great shadow loomed outside the shattered glass.
The engine caught, rumbled to life. Syd jammed his foot
to the gas, felt it roar in response. The door clattered,
started to open. Syd threw the shifter into gear, popped the
clutch.

The Mustang's rear wheels spun, sent up a roaring
granite spray. Syd wrenched the steering wheel to the left,
sent the car into a hard three-sixty across the barren space.
The door clicked shut. The thing held on. Syd seesawed
the wheel back, whipping the car so hard to the right that
he thought he would roll it as he did a vicious figure eight.

Somewhere coming out of the second turn the creature
lost its grip, went sailing off into space. Syd didn't see it
land. He didn't need to. The road was directly before him.
He had his shot.

He wouldn't get another.

Gunning it for all it was worth, Syd aimed for the entrance. The Mustang slalomed and slid, picking up speed.
By the time he cleared the entrance he was doing fifty, and
he went screaming onto the road without letting up or
looking back. If anyone had been coming in either direction he'd have been hamburger.

But luck was with him. It was late. The road was
empty. The Mustang made the turn, missing the guardrail
with inches to spare. Syd straightened out and floored it,
the speedometer arcing past sixty, seventy. The Chameleon's sign disappeared in a cloud of dust and smoking
rubber.

Syd drove and drove: going nowhere but *away*, his
body shaking, his thoughts slam-dancing between shock
and shrieking terror. The straight road gave way to twisting mountain curves. Syd's hands white-knuckled the
wheel as his mind rebelled, tried to strike deals with the

unreal. This couldn't be happening. This couldn't be denied. The details were too clear: burned into his gray matter, stark and garish in his mind's eye. The steaming blood.
The lifeless form strewn across the cold ground.

The thing that hovered above it . . .

From behind, the glare of hi-beams and flickering
light. It was Jules's sedan, jerking and weaving as it hurtled forward, eating up the distance between them. Syd
screamed, punched it again. The speedometer climbed,
leveled off at eighty. The road snaked out treacherously
before him. The sedan's headlights disappeared momentarily as he hooked around the next bend.

But by the time he went over the last rise that marked
the beginning of the downgrade the Chrysler had caught
up, its big angular bumper riding up his ass as they roared
down the road. It nudged him, a two-ton kiss that
crunched metal to metal and crumpled his flimsy rear end.
The Mustang screeched and skidded; Syd jerked and
screamed again, almost lost control. He was drunk and
scared shitless. He was losing his mind.

A sign flashed yellow, illuminated by the headlights as
it whipped by. NO PASSING. DANGEROUS CURVES AHEAD. The
Chrysler crossed out and into the oncoming lane. As it did
Syd heard the stereo, maxxed and blasting, some wild-ass
Stevie Ray sonic assault so loud it penetrated the slipstream, the roar of the dueling engines. The sedan pulled
abreast of him.

Syd glanced over, blood thudding madly in his head.

The dome light was flickering, so he couldn't clearly
see the interior. But something very large was behind the
wheel, and a very dead Jules was riding shotgun: his face
pulped and mangled, his head puppeteered by the monster
beside him. His throat was completely gone, from Adam's
apple to spinal column. Syd watched in horror as Jules's
face twisted around, smacked and slid against the glass.
His dead friend stared blindly at him, his features smushed
and distorted.

Then the monster flicked its wrist.

And Syd lost it completely.

Jules's face was still stuck to the glass: skin sloughing off his skull like a cheap Halloween mask as his body slumped. The flesh hovered on the window for a moment before sliding away, leaving a gore-streaked smear in its wake.

The road hooked to the left. The thing behind the wheel accelerated, veering back across the double yellow line.

It smacked into him, crushing the left front quarterpanel as it tried to force him off the road. Syd felt the Mustang pitch to the right, saw sparks fly as the guardrail connected like a can opener, peeling sheet metal into jagged, razored ribbons. The blackness beyond the edge of the road yawned beside him.

Syd countersteered, throwing his weight into it. The Mustang groaned and pushed off the rail, tires screeching as it bit back into the lane. The Chrysler lurched and surged, swerving away as Syd cursed and downshifted, dropping back one car length back as the Chrysler rocketed ahead.

He was behind it now, the big black sedan weaving back and forth as they slid through the next set of turns. The Chrysler cut to the right; Syd hit the gas and steered left, trying to go around it. The road hooked and swooped. The Mustang's engine screamed as he took to the outside lane, roared past his tormentor . . .

. . . and that was when the big sedan came careening back, swatting into him at seventy miles an hour. Syd felt his right rear end buckle as the tire disintegrated, throwing smoke and chunks of rubber all over the highway. The wheel jerked out of his hands and he lost control completely: the Mustang fishtailing, g-force and momentum carrying him clear across the road and into the concrete retaining wall on the other side.

There was a grinding trash-compactor roar, a white-hot blast of pain as the driver's side door buckled and caved in on him and a lacerating shower of glass swarmed like hornets in the air. Syd's mind dislocated, felt reality go molten, elastic. The car was still moving, wholly of its own volition. The sound was deafening. The car was still moving.

The last thing he saw was an enormous tree, rushing madly toward him.

Then, impact.

And blackness.

THE CHRYSLER SLOWED to a stop, some two hundred yards down the road. Vic turned the volume down and hit the power-window button. He listened for the sound of fire, or maybe a nice explosion.

But aside from the tortured rumble of the sedan's engine, all was quiet. He'd lost sight of the Mustang shortly after it hit the retaining wall. The curve obscured the rest. He put the car into reverse, began backing up. He'd gone maybe three or four hundred feet when he saw a wheel, upright and wobbling as it rolled all on its lonesome down the darkened road. Another fifty feet back, and the wreck came into view.

The Mustang had wrapped around a gnarled old oak. The front end was crushed from bumper to windshield, the rest of the car mashed like an old beer can.

Vic smiled. He could see steam wafting up, hear the groan of metal settling. He watched for a minute, didn't hear anything else. He'd kept his promise, all right. Just like he said he would.

Never laid a hand on 'im, he thought, and began to chuckle.

And the chuckle became a laugh, the laugh a full-scale belly-buster. He looked up, saw the waning moon, dolefully observant. She was the perfect lover, he mused. She kept her opinions to herself. This time when the urge to bay rose up inside, Vic gleefully gave in.

Then he turned the stereo way up high. Put the car into drive.

And together, they howled off into the night.

PART TWO

Jane

PART TWO

EIGHTEEN MONTHS LATER

26

AH, HOW THE mighty had fallen.

The name on the sign hanging over the door was Big Dan's Deadbeat Bar & Grill; and whether that was simply truth in advertising or actual self-fulfilling prophecy, the end result was the same.

It didn't matter that it wasn't the actual name of the bar—which was Danny D.'s, for anybody who cared. Once upon a time, some whiz kid had scrawled the words on the flap off a case of Gennie Cream Ale, found a stray nail poking halfway out above the door. The rest was not so much history as irony, or entropy. Dan didn't much care for the sign, but he couldn't be bothered to climb up there and take it down. And neither could anyone else.

Which pretty much summed it up. The bar wasn't just a dump; it was a black hole. And moreover, a virtual loser magnet, ground zero for bottom feeders, with a rich redneck history of shootings and stabbings to go with its watered-down booze and lobotomized IQs. It had the kind of desperate dog kennel vibe you made cruel jokes about when your life was on track, but found yourself naturally gravitating toward when that same life horribly disassembled.

Syd had spent a good bit of the last eighteen months there. It somehow spoke to his condition.

Ever since the crash and burn.

The door opened without warning. Another loser, coming through. Syd winced against the light, the dark shape it framed. He couldn't see who it was, nor imagine that it mattered. It was three o'clock in the afternoon. Syd was on his seventh beer. On the outside, yet another Pennsylvania spring had sprung: a bright, shiny, sun-spackled chlorophyll explosion, draping the world in its first blush of green.

He knew it was beautiful, and that it should be inspiring; but, frankly, at this point, it just gave him a headache. The sun was too bright, and what it revealed was too damaged. The world didn't bear up to such close scrutiny. The shadows made a lot more sense.

Just as it was easier, in the long run, to bury the truth. . . .

The door shut. Syd blinked back the little floating dots, let his gaze flicker across the room. There was Doris the troll, on her perch by the corner, with her bottle of Pabst and all those hairs in her chin. There was Big Dan himself, a blubbery mountain of caked sweat and whiskey-soaked lard. A couple of big-mouthed Blutos—Syd had nicknamed them Bo Hunk and Dick Weed—slowly pissed each other off as they argued last night's pre-season game. Maybe a half-dozen others, mostly regulars, were scattered around the bar. He didn't know their real names, didn't want to; it was easier to make up his own.

The guy who'd just come in was small and balding. It took Syd's eyes a moment to completely readjust, make the face come clear. In fact, it wasn't until the little guy stopped and said, "Hey, man. How ya doin'?" that Syd realized who it was.

And by then, of course, it was far too late.

Oh, christ, he thought. Staring at the legendary figure

before him. There was no time to do anything but react. His grimace and shrug were completely automatic.

"I know," said Marc Pankowski, "exactly what you mean."

For a moment, they exchanged what Syd knew was meant to be meaningful eye contact. It was hard not to laugh, but the dread in his stomach went a long way toward counterbalancing his reaction. Syd wasn't sure if Marc could read him, because Marc looked away and then kept going down the bar.

But the horrible thing was that, under the circumstances, maybe Marc had a point.

I know exactly what you mean. It suggested a commonality of experience, a new link forged of understanding in the brotherhood of man. *I know exactly what you mean*. Was it true? God help him: in some ways, yes. They had both flamed out and lived to smell the ashes. They had both been drunk when they did it, and had pretty much stayed that way ever since. They had both become monsters, then turned to shit. So, yeah, there were a couple of similarities.

Only I never took anyone out with me, Syd thought.

But that wasn't exactly true.

Suddenly, Syd was staring at his hands and the fifty-cent draft on the bar before him. The TV behind the bar was tuned to "The Love Connection." Chuck Hillary—or Willary, or whatever—was smugly leering. He tried to make himself watch, couldn't. It was just too fucking grim. There was nothing here to feed his soul, nothing here to give him solace.

When the first tear welled up, he was almost surprised. It had been so long since he'd even cared.

Syd picked up the beer and drained it, wiped his cheek as an afterthought. Then he motioned wordlessly to Dan for another. It was still very difficult to think about Jules, even after all this time. What was worse: once he'd started, it was impossible to stop. The fact that he'd never told a living soul just compounded the matter, upped the ante on his shame.

When the cops had shown up at the scene, he was fucked up and far from home, with a concussion, six cracked ribs, and his left arm and leg broken in seven places. Syd was pinned beneath the steering column. It took two hours, an extra EMS team and the Jaws of Life to finally free him from the wreckage, and the whole time he was fading in and out of resolution: from teeth-chattering shock to utter black and back again. He was babbling, too, about chases and bodies and mysterious monsters trying to run him off the road.

The police listened to every word he said, and didn't believe a bit of it. Chief Hoser, in particular, shook his head dismissively, his stern, gaunt features conveying the essential message: I always knew you'd turn to shit.

In any event, all of their most pressing questions were answered by his Breathalyzer test. Never mind the crash, they said: his blood-alcohol level alone was enough to have killed him.

It wasn't until Jules turned up missing, and the blood in the parking lot was found, that they seriously started asking questions. But by then, Syd had sobered up and had time to think. Think about the thing that had chased and destroyed him. Integrate and assess the astonishing facts of his condition, the essential unbelievability of his experience.

Compounding his predicament was the fact that the car that Nora left parked outside his apartment turned out to be registered to a thirty-two-year-old white male by the name of James Whalen, late of Shreveport, La. James had been missing some seven months now. The police were real *curious about that little development.* Well, you see, officer, my friend Jules got killed by a werewolf, the same one that ran me off the road. It all happened because I fucked its girlfriend, who just happened to be *another* werewolf, probably the one who did your boy down in L'weeziana. Oh, yeah, and in the process *I* got turned into one, too. Swear to Christ.

So much for the truth, the whole truth, and nothing but the truth.

In the end the only way to deal with it was to swear complete ignorance: of what had happened to Jules, of what had happened to Nora, of absolutely everything. Nora's things were confiscated, but like the car, they yielded no clues, not even a fingerprint. Chief Hoser dragged Syd in for questioning yet again, this time with detectives and State Police in the room, and asked him why he thought that might be.

Syd could only shrug.

In the end he got a lot of hard looks and intimidating questioning that went nowhere; Jules's case was left open, but past a certain point they just stopped looking.

Of course, the rumor mill took it through every conceivable mutation, mostly centering on Jules's pent-up wanderlust and the mysterious redhead. Syd kept his mouth shut and his head down; he had other problems to worry about.

Eventually he went to court for reckless driving, driving under the influence, and reckless endangerment; he pled guilty and got socked with a two-thousand-dollar fine, eight weeks on the D.W.I. program plus four months of A.A. and personal counseling, and a year's suspension of his driver's license.

All of which mattered not in the slightest, being that he had no car to drive, having wrapped his wheels around a tree. And he had no money to buy one with, because he'd just quit his job. Bobo was predictably compassionate; after their little encounter, this was not a surprise. But it meant no disability, no workmen's comp, no nothing.

He had managed to hold on to the cheesy hospitalization plan attached to his long-beleaguered Visa card; it constituted the sole bright light on his medical horizon. It had, at least, covered a chunk of his physical therapy.

He healed incredibly fast, of course.

Surprising everyone but himself . . .

Suddenly, Dan appeared with another glass of suds, scooping four bits out of Syd's loose change. Syd pulled back to the present, looked at Marc Pankowski, who had picked out a table near the back. Marc smiled at Syd. Syd looked away quickly, wondered what *Marc's* excuse was for surviving all those crashes.

It had occurred to Syd that maybe he wasn't the only amped-up critter in Monville. If Marc's inner nature did reveal itself, what would he be? A were-weasel, maybe? A were-slug?

Syd felt the pain resurging, downed another insulating gulp of beer. Nowadays, at least, his senses were so dulled by ritual sedation that he could no longer be trusted to pick one out of the crowd.

But one thing seemed certain: there were very few wolves running loose in the wild. He felt pretty sure he was the only one in town, broken or otherwise. Most people were herbivores at heart: unrealized were-cows, sheep, and pigs. If they reached in far enough to tap their true natures, you could probably sneak up and tip them in their sleep.

Syd couldn't worry about them at this point. For the last year and a half, he'd been mostly concerned with how to keep his own animal down. . . .

WHEN THE FIRST full moon came, he hadn't known what to expect. Either he was a monster, or he was insane, or both. Not exactly a prime set of options.

Syd had spent the day alone and afraid, pacing crippled through the apartment that now functioned as his cage. It was just prior to his eviction, early on in his physical therapy, and absolutely everything hurt: from the bodily damage he'd sustained in the crash to the permanent loss of the woman he loved.

Of the two, the pain with Nora's name on it was by far the worst. The physical damage would heal, at least; the emotional destruction was beyond salvation. At first he thought the shock of her absence alone would kill him; it was impossible to sleep or eat or even think clearly.

In the end Syd had resorted to a sort of traumatic amputation of the soul, cauterizing the wound at every point where they'd connected, focusing every ounce of will he

could muster on eradicating all memory of her. It left him
dead inside, but at least he could sleep at night.

He was no longer afraid of his dreams: in the aftermath of the accident his sleep was black, devoid of images. As if a concrete lid had slammed down on his
subconscious: shutting off the dialogue, refusing all contact.

But that didn't mean that it didn't want out. . . .

As the full moon neared he grew more restless. He'd
been feeling antsy for days, fending off the now-familiar
rushes of power that came with increasing frequency. They
were tied to his anger, most clearly; but day by day, they
were coming on stronger. He felt like the guy in *American
Werewolf in London,* just before the big transformation
scene. Only there was nothing funny about this. Not a single goddamned thing. As he paced he fingered his gun,
wondering whether or not he should just stick the barrel in
his mouth and get it over with.

More than once, he came close: hefting the blue-black
steel in his hands, imagining the click and the bang, the
deafening sensation of his skull exploding and spraying
the back wall with brains and bone and red red rain, the
subsequent headlong hurtle into . . . what? The void?
Some mercifully blank oblivion? How could he know that
would even end it? What if this thing went deeper, was
somehow embedded not just in his flesh, but in his *soul*?
There was no guarantee that this would all be over, or that
wherever he ended up would be one bit better than this.

In the end, his questions remained unanswered, rendered academic by the simple fact that he just couldn't do
it. No matter how much he hurt. No matter how bad it got.
The part of him that still loved life wouldn't let him, and
it was ultimately stronger than he was.

Which effectively left him right back where he'd
started.

All day, he had dreaded the sun's descent.

When it finally came, so did the Change . . .

*. . . and he saw enough in those first moments to know
that it had not been a hallucination. For hours he stood*

naked before the mirror in his bedroom: his leg shackled to the steam radiator, sweat rolling off of him in waves. He tried to stay focused on the reflection of his eyes. His eyes were his sole anchor point, the only things that seemed stable in a universe gone mad: even dilated and bugging with fear, they were the key. He fixed and focused on them as the Change moved underneath his skin like a school of minnows. Swarming. Crazed. His muscles and tendons shifting and straining, fighting at their accepted boundaries.

His face tensed and contorted, a manic parade of primal impulse pushing up from his subconscious. His hands clenched and clawed, came up to feel the rupturing flesh of his torso, his neck, his arms and legs and back.

The whole time he told himself: he knew who he was, knew what he was. He was not a monster. He would not become a monster. He would not give in.

He would not let it out.

The rushes intensified, became pain. The pain blossomed into agony. And Syd began to scream, his will locked in mortal combat with the ravening power inside. And his will said NO! to the rushes that pummeled his body, said NO! to the howling that wailed in his brain. He watched them surge, fall back, resurge and counterattack.

For twelve hours, he wrestled the monster within.

But when dawn came, and he realized that he didn't *have* to Change—that it was still, ultimately, something he could control—he no longer felt like the Lawrence Talbot character in a third-rate Universal Pictures sendup, bemoaning dat horrible wolfman curse what had been visited upon him. This wasn't the movies, and there were some fundamental differences. What, exactly, those differences *were* was something he determined to figure out.

And thus Syd entered his In-Search-of-the-Magical-Werewolf-Within phase: a phase that carried him through the spring and summer, clear into the following fall. Most of that time was spent based out of Tommy's basement rec room, which was where he gratefully crashed when his eviction came through. He didn't have a job, couldn't bring himself to try and find one. He still had his stereo and album/CD collection, though he couldn't bring himself to listen to the music anymore. When Syd insisted, Tommy reluctantly took it in trade.

During that time, Syd studied everything he could get his hands on. By day he limped down to the Monville Public Library or hitched up to Pittsburgh to haunt book-stores and pore over werewolf stories, from Native American wolf rituals to northern European legends to classical Greek and Roman myths and on, as far back as ancient Syria.

Some were benevolent; most, malign. For every Rom-ulus and Remus-style recounting of feral children raised by loving mother wolves or beneficent lupine-spirits aid-ing a Pawnee hunting party, there were dozens of darker tales. In Aristotle's *Historia Animalium* and Pliny's *Historia Naturalis*, in the *Physiologus* or Olaus Magnus's *History of the Goths, Swedes and Vandals* nightmares abounded: of werewolves that fed on human flesh, were-wolves that raided villages and feasted on the succulent meat of babes, werewolves that gathered together for drinking bouts and raided the wine cellars of the devout on Christmas Eve. Navaho werewolves raided graveyards to mutilate the corpses of the dead; in White Russia, they struck men dumb with their gaze and caused deformed children to be born of women who crossed their tracks.

In medieval lore, it was even worse. Haunted by the Plague, molded by the Church, and enforced by the Inqui-sition, the hysteria burgeoned to new heights of insanity: wolves were nothing short of the Devil's hounds, agents of debauchery and sacrilege, symbols of everything vile and depraved in the soul of man. Stoked by the dictates of the *Malleus Malefaricum*, thousands were accused of were-wolvery at the slightest provocation, convicted on the flimsiest of evidence, tortured to grisly confession and burned at the stake. The legends even migrated to America with the settlers, became the foundational basis for the great wolf purges of the nineteenth and twentieth centu-ries, where the systematic slaughter of tens, even hundreds of millions of animals, drove them to the brink of extinction. What Nora had said came back to haunt him.

Theriophobia. Fear of the wild thing inside.

Having read himself to death each day, Syd would hobble over to Blockbuster Video, then head home, tapes in hand, to watch every movie that even alluded to his condition. From *Wolfen* to *Werewolf of London* to *The Howling* parts one through one million, from *Altered States* to *Teen Wolf* to Cronenberg's remake of *The Fly*, Syd religiously sifted through the garish and distorted Hollywood hokum for some grain of usable truth.

But did it give him the answers he needed? Not really. Every once in a while, he'd stumble on an interesting scrap, but it was obvious that most of the available information was a mishmash of old wives' tales, folklore, or out-and-out lies.

After a while, even thinking about it made the pain in his head throb mercilessly, like a never-ending migraine from hell. And as his frustration mounted, one thing became clear: he had a lot more to fear from his worsening temper than he did from any stage of the moon or nocturnal nightmare.

It could well up at any moment. Whatever peace he found in the knowledge that he need no longer live in fear of a particular time of the month or getting a good night's sleep was instantly mitigated by the understanding that, at any moment, he might hit some emotional trip wire and go off.

It was like walking a tightrope twenty-four hours a day. And he found, to his dismay, that the longer he spent in that state, the less it took to set him off. A harsh word. A busy signal. A bum hitting him up for change.

One morning when Tommy's new girlfriend Annette had chastised him for some inconsequential domestic crisis—leaving the toilet seat up or squeezing the toothpaste tube in the middle, or some such triviality—Syd had very nearly lost it.

He flipped out, ranted and raved, and totally terrorized her for over an hour, ended up breaking a kitchen chair into kindling with his bare hands before storming out screaming. It was all he could do to not rip her throat out.

He came back later, apologizing profusely, and confessed that he couldn't remember exactly what she'd said that had set him off. He chalked it up to stress, made nice in the worst way, and tiptoed around her for weeks. Annette eventually forgave him, but the damage was done. From that moment on, she was genuinely scared of him. And Tommy never looked at Syd the same way again.

It was at that point that suicide started to seem like a viable alternative.

But what could kill him? He had no idea. Evidently not the same things that, for example, went into totaling cars. Or maybe he'd just been lucky; he really didn't have a clue. He wasn't particularly into the idea of hanging himself or sticking a gun in his mouth just to find out.

At one point he'd wandered into a jewelry shop, asked the perplexed shop owner if he had any silver bullets on hand. The guy looked at Syd like he was crazy, which wasn't far off the mark. Syd found himself helplessly, morbidly staring at the glittering bits of metal that lined the cases. *Can that kill me?* he wondered, his hand reaching out like a tentative child's first encounter with flame.

Nothing happened, of course. It was kind of like learning that your mom's spine wouldn't actually fracture if you stepped on a crack, or that golf balls weren't actually filled with a powerful explosive.

And he didn't have no pentagram on the palm of his hand, neither.

So much for Hollywood.

Once his search had exhausted every possible lead, slammed up against every conceivable wall, his mind simply shut down. Syd became zombielike, simultaneously distracted and stupefied, like he was perpetually tuned to a station that was off the air. By that time his welcome at *Casa Kramer* was pretty effectively worn out, and Tommy had asked Syd to leave. He did so without complaint.

The next stop was a room at the Y, where he stayed afloat doing odd jobs for Manpower and other menial employment agencies. As bad as the economy was, there was always grunt work for garbagemen, moving men, general unskilled labor. It kept him marginally solvent, even as it reinforced his faltering self-image. He worked as much as he could, never said a word to anyone, and wandered the streets and slept in his spare time. He never went into the woods anymore, eschewing even parks for fear of waking the sleeping beast. Syd hid in a world of concrete and shadow. Blocking his memories. Shut off from his dreams.

Then one night he wandered into Big Danny's Deadbeat Bar & Grill. It was conveniently right around the corner, and it gave him everything he needed, including a surprisingly effective recipe for keeping things submerged. It called for lots of beer, but no hard liquor; a mind kept distracted, sedated, and numb; people he couldn't care less about; and absolutely zero point zero romance.

He'd found that beer worked best, as a control mechanism: carefully regulating the dosage of numb. Somewhere between nine and fifteen cold ones, he slipped into the dead zone. Any more than that, and it was anyone's guess. That was why Nora had always insisted upon Comfort: it took you over so fast, you never knew what hit you.

Numb was the ticket: freed of both his monster and his rational mind, it made circular thinking easier, and put him on an even intellectual keel with the rest of Big Danny's highbrow clientele. After a while, even his temper subsided: these people were simply too stupid to argue with.

As for sexual abstinence, it was no longer a problem. The kind of females who frequented the bar were about as appealing as cheese mold. And by now, he was utterly terrified of women. Their effect *on* him. His reaction *to* them. Their power *over* him.

Nora had been his final lesson.

He had never gone back to Chameleon's again.

BUT NOW—SITTING here with his eighth glass of Pabst, surrounded by burnouts and hopped-up human dregs—Syd felt the first stirrings of a shift within him, like a tiny switch flicking at the back of his brain. Right in the vicinity of that long-forgotten itch.

Enough, it seemed to be saying.

Enough ...

And that was when he felt the presence, stalking him from behind. The one and only Marc Pankowski, here to feed on his malaise. Syd had almost forgotten how evil he was: what a soul scavenger, what a parasite of sorrow. The simple fact that Marc was stalking him let him know how far he'd fallen, how totally screwed-up and vulnerable he must appear from the outside; and that was the most terrifying realization of all.

At that moment, his dread resurged. But with it, for the first time in ages, *conviction*. Suddenly, he was remembering something that Jules had said, way the hell back in the post-Karen, pre-Nora days. A vintage piece of Jules-style wisdom, replaying once again behind his eyes. It was, quite naturally, on the subject of depression; and Syd couldn't help but wonder why he'd forgotten it so long.

Maybe it had just been waiting for the right moment to remind him.

Maybe that moment had finally come.

When the blues hit you bad, Jules had said, *sometimes you've just got to roll with 'em, just let life run its course. And if it knocks you down so hard that you can't get up, then sometimes you've just got to lay there and let it kick you around for a while. That's the way of the world, my man. Anybody who knows will understand.*

But a lot of times, you'll wake up one day to find that the blues have wandered off to greener pastures, found some other fool to kick around; and that in fact, you've just been laying there kicking yourself *for God only knows how long.*

At that point, it's probably time to get up. Dust yourself off. And get on with your life.

Eighteen months, he realized now, was an adequate period of mourning: for Jules, for Nora, for the life that might have been. He did nothing to honor their memory

by hiding in this hole: drinking himself stupid, slowly
wasting away.

A year and a half.

Maybe that was actually long enough.

Then Syd looked up, and Marc Pankowski was there:
Depression Incarnate, etched in living weasel-flesh. Suddenly, Syd was actually almost happy to see him.

It wasn't every day you got to face down your demons.

Now if we were at Chameleon's, Syd found himself
thinking, *it would probably be time for the ol' "Band
Gambit." He'd try to guess what I thought of the tunes,
feed me back precisely what I wanted to hear.* The mere
act of thinking blew dust off Syd's brain. He felt himself
starting to smile.

But if there's no music playing, he mused, *what will
Marc try to use?* Syd did a quick mental inventory. Good
ol' Messrs. Hunk and Weed were still having angry words,
at the far end of the bar; that might be good for a Pirates
reference. Beyond that, Syd got a little fuzzy. *This bar is
smokin'? This dive really sucks?*

It was hard to imagine. Marc took a seat beside him, his
mouth already beginning to open. Syd braced himself, did a
little psychic drumroll. It was the moment of truth.

"I hate the fucking 'Love Connection,' " Marc said.

Syd laughed, a single hard bark of absurd comprehension.

It was all so very casual: as if they were good friends,
or the most perfect of strangers. Marc had that way of *insinuating* himself: a remarkable confidence that came from
being ahead of the game because he was making it up on
the spot.

Syd said nothing, let him play his hand.

Marc reached into his jacket pocket, pulled out a pack
of smokes, offered one to Syd. Marlboro Lights. Syd de-
clined. "You didn't quit smoking," Marc said. It was
nearly a question. To which Syd pulled out his pack of unfiltered Camels. Marc smiled, showing little yellow teeth.
"I was gonna say. You always have a cigarette in your
hand."

Marc paused to light one up, Syd watched him, waited. If Marc noticed Syd's watchfulness, he gave nothing away. He was used to fielding attitude. It was part of his job description.

On the tube, a vacuous blonde Malibu Barbie described the intimate details of her "love connection" with the grinning goob to her left. Marc grimaced and shook his head, as if the sight physically pained him. "Jesus God," he moaned. "Look at the rack on that bitch. Can you imagine getting your hands on something like that?"

Syd looked at the blonde, did the inevitable comparison. Now it was Syd's turn to look physically pained.

"Oh, man, I'm sorry." Marc really looked it, too. Very slick. It was a measure of how good he was that he'd cut straight to the core of Syd's pain in less than thirty seconds. "Oh, shit. You're still thinking about her, huh? I didn't know, man. I really didn't. I'm sorry."

And it wasn't just the manipulation Syd minded— wasn't just the fact that the buttons were still there to be pushed. It was the *presumption* of intimacy: the bogus, unclean transition from stories passed on the rumor mill to deeply shared personal experience. He knew that Marc had never even *seen* Nora, much less watched them together. That Marc should feel free to yank on those chains triggered something in him. Something he hadn't felt in a long long time.

It was clear that Marc saw it; his big show of contrition kicked into overdrive. "Hey, whoa, man. Lemme buy you a drink," he said at once, didn't even wait for Syd to respond. "Danny! Hey, Danny! Set up my buddy here!"

Syd watched the bartender lumber toward him, fought down the urge to laugh. He didn't want a beer off this guy. He didn't want another drink at all. What he wanted, more than anything, was just to get the hell out of this place. He felt, all at once, both unhinged and hyperclear, as if suddenly awakening from a dream. He looked around the bar, at all those bleary-eyed faces, and he thought *MY GOD WHAT AM I DOING HERE?*

And through it all burned the image of Nora: the

woman who had so undone his life and reduced him to
this. In that moment he wished: if only he could *take back*
those seconds, excise them strategically from his life—
from the moment she first stepped through the door and
her eyes found his face. And that sly smile beguiled him.

And she walked right up and said . . .

"Holy shit." Syd paused for a moment, stunned, while
a little light bulb went off over his head. "Holy *SHIT*."
Putting together a vision out of intuition and dime-store
magic.

"You know what?" he said, addressing Marc for the
first time. He clapped one hand on Marc's shoulder, and
Marc visibly contracted, as though flinching in advance.

But Syd only smiled. "I *would* like a drink, now that
ya mention it," he said, in deadly earnest. "But beer's not
what I need."

Then he turned to Danny and said, "Dan, muh man. I
need my brain back.

"Make me a Hemorrhaging Brain."

"Huh?" Big Dan said, utterly clueless. "Whuzzat?"

"That's what I thought you'd say," Syd replied, as the
last piece of the puzzle fell smack into place. He smiled as
he got up off his stool. "May I?"

The whole room went silent as Syd went around the
bar. Big Dan stared, too amazed to react. Syd, for his part,
was just as amazed that Dan even had the ingredients. It
was a good sign. As he pulled them out, whipped down a
glass, and started to pour, he realized that it felt *more* than
natural. It felt absolutely right.

He thought about Jules, and the road to redemption.

The brain came out perfect.

And Syd began to live again.

27

IT TOOK ABOUT ten weeks to ready himself. Syd had fallen into more than just psychological disrepair. The first law of bartending was *you gotta look good;* and right now, quite honestly, he looked anything but. He had a dumb-looking beard and an even dumber-looking beer gut, and he could pack two weeks' luggage into the bags under his eyes.

It was considerable damage. But not irreversible.

One step at a time was the way to go.

There was no small irony in Syd's selection of the phrase; his exposure to the grinding machineries of the State had not sold him on the earnestly lockstep programming of the Twelve Step hordes. He had no interest in becoming just another A.A. addict, sweet and well-intentioned though so many of them were. He'd been to enough meetings now to know of what he spoke. They were a tight-knit circle of folks who were *hanging on to hanging on:* strung out on mutual confession, circulating the bottomless pipe of shame. In that sense, A.A. was like a gateway drug to Jesus that they just kept passing around and around.

Syd understood the attraction, didn't fault them for their reliance upon it. It just didn't speak to him. Not to mention the fact that he had *other* problems to contend with that were best not shared with a group.

No, Syd's personal journey back from hell was by necessity a solitary one. But he did borrow from them their most important rule. The fundamental keystone of recovery.

One step at a time.

Syd's first step was to leave Danny D.'s, thank them for their hospitality, and never look back. It was one of the most painless procedures Syd had ever undergone. The next step was only eight trillion times harder: quitting drinking.

At first he'd balked at the concept. He'd always felt that, in a binge-or-cringe culture, moderation made more sense than abstinence *or* excess. And moderation was the *hardest:* both to achieve, and to sustain.

In the beginning he tried to weasel deals with himself. *Well, I'll just have* two *beers a night, except for the nights when I have* four. *And I won't start drinking until at least* nine *each night, except of course on those nights I start at* six. . . .

Ultimately he realized that he was only fooling himself; that moderation was great in theory, but that he had developed a very real problem—maybe not full-blown alcoholism yet, but well on the way. And that until he could muster the will to break his reliance upon alcohol on a daily basis, *to not need to have it in his life,* moderation was a joke.

He quit that day.

The next month was hell. But he did it, by sheer dint of will. In the process, he dropped twelve pounds, all of it bloat. And he broke the constant craving, the knee-jerk reflex that made him squirm in his seat every time a beer commercial came on. He felt stronger.

That strength made it easier to take the next step: starting—and sticking to—an exercise program: running, swimming, lifting weights, working his way up from fifty to three hundred sit-ups a day. There was plenty of stuff at the Y to work with, now that he was of a mind. As he acquired a taste for the pain of exertion he realized it was a pleasure to feel the intricate mechanism that was his body at work. The subtle play of muscle and sinew made him feel more human, helped to beat back other, darker memories. It was worth the effort.

It was still incredibly hard. But he did it religiously. And it got easier.

The next step was to pick up every bartending guide and mixological dictionary on the market. He studied and crammed and crammed and studied every nuance of bartending protocol and lore: comparing every recipe to his memory of Jules's; cross-referencing every suggested technique with the ones that he'd watched in action a thousand times.

He locked down the difference between Collins and Highball, Sour Rocks and Cordial, Sham Pilsner and Goblet. He learned that the difference between Seagram's 7 and Seagram's V.O. was the Canadian border and six-point-eight proof. He practiced slicing and arranging fruit till he had it down to an art.

Meanwhile, of course, he continued to work. He became a regular at Manpower and every other temp agency in town: taking any job, no matter how seemingly demeaning, finding the value in it. He worked steadily, slowly paid off his bills. The day he zeroed out his credit card he even splurged a little, bought himself a little Sony CD/cassette boombox. With cash. Otherwise, he lived on very little.

Frugal living allowed him to save. When a '68 Cougar showed up in the papers for three hundred dollars, Syd checked it out. His suspension was up; he had his license reinstated. His insurance premiums were brutal; he paid in full and on time, and didn't lose any sleep over it.

By the end of ten weeks, he had lost both his beard and the puffiness that had buried his cheekbones. His gut was tapered. His clothes fit for the first time in ages. His body felt strong, his mind alert. Except for the eyes, he looked five years younger.

As a bartender, he had everything he needed but experience.

Then, and only then, did he take the next step.

THE ROAD TO Chameleon's looked completely the same. It was almost as if that nightmare year-and-change had never happened. He didn't know why he felt so surprised; the world, of course, had kept right on going. It was only his life that had gone up in flames. His and Jules's.

And possibly Nora's, as well.

No, he told himself, quashing the spiking pang of memory. *Forget about her.* He couldn't allow himself to think about Nora; at least not anymore than he could help. *She's history, she's gone, and good riddance.* Eradicating her from his mind was excruciating but necessary, like scraping an infected wound clean. He blotted out all thought of her, told himself that if he never saw her again, it would be way too soon.

But it was hard, it was hard, to negotiate the turns where he'd watched his friend's face smack and slide against the glass. It was hard to keep driving and try to ignore the ruthless tug of memory, atrocity and rage.

It was important, at this point, to keep himself focused. That was all in the past. He was here for a reason. It would not do to derail.

But, God, did it ever make him want a drink.

It was slightly easier going on the straightaway, with the familiar sign in the narrowing distance. Nostalgia began to replace the harsher memories, whittle away at the pain. He started thinking about the people he was liable to see—Trent, Jane, Red, the regular crowd—and it took a little tension off the edge of his smile.

Most important, of course, was Randy Sanders: the owner of the bar, with whom Syd had set up this appointment. Randy always did the hiring and firing, even if he did leave the lion's share of responsibility to Jules—or whoever had taken his place. He was a good guy, and they'd always gotten along, though in reality they were no more than pleasant acquaintances. There were no illusions of loyalty or enduring friendship to bank on. At least not at this point.

At least not from Randy's side. Syd's agenda, on the other hand, rested almost entirely on those essential building blocks. He had loyalties to honor. Sins to atone for. And a friendship to redeem. Even if that redemption came after the fact.

Even if it was a matter of too little, too late.

Pulling into the parking lot, Syd felt his throat tighten and his stomach constrict. Jesus, he was nervous. He took a last drag off his Camel, snubbed the butt in the ashtray. He'd cut down a good bit since he'd started working out. But for all his overt healthifying, he still couldn't bring himself to quit, much less suck on a filtered cigarette. Might as well snap a nipple on a bottle of Bud, toss a condom over your pecker just to jack yourself off.

Syd caught himself automatically steering for his old parking spot, froze with his foot on the brake. There were a trillion other available spaces in the near-empty lot, most of them closer than his traditional spot. And none of them made him feel like he had just danced all over his own grave. He wheeled right up to a spot by the door, parked, and took a long sixty seconds to calm himself down before cutting the engine and heading inside.

The tunes, as always, were booming: at the moment, a bit of vintage Sonny Terry and Brownie McGee. Scared as he was, it brought a smile to his face. He took off his shades, let his eyes adjust to the dimness.

He didn't see her until she was almost upon him.

"Wow." Coming to a stop three paces away and staring at him, head cocked in thoughtful scrutiny. "I was starting to think we'd never see you again."

"Hi, Jane." He was almost afraid to meet her eye-to-eye. He forced himself to, was glad he did. Her gaze was penetrating yet open, questioning without the overreaching taint of suspicion.

"Hey, stranger." She smiled, and it was clear that she

was happy to see him, too. He smiled back, and they hesitated awkwardly, on the brink of friendly embrace, just long enough to make them laugh at the absurdity before at last they came together. He squeezed her hard. She squeezed back.

"It's *so good* to see you," he said.

"Good to see you, too." She punctuated the hug with a kiss on the cheek. It had been ages since anybody had held him close, even for a second. Nine months ago, Tommy'd given him a terse little hug—a stiff upper-body, two-slaps-on-the-back, *soldier, may God go with you* sort of male-bonding embrace—just before showing his ass the door.

Syd didn't want to break the connection; he had forgotten how much he craved the contact, body and soul. He rocked her back and forth, went *mmmm*. She laughed, gave one last punctuating squeeze, and gently pulled away.

"You've changed," she said.

She looked at him, frankly scrutinizing. It unnerved him, just a little, as he met the gaze; it had been a long time since he'd engaged in such open, direct contact with another living soul. As he did he realized that the past year didn't appear to have diminished her in the slightest. Her wild, dark hair was a little longer. Her wise, dark eyes were just the same. And her smile was as warm as ever.

"You look great," he told her.

"You don't look so shabby yourself." He pshawed, but she persisted. "No, honest. We were all real worried about you. . . ." She realized she was going down the wrong mountain path, but it was too late. The awkwardness returned in force. She wouldn't have a bit of it. "What I mean is, I'm glad to see you looking so . . . together."

Syd nodded. "Thanks. So did Randy tell you why I'm here?"

"Sure did." She grinned conspiratorially, leaned close. "You couldn't have picked a better time. See that guy behind the bar?" Syd looked. "That's Tony. What a douchebag." "You know what the first thing he said to me was?" She adopted a macho swagger, the witless neanderthal voice to match. "Yo, didn't I see you in the December issue of *Hustler*?"

Syd groaned, checked the guy out again. He looked sorta like a cross between Jon Lovitz and Ron Jeremy: pudgy, dark-haired and mustachioed, with an oily quality that just got funnier the harder you tried to take it seriously. "So how is he as a bartender?"

"Sucks," Jane said plainly. "He's slow, he's a sleaze, he's got no talent at all, unless they give out points for being an asshole. Of course . . ." and here she paused, as if debating for a second the wisdom of the words, ". . . anybody who tends bar here has got some pretty big shoes to fill."

Jane looked straight in Syd's eyes when she said it; she wasn't about to miss one little scrap of his reaction. He wasn't sure how much he gave away in the split second of reaction time he had; but he knew for a fact that she knew that he knew more than he'd ever told the cops, or anyone else.

Syd understood. She and Jules had been tight; there was a lot of love between them. And she wasn't exactly prying; there was nothing pushy about her manner. But her unspoken message was clear: *one day, I'm gonna need to know what happened.*

"I know," he said. He could have been responding to any part of her message and inquiry. When he left it at that, so did she.

Then Randy came out of his office, spotted Syd, waved. Syd smiled and acknowledged him. Saved by the boss. "I wouldn't be at all surprised if you get the job," Jane told him.

And it was true. She wasn't.

And he did.

28

IN THE WEEKS that followed his hiring, Syd acclimated quickly to the bartending life. He'd gotten around the lack of a diploma from Famous Bartenders' School on a combination of his own *chutzpah* and Randy's desperation, along with a rock-solid recommendation from Jane and the promise that she'd show him the ropes. It did wonders for his ego, was a milepost on the road to rebuilding his life. Chameleon's was exactly what he needed, and even better than he'd hoped. It was like a crash course in the discipline, an earn-while-you-burn proposition.

He started by second-stringing behind Trent on the Thursday-through-Sunday rush. On those nights, the bar was an utter madhouse. From a consumer standpoint, he'd always recognized the pandemonium factor; but once you stood on the flip side, there was absolutely no comparison. The orders never stopped coming. The collective thirst was never quenched.

Beyond that was the fact that you were a *team* out there: the bartenders, the waitresses, and the cooks in the back. Which meant that if you let your end slide, everybody paid for it, all up and down the line. Fortunately, they had a pretty well-oiled machine already up and running. All Syd had to do was plug in and get up to speed. This he did, in record time.

Trent was not only extremely helpful, but extremely grateful for all Syd's help; and when word got back to Randy, not only did Syd get Wednesday nights to himself, but it was curtains at last for Jane's oily bartending nemesis. Jane was so pleased, she did a little whooping war dance, much to the delight of all in attendance.

On the weekends, Syd and Trent split the bar in half, with a waitress station and fifteen seats apiece. They were each responsible for three waitresses, the people at their seats, and whoever wandered up from the floor. This was more than enough to keep them buzzing for eight to ten hours at a stretch.

Syd's life at those points became a flurry of bottle caps flipping and pitchers filling, intermittently punctuated by coolers, spritzers, orders of cheese fries, and Rum-and-Cokes galore. Fortunately, this was primarily a beer-drinkin' crowd—not a lot of Martinis, Banana Daiquiris, or trendy quaffs bereft of staying power—but there were just enough eclectic characters and tastes to present a challenge and keep him guessing without driving him nuts.

Of course, people-watching was a major attraction, even if it sometimes made him feel like a cultural anthropologist doing fieldwork. For a guy who'd been isolated and out of the loop as long as he had, it was like a feast to a starving man. He saw familiar faces and utter strangers perform at both their best and worst, watched relationships blossom and shrivel in the course of a week or a weekend, sometimes a single night.

Most of all, he established relationships with the people he served: learning through conversation and observation their dreams, their failings, their prejudices and prides, the things that they wanted and the things that they got.

Which meant that, for the first time in ages, Syd felt like a member of a community. And he found that—despite the small-town setting, and the gossip-web that the

last year or so had spun up in the wake of his flameout—
most people were quick to accept him in his new role.

Probably because he had so completely changed.

And Jane's first assessment was dead-on: Syd *was* a
new man, no question about it. His mind was clear. His
body was pumped. He radiated a quiet competence that
made people comfortable in his presence. He learned to
listen without comment, to tune in to the lives unfolding
around him. It was no time at all before people were joking with him, trying to drag him into their political de-
bates, unloading a measure of their burdens on his
nonjudgmental shoulders.

Syd found that he enjoyed the intimate anonymity, the
ability to commiserate while still keeping everyone at
arm's length. Between that carefully maintained safety
zone and the realization that for once *other* people's personal lives were providing the requisite grist for the rumor
mills, Syd had to admit that, all in all, life was good.

There was only one little problem.

And that problem was the ongoing hole at the center of
his soul: the one arena in which he had not yet prepared
to engage. Everything was great, you bet, except for the
fact that he was alone, and there was simply no substitute
for the warmth of another human touch. He tried to draw
the philosophical distinction between *alone* and *lonely;*
somehow it seemed a little too intellectual for his tastes,
considering the emptiness he felt.

He tried to take it in stride, part of his penance. Soli-
tude was a cruel, if somehow fitting fate. When he was
working, it was easier to screen out, distracted as he was
by the ceaseless flow of work, the endlessly entertaining
throngs.

The flip side, of course, were the women, and the var-
ious temptations they posed. Band nights were the worst,
especially when acts like Brave Combo or the Flamin'
Caucasians booked in and the crowd got all hot and bothered.

Watching women was troublesome enough; watching
them *dance* was downright painful. Something about a

roomful of undulating female flesh set off an ache inside him that went all the way down to his bones; every so often Syd would catch a stray whiff of perfume and sweat that would jump-start memories he'd fought long and hard to bury, make him nervously start cleaning ashtrays or checking the taps.

But very rarely did it actually come right at him.

So the first time Syd got hit on it took him so off-guard that he deflected it with a dazed *who, me?* attitude that came off as practiced indifference but was in truth utter disbelief. It had been so long that he felt like he'd gone from monogamous to *non*ogamous, become asexual, fundamentally incapable of inducing desire.

Her name was Elaine, and she was very attractive: raven-haired and buxom, and just drunk enough to trip his *danger* circuit breakers. She spent the better part of the night flirting with him, downing six Tequila Sunrises as she explained that she had broken up with her boyfriend once and for all, on account of he was a skeevy, dickless little miserable two-timing bastard. Or something to that effect.

When midnight rolled around and Syd cut her off at lucky number seven, Elaine told him he had a nice butt. Syd thanked her and left it at that. Elaine asked him if he was seeing anyone. Syd said no, he wasn't. She said that seemed a waste. Syd smiled and said nothing.

As he cleared her glass away she took ahold of his arm, and with inebriated single-mindedness offered to take Syd home and fuck his brains out. Syd gently disengaged, offered to call her a cab. She promised him a night he'd never forget. He promised her that come morning, she'd never remember. In the end, chivalry and common sense won out, and the only thing Syd ended up picking up was the phone.

When the cab arrived, Syd walked her out, paid for it out of his own pocket. Just before getting in she drew him aside and said thanks, that he was a really nice guy, that most guys would have taken advantage of her. Syd shrugged, said he wasn't like most guys.

Elaine embraced him. Then she stuck her tongue in his ear.

He was still shivering as the cab pulled away.

When he came back in, Jane was at the waitress station, watching him. She smiled at him and nodded. Her smile lingered with him long after she headed off, tray in hand.

It was another three days before he realized he was seeing it in his sleep.

SUNDAY NIGHT WAS Ladies' Night: yet another brilliant Randy edict, aimed at squeezing every last discretionary dollar out of the weekend crowd. Drinks were two-for-one till nine, ladies half-price all night. Jane explained to Syd that "ladies" was a term Randy applied to anything that ovulated.

Judging from the crowd, Syd was inclined to agree.

By eight forty-five the bar was bustling, with hordes of horny guys lining up for the last of the bargain beverages. The music was blasting. The bar line was bedlam.

And that, of course, was when it happened.

Syd had been minding his own business, dispensing shots and beers for a gang of gap-toothed locals who were eyeballing a gaggle of big-haired babes fresh off the second shift at the local Big Boy restaurant. The jukebox finished up with a Bonnie Raitt tune, kicked in with something by Treat Her Right. Syd looked up, a big shit-eating grin plastered across his face.

"*All right!*" he cheered. Treat Her Right was one of his all-time favorite bands: four white boys from Boston, doing the funkiest down-home blues-based swamp-rock he'd ever heard. So when David Champagne's nasty skank-boogie guitar line came up Syd's body started bopping in place. It was "Hit a Man," an old Captain Beefheart tune. The drums and mouth harp came next, rumbling and dirty, and by the time Mark Sandman's gravelly voice chimed in, Syd was in full-tilt auto-boogie, shaking his butt as he filled the mugs. He turned . . .

. . . and there stood Jane.

She was at the drink station with a big smile on her face and the most incredible sparkle in her eyes. She was also practically jumping up and down with excitement. He stopped, straightened up, felt his face go beet-red. Jane motioned urgently for him to come over. She obviously had something she was dying to tell him. Syd nodded, as a vertiginous feeling welled up in his stomach.

It was a quick couple of seconds from the bar to the register and back. The money-counting part of his brain was not impaired. But the whole time he was gathering and dispersing hayseed change, he found himself helplessly wondering about Jane. What was she so excited about? What had her jumping up and down? A couple of ideas sprang unbidden into his head.

And suddenly he was nervous.

His first thought was: *she's leaving town.* He recalled a leftover bit of counseling-speak. *Projecting.* As if *his* fantasies were shining out onto someone else's face, like a cheesy stag movie on a stranger's cellar wall. It made him feel exposed and stupid. Plus, it was unlikely. Getting the hell out of Dodge might put that expression on *his* face, but Jane had never expressed that kind of caged-animal antsiness at the possibility of an open ticket out of town. After all, he was born here, and hence was entitled to his contempt. But Jane had come from someplace else; and in the three years he'd known her, she'd never expressed a complaint.

But the second his brain rejected that, Possibility Number Two reared its fat ugly head: *she met a guy.* Or a girl, for that matter. What did *he* know? Either way, the mere thought of it instantly sucked the wind from his sails. His mind didn't go off, as he might have expected, spontaneously erupting in a volley of who's, where's, and why's. He just suddenly felt like he was down the doom flume to nowhere.

And that was when he knew he was starting to fall for her.

Oh, shit, said a voice in his head. It was a ballpeen-hammer moment: Syd went away, snapped back, the multicolored cartoon constellations twirling over his head. He realized he was staring blankly at the big black birthmark on the nose of some guy who was waiting for a drink. The guy did not look real happy about it.

He held one finger up, said "Just a sec," and regained his composure. Jane was still waiting. She gave him one of those Earth-to-Syd looks, and he realized she'd been watching him the whole time. *Oh, shit,* he thought again, this time more subdued. Or maybe it was just that he was still in shock.

It was a big seven steps down to the drink station. He barely felt his body as it carried him to her. It was hard, once again, to look her in the eye, given the feelings he now knew he possessed; and it struck him as odd—no, make that ridiculous—that the simple act of her smiling should send him off into such a lobotomized funk.

"What's up?" he said upon reaching the end of the bar, trying like hell to appear nonchalant. She automatically slipped him her drink orders, which gave him a place to put his eyes. Two Bud drafts and an Amstel light. Okay. Unfortunately, she was jumping up and down again.

He steeled himself and met her gaze.

Jane's features were radiant, animated, downright conspiratorial. Her eyes shimmered with excitement. There was no restraining her grin. She leaned forward, her breasts pressing against the bar top. Syd felt a quivering rush echo through him. It was loud in the club; mouth was nearly touching his ear. His cheek brushed up against her hair, and Syd was instantly filled with the smell of her, like woodsmoke and roses.

"I got tickets for Eric Clapton!" she said.

"Huh?"

"Eric Clapton!!" she repeated. "Pittsburgh Forum! Third row seats!"

"Wow." Syd found a grin beginning to crack through his brittle composure. "Sounds like fun." His body untensed a few clicks, and he mentally kicked himself for being such a jerk.

Jane was shifting her weight from one foot to the other

and back again, dancing in place. He pulled back, found himself staring deeply into her eyes, and understood why he'd restrained himself earlier. It would be easy to fall in there. Too easy, perhaps.

"So," she said expectantly. "You wanna?"

Syd immediately misinterpreted. Projecting again. Before he could hide it Jane picked up on his misread. "The concert, I mean," she said. And it was *her* turn to blush.

"Oh," Syd began. "I, uh . . ." He cast a quick glance across the bar. People were piling up, waiting for drinks, the guy with the nose included. Jane's order was still in front of him. Syd busied himself: opening the beer cooler to get the Amstel, then pulling a couple of pilsner glasses off the overhead rack. He began to fill the first one. He could feel her eyes upon him. Syd capped off the first draft, slipped the second in without spilling a drop. Very professional. He cleared his throat, slipped a quick glance in her direction.

Jane was smiling.

It was a very interesting smile.

Syd poured a little head off the second beer, watched it slowly cave in as it dissolved down the drain. He started to laugh. He couldn't help it. Picking up both glasses, he walked back to her, put the beers on her tray, readied himself to speak.

"I, uh . . ."

"Hold that thought," she said.

And then she turned away.

But . . . he thought, watching her depart. An astonishing warmth pulsed through him, emanating from his heart. He closed his eyes, and her face remained.

Hold that thought, she had said. As if he any longer had a choice in the matter. *So you wanna?* she had asked him; but to his way of thinking, the more wholly pertinent question was, did *she* wanna? From the look in her eyes, he was suspecting that maybe she did.

I love my life, he thought to himself. *My life is great.*

But, for the first time in ages, he actually meant it.

Syd turned his attention back to the spotty-nosed man and all the rest of his quaff-craving clientele. He sighed.

It was gonna be a long, long night.

AND INDEED, THE remaining hours till closing had that timeless quality one usually associates with purgatory. In other words, they seemed to take for-fucking-ever. Syd kept busy—a function his customers were more than happy about—while simultaneously, endlessly flagellating himself with fruitless speculation as to the nature of Jane's personal life.

The truth was, he had very little to go on, beyond the limited evidence of his deliberately reined-in senses. She was not a local; as a result, her past was not a matter of public record or scrutiny. She lived somewhere up in the boonies. He knew less than nothing about her family or upbringing, but she talked as if she'd traveled a good bit in her young life.

More to the point, and to the best of his knowledge, she'd never had anything like a steady boyfriend. If she had, she'd never mentioned it to anyone he knew. The one thing he *did* know was that she had a policy regarding people who did nothing but get drunk and hang out in bars. *Oh, yeah, they make ME wet* were her exact words. That probably helped explain why she'd never, in the past, exhibited anything more than a friendly-but-unmistakable distance with him. There was always that invisible line that was never crossed.

But now the line was gone. Or so it would appear.

It was clear, at any rate, that she had a lot of respect for the way he was pulling his life together. Working side by side for the past month had something to do with it, he was fairly sure. Confidence, hard work, and success—however humble—were definite turn-ons in *his* book; so maybe she was responding to that.

Did he know anyone who'd ever slept with her? He dug around in his memory, came up with a blank. Did it matter in the slightest? No, probably not. Did he have any idea why he was asking himself all these idiotic questions?

Well, actually, yes.

One very good idea.

Because comparisons were inevitable; and unfortunately, he didn't have a lot of good comparisons to make. Maybe if his last girlfriend hadn't turned out to be a fucking werewolf, *his subconscious would be singing a different tune. Not to mention his ex-wife, who was such ancient history at this point it seemed like she was a character in a movie he once saw, screwing over some actor he vaguely recognized.*

Which led to the deeper issue of his own *little secret; and how the hell was he supposed to break* that *to Jane?* Honey, there's one thing about me that I think you should know . . . *Or like Michael Jackson in* Thriller, *before he turned into that were-kitty or whatever the hell it was.* I'm not like other boys. *Wasn't that the goddamned truth.*

His mind made light of the matter, but the fact was that he was scared shitless. Was it even responsible to consider making love with someone, under the circumstances? Nora had awakened the animal in Syd; would he, then, do the same thing to Jane? Was there any way around it? Would condoms help? Was lycanthropy a communicable condition: a kind of supernatural-AIDS-in-reverse that turbocharged not only your immune system, but everything else?

The more he thought about these things, the more his brain hurt. But *not* thinking about them certainly wouldn't help; and besides, it was impossible to do.

Just as it was impossible to not watch Jane, every time she passed his field of vision. She was making a perverse game out of it: watching him whenever he had to take his eyes away from her, refusing to meet his gaze when he *did* turn back to look. When she came to the drink station she was all business; but as he turned to fill the orders she would do it again.

In short, she was torturing him.

Unless of course you're blowing this out of proportion, came that nasty little nagging voice in his head. *She did, after all, only ask you to a concert. . . .*

And that really got him started. What if she was just being a pal, and he was taking it all wrong? And just how *was* he supposed to know the difference? Instinct? Yeah, right; he had a fabulous track record in that department. He'd rather trust the divination of goat entrails.

So what, then . . . read the signs? They were just ambiguous enough to worry him. And getting it wrong meant facing rejection and loss, however polite or gently executed. And that was something Syd categorically refused to risk.

His walls were too hard-won, the peace too fragile. The battle between *aloneness* and *loneliness* was being waged on a daily basis.

And he asked himself, how long does it take before the dread spectre of *rebound* stops rearing its ugly head?

He wondered what Jane would make of all this, if he told her. On the surface, at least, she seemed to be free of this sort of stupidity. Just like she seemed, on the surface, to be interested in him.

But then, of course, she didn't know what he was.

And so around and around he went, making himself insane behind a cool veneer of bartenderly efficiency and calm. It went that way until just around two ayem.

And then, once again, the course of his life was dramatically altered forever.

It was one forty-five, and the bar had already thinned out, maybe a half-dozen stragglers nursing their last calls. Trent, being the head bartender, was in charge of closing up; his wife was home in bed, nursing a case of extreme pregnancy.

Then the phone rang. Trent was hauling up a fresh keg from the basement when Syd picked up the line. He stuck his head through the double doors leading to the kitchen, spotted Trent wrestling with the keg as he came up the stairs.

"Trent! It's Leslie!"

Trent groaned, bracing himself; her weird cravings had extended clear into the ninth month, and it was not unusual for her to hit him with last-minute late-night requests for anything from chocolate raisins-and-pork rinds to black licorice-and-pickles. "Tell her I'm already gone for the night," he grumbled.

Syd shook his head. "She says you better be on your way to the hospital, then," he deadpanned. "Her water just broke."

Trent's face went white, then gray, then red. "HOLY SHIT!" he yelped. He dropped the keg and bounded up the cellar steps, grabbed the phone from Syd's outstretched hand. Jane came up, wiping her hands.

"What's going on?" she asked. She took one look at Trent's face.

And thus did Syd graduate to closing up.

At two twenty-five, Syd looked up to see the other waitresses ducking out. He was just finishing closing out the books; they were through with cleanup and the ritual splitting of tips. They each said 'bye and waved on their respective ways out. Jane was still at the bar, lingering behind. Bonnie, the last one to leave, threw him a sly look as she headed through the door.

And then he and Jane were alone.

As Syd totaled the receipts Jane went over to the juke-box, punched up some tunes. The first muted chords of ZZ Top's "La Grange" came on, low and thrumming as Jane sidled up to a stool directly before him, took a load off her feet; as she did she rocked her head back and forth, working the kinks out of her neck.

"God," she groaned. "I hate Ladies' Night. Why don't they just call it 'Drunken Hell-Sluts Night' and get it over with?"

"Guess people are just afraid to say what they really mean," Syd replied, trying not to watch.

"Yeah," Jane said. "Where would we be if we all started telling each other the truth?"

Their eyes made fleeting contact, and then Jane looked away, as if she wanted to say something further, opted not to. She turned her attention to the books.

"All done?" she asked. Syd nodded. "Lemme see."

She scanned the register readouts, cross-referenced them against the night's receipts. After a moment, she nodded. "Looks okay to me," she said. "You sure you didn't go to Famous Bartenders' School?"

"Nope," Syd shrugged. "Just have years of experience," adding, "most of it on the *other* side of the bar."

"Yeah," she replied. "I noticed."

Syd felt his face go red, hoped it didn't show; Jane cut him a little slack. "Anyway, that was a long time ago," she said. "Just for the record, everybody 'round here thinks you're doing a great job."

"Thanks." Syd stopped, thought about Jules, and the shoes he had to fill. Jane said nothing, started rubbing her neck again. Suddenly she hunched her shoulders. "Ow! Shit!" She winced.

"What's wrong?"

"My neck," she replied. "Sometimes it gets like this after a shift."

"Hang on."

Syd hustled around the bar, came up behind her, placed his hands on her shoulders, and began gently massaging the muscles there.

"Oh god," she murmured, spontaneously melting as the knotted tissue gave way beneath his touch. *"Ow . . .!"* She flinched, tightened up again.

"Sorry," he said, backing off a bit, as his heart did cartwheels into the stratosphere. She relaxed, leaning back 'till her head just touched his chest. Syd worked his way along her shoulders, around the base of her neck, and up to the apex of her spine. Her skin was warm and soft, the flesh beneath firm and supple. He was certain the pounding of his heart would give her a concussion as it gave away his feelings, revealed the depth of his desire. Any minute she would stand and shake off the contact, redraw the line between them. . . .

But Jane showed no sign of leaving. She stayed put, letting her weight lean into him. When she spoke, her voice was soft, cautious.

"You've really changed. . . ." she began.

Syd kept silent, kept working: feeling her breathe, drinking in her warmth.

"I used to think you were kind of an asshole, sometimes," she continued. It was Syd's turn to flinch. He thought about it, then nodded.

"Me, too," he confessed.

Jane echoed the gesture, her head still against his chest. She relaxed a little more, let her full weight lean into him.

"For the record, I like you better this way."

"Me, too."

There was another long pause, both lost in their own thoughts. Syd kept massaging her: holding the line, afraid to either break the contact or press forward. Knowing that, either way, the next move was hers.

"That feels great," she said dreamily.

She brought one hand up to join with his; the second their fingers touched it sent a charge directly to the green light in his soul. He felt a warm light glow there, begin spreading through him.

His fingers gently disengaged, traced the back of her hand to the outside of her arm and up to her neck. As they found the line of her jaw, she tilted her head in response, leaning into his hand. His fingertips came up, brushed against her lips.

She kissed them.

It was another few seconds before he could even think. He cleared his throat to say something, changed his mind, simply leaned forward. She turned to meet him halfway. Their lips touched, hovering exquisitely before parting to reveal softly darting tongues. His eyes fluttered closed. Her lips were feather-soft, wonderfully smooth. His hands slipped beneath her hair, cupping her head. She let out a little groan of pleasure and hunger, and her mouth opened wider, drawing him in . . .

. . . and it was as if the entire universe whirled and spun and stopped altogether, obliterated by the ecstatic rush that rose up to envelop them. Syd felt the walls melt between them, the line disappearing completely . . .

. . . and then she was pulling away, grudgingly breaking the contact as Syd opened his eyes, felt the room rematerialize around them. Reeling, Syd looked across the room to the booths, then back to Jane.

Jane met his gaze, her dark eyes smoldering.

"Let's get out of here," she said.

29

T HE NIGHT WAS alive as they drove, the big knobby
tires of Jane's Jeep Renegade humming down the
road. It was a battered, weather-beaten little vehicle, with
a combination tow winch/snowplow attachment mounted
on the front bumper. The wind whipped through the open
top and windows. Syd looked up and saw stars twinkling
through the budding foliage, looked over and watched her
long hair flying back, wild and alive as well.

The whole way there they didn't speak, or at least no
words were exchanged. But the heat of her hand spoke
volumes: the way it drifted from his grasp to the gearshift
and back again, continually maintaining the contact. Keeping the excitement level high.

And Syd was excited; of this there was no doubt.
There was promise in her touch, in the way she glanced at
him as they rolled down the winding mountain road. A
steadily mounting buzz had taken hold of his senses,
heightening everything, rendering it crystal clear. It was
the sweet taste of anticipation, the knowledge that something very, very good was happening. It was a feeling he
hadn't had in a long, long time.

And it was getting better by the second.

They rounded a curve and Jane's hand slipped from his, grabbed the gearshift. "Hang on," she said, downshifting into the turn and cutting across the road into a black hole in the trees.

"Whoa," Syd cried, reaching up to grab the passenger side panic bar. The Jeep rumbled and thumped as it left the road, and the next thing he knew they were climbing a rutted, pitch-black private drive. The woods closed in on all sides; Syd glanced back, saw the main road disappear behind them.

A shudder of irrational fear came over him; it had been a long time since he had been in the woods with a woman at night—been in the woods at all, for that matter. The Jeep jerked and bumped, as the drive hooked sharply to the right, angled even more steeply. It was clear that nothing short of four-wheel drive would stand a chance of making this jaunt; even in good weather, his Cougar would have bottomed out a long time ago.

But Jane took it all in stride, tearing up the path at speeds he found genuinely disturbing, rocks and dust billowing up behind them as she navigated the rugged terrain.

They passed a rough-hewn sign reading PRIVATE PROPERTY: NO HUNTING! NO TRESPASSING! The path widened, leveled into a clearing. Jane slowed to a more leisurely and altogether quieter speed.

Up ahead, a light appeared through the trees. As they drew closer Syd saw that it was a porch light, softly illuminating the rambling structure that nestled in the clearing.

To call it a log cabin was like calling the America Cup winner a sailboat: it was split-level, rustic and sprawling, all stone and thick-beamed wood, with a gabled roof, a big wraparound porch and lots of windows. There was a neat little gravel parking apron just off to one side. Jane pulled up, crunched to a halt, shut off the engine. Then she turned to him and smiled.

"Well, here we are," she said.

"Wow," Syd murmured, looking around. "This is incredible."

"Yeah," she said. "You should see it in the daytime."

There was a pause, in which the stillness of the night enfolded them. No sounds of civilization intruded up here, not even the hum of a distant highway. It was strangely unnerving, like seeing the last glimpse of land slip over the horizon as you set out to sea. Syd found that his excitement had changed to nervousness; as he looked at her he realized that he hadn't the slightest idea of what to do or say next.

Jane, too, seemed to hesitate, like there was something important she wanted to tell him and she didn't know quite how to put it. "I'm not very good at this," she offered at last.

"Me, either," Syd replied. There was another pause.

She took a deep breath, then leaned over and kissed him.

Her mouth was hot, incredibly sweet. Her lips moved from his mouth to the hollow of his neck, nuzzling him, and it was as if his head disconnected, became a balloon hovering somewhere above his body, held in place only by a single strand of desire. She leaned up, whispering into his ear.

"Let's go to bed," she said.

IF ANYONE HAD suggested that Syd would ever find a lover to compare with Nora, he would have laughed out loud. It was a little like losing your life's fortune, only to discover that you'd been using the Hope diamond as a paperweight. Jane was that good.

And not just physically, although Syd was certainly as pleased as he was surprised. Jane unclothed and unbound was a creature roughly a million times more provocative than her work persona ever let on. Her body was wonderfully full and feminine; her skin soft and very pale, almost translucent. It offset her dark hair and even darker pubic thatch, gave her a striking, almost ethereal quality.

And once revealed, Jane's sexuality was stronger than

he'd ever imagined. The word *grounded* came to mind; as she kissed him Syd felt like he had been plugged into a pipeline to the center of the earth. His nagging anxieties melted under her touch; she thoughtfully provided him with a condom and then made him forget he was even wearing one.

And where Nora was a midnight joyride that continually threatened to skid out of control, Jane's lovemaking was marked by an intense *serenity,* an air of caring that calmed him even as it brought him to the brink, made him feel like he could go on forever.

And indeed, they went round and round for hours; Jane's climax building and peaking repeatedly as they moved into and out of each other, becoming intimate with each other's mechanisms of ecstasy.

And when Syd could go no longer, as he finally shuddered and exploded inside her, Jane took him in her arms and kissed him: accepting his release as she welcomed him home.

And as Syd collapsed in her arms a wave of anguish billowed up in its wake, venting raw emotion like a hurricane slamming a placid shore . . .

. . . and it felt as if everything he had ever done, or tried to do, or would ever try to do was ruined from the start; that no matter how hard he tried or how long he struggled, the end result would always be the same. That Jane was there with him only served to underscore his terror. She didn't know his secret. He didn't know how to tell her. He was putting her at risk by even being here, by letting her get close.

And he feared more than anything that he would lose this, too: that one way or another she would be taken from him. That he would destroy her. That she would desert him.

That he would come to need her, only to lose her in the end.

That it would always be this way . . .

. . . and suddenly she was there, she was there, her hands reaching out to hold him, pull him into her warm embrace. He heard a distant keening noise, realized the sound was coming from him, a wordless lament.

He heard words, too, softly repeating over and over. It was Jane, talking to him; and her voice moved in concert with her hands, her hands that kept moving over his back and shoulders and neck and head.

It's okay, she was saying. *Let it out. Let it all out. It's okay. . . .*

And the words were an invitation, as Jane held and rocked him. *Let it go,* she said. Syd curled naked between her legs, fetal and defenseless.

And he began to cry: a heartfelt human sobbing that had nothing whatsoever to do with self-pity and absolutely everything to do with the simple honest expression of sadness. It was the first time in years he had been able to let himself cry without embarrassment or reservation, untainted by bitterness or anger. He cried to say good-bye to Karen, and Nora, and the lives that might have been; he cried to say he was sorry for all the pain with his name on it.

Ultimately he cried simply because it hurt, and tears were the only honest reaction.

And that was the most amazing thing. The pain felt *good;* not because he enjoyed it, but because it was real, and to not acknowledge it was to cut himself off from a vital side of himself. Syd hugged Jane fiercely, gratefully. It was as though she had taken all of his anguish and transformed it, by nothing more than the force of her caring. Syd buried his face between her breasts; Jane stroked his hair and kissed the crown of his head, told him to sleep. They stayed like that until the first light of dawn crawled across the sky, until they finally fell asleep, enmeshed in a tired and gentle tangle of limbs.

It was an altogether wonderful feeling, one that he would carry with him always.

Until the day he died.

30

SYD AWOKE ALONE and naked, in the middle of a big brass bed. The covers that bunched around him were fragrant with musk and scented sachet.

He tried to move, but his body refused to cooperate. He felt drained, utterly spent. The drapes were drawn, dimming the room, but he could see a ribbon of bright sunlight threading along the seam. He had no idea what time it was. He looked over to the dresser, then to the table beside the bed. No clocks. There was a picture on the nightstand, showing a years-younger Jane, standing next to a smaller, silver-haired woman. Together they looked like before and after versions of the same person; the family resemblance was that strong. They were standing in the woods and hugging each other. They were smiling.

From somewhere downstairs came the clatter of pots and pans, and the smell of cooking. Even better was the fragrant bouquet underlying the food smells. Even more important than food. The smell of life itself.

Coffee.

"Hmmmmm," Syd moaned, thinking *god, this woman is wonderful, may she live a hundred years*. He still had no idea what time it was, or how long he'd been out. He sat up, was pleasantly surprised to find that he felt cleaner, lighter somehow, as though he'd been unburdened of a great weight. He realized anew how much scar tissue he'd been carrying around, how crippling it was.

But for the first time in ages, he actually felt freed from it. That in itself was nothing short of a miracle. He could see the headlines now: *The blind see! The dead speak! Syd Jarrett learns to let go! Film at eleven* . . . Hell, it was more than a new lease on life.

It was a new life altogether.

"Yahoo," Syd murmured, hoisting himself from the bed. He stood and his bladder ballooned, warning him that if he didn't piss in the next sixty seconds, he was going to explode.

Fortunately for all concerned, it was the first door on the right, once he cleared the bedroom. The bathroom, like the rest of the house, was a funky hodgepodge of country-rustic and nineties hip. The floors were rough-hewn hard-wood, the fixtures all antique, down to the old-fashioned claw-foot tub. As Syd slid inside, the thought of a roman-tic bath-by-candlelight posed itself. They both had the day off. Anything could happen.

He hustled over to the john, lifted the lid and let fly. As he peed he noticed a burgeoning magazine rack, blithely perused its contents. Syd had always felt you could tell a lot about the inner workings of a person's mind by studying what they kept around for bathroom reading, and Jane's taste was as eclectic as it was infor-mative: Robert Bly's *Iron John* and Margot Adler's *Draw-ing Down the Moon* side by side with Zippy the Pinhead, Harlan Ellison's *The Essential Ellison* and Paul Williams's slim-but-deadly *Nation of Lawyers*. There were a few well-thumbed Bloom County and Far Side compilations thrown in for good measure.

Syd cracked a grin, felt a warm glow blossom in his heart. The more he found out about this girl, the more in-trigued he was. He was struck again at how amazing it was that they connected with each other, at how good it felt to actually be friends with the person you slept with. At how good he felt, in general.

He finished, reached down to flush the toilet; as he did, he caught a glimpse of himself in the mirror over the sink. His chest and shoulders were covered with little bite marks and scratches. For once, he could account for all of them. He remembered getting every single one, greatly looked forward to acquiring more.

The handle depressed; the commode rattled and swirled. Syd went to the sink, splashed some cold water onto his face and through his hair, which he finger-combed back. He did a quick check in the mirror, assessing the damage. He could definitely use a shower, and he definitely looked his age, but all in all he felt pretty damned fine.

Syd stepped into the hall and turned back toward the bedroom to search for his clothes, when the food smells assailed him again. The coffee was cinnamon-scented and wonderful; there were eggs and potatoes and some kind of sizzling meat. He caught the whiff of fresh-baked bread, and his knees went weak. *Oh, man,* he thought. *This is too much.*

He looked at the stairs, was struck with the impulse to go down and jump her right there in the kitchen. The thought of her stirred his loins. Syd turned, a sly smile on his face, and started creeping down.

The kitchen was just off the entrance hall to the right of the staircase. The stairs themselves were old and creaky; Syd paused twice on his way down, once after hitting a particularly noisy plank, the second time when he stubbed his toe. He hugged the wall and held his breath, biting back the urge to curse.

The noises from the kitchen continued unabated. The meat was still sizzling away, effectively covering his stalking sounds. Syd was two steps from the door. The sizzling stopped, and there came the sound of a pan being lifted from the stove. A shadow moved across the kitchen floor, giving away her position. Syd grinned, anticipating the look on her face, as he coiled himself, preparing to spring.

Syd leapt around the corner, arms outstretched, let loose with a fiercesome snarl . . .

. . . and came face-to-face with an old woman holding a hot frying pan.

"Oh shit!!" he gasped, hands scrambling to cover his exposed crotch. The old woman looked at him, utterly unfazed. She was gaunt and stooped, with leathery skin and long silver hair pulled into a thick braid that hung halfway down her back. Her eyes were Jane's eyes: kind and dark and sharply focused, the sort of eyes that took in everything and missed nothing. She cocked her head, curiously regarding the naked madman standing in the middle of her kitchen.

"I'm sorry!" Syd blurted. "I thought you were someone else!"

The old woman raised her eyebrows, gave him a quizzical look. Syd turned fifteen shades of red, started backing toward the door. "I, uh, I was just, um . . ." He backed up, stumbled against a chair, reached out for balance, exposed himself again. "Sorry!" he said, covering up again.

The old woman shook her head. "We were beginning to wonder if you'd sleep all day." She proceeded to carry the pan to the table, set it down. As she turned, Syd recognized her: a somewhat older version of the woman in the photograph. "My name's Mae," she said. "I'm Janey's gramma."

"Syd," Syd replied sheepishly. "Syd Jarrett."

Mae nodded. "Janey's told me all about you."

"Ah," Syd said, feeling like a complete idiot.

Mae turned her attention back to the table, sparing him further embarrassment. Syd saw it had been set for one. "Thought you might be hungry," she said, very matter-of-factly. "Janey's out for a walk, just yet. She'll be back shortly. How do you like your coffee?"

"Uh, black," Syd said. "One sugar."

"Mmm-hmmm," Mae replied. She turned back to the counter, where a Mr. Coffee sat. Syd remained frozen in place, afraid to get up or move. She poured a steaming mugful for herself, then got a fresh mug down from the cupboard for him. As she did, the tiniest flicker of amusement flitted across her features.

"Best you find your clothes," Mae said, " 'fore your food gets cold."

"Yes ma'am," Syd replied, easing his way toward the door. He bolted upstairs, found his pants and shirt balled up in the corner of the bedroom where he'd thrown them. By the time he came back downstairs his embarrassment had receded to a manageable level. Gramma Mae served him a steaming plate of food and retired to another part of the house without saying anything more.

Syd seated himself, feeling simultaneously awkward and strangely accepted, a guest being treated with casual, comfortable neglect, almost like family. The breakfast nook was sunny and filled with plants; bundles of drying herbs hung from the eaves and rafters, filling the air with their aromatic scents. The woods outside the window were thick and lush and alive, and sparkled with a thousand shades of green and gold and russet brown.

All in all, it was the kind of room that invited hours of peaceful contemplation on the essential goodness of life, and like the rest of the house it resonated with a sense of rootedness, of home and hearth and family. Syd found himself fending off the bittersweet longing for something like that in his own life. . . .

Then his stomach growled, drawing him back to the present. He scooped up a fragrant forkful, brought it to his lips.

And it was delicious.

31

THE DAY THAT awaited was warm, laced with the sweet smell of green things growing and an underpinning of moist, verdant earth. It was mid-afternoon, almost three-thirty, and Jane still wasn't back.

Syd had finished eating and then washed his dishes, killing time until she returned. After tending to his needs Gramma Mae had disappeared, leaving Syd to his own devices. But as he rinsed and racked the last plate, he began to feel more than a little bit awkward lounging around by himself. He decided to get some fresh air, maybe actually take a little walk. Maybe use the time to figure out how he was going to broach the subject of his little secret.

There was a trail off to the side of the house that looked promising. Syd took a deep breath and ambled off, picking his way through the vibrant greenery. He hadn't gone more than twenty yards before the house had completely disappeared from view, lost in the wild sprawl of trees.

The path sloped down, turning twisted and rocky as it threaded across the mountainside. Syd hiked along, weaving around moss-laden storm-fall and scuttling over craggy

outcroppings. As he did he was struck by how it felt to be
outside again: familiar, yet unsettling, like coming home
after a long journey to find everything you owned moved
three inches to the left.

Syd took in the sights and smells, weighed them
against his own mixed feelings and marveled at how the
play of light and shadow could simultaneously be so innocent and so foreboding, so ripe with threat. All of nature,
for him, had taken on a strangely sinister cast: where before he would have heard nothing but the birds and insects
and blameless wind rustling leaves overhead and sending
them skittering beneath his feet, now he was acutely aware
of the countless desperate daily struggles for existence going on around him. A million myriad forms of life, each
locked in its own private fight for survival in the food
chain. Syd caught a glimpse of a field mouse, darting from
the safety of an elm and disappearing under a log. He
wondered if it slept in fear, and if its dreams were haunted
by the sound of snapping jaws.

Then a twig cracked as loud as a rifle shot right behind
him. Syd turned, startled, and Jane was there: bopping
down the path in sneakers and a loose Indian cotton print
dress.

"Hi, stranger," she said, wrapping her arms around
him, giving him a big hug. As she kissed him he felt the
pleasant tautness of her flesh under the sheer fabric,
caught the scent of rose oil and wildflowers, the faint mus-
cular tang of sweat underneath. It only took him a second
to relax and respond fully, but it was enough for her to
pick up on.

"What's wrong?" she asked.

"Nothing," he answered a little too abruptly, then
looked away, shaking his head. "I was just thinking back
on the last time I was out in the woods." He didn't elaborate. She let it slide, instead wrapped his arm around her
shoulder and began to stroll. "So where you been all
morning?" he asked.

"Oh, out and about," Jane said. "I stopped back at the
house—I must have just missed you." She bumped hips

with him, nudging him off the path. "I figured you probably needed the rest."

"Oh, yeah," Syd replied, letting out a chagrined
chuckle. "Yeah, I guess I did." There was an awkward
pause. *Tell her,* said the voice in his mind. "Listen, about
last night . . ." he began. "Um, I don't usually go to pieces
like that. . . ."

"You mean you don't have a nervous breakdown with
every girl you go to bed with?" Jane chided. "I'm glad to
hear it."

"Yeah, right," Syd said, his face flush with embarrassment. "It's just been a long time since I felt that good, and
it brought back some memories I'd kinda buried. . . ."

He stopped, not knowing if he could continue. Jane
gave him an understanding squeeze. "S'okay," she said,
meaning *you don't have to talk about this right now.* "Just
so you know, I had a pretty great time, too." She nodded,
gravely serious. It cracked the tension, brought a smile to
his face.

"Much better," she said. "You know, you're kinda cute
when you're embarrassed." She reached around and
grabbed his ass "Even Gram thinks so."

"Oh, god," he groaned. "She told you."

Jane shrugged. "She tells me everything."

"Oh, god," he repeated, mortified.

"Don't worry about it," Jane added. "Gram's seen naked men before."

He winced, tried to change the subject. "So," he said,
"is it just you and her here?"

"Yep," Jane nodded. "I came here after my folks
died." She said it plainly, and it made Syd aware of exactly how little he knew about her, how much he wanted
to know more.

"I'm sorry," he said. "How . . ." he stopped, unsure of
whether he should ask.

"Hunting accident," she replied. "We were up in the
Poconos, and they got shot by a bunch of drunken
assholes." She shook her head sadly. "People can be so
fucking stupid."

"I'm so sorry. I had no idea . . ."

"Yeah, well," she sighed. "It's not something I usually talk about."

She grew quiet, and Syd sensed that they were in delicate territory. He said nothing, but drew her a little closer; she responded, leaning into him as they walked.

Just ahead the trail ended and the trees opened up, revealing a spectacular view of the valley below. She took his hand, led him over to a rock ledge next to a big gnarly oak. As they sat Syd scooted up until his back was against the tree, then Jane hopped up and leaned into him.

"This is my favorite spot," she said. "You can see practically the whole valley."

Syd looked out, saw that, indeed, the whole town was visible on the middle horizon: nestled in the folds of the green earth, its grim industrial decay rendered picturesque by distance. The huddled houses and squat buildings became magical, pristine; the mill works' gray smokestacks thrust skyward, still and silent; sunlight gleamed diamondlike off a thousand empty windows. The river snaked below them like a fat golden ribbon, shimmering and alive.

They sat there for a time in silence, watching nature unfold. The day was perfect, the scenery breathtaking. The sky was a pure cobalt blue, the clouds casting fat shadows on the floor of the valley, the coming moon a faint ghost overhead. A hawk swooped and soared not a mile away, riding the thermal currents coming off the mountainside. It was hundreds of feet above the valley floor but level with the two of them, hanging effortlessly in the sky.

"It's so beautiful," Syd sighed. "Hard to believe it's so ugly up close."

"That's why I like it here," Jane said. "You can't see all the bullshit." She nodded to herself. "I think everything looks better from a distance."

Syd grew quiet, torn between enjoying her presence and trying to ignore the voice in his head. *You have to tell her,* it said. *You have to do it now.* He leaned forward, tried to hide in the solace of her smell. She was so beautiful.

This felt so good. This was a mistake. It was unspeakably selfish of him to hide the truth, unthinkable to reveal it. She would think he was joking, or think him deranged. She would hate him.

Then she would fear him. . . .

In the sky above, the hawk banked and dove, descending on some unsuspecting prey. Syd wondered if its intended victim could feel it coming.

"Hell-o?" Jane's singsong sliced through his silence, brought him back. "Anybody home?"

"What? Oh. Sorry."

"If you're gonna keep going away like that," she told him, "the least you could do is rub my shoulders." He could hear her smiling.

"No problem," he replied, and Jane tilted her head forward as he brought his hands up and under her hair, then settled back as he began to knead the soft skin there. She gave out a little growl of pleasure, and Syd felt a horrible rush of sadness well up in his soul. *You can't have this.* He wanted her so badly. *You can't ever have this.* . . .

"Tell me what you're thinking," Jane said.

Her tone was earnest, softly insistent. It invited the truth.

"I don't know . . . I guess I was thinking about why shit happens . . ." he said. As poetic replies went, it fell way short of the mark. ". . . wondering why life goes the way it goes." He stopped, overwhelmed by his own inability to articulate his feelings. "I guess maybe I was wondering why we never got together before."

"I never would have gone out with you before," she said. Her candor threw him a little.

"I was always attracted to you," he confessed.

"I always *noticed* you," she acknowledged. "But I still wouldn't have gone out with you."

Syd paused, letting her words sink in. It begged the obvious question. "So why are you with me now?"

"Like I said," she told him. "You've changed."

She thought about it a little more, elaborated. "The whole time I was growing up, my folks never stayed in one place more than a couple of months. We were always either just leaving someplace or just arriving someplace else. Kind of a hippie-nomad thing, I guess. God knows we weren't exactly the normal American family unit. . . ." Jane picked at a blade of grass, stared into the distance. "Anyway, I never got a chance to get close to anyone but them. When they died, I was alone. . . ."

"So why'd you come here?"

Jane gave an offhand little shrug. "Guess I got tired of being alone," she said.

Maybe it was the way they were touching: the intimacy of physical contact softening the pain of opening up. Or perhaps it was the presence of the scenery, providing them with a mitigating focal point, allowing for a heightened sense of perspective. Or even just that it was a continuation of his healing process, the next step in unburdening himself of years of brittle ego-armor.

For whatever reasons, it was his turn. Syd took a deep breath, fumbled for the words.

"I've really fucked up my life," he said. Jane went very still in his arms, listening. "It's like there's this thing inside me that knows that there's *more* to life than what everyone tells you," he said. "More than just being a good little robot and playing by the rules and doing what you're told. I've always known it. Only I never knew what to *do* about it.

"I mean, I tried to find it when I was a kid, and I just got into trouble. Like people don't *want* you to know about it, and they punish you for trying to let it out."

Quit weaseling, the voice warned. *Tell her.*

Jane nodded, listening.

"I tried to bury it, just do what everyone told me was the right thing: get a job, get married, have a *normal* life. . . ." He laughed, putting bitter emphasis on the word. "Then," he said, "when you least expect it, someone comes along and shows you what it is you've been denying all along."

"Nora," she said, her voice flat, very small.

"Yeah," he nodded. *"Nora."* It was the first time he'd spoken her name in ages. It felt strange on his tongue.

"So what is it she showed you?"

"It's something wild," he said. "It feels like, I don't know, like this animal side of me that's always been there, only I'd kept it locked away. And once I realized it I felt like, for the first time in my life, I knew who I really was.

"The problem is, I'd starved it so long that when I *did* finally let it out, it tore my whole life apart." He paused, as a chill rush passed through him. "And I'm afraid of it now."

Syd stopped, tears welling up in his eyes. "I mean, I feel like now that I know what it is, I'll die without it, or be as good as dead.

"But if I let it out again, it'll kill me," he said. "Or else it'll hurt the people I love."

Like Jules, he meant to say. *Like you . . .*

Jane sat up then, turned toward him. The setting sun was just kissing the mountain's ridge: throwing long shadows across the valley, bathing her features in red and gold. She studied him skeptically, shook her head emphatically.

"Bullshit," she said.

Syd looked at her, shocked.

"Being an animal isn't your problem, Syd." Her tone was matter-of-fact, unwavering. "Being an animal has nothing to do with it. Everyone's an animal. It's the natural order of things.

"But it's not a license to be a *jerk.*"

Syd opened his mouth, closed it again. Her gaze was hot upon him. He was about to tell her *no, you don't understand,* but she stopped him before he could speak.

"Your problem is that you think too much," Jane said, "and you get way too bent out of shape about shit that shouldn't even matter. Some things you just *know,* like you know them in your gut. Nora was nothing but trouble, Syd, you'd have to be blind not to see that. And as for Karen, *Jesus . . .*"

Jane stopped, caught herself. Syd read her look, sensed

some secret knowledge hidden there. "What about Karen?" he asked.

"Nothing," she said. "It doesn't matter."

"No, tell me," Syd insisted, suddenly annoyed. "What about Karen?"

The question hung in the air like a threat. Jane looked around as if there might be some way to deflect his attention. Syd followed her gaze, offering no escape. "It's nothing," she reiterated. "I just *saw* things, okay?"

"What *kinds* of things?"

"Things I didn't like very much."

"Like what?"

Jane paused, not liking the interrogatory shift the conversation had taken. "She came into the bar a lot," she said finally, the last word pregnant with meaning.

"What, like with Vaughn?"

"Yes . . ." she said, then, ". . . and with other people."

"Like *who?*" Syd stared at her disbelievingly. The tension level skyrocketed, as Syd's expression changed from *I can't believe I'm hearing this* to *I can't believe I'm hearing this NOW!*

"*Who'd* she come into the bar with?"

"I don't know," Jane replied, annoyed herself now. "Other guys. Some guy named Doug. Another guy, an artist . . ." She thought about it. "Philip something or another. He was from New York, I think. . . ."

Syd flipped back through his internal Rolodex, searching for all the Dougs and Philips that might fit the bill. The only Doug he knew was this dweeby guy that hung on the periphery of their acquaintance pool, a harmless would-be hipster who got shit-faced at parties and wore T-shirts emblazoned with catchy slogans like *ten reasons why beer is better than women*. And as for the other guy. . . .

"What about this Phil?"

"What about him?" Jane said.

"Tell me about him!" Syd demanded.

"I don't *know* anything about him!" she cried. "What does it matter?"

"IT *MATTERS!!*" he roared. Jane backed away instantly, recoiling from his explosion. Syd pinned back his rage, beat it down, tried again. "I'm sorry," he said. "I just have to know, okay?"

Jane shook her head. "Some of them I knew, most I'd never seen before." Syd winced at the word *most;* Jane sighed and continued, her gaze painfully intense. "She did it a lot, Syd. She did it all the time."

"Jesus, Jane!" he said. "Why the hell didn't you *tell* me this?"

"I didn't *know* you!" she shot back. "I didn't know what your *rules* were. You work in bars long enough, you see some pretty strange shit. Maybe you knew. Maybe you got *off* on it. How was I supposed to know?"

"You could have asked me!" he said bitterly. "You could have said something."

"Yeah?" she replied sarcastically. "What the hell did you want me to say: hey, Syd, how's it hangin'? By the way, did you know your wife is a *slut*?"

Syd stood then, started pacing and shaking his head. There was one final question, burning in the center of his brain. Syd took a deep breath, faced her.

"Did Jules know about this?" he asked. His voice cracked, as dry as dead leaves. The look in Jane's eyes telegraphed the answer before she even opened her mouth.

"*Everybody* knew, Syd," she replied softly. "It was happening right out in the open. There was no way for us *not* to know.

"The only reason you *didn't* see it," she said flatly, "was because you didn't *want* to."

Jane stopped then, regret implicit in her tone, as though she wished there were some way to take it back, or at least soften the impact of the knowledge. "I'm sorry," she said. "I didn't mean to . . ."

. . . but Syd was no longer hearing anything she said, so busy was he listening to the sound of his own blood roaring through his veins. His breathing was quick and shallow; when he next looked at her he saw a red that had nothing to do with the setting sun.

And then he was moving, he was moving, away from Jane and up the path, into the darkening woods. She called out to him, but Syd ignored her. One thought alone held sway in his mind, a single snarling impulse behind it.

She lied, he thought. *She fucking lied to me.*

Syd gave himself over to the impulse, under the setting sun, as the night descended upon them.

And the luminous moon rose high.

32

MEANWHILE, SOME FOUR hundred miles away, the beat of business-as-usual was wearing very thin.

In fact, Vic thought, *if she doesn't shut up pretty soon, I'm gonna rip her fucking head off and piss down the stump.*

Not that Nora wasn't being just as nice as pie. Of course she was. Now that she had what she wanted. The fact that Nora's nicey-nice had been totally purchased at his expense just served to expand the already-yawning emotional abyss between them.

Vic glanced at the neon clock on the wall. Eleven thirty-five, on a dead Wednesday night. They were sitting on the patio of a tacky little tourist trap called Viper's, just off Atlantic Avenue in beautiful scenic Virginia Beach, Va. It was the second week of their little oceanside vacation together: Vic's latest attempt to make her happy, salvage what was left of their hopelessly fucked-up relationship.

The trip had been bankrolled by one P. Clinton Melhorn: a resourceful, fun-loving Baltimore businessman with thousands of dollars' worth of available credit on his battery of credit cards, not to mention a bitchin' Mercedes with a truly breathtaking Blaupunkt sound system. Clint had recently relocated—rather abruptly, in fact—to a celestial condo in the great Hereafter, but his legacy of quality spending lived on. Their suite at the Seaside Hideaway Resort Inn—complete with Jacuzzi, jumbo king-size bed, oceanfront balcony, wet bar, the works—was a tribute of sorts to the man's spectacular earning power and upscale tastes.

It should have been a world-class vacation. And had Vic done it by himself, he would have had the time of his life. But no, he had to bring *her* along; and damned if she hadn't done everything in her power to make sure that this was not the best, but the absolute *worst* time of his life.

All because of one little indiscretion.

One little potentially life-changing indiscretion.

Oh, you bitch, he silently fumed. *How could you do it? How could you make ME do it?*

But of course he couldn't say anything, because it would just tip Nora over into another psychotic episode, and god knows he didn't need another one of *those*. After everything she'd already put him through, this little pocket of peace was almost worth the sound of her voice. It brought him a couple of seconds to think.

And, perchance, to plot and scheme . . .

"Baby?" It was her *I'm talking to you* voice, modulated for easy listening. He could pretend not to hear her for another second at the most. It wasn't worth the bother.

"Yeah," he said, carefully diffident.

"I was just thinking," she said, "about how we first met."

Oh, great! he thought bitterly. *And just in time, too!* It was all he could do to keep from smashing his glass into her face. He resisted the impulse, went for a noncommittal nod of the head.

She sighed. "It was a night like this, remember? Moon almost full, shining over the mountains . . ." She paused to look out past the boardwalk to the ocean beyond, the bright slick of light that washed across its infinite rippling surface. "I took one look at you and thought I would die.

I just couldn't believe how beautiful you were, like some sort of pagan god. . . ."

She paused to chew softly on her ripe lower lip, an automatic gesture he had always found maddeningly erotic. Now it merely repulsed him. In the dim light, she looked suddenly very much as she had twenty years earlier, or twenty years before that, before the terminal toxicity had set in. Vic looked past her to the ocean and the moon, did his damnedest to resist nostalgia's tidal pull.

". . . you turned my whole life around." She was still speaking. "*God*, I was so in love with you then." She bowed her head, eyes closed, as if mourning the loss. "Of course, that was before you started to hate me. . . ."

"*Jesus.*" Vic groaned wearily. "I don't hate you, Nora."

She looked up, shook her head, and sadly smiled. "You *lie*, you *lie*. But, hey, why am I surprised? Everybody knows you can't tell the truth to ol' crazy Nora. She'll just flip out." She paused, took a swig off her drink.

And he wanted to say *that's exactly right, Nora. You'd be great if you were deaf, dumb, and blind, and then maybe we did something with your goddam sense of smell. Then maybe you wouldn't have to FLIP THE FUCK OUT every time I just happen to casually notice that you aren't the ONLY WOMAN IN THE WORLD . . . !!!* He felt the anger mount in him, enjoyed the sick thrillrush of savagery it inspired. *I mean, it's just a thought, baby—and I wouldn't want to knock the planet out of orbit or anything—but has it ever occurred to you that I might not even LOOK at another woman if you weren't such a psychotic fucking manipulative BITCH—*

He wanted to say it, but instead he turned his head. His whiskey beckoned. He drained it in a gulp, spotted his waitress, held the empty glass up for her to see. When she nodded her bovine head, Vic went back to looking at the clock. Eleven forty-one. And way too slowly counting.

Nora just sat there, deep in Noraland. Evidently, she was waiting for him to refute her claim. When he could stand the silence no longer, he said, "Listen. If I really hated you that much, I wouldn't still be sticking around now, would I?"

She got a rich, automatic little chuckle out of that. It really pissed Vic off. This time, it showed very clearly in his eyes.

"What?" he hissed, showing teeth.

Nora's eyes went wide. "I'm sorry," she said. All at once, she was Ms. Contrition. "Vic, I understand. You're very upset. And I know how hard it was to do . . . to do what you did." He tensed; she sensed it, and her little speech grew even more saccharine and heartfelt. "I just want you to know that . . . oh, god. Just that it *meant a lot to me*."

It was Vic's turn to chuckle: an ugly little bark that felt good coming out, like dislodging a psychic hairball. It should have been enough to warn anyone away. But when she reached out and took his hand, he felt himself go cold and still.

Her emerald eyes had lit upon him. Reluctantly, he brought his gaze up to meet hers.

And in so doing, found himself pulled back through the year and a half that had brought them to this place . . .

PRACTICALLY FROM THE moment they'd left Pennsylvania, the hell had begun in earnest. Nora may have been back in the fold, but she'd made it painfully clear that she was not there of her own volition. And while she never tried to run away again—some fundamental aspect of her spirit had been broken, evidently for good—Nora was living proof that there was always more than one way to escape.

She began to drink; and Vic wasn't talking normal drinking here. He wasn't even talking normal *Nora* drinking, which would be enough to put most light infantry divisions under a very large table. No, her jacked-up metabolism required alcohol in superhuman doses to achieve the oblivion she craved.

Vic understood. She'd somehow gotten it into her head that it was *his* fault that she couldn't have pups, and it was hard to let go of the fantasy. The only conceivable antidote was a customized blend of patience, persistence, and just the right amount of iron-handed discipline: three qualities that, in those days, he had in seemingly infinite supply. It didn't matter how many times she descended to her lowest, most venomous liquored-down state. He loved her, and *that* was what mattered. Everything else was irrelevant, would burn away with time and the heat of his unlimited devotion.

Still, it was hard, keeping up the good fight in the face of her unmitigated rage and despair. The months dragged on, spring turning to summer, fall to winter, and their predatory lifestyle saw them drifting from state to state to state without any real change in their dynamic. Except for maybe a change for the worse ...

Nora was getting increasingly sloppy on him, for one thing: when they would go to tag-team some poor dumb bastard she would play along just fine through the stalking and the pickup and the setup, only to blow the sting a split second before Vic made his entrance. Vic could recall six occasions when he had found himself staring down a gun barrel at the critical moment of truth, mostly as a result of her newfound bad timing and her big fucking mouth.

Sure, he could take care of himself. And sure, it would take more than a stray round from some redneck pecker-wood's Saturday Night Special to put him down. But that was hardly the point.

The point was, it was just her little way of rubbing his previous fuckup in his face. She would never let him forget how the ox snuck up on him that night, the cold steel kiss against the back of his skull. Like she wanted to remind him that he was slipping, or losing his touch. Or maybe it was a genuine death wish. It was hard to tell.

At any rate, as time wore on he found himself growing increasingly frustrated with her carelessness, and her intransigence. What was the fucking deal here he wondered. What had he done that was so wrong?

You really don't know, do you? She'd practically spat it in his face. And he'd said well, no, I don't. To which she'd replied, *you didn't have to kill him.*

Kill who? he wanted to know. He knew damned well she didn't know about whatsisname back in Pee-aye. She clammed up again. And again, he pressed: so who the fuck did I kill that was so important he could get between you and me?

Michael, she said.

Michael who? he asked, genuinely perplexed.

Mississippi, she replied, and would say no more. Tears were in her eyes. Tears that had nothing to do with Vic.

Then, and only then, did he realize the extent of her betrayal.

At that point, it required a superhuman effort on his part to keep from Changing on the spot, going absolutely berserk. The scar on his face was burning. He suddenly remembered all too well. From his perspective, it had always been just another dumbshit fucking *pick,* albeit slightly further along than the rest. Now he realized that it had run deeper than that.

He demanded to know if she'd been in love with him. She looked him dead in the eye and said *yes.* She might as well have just stabbed him in the heart, for all the compassion implicit in the gesture. He asked her how dare you, how fucking *dare* you give your heart to someone other than me?

And this was what she said:

Because he loved me. He genuinely loved me. Not like a toy, or a possession. Not like you. *Michael cared about me.*

Oh, said Vic. And I don't.

No, she told him. *No, you don't. You don't even know how. He was good to me, Vic. I never would have left him if you hadn't come along. But even if I did, he wouldn't have tried to force it. He wouldn't have chased me down like a dog. He would have taken the fucking hint.*

That's because he didn't love you for shit, Vic hissed. Little fuck didn't even know what love is.

No, Vic, she went on, working the knife deeper and deeper into his heart. *You're the one who doesn't know*

*what love is. If you did, you wouldn't have to chase after
every piece of ass that comes down the pike. . . .*

At which point he went whoa, whoa, whoa. Excuse me
just a goddam minute here. Do you see me chasing after
anyone now? Do you see me even *looking* at anybody
else?

And she said *of course not. Of COURSE you want me
now. You want me because you know you can't have me.
But if I was to give in for EVEN ONE SECOND, you'd
start chasing around again the minute my back was
turned. And you know why? Because this isn't about us at
all. It's about YOU. It's about what YOU want.*

You're wrong, he started to say; but Nora would have
none of it. *And you know how I know?* she continued, setting up the coup de grace. *Because for all your big talk,
you'll never give me what I want.*

Oh? he said snidely. And just what the fuck *do* you
want?

I want you the fuck out of my life, she said. *I want to
never have to see your face again. Because I hate you, you
lousy son of a bitch. I hate you for stealing my life from
me. I hate you for stealing Michael from me. Every decent
thing I ever tried to have in this life, you stole from me, or
you destroyed.*

And I will never forgive you. Not now.

Not ever.

It was impossible to quantify the depth of his damage
at those words. There was no bottom to the pain. He tried
to speak, could not. He wished he could cry, but that too
was beyond him.

You ever mention his name again, Vic had managed at
last, and I swear I'll kill you.

To which Nora had answered *I wish you would. . . .*

SHE HAD BEEN looking in his eyes when she said it. She
was looking in his eyes now, as well. And if there was any
difference at all, it was probably because now the shoe
was entirely on the other foot.

He looked at her, in the dim light of the boardwalk

patio, while the salty breeze rustled through the tangled mass of her hair. Nora's hair was like dancing snakes of fire in a ratty nest of their own device, framing the exquisite face gone pinched and sour with too much drink and unquenchable despair. A year and a half was a very long time to live with such vehemence burning within.

She had let herself go, to an extent far beyond what Vic would ever have dreamed her vanity would have permitted. Bitterness and gravity had done the rest, minutely resculpting her features with delicate inlaid spider lines of startling unpleasantness. She was still technically beautiful—at least in the right light and under the right influence. But she did not look good.

"What are you thinking?" she asked him now; and if she didn't know exactly what was on his mind, she at least had gotten a whiff of its tenor. Vic had never been good at muzzling his rage; a tight rein on it was about the best he could do.

"To be real honest," he said, lying only slightly, "I was thinking it would be real nice if you just stopped asking me what I was thinking. Do you think that might be okay?"

Nora nodded her head, understanding completely. "That's okay," she said, then added, "I gotta go pee." When she stood, the look in her eyes was a powerful mixture of compassion and regret. He found himself thinking of his glass and her face again—just a stray, pleasant fantasy—even as he smiled and nodded his assent.

She crossed to his side of the table and, surprisingly, leaned over to kiss him on the mouth. As she did she ran one hand across his chest, down his torso to his lap. It sent a cold rush of numbness arcing through him, made something clench in the vicinity of his heart.

"I'll be right back," she said; and when he didn't respond, she just headed for the patio door and the rest rooms within. She was weaving slightly, as was normal these days. Vic didn't even bother to watch her go.

Once he was alone, he exhaled heavily and leaned his head in his hands. Christ, but he was tired. Tired of her, tired of life, tired of the miserable endless hamster wheel his existence had become.

He had to think of something. Whatever it was, it would have to be slick. Nora's instincts were good; even drunk as a bitch, she was light-years beyond the precocious farmgirl cunt he'd happened upon in the Bitterroot Mountains, oh so long ago. If only her daddy could see her now . . .

Probably his best bet, Vic mused, would be to kill her when she nodded out. It wouldn't do to have her fighting back.

Besides, why the fuck should I give her the chance? he added, thinking bitterly back on last night. What a waste. What a goddamned tragedy. Nora didn't give out second chances. Why should he?

The clock read eleven forty-six. He wondered where his waitress was, that miserable stupid cow. He needed his drink, and he needed it now.

Vic ran his tongue idly over his teeth, tasted whiskey and a little something else that was wedged way in the back, between his rear molars. It took him a second to place, another to index, yet a third for the pain to set in.

It was the pain of intimate recognition.

HER NAME WAS Tristana, or at least that's what she said. She was working as a dancer at one of those 17th Street titty bars when he'd wandered, quite by accident, into her life.

It was his fifth night in Virginia Beach, and Nora had remained true to her now-established nightly pattern of drinking herself insensate and blacking out by twelve-fifteen. Vic, to be honest, had been pretty damn good over the very long year since that fateful dialogue had transpired, not even scarfing so much as a bit of stray poontang, even when he thought he could get away with it.

Still, he had to admit that at this point it was more a matter of principle than of actual fidelity. And with all this excess cash and free time on his hands, he would be good and goddamned if he was gonna sit on his hands for two weeks, watching the Playboy Channel and listening to her snore.

Fishnet's was your standard rubbernecking flesh market, designed to squeegee greenbacks off the tourists and trillions of horny grab-ass sailors who regularly poured out of Norfolk Naval Base. The latter were pejoratively referred to by the locals as *squids,* and they were absolutely everywhere you looked: roaming in packs, sniffing for action. Trying to scratch the itch.

They were tough, drunk, rowdy sons of bitches, but Vic waded easily through their ranks; even the dumbest and meanest among them seemed to sense that he wasn't someone to be messing with. The masculine reek of barely bridled lust and lonely desperation was thick enough to choke on, but Vic enjoyed adding a little fear to the mix. The old city ordinance that only allowed bikini dancing had recently been repealed, so there was plenty of what he was looking for on display.

But out of all the hydroponically grown beach bunnies, obvious tit jobs and aerobicized abs of steel, there was one that stood out from the pack. She was a lithe punk bitch with a dangerous body and attitude to burn. He liked her aggression, her pantherlike strut. He liked her china-white skin, her leather G-string and close-cropped blue-black hair with the long braided forelock that she could crack like a whip. Most of all, he liked the fact that she utterly *intimidated* the natives, even as she got them off.

And she even came with her own nose ring.

Her first time past, he slipped her a fifty and gave her a bemused look. The rest of the night, she played to him whenever she was up. He made it worth her while. Still, the vibe was there, the unmistakable underlying message: *yeah, so you're hot and you're loaded, but I'm working and this is* business. . . .

Vic watched her all night, then left, ten minutes before closing time, without even learning her name. He made sure that she saw him go, though, nodded to her as he waltzed out the door.

The next night he was back, with more cash to flash

and more casually smoldering glances. Vic dropped another couple of hundred or so, this time in tens and twenties, drawing it out for effect. As before, his attention was
focused solely upon her, as though the other dancers were
nothing but background detail, shifting shapes and colors
that only served to highlight *her* presence, *her* perfection.
And again, at the end of the night he left, with no more
than a glance and a nod and that sly, knowing smile.

When he showed up the third night she came to him
during one of her breaks, introduced herself. Vic said he'd
like to talk to her, maybe take her out for a bite to eat. She
gave him a look—part cynicism, part intrigue—and said
she'd think about it.

When closing time came, Vic hovered at the door just
long enough for her to see that yes, he was leaving now.
Then he departed, winking at the sumo-sized bouncer at
the door on his way out. He enjoyed watching the seismic
tremor of confusion as it rumbled through all that blubber.

She emerged, some twenty minutes later. Vic was waiting. When he asked her to walk with him, she raised an
eyebrow warily. Vic smiled his most disarmingly dangerous smile, pouring on the charm.

But in the end, he got the feeling that she came not because he had bamboozled her, but because she'd *decided*
to. She had weighed the risk, decided that yes, she would
take the chance. Her attitude was a refreshing change of
pace.

As they strolled down to the boardwalk Vic played the
part of the perfect gentleman, bereft of even the tiniest
whiff of sleaze. And though he never so much as laid a
hand on her as they walked along the moonlit beach, he
touched her nonetheless. He asked just the right amount of
questions, gave the impression of being genuinely interested in her responses. Which, in fact, he was.

She said she was twenty-three, though she looked
more like seventeen. She told him that dancing was a tem-
porary fix, a fallback position to get her through this little
rough patch in her life. It appeared that, up until three
weeks before, she'd had a lucrative gig as a dominatrix at

the only first-class dungeon in town: whipping the flaccid
butts of upstanding Southern businessmen, administering
serious cock-and-ball discipline to lawyers, evangelical TV
hosts, local politicians, and touring music stars. These
were people who wielded power in their daily lives, and
then paid dearly to pretend to relinquish that power for a
couple of carefully controlled hours at a stretch: being
made to crawl and beg and squeal, to excrete on command
or swallow disgusting things, to admit what slime they really were without having to change their methodology a
whit. *Mea culpa, mea culpa,* my transgressions are legion.
And then back to ruthlessly ruling the world.

Vic was utterly fascinated. He asked her what had
gone wrong. A cloud passed over her features as she described her fall from grace. It had basically to do with a
long-standing problem of hers: an intense contempt for authority figures. Basically, if she couldn't beat them senseless, she had no use for them.

Unfortunately, the madam who ran the place didn't
double as one of Tristana's clients. This was a woman who
desperately needed to be tortured, then mangled, then shot;
but reality, in this instance, was not willing to oblige. In
the battle of wills between Tristana and the dragon lady,
there was no god or goddess to turn to, nor any justice to
be found. The next thing she knew, she was out on her ass,
hustling up sexual grunt work just to keep the bills paid.

Vic was more than sympathetic. He was strangely
touched. There was something about this girl that spoke to
a very deep part of him. He admired her soul-fire, her innate survivor's instinct, her disarming lack of confusion
and pretense. At first he thought maybe she reminded him
of Nora, back in the good old days: before Nora'd gone
and changed the rules on him.

And then, he realized: this woman was nothing like
Nora, with her constant whining about fidelity and her nat-
tering biological clock. Tristana was no good-girl-gone-
bad bullshit artist; Tristana was just *bad.* She knew who
she was, apologized to no one for it, and reveled in her
edgy identity.

In short, she reminded Vic of *Vic*.

For the first time in decades, Vic felt the internal stirrings of something profound. They walked and talked for hours. And then, just when the vibe built to a head and he was about to make his move, *she* surprised *him* by taking his hand and leading him down to the shadows beneath the abandoned steel pier. It was there that she pulled him down onto the cool, damp sand. It was there that they did the raging bone dance ceaselessly till four ayem, their screams buried by the pounding surf. She was so fine, so wet and savage, that he never wanted to stop thrusting inside her.

But alas, reality beckoned with the first hint of sunrise. Reluctantly, he bid her adieu, then rinsed himself clean in the ocean green. He was back in his hotel room by a quarter to six, her phone number tucked in his pocket, his head still humming from the glory of his new lust for life.

When Vic awoke, sometime after noon, he was unsurprised to find Nora rapidly losing her appeal. There was something about women who no longer gave a shit. When she finally dragged herself out of bed at four, Vic hustled her out for a late margarita brunch.

She was out like a light by ten.

And Vic was on his way.

As fate would have it, Tristana had the night off. She met him on the boardwalk, led him to a seedy little motel on Baltic Avenue, the kind that featured kitchenettes and weekly rentals and catered to a transient clientele. And indeed, Tristana's space gave no indication of rootedness; everything was geared to up and run at the drop of a hat.

The apartment itself was spartan and spare, the sole nod to individuality evident in the photos she'd plastered across the bedroom walls: a variety of Tristana-in-bondage poses, playing both dominant and submissive roles with equal skill and fervor. As she showed him her collection of whips and dildos and nipple-clamps, she went on to explain that you couldn't really top until you'd bottomed, felt the experience from the pay-end of the whip.

Vic was fascinated; so much so that when she brought

out a pair of handcuffs he actually let her slip one on him, click it shut. Something stirred in the silt of his soul; he took the other side of the cuffs and fastened it on her wrist. When she led him to the bed, he let her.

As she laid him down she asked about his many tattoos, who the mysterious woman was who ruled over so much of his body.

No one important, he replied. *Not anymore.*

She regarded him skeptically, searching for clues. He gave her none. *She's in the past,* he said. *Now there's only you.*

Only you.

They spent the rest of the night driving each other completely insane. The sex was phenomenal, worlds away from his standard prey. In the space of a single night Tristana taught him not so much the art of *give-and-take* but how to *take and be taken.* It was a first for him, a revelation. She taught him to trust, as she did things with ropes and whips and hands and mouth, showed him a whole new dimension to pleasure in pain.

And when they were done and spent and sated, she had actually kicked *him* out, saying she had to be somewhere in the morning. Vic was frankly amazed: it was the first time a female of his choosing had shared his bed and not become a brainless slave to his dick. The look on her face as she shut the door in his was a thing of beauty. What was the old saying? *A man chases a woman until she catches him.*

He was hooked. As the door closed Vic realized it was very possibly the best time he'd ever had.

But, of course, it was too good to last. . . .

VIC LOOKED UP. "'Bout fucking time," he snarled.

"Sorry about that," the waitress said, placed a fresh drink before him, beat a hasty retreat.

Vic sipped thoughtfully and stared at the ocean. What secrets it contained. And now it had another. He found himself replaying a bit of dialogue he and Tristana had shared on their last good night together. Out of context, it was horribly ironic and tragic ... all the more so because of the hopeful spirit in which it had originally been played out.

On the night before it all blew up, he was already contemplating the realities of turning Tristana. It would have been another first—generally he ate his conquests. Nora was handful enough, and the last thing he needed was a bunch of pissed-off werewolf one-night-stands chasing him around. But Tristana was different.

The more he thought of her, the less important Nora seemed. The very thought of roaming the night with Tristana at his side left him nervous, anticipatory, excited. He doubted that it would even be that hard to awaken her. She was halfway there, in spirit anyway, and she didn't even drink. And it was a fact that she had his juices flowing; already it was all he could do to keep from Changing every time she touched his cock.

No, her animal would emerge, and beautifully; of that, he had no doubt. Tristana was a natural. In fact, she was more than just a likely protégée; everything about her told him she could actually become his equal, someone to rival and complement his appetite. Once awakened, she would be magnificent. And together, they would be unstoppable.

They just needed a little more time.

And a couple of key issues cleared up.

So after spending hours drenched in each other's passion, he pulled her close and looked her in the eye. She met his gaze fiercely, awaiting the words she seemed to sense hanging between them. Lord only knew what she was expecting to hear—I love you, I need you, I want you forever—but he was impressed by how she took it in stride when he asked:

"So ... what do you think about eating human flesh?"

Tristana did a double take, then laughed: a low, evil chuckle that never failed to make him smile. "I guess that depends on who's doing the eating," she said. "And who's being eaten."

"Seriously," he persisted, and let her know he meant it. She was about to say something else glibly transgres-

*sive; he watched the impulse flare up and fizzle, becoming
suddenly thoughtful.*

*"Well, if it came down to a choice, I'd rather be the
one who eats," she said, and with a sudden faraway look
in her eye. "But if I was to be eaten, I'd want to be eaten
by someone I loved. Like 'Stranger in a Strange Land,' if
you know what I mean." He had no idea, but nodded anyway. "To be part of them forever," she continued. "That
would be cool. . . ."*

He had kissed her then, as if sealing a pact.

If he had only known . . .

Vic took another hit of whiskey, felt the sorrow bloom
inside his chest and well up in his eyes. Hindsight could
be so incredibly cruel. He looked at the clock. Twelve oh-
seven. Briefly, he wondered what was taking Nora so long.

But even the thought of her name was too much to
bear. Suddenly, he couldn't stand to think of her at all. It
flashed him back to last night, flashed him back on his
guilt, his own culpability in what had gone wrong. It made
him wish he had killed her first.

Before it was too late. . . .

IN RETROSPECT, HE realized she'd probably been sensing it
coming. The clues were certainly there: his increased impatience, his mounting detachment, his sudden indifference
to her aloofness. Vic cursed himself for not having worked
harder to cover his tracks.

Tuesday night had gone pretty much like every other:
Nora reducing herself to catatonia with the television on,
snoring through some Cinemax soft-core porn with a
warm bottle still in her hand. Vic had felt nothing but contempt for her as he slipped out the door, heading for the
tenth-floor elevator banks and the big wide world beyond.

It was just a couple blocks to 17th Street, with its garish neon and carnal, neo-carnival atmosphere. The streets
were teeming, the tacky sidewalk souvenir shops bright-lit
and bustling with life.

When he got to Fishnet's, Fernango the bouncer nodded. Vic had been acknowledged; a regular now, practi-

cally part of the family. There was, as always, a good-sized crowd, but he had no problem finding a place at the bar. The bartender saw him coming as well, set him up from the second he landed.

When Tristana came out, she was easily five times as hot as when he'd first seen her take the stage: writhing with shamanic abandon, firing unadulterated lust over the heads of the overheated throngs. Where before she'd been going through the motions, now there was a genuine burning passion.

But she only had eyes for Vic, and vice versa. The rest of the patrons didn't seem to notice their hidden dialogue; they were too busy responding to Tristana. As sexual totem, as *fuck muffin-slash-fantasy figure par excellence.* They were mesmerized.

Vic scoped the crowd as he watched her work, decided to play a little impromptu fiscal dick-measuring game called *up the ante.* He would target some sweaty, fervid herbivore with a fistful of dollars and a bellyful of beer, then sidle up adjacent to him and proceed to hand Tristana fives to his ones, tens to his fives, twenties to his tens and so on, making the clown pony up to match him for the illusion of her affections.

Tristana sensed the scam instinctively, played up to the sucker like crazy, giving him the extra smile and flash that told him beyond the shadow of a doubt that *he* was the one she really wanted, *he* was the one who made her all hot and sticky, ooh baby, ooh baby gimme another twenty to show me that you love me. . . .

In between sets, she would come down and sit with each mark in turn, keeping their libidos greased, before toddling off to the shadowy corner table where Vic lay waiting. Physical affection was strictly *verboten* on the premises—especially where boyfriends were concerned—but the look in Tristana's eyes told him that she was pleased. They made a beautiful team, and they both knew it.

So when he told her to give him her money, there was but a split second of doubt that flitted across her features before she dipped into her bag and forked it over. Vic slipped the wad of bills into his pocket and smiled.

Trust.

The second set was even better; Vic and Tristana tag-teaming the crowd as he fed her back the cash in ever-increasing quantities and she pushed her own considerable sexual repertoire to the limit, all with astonishing results. The bar grew even more packed: men began streaming through the door in droves, driven by an unseen impulse. Like cattle to the slaughter, like lemmings toward the cliffs of their collective desire, it was as if they could smell the charge from blocks away, knew instinctively that *this* was the place they needed to be. While up on the runway, Tristana whirled and gyrated, pushing psychic buttons they never even dreamed existed.

Vic hung back, sending her the subtlest of cues, picking each successive mark with a nod and a glance. Thoroughly enjoying himself, and the show. Completely in awe of her power.

All the while seeing a new world unfurl in his mind.

By the middle of the third set, Tristana had raked in close to six hundred dollars, and she was riding high: strutting up and down the runway in complete control, crossing into other dancers' kill zones at will, exerting her utter dominion over all. The crowd hooted and roared and drank with abandon; the other girls grumbled and gave way, trading knife-edged glances even as they yielded her ground. The management counted the profits and happily turned a deaf ear to their complaints.

The hours unfolded, wending inexorably toward closing time and the fulfillment of their hearts' desires. Vic had never felt quite so happy. He decided he would ask her to come away with him tonight, felt certain of her reply. Tristana was tough, and as such, she was unused to exposing herself emotionally. But love is willing vulnerability, under any other name; and she didn't have to say a word for him to know she loved him, too. The look in her eyes said it all.

For the first time in what felt like forever, all was right with his world.

And then Nora came walking in.

It was to Vic's eternal shame that he never even saw her coming, didn't have a fucking clue. One second, he was watching his new love dance, a big grin pasted across his kisser; the next thing he knew, Nora was standing beside him with the coldest, craziest expression on her face he'd ever seen. Her breath reeked of liquor, blood, and rage. She hissed at him.

You sonofaBITCH.

Every drop of stripjoint sweat on his body went instantly frigid. Every hair stood on end. He knew what was coming before it came, what she was going to say before she even said it.

Are you gonna take care of this? Or do I have to do it for you?

Tristana was at the far end of the runway, oblivious to the exchange. In desperation, Vic tried to feign ignorance. No chance. She knew, she knew, there was no way around it; denying it only made it worse. He found himself wracking his brain, searching out escape routes that didn't exist. He could feel the terrible killing power of the Change, surging through Nora and radiating outward.

And he knew, in that moment, that it was too late. She would stop at nothing. She had nothing to lose. She would do it right here, in front of everyone, bring the whole place crashing down around their ears—put the cops on their trail, kill herself, kill *him*—before she would let this violation go unavenged.

You can't make me do this, he tried to say, but he knew it wasn't true.

You OWE me, motherfucker, she spat. *We were meant to be together, remember? Well, now we are. For better and for worse, in sickness and in health, forever and ever and you fucking OWE ME THIS!!!*

And then she turned and stormed out, leaving Vic to his choices.

When closing time came, he tried his best to pretend

that nothing was wrong. Tristana, of course, was way too smart to buy it; and so she followed him around to the back of the club in a desperate attempt to pry loose his sudden, terrible secret. The Mercedes was parked back there in the alley, the trunk ajar and waiting. Nora was nowhere to be seen. She had thought of everything.

He brought them to a halt by the back of the car, making it look entirely coincidental. To his surprise, he found that he was shaking. She asked him what was wrong, slipped deftly into his embrace. He nestled her head against his chest.

Nora stepped out from around the corner.

Just remember, he whispered, *that I love you.* Kissing her lightly on the forehead. He cradled her face in his hands. She made a soft sound of unmistakable passion.

Then he seized her skull, twisting viciously. . . .

And it should have ended just like that.

But, of course, it didn't.

Because Tristana's instincts were strong, and she picked up on Vic's intent a split second before he could do the deed. Fear and confusion flared, were instantly incinerated by a single overriding impulse.

Tristana locked her neck, began to fight.

She was much stronger than he'd expected; she kicked and thrashed and raked her nails across his face. It bought her maybe another ten seconds of survival. Long enough for her to twist her head to come face-to-face with him. Long enough to see the tattoo on his bulging forearm, see Nora emerge from the darkness, see it all for what it was.

The look of sorrow in her eyes was matched only by the contempt, in the moment before she died. They fused together to burn into his brain forever, transmitting a single indelible message:

You pussy.

And then her neck muscles gave out, with a slingshot bonecracking snap. . . .

And it was done. One second, she was a living, breathing embodiment of all his dreams; the next, she was a hun-

dred and twelve pounds of limp and sagging meat: forever
gone, useless in his arms.

It had been years since he'd allowed himself to cry,
and it seemed strange to be doing it now. Her dead weight
knocked him back a step, as if her flesh knew its final destination, was only trying to help. He kissed her once more,
mouthed the words *I'm sorry*. Then he gently laid her out
on the plastic trunk liners that Nora had so thoughtfully
provided.

Suddenly, he was being elbowed roughly but indiffer-
ently aside. He fell back without protest, though he felt his
heart constrict. Nora was there—half-human, half-beast,
completely deranged—looming over the body, her features
lit from the trunk light below. Without hesitation, she slit
Tristana's dead throat, peeling upward in an ugly, brutal
swipe. The face came clean away, leaving behind a
deathmask of muscle and skull that could have belonged to
anyone.

This is mine, Nora said, holding up her souvenir.

Then she reached down with her free hand and slit the
carcass from vulva to sternum, viscid tubes and exposed
organs flopping to either side. A final desecration. Her last
disrespects. Nora dug up under the breastbone to wrench
the dead heart free, then helped herself to a big steaming
bite.

Savoring the spark. Getting off on it.

You can take care of the garbage, she told him, as she
tossed the leftovers into the trunk. Nora stalked off into
the shadows.

Leaving Vic alone, moaning over the seeping remnants
of his dream . . .

OVER THE OCEAN, a storm front was gathering. Already, its
dark clouds had swallowed the moon. He felt its immi-
nence in the pit of his stomach. A sinking sensation. Too
appropriate for words. Vic wiped the last of this evening's
tears on the back of his hand, snuck a glimpse at the clock.

It was twelve-fifteen.

For the first time, it fully occurred to him that Nora

had been gone an awfully long time. Nearly half an hour. What the fuck was that about? Not that he was in any hurry to experience her return—just the thought of her, at this point, made his blood congeal in his veins—but it struck him as strange. She'd told him she'd be right back.

Oh no, said a voice in his head.

Vic looked at his half-empty glass of whiskey, then across the table at Nora's drink. She had drained it before she left for the bathroom. She hadn't ordered another.

Oh christ no, said the voice, more emphatic.

He clamped down hard, methodically ran down the list of reasons why panic was pointless, the worst of his options. He thought about the last year and a half spent together: eighteen months in which she'd never once tried to run away. He thought about the permanent shattering of will, her terrible crippling resignation. He thought about the words *forever and ever.*

He thought about the way she'd looked while gutting Tristana.

He looked at the clock again.

A sickly churn began to cycle in his gut, physical corollary to the voice in his head. A second voice chimed in now, infinitely more practical. *Go look for her,* it said.

He stood, a bit unsteadily. Something slipped from his lap, tumbled to the floor. Vic looked down, struggling to focus. Something shiny lay coiled at his feet. It was fine-tooled and delicate, easily five feet long, with a tiny silver clasp on the end.

Her chain.

Oh god.

Vic stood paralyzed, unable to accept the evidence of his senses. He suddenly realized how completely he'd been suckered, how very deeply he'd been spiked.

"Oh, fuck," he muttered, half-falling back against the wall. "Oh, fuck." Waiting for the dizziness to pass. The thought of dragging himself another step farther was incredibly difficult: a deep soul-exhaustion settled over and through him like a fog that freezes bone.

But beneath the killing fog was the understanding that

she had *planned* this, she had deliberately done this to
fuck him up; and what was worse, she had waited until tonight. Which meant that she'd known she was going to do
this even *before* she made him kill Tristana.

Which meant that Tristana had died for nothing.

No, *worse:* as an instrument of Nora's revenge.

And she had used his hands to do it. . . .

"You bitch." Feeling the fog burn off, the withering
lethargy disperse. "Oh jesus god you fucking BITCH!"
His strength returned in a bloodred tidal wave. Suddenly,
it was standing still that had become impossible. Vic
pushed off from the wall, fists clenched and teeth bared,
his whole body coursing with murderous animal rage. He
stormed into the bar, following her trail. It went right past
the rest rooms, and straight out the door leading to the
street.

Oh, you bitch. You didn't . . .

But as a matter of fact, she did.

Vic did the mental math. She had roughly a thirty-
minute lead. He didn't want to think about how far behind
the eight ball that put him. He went out the door, moving
fast, and did not look back.

Atlantic Avenue ran parallel to the boardwalk, all the
way up and down the length of the beach. Hotels loomed
huge along the seaward side; clubs and tourist traps hawk-
ing doodads or overpriced drinks festooned the inland side
of the street.

Nora's trail headed south. There was not much traffic,
either by car or on foot. All the trawling young college
meat that he passed on the street meant nothing to him.
They were, to his eyes, less substantial than ghosts.

At the Hilton, Nora's trajectory shifted inward. He
practically blew through the glass revolving doors. The
sound of canned Top 40 dogshit emanated from Chico's,
the hotel lounge; a cow-eyed couple quickly ducked to one
side as he barreled through the lobby toward them. He
peered through the giant aquarium to the dim-lit interior.

A complete waste of time. Nora hadn't taken off running for a drink with an umbrella in it and a slow dance

to the sound of Wilson Philips wannabees. He turned, heading out the door that led to the boardwalk.

And as he ran and he ran, tracking her from one bar to another to another, it didn't take long to figure out that she was leading him on a wild-goose chase. And in the process, leading him farther and farther away from the Seaside Hideaway. Away from his room, his car, all his belongings . . .

. . . including all those credit cards he hadn't felt like carrying . . .

"GODDAMMIT!" he screeched, as he spun on his heel, using every last molecule of strength at his disposal, going *fuck fuck fuck you conniving little CUNT!* as he pushed himself harder, hoping against hope that she had played the thread too long, was still trying to throw him off the trail instead of doubling back and doing what *he* would have done . . .

. . . and it took him less than four minutes to travel the mile-and-a-quarter distance: some kind of record for a biped, even without the human and hurtling metal obstacles in his path. He arrived at their hotel, slipped in a side entrance, not wanting to be seen. There was nobody at the elevator when he got there. No one to distract him. No one he would have to kill. He thought about how long she'd been gone. Easily an hour and change, more than doubling her lead time since he'd left Viper's.

Vic took a deep breath, tried to keep it in perspective. These things had a way of balancing out. She might have a head start, but he excelled at playing catch-up.

And he had a pretty good idea where ol' Nora might be heading. . . .

The elevator came. There was nobody inside. So much the better for the human race. *And when I find you,* he mused, stepping in. *Ooh baby, when I do . . .*

He didn't hear the first police sirens till the doors were almost closed. All the way up, he kept telling himself *it's okay, it doesn't matter, it has nothing to do with you.* Which worked just fine and dandy, right up until he began to hear the caterwauling voices from above.

And all the smells of death assailed him.

Vic numb. The jumble of screaming, shouting, heaving voices told him less than the stench in the air. He smelled brains—two, maybe three—and yards upon yards of unfurled digestive tract.

The doors slid open on ten. Blood and meat had graffitoed the corridor walls directly across from Room 1019. She hadn't even kept it contained to their suite. But then again, why would she? She was a bright girl. She'd sought maximum impact, in the shortest possible time.

He elbowed aside a hurling coed and came to a stop in front of the door. "Holy shit," he hissed softly, surveying the carnage. He saw shreds of Navy white, mostly stained with Navy red, put the jigsaw pieces together in his mind. Three squids. She had picked up three sailors, brought them back to her place for a groovy gangbang.

Well, they'd gone off with a bang, all right. Actually, more like a groovy *ka-BOOM!!!* He almost laughed when he thought about it; in fact, one split second later, he did. He found that he couldn't help it. It was just so fucking perverse.

He realized that he should be very upset—that li'l Nora was already gone—and moreover, that he was standing in the middle of Setup City. He had to admire the beauty of how she'd spiked him; and besides, he needed a place to put all this fresh psychotic energy.

A storm was coming, that much was for certain. And the cops would be here any second. Vic hoped she'd be listening to her dashboard radio.

The elevator doors opened. Vic smiled.

It was time for a Change.

33

I T WAS JUST past midnight when the front door to 716 Raymire Street exploded in a shower of oak and leaded glass. The sky to the east had clouded over forebodingly, peals of distant thunder rumbling down the windswept, empty streets.

The door was heavy and strong, painstakingly stripped and refinished. It gave way practically on the first blow, sent long shards of destruction raining down on the patterned Italian tile of the entrance hall.

Syd came roaring in through the wreckage, his every move crackling with murderous intent. The house was dark and still, but otherwise amazingly unchanged: its warm wood floors and cool white walls almost exactly as he'd left them, another lifetime ago.

He roamed from room to room, spreading annihilation in his wake as he smashed and gouged and tore his way across the face of what was once his home. All the while howling out her name.

Calling for Karen, in a voice no longer human.

Because Syd had changed; oh, yes, indeed. As he'd fled the mountain, a wildfire had lit in his soul: fueled by the sudden revelation of futher betrayal, unchecked by sanity or reason. Mental tinder, ignited by the spark of betrayal, magnified a millionfold until it burned out of control in his brain. The fire spread through his body, raced under his quivering skin.

By the time he reached the house, it was a raging inferno.

And it would not stop until it had consumed all in its path.

A ceiling fan spun lazily in the living room, blades slowly slicing the air. He had hung it there himself, the week they moved in. Syd yowled, vaulted skyward, did a manic slam-dunk. The fan came down, trailing hot sparks and live wire.

"KAAHHREN!!"

His voice was harder than nails: an unhinged and inchoate asylum of sound. He moved into the dining room, upending the heavy deco table they'd found at a flea market on her twenty-fifth birthday. The table flew through the air, exploded into splinters and shrapnel against the hutch that still housed the wedding presents: china and *tsatskes,* nuptial relics. The hutch came next, tipping free from the wall, disgorging its contents to shatter on the floor. The walls grew great gaping holes, as his misshapen fists lashed out again and again. Forensic foreplay, warm-up to the main event.

All the while, calling her name.

Upstairs, a flurry of footfalls: panicked-sounding, crazed. Syd growled and spun, loping down the hall, ripping rungs from the banister as he vaulted over it. Taking the stairs three at a time.

A pajama-clad figure stood paralyzed at the second-floor landing, a nine-iron quivering in one upraised hand. One glimpse of Syd and the pajama-man fled for the bedroom, golf club clattering to the floor.

Syd hit the landing, hot on his tail. Seeing Vaughn Restal, Doug-the-dweeb, Phil-from-New-York all rolled into one: one screeching, scuttling everyman who had ever snuck behind his back and slithered between her legs. The fear in the air was napalm perfume, pointedly fanning the flames.

Pajama-man reached the master bedroom, slamming the door. A split second later, Syd landed full force upon it. The door folded and fell inward, careening off its hinges. Pajama-man fell back, screaming.

More screams, erupting from the darkness: pitiful animal shrieking sounds. A low growl spilled from Syd's lips as he bounded over the threshold. He found Karen there, huddled in the middle of the bed.

The same bed they'd once shared.

The one she shared now with this *sniveling little shit*. . . .

The comforter was gathered cocoonlike around her. He remembered it well, down to how much it cost. But not like he remembered *her*. It had been two and a half years since last they'd spoken. Even in shock, she looked very much the same. Perhaps her hair was a little bit longer; her pupils larger, huge and brimming with fear.

As he approached the bed, her boyfriend rallied, launching a desperate counterstrike. Syd snarled and backhanded him, felt the satisfying crunch of shattered meat and bone. Pajama-man crashed to the floor in a heap, his jaw dislocated, retching up blood and teeth.

Karen screeched, vaulting off the bed to shield her wounded lover. Syd snatched her leg, pulled her kicking and screaming toward him. She scrabbled and thrashed, clawing at the floor. Her nightgown rode up, exposing the bare flesh of her buttocks.

Syd flipped her over, lips skinning back, ready to bite out her tiny, scabrous heart. . . .

Then he saw the small but unmistakable bulge in her belly: the hard, round swell of life now growing in that once-desolate place.

It was like ramming an iceberg: cold truth punching a hole in his rage, leaving him suddenly adrift and sinking. Syd stopped, staring at her nakedness. He let go of her ankle, let her leg drop. Karen hit the floor, scuttled back to her fallen lover. The new king of the castle.

The father of her child.

Two and a half years. Time enough for ghosts to fade, for lives to start over. *Two and a half years.* Syd cast a wild eye around the room, as the difference in his surroundings suddenly assailed him. He saw stuffed animals lining a shelf on the wall, bright plastic eyes bearing blind witness to the slaughter.

A crib waited beneath them, empty and expectant.

There was an antique mirror on the bureau by the bed, another flea market flashback to their former life. Syd turned, caught a glimpse of himself, hovering in the blue-black shadows of the room . . .

. . . *and he saw himself bearing down mercilessly on her, his features predatory, contorted with bitterness and rage* . . .

. . . and the face that stared back at him was monstrous, deformed into bestial caricature: his mouth grown huge and leering, his skin crawling and crisscrossed with the scars of a thousand inner battles . . .

. . . *and he saw Karen, her own features frozen in that perfect, blank mask: withering under the force of his boundless anger, his endless torrent of bile* . . .

. . . *and he saw Karen, her eyes like bright mirrors, reflecting back the face that he had shown her, time and time again.*

The face of the monster he kept inside . . .

Karen's lover moaned and brought a hand up to his broken face. A glint of gold shone on his ring finger. A wedding band. Karen mewled, protectively cradled his head. There was a wedding ring on her finger, as well. Syd turned away from his reflection, watched them quiver on the floor: huddled together like bunnies, like frightened deer, Bambi and Thumper caught in the onrushing headlights' glare. It felt suddenly shameful to torment these harmless creatures. They were not of his kind. Never would be. Never were.

And as her eyes flickered up to his, tearful and doomed, he saw clearly now that she didn't have a clue:

no understanding as to who he was, why any of this was happening, why any of it had ever happened at all.

But for all her lack of understanding, one other thing was clear: her life had gone on, while he had remained chained to his past, unable to let go of the pain. For better or worse, she had a new life; and so his presence here was reduced to senseless madness. Laying waste to her world. For no reason at all.

It was that simple, and that horrifying. It left Syd standing frozen there, trembling and torn. He could kill her, yes—kill *both* of them—and murder the promise sleeping inside her. He could destroy her life, make her suffer, make her die. But he could never make her *understand*.

In the end, it would mean less than nothing.

And he would never be healed.

I'm sorry. . . . he tried to say. The words, when they came, made no sense at all; guttural gibberish from the mouth of a monster. *I'm sorry. . . .* Karen flinched and heard only threats. She lashed out weakly, clutched at her husband, began to cry.

He watched her for a moment, a shadow passing over his face. Then he was moving: away from them, down the hall and down the stairs, then out of the shattered portal of his long-dead dream.

Outside, lights had flickered on along Raymire Street. Anonymous shadows watched from furtive windows; psychic scavengers, feeding on boudoir secrets. In the sky, lightning flickered ominously. The wind had picked up, bringing with it the first faint drops of the coming storm. It would be upon them soon.

But for Syd, it was already here.

34

THURSDAY PLAYED OUT for Nora behind a ceaseless curtain of rain: a blinding, torrential downpour that started forty miles out of Virginia Beach and dogged her all the rest of the way. The windshield wipers bravely flailed against the flood, could not keep up. The Mercedes was frequently forced to a slogging 25-m.p.h. crawl that seemed to last forever.

She had chosen the most direct route: straight up I-64 out of Norfolk, past Richmond and Charlottesville, then across the Blue Ridge Mountains to Staunton, VA. It should have taken five hours, wound up taking nine. By the time she pulled off the road and checked into a Comfort Inn sometime around ten-thirty the next morning they were just packing up the free continental breakfast; and despite all the speeders she'd gobbled, she managed to scarf three half-stale Danishes before collapsing on top of her still-made bed.

She awoke around four, to the sound of rolling thunder. The storm had settled in, lashing the windows monotonously, turning the parking lot into an asphalt lake. She sat up and reached for the remote control, immediately turned on the news. The car's radio reception had been lousy, between the mountains and the rain; but cable TV was a whole 'nother story. As she flipped through the channels, she caught a bit on CNN about a fairly spectac- ular bloodbath that had taken place late Wednesday in none other than beautiful scenic Virginia Beach. Official reports now put the death toll at thirty, including four po- lice officers and several members of the hotel staff. The rest had been guests who stumbled onto the scene, as well as three unidentified sailors whose presence there still had not been explained. Reporters on the scene described it as a "grisly slaughterhouse tableau." There were no survi- vors.

The man whose suite had been the locus of the may- hem was identified from hotel records as one P. Clinton Melhorn, although subsequent investigation cast some doubt on that. CNN had an artist's composite of the man being sought for questioning, along with a rendition of the "female companion" who had checked in with him. Vic's sketch looked more like a scar-faced cartoon pirate than the real thing, but that was hardly the point. Hers was close enough for folk music.

And she was driving the Mercedes.

Nora was wide awake now; she leapt off the bed, be- gan pacing the room as she flipped channels, searching for more clues. She caught the local news in time to hear about a seemingly unrelated incident some one hundred and eighty-seven miles to the west. A routine speeding vi- olation spotted by State Police had led to a thirty-seven- mile-long chase, culminating in a five-car pileup in the Allegheny foothills just outside of Swift Run, Virginia. The chase had continued on foot into Shenandoah State Park before the police lost the suspect; authorities reported the deaths of two of the officers in pursuit. A third trooper reported having fired upon "a large, wild animal" that then disappeared into the woods and the blinding rain. He was treated for severe lacerations and shock, and was reported in serious but stable condition.

The news switched gears then, offering a startling new

update on breast implants, but Nora was no longer listening. She was busy thinking about Vic.

He was sending her a message. And Nora was reading it loud and clear. No question about it, he was hot on her trail, and the gloves were off for good. All this mayhem was just his little way of saying *prepare to die real bad*.

Judging from the time of Vic's last sighting, the weather conditions, and the distance between them, she gave herself ten, maybe twelve hours before it might be time to start seriously worrying again.

Nora considered her options. It was definitely time to ditch the car. Worse yet, she was running short of cash. A fresh credit card wouldn't hurt, either, plus some makeup and toiletries. Then she could be on her way.

These courtesies were provided by Mr. and Mrs. Ralph Landry of Cincinnati, Ohio. Nora found them in Room 117, where the motel staff would eventually find them, as well. Mrs. Landry was a plump little thing, and her taste in clothing was strictly Jaclyn Smith K mart collection, but her makeup at least was decent, Elizabeth Arden and Lancôme. They also were kind enough to provide her with an American Express card, a Gold MasterCard, Amoco and Sunoco gas cards, plus a neat six hundred in cash, the keys to their slate-blue '91 Acura Legend, and their souls.

Granted, the two of them strapped together didn't stack up to much, lifeforce-wise; the Navy-boys were much stronger. But she did get a tepid buzz; enough to sharpen her up a bit, get her where she was going.

From Staunton, she hooked north onto Route 250, a snaky little secondary highway that traversed both the Appalachian and Allegheny mountains. The Acura handled nicely—almost as good as the Mercedes—and it should have been a scenic route, but she was in a hurry and the rain wouldn't give her an ounce of slack. Again, she found herself crutching half-blind through eight hours of solid driving that should have taken less than half that time.

In Fairmont, West Virginia, the final leg of the journey began: heading straight up I-79 to Pittsburgh and the surrounding environs. By then, she'd been plowing through sodden darkness for hours. She wondered if Vic had laid low till sunset, given the heat on his tail. Or perhaps he'd just transformed and traveled through the woods on foot. He could cover a lot of ground that way. She took small comfort in the fact that the storm was doubtless slowing his course as much as hers.

Ten miles out of Monville, radio reception finally cleared enough to give her an update. And what an update it was. Seven more butchered tonight along the Chickahominy River, right outside of Roxbury, Virginia. Vic hadn't even made it to West Virginia yet. This was very good news indeed. State Police were already casting a net, setting up roadblocks on all routes leading out of the state. Nora smiled. If he kept it up with these hotdogging grandiose displays, she might get lucky and someone would shoot his ass. Then maybe she wouldn't need Syd, after all.

Which just left the other burning issue: did she even *want* Syd now? It was a damned good question. In truth, it had been so long since she'd dared to even think about it that she really didn't know. She remembered his kisses, the heat of his touch, the exquisite feel of him coming inside her. They were great memories, to be sure; but she couldn't help but wonder if they hadn't been enhanced somewhat by the last year and a half's travails. Was he really that good, or had she just wanted to remember it that way?

And then there was the issue of his straight-arrow domestic impulse. Did she really want to play house anymore? She wasn't quite sure, but her wild side had a definite feeling on the matter, and that feeling was *AIEEEE!!!* After eighteen months imprisoned in the dungeon of love, she was fairly chomping at the bit for some action. A little craziness. Was that too much to ask?

There were thoughts in her head that were threatening admission, feelings burbling volcanic beneath the surface of all this; and they were dangerous things, so supercharged and volatile that if she allowed herself to let go and *really experience them,* she might literally tear herself apart. Key among them was the issue of *love;* an emotion she'd been forced to suppress so deeply that she'd almost forgotten what it was.

She knew, from cruel experience, that nothing could wound and savage like love. Nothing else left you quite so open, so vulnerable to the damage. Nora's defenses, by and large, were pretty formidable: she'd chewed her way through those sailors like so many Sta-Puf marshmallow boys, and she could easily have done a dozen more if the matter had come up. But slap a little *love* into the equation, and watch her just fall to pieces. It was truly pathetic.

And what's more, it never failed.

Because once you let them in, there *were* no more defenses. No teeth or claws on the inside. Just tender vittles and soft bellyflesh. They could do anything they wanted then; without even trying, they could eat you alive.

And she, in turn, had spread for them at every conceivable opportunity: welcoming them inside, literally inviting them to feed. And why had she done this incredibly stupid thing? *Because she was in love.* Because she was perpetually starving for that essence. Because she needed what they had. No matter how shitty they treated her. No matter how destructive it became.

The most important thing, she reckoned, was to get Syd back in the fold. Between the two of them, they could handle Vic; and this time, she would not hold back. If they survived, they could take it from there. Or *not.* Depending on how she felt.

It was just past midnight when Nora pulled onto the Mt. Haversford Road. She still couldn't see squat, but memory alone was enough to propel her through the familiar twists and turns. She had just driven through over five hundred miles of rain-smothered, interminable hell. It had taken her nearly twenty-four hours. She had done this with a single-minded clarity of purpose, a nearly preternatural calm. From the outside, she was sure, she looked stable, completely in control.

But she was just keeping the lid on tight; and all the way across the Eastern seaboard, there had not been a single second during which she hadn't been aware of the forces raging within her. Like the storm that had dogged her every step, she was unable to escape their power. Just as she was unable to escape her need for the prison-keepers of the opposite camp.

Do I still love Syd? she asked herself. And instead of an answer, a question came back:

Did I ever?

And then, all at once, she was there: the twinkling sign directly ahead. She swallowed hard and pulled in to the lot. It was nearly empty; in weather like this, people rightly stayed home. Nora pulled in maybe ten spaces from the door, parked under the neon flicker of the Budweiser and Stroh's signs.

She turned on the dome light in the car, did some last-minute adjustments. Her hair was a lost cause, under the circumstances. Likewise her wardrobe. Ah, well. She unfortunately didn't have time to wait around for the optimum conditions. It was already twelve forty-five.

"You're beautiful," she told herself, desperately hoped it was true.

Then she opened the door, and stepped out into the night.

JUST WHEN JANE thought things couldn't possibly get any worse.

All day she'd felt like shit: wandering around in a state of complete agitation, torn between kicking herself for not stopping Syd and the knowledge that whatever he was going through was *his* battle, not hers. That he would have to come to grips with it on his own, and on his own terms. Only then could she hope to help him. Only then would it do any good.

Of course, you could have told *him,* said the nagging voice of conscience. She winced at the thought. How could she have? It was part of her upbringing, the involuntary common sense by-product of living life as the perpetual outsider, of constantly moving from place to place to place. It had seemed the most natural thing in the world as

a child, but more and more lately she had come to realize
how weirdly socialized it had left her. She never even
went to *school*, for god's sake; educated instead by her
mother, taking her lessons in the back of a jostling Winne-
bago as they rolled down one faceless stretch of highway
after another.

Privacy was second only to toilet training in her lexicon of familial programming. *Stay out of other people's
business* was the Mason family edict, *and keep them out of
yours. Always be friendly. Never get close. They'll hurt
you if you do, even if they don't mean to.*

They just can't help themselves.

It made tons of sense, considering how the world was,
and their place in it. As a child, it hardly even mattered.
She had love and caring to spare. She was cherished and
protected. The family was all that mattered. The family
was all there was.

But now Mom and Dad were gone, and the program
was still in place, chugging away like the runaway lawn
mower of a suburban heart attack victim, cutting random
swaths through the rest of her life. It wasn't until Syd had
fled that Jane fully realized just how much she cared about
him. And just how tired she was of being alone.

She loved Gramma Mae, but it just wasn't the same:
Gram had her own life, and liked it just the way it was.
Gram was a loner by nature, and though Janey would always be welcome in her house, it would always be exactly
that. *Her* house. *Her* life. Jane needed her own. Now, more
than ever.

She was worried about Syd, and what he was going
through; she wanted to talk to him *so bad*. But god, was
it hard to let down her guard.

So when he showed up for work, looking ragged and
haggard and genuinely *haunted*, she approached him immediately. *Are you okay?* she asked.

Fine, he said. *I'm fine.*

And she knew it wasn't true, that it was anything but.
His tone was chilled to the point of numbness; he worked

robotically, not smiling, not talking, deflecting her every
overture of concern.

Jane finally determined that she would get inside his
defenses, even if she had to let her own down to do it. She
would do it tonight.

Just as soon as they got out of there.

Fortunately, it was deadly slow, business-wise. What
with the storm battering the valley, there were maybe two
dozen people in the whole damn club. Jane let Bonnie go
home early, kept herself nominally busy, waiting for the
opportunity to talk to him. At eleven forty-five it looked
like her chance had come.

Then the front door opened.

And everything went straight to hell.

Oʜ ᴍʏ ɢᴏᴅ.

Syd looked up from rinsing glasses, saw her reflection
in the mirror. *Oh my god.* Watching her descend the steps
like Marley's ghost in heels. The feeling struck like an ice
pick to the back of his skull, made the blood drain from
his face. *Please don't do this,* he silently pleaded. *Oh
please . . .*

But there wasn't a force on earth that could stop what
was already in motion.

Syd turned and saw Nora moving toward him, all her
calculated sexual ferocity firing point-blank in his direction; and watching her, he couldn't help but be thrown
back on those long-buried memories he'd worked so hard
to inter. The way she'd first appeared, like Rita Hayworth
descending from the screen. The revelation implicit in her
presence. The astounding tug on his body and soul.

He remembered swearing his undying love to her, being ready to follow her wherever she might go.

And now she was back . . .

*. . . but there was something wrong with the picture
this time. Or maybe he'd just finally learned how to see.
The wrongness extended far beyond mere physicality: the
rain pasting her clothing to her body, slicking her hair*

back on her head. Those things could just as easily have worked to her advantage.

But they didn't, and the reason became clearer with every step she took. He bristled, sensitized to her severe stimuli; and as he did he realized that she had a reek *to her—a rotting spirit-smell—that had far less to do with physical senses than with soul-antennae. It was the stench of her dissipation, the stink of corruption beyond repair, and he couldn't help but respond.*

The closer she came, the more his flesh began to crawl.

Nora crossed the room, the illusion peeling back in *déjà vu* detail. Her beauty was still there, still powerful. But her beauty was utterly subsumed by the infinite, minute striations of character etched indelibly into the tiny lines of her face, the strips of light and shadow that demarcated her flesh.

They said that God was in the details.

Perhaps this was what they were talking about.

Because as Syd beheld her entrance all the Marc Pankowski-esque metaphors came instantly, incandescently clear. No evasion. No mistake. No way to deny it. She was responsible for all those lines—*every single one*—and they told her story like karmic hieroglyphs, roadmaps of the journey of her soul.

And, dear God, there was so much ugliness there. . . .

He saw it in the lines that framed the mouth that parted now to speak. So much bitterness. So little mercy. He saw it in the lines that surrounded her eyes: lines both cruel and tragic, born from both sides of betrayal.

Most of all, it was in the eyes, which could no longer mask her insanity.

Nora stepped up to the bar. "Nora," he said.

"Syd," she said. "I'm so sorry."

And it was as if the entire last year and a half of hell had been nothing more than a trip to the bathroom, and now they were late for a previous engagement.

"What?" he replied.

"I'm sorry," she repeated. "I know this seems crazy,

but I've missed you so much, and we really don't have much time," she continued. "I promise, I'll explain it all later."

"Nora, I can't—"

"Syd, please," she interrupted, impatience underlying the urgency in her tone. "I don't understand what the big deal is. If you'll just come with me I swear I'll explain everything. . . ."

"Syd." Jane's voice, behind him. "Syd, is everything okay?"

Oh god, he thought. Jane. He glanced at her nervously, then back to Nora.

As her features went icy and hard . . .

. . . AND SUDDENLY ALL of her plans were in jeopardy, igniting to sizzling flame in her brain.

The sight of Syd on the other side of the bar was weird enough, the idea that he would not want to leave with her had never even entered her mind. There was, after all, the reality of Vic to buttress her story: one twist of the radio dial would confirm that.

Beyond that, there was her vast repertoire of skills. Nora could cry; she could browbeat; she could lie; she could intimidate; she could plead, cajole, caress, extol, impress, distress, and suck cock like a pro. And because there was nothing she wouldn't do, there was virtually nothing she *couldn't* do. It was the essence of her strength.

Right up until the moment the little bitch came up behind him.

She hadn't planned for this, hadn't considered it at all. She had saved his goddamned life, and he had just gone on without her. She vaguely remembered this second-string cunt from way back, recalled the way she'd so wisely deferred. Now she wasn't being nearly so smart.

"Syd, you gotta believe me," she continued, negating the intrusion. "I tried to get back to you, I really did. Baby, I missed you *so much.* . . ."

"Syd." The cunt was speaking again. "Syd, what—"

"Shut *up!*" Nora snarled. Jane visibly recoiled, but did

not move. Nora turned her attention back to Syd. "Quit fucking around, baby." She reached out to take his hand. "C'mon, we gotta go. . . ."

"No."

"Seriously, baby, we—"

"NO!"

He yanked his hand away, out of her grasp. Nora's eyes flared, then narrowed to flinty slits. "What did you say?" she asked incredulously.

"He said, 'No.' "

Nora glared. Another cunting intrusion. Bad enough she should speak; Nora then watched in amazement as the little slut actually *insinuated* herself: placing a protective hand on Syd's shoulder, trying to pull him away. Nora's eyes locked on the offending hand before flitting back to Syd's face. For the first time, she realized how different he looked. How much he had changed.

But she didn't miss—*couldn't* miss—the way Syd moved, not back, but instinctively *forward* to shield the bitch. She saw the way his body language so eloquently revealed his betrayal. Syd took position in front of his barmaid bitch, his entire body tensed and ready.

Ready to defend her, Nora realized. *Defend her against me . . .*

And it was all so suddenly, terribly clear. Nora realized with a slick rush of horror that they were completely, unassailably in love, and they didn't even know it yet.

She started to laugh then: a caustic, acid-tinged explosion, devoid of mirth. "You gotta be kidding," she said. "What'd she do, Syd, wrap your dick around her little finger?"

"Nora, stop it."

"Do you have *any idea* what I've been through?" Nora hissed, tears beginning to well in her eyes. "I fought my way through hell to get back to you, you miserable sonofabitch; you'd be *dead* if it wasn't for me. . . ."

"Nora, please . . ."

"I put my ass on the line for you, and now you're telling me you're gonna throw me over for this . . . this—"

She gestured dismissively to his little squeeze. "I *love* you, goddammit! I need your help! Now, are you coming with me, or what??"

But Syd just stood his ground and stared at her: not speaking, not moving, not giving her an inch. He didn't have to. The light in his eyes said it all. There was fear there, yes, and confusion. But there was something else, too: and its mere presence made Nora crazy, made it very hard to keep from just slaughtering him on the spot, slaughtering them both.

She looked in his eyes, and saw *pity*.

"I'm sorry," he croaked.

"Mother*fucker*," she spat. "You *had* your chance. Just remember that. You *had* your chance. . . ."

. . . AND THEN SHE was whirling, stalking off toward the door while the feelings surged up inside him, yanking at the far end of his chain. There was no getting around how powerful it felt . . .

. . . just as there had been no getting around the look in her eyes, in the moment before she turned . . .

. . . and then she was gone, her memory burning a free-way of fire through his brain. He had seen the murder in those eyes—had seen, there, what she was capable of—and it flashed him back on Jules, and that night of blood and destruction.

The door hissed closed behind her. Syd felt Jane shudder beside him, slipped his arm around her.

"It's okay," Syd murmured; and that was when Jane pulled away. As she did he saw that it was anger, not fear, that made her tremble. "It'll be okay. . . ."

"Don't bet on it," Jane said. "That bitch is crazy." Syd nodded, thinking *you don't know the half of it.*

"If she comes around again," Jane added, "I'll fucking kill her."

Syd looked at her. Thinking *you don't know . . .*

The time for revelation had come.

It was twelve fifty-one.

35

R EVELATION, HOWEVER, DIDN'T come all at once;
nor did it come easily. The first order of business
was to get Jane home, alive and in one piece. He could
worry about the rest from there.

Closing up early, by comparison, was a given. Under
the circumstances, it was the only thing to do. Syd an-
nounced last call practically the moment Nora left. Jane
backed him up completely, scooping half-finished drinks
off of customers' tables, hustling everyone out the door as
quickly as they possibly could. By the time the last stragglers were ready to go, Syd and Jane were ready as well.

Throughout the whole ordeal, Jane didn't utter a single
word that wasn't entirely job-related. Whatever she was
feeling, she played it close to the vest. That was fine with
Syd; he couldn't talk about it, either, though he suspected
his reasons and hers were maybe *just a little bit* different.

Her concerns, he was forced to suspect, were probably
just a touch more terrestrial than his. The odds were pretty
good that, when she thought about this, she wasn't fac-
toring in the supernatural. In fact, he found himself thinking about asking her *jeez, honey, you ain't scared of no*

werewolves, now, are ya? But then again, it probably wasn't the best idea. Whatever was going to happen, he sure as shit didn't need her doubting his sanity.

Lord knows, she'd soon have reason enough to doubt her own.

At one-thirty they chased out the last stragglers. Jane didn't complain when he left on the parking lot lights; she seemed to instinctively grasp that it was best to leave with all the lights on and as many people around as possible. As the last customer filed out Syd darted behind the bar, reached behind the ice chest and grabbed the shotgun, wrapping it in his jacket like so much fresh fish from market. Jane flashed him a worrisome look as he rejoined her, but said nothing.

Even in the company of others, the parking lot felt both treacherous and terrifying. The relentless, pounding rain didn't help matters. Syd held the jacket-wrapped gun in one hand, clutched Jane's hand in the other as they exited. He wouldn't let her leave his side, not even for a second. The memories were far too vivid, his recollection of them far too clear.

And it was so easy, so easy to let his mind slip horribly back. The pool of blood. The growling beast. Jules's dead face sliding across the window. It would paralyze him if he let it, this fear: freeze him right in his tracks. Another thing he could not allow. He feared for these people, knowing they could just as easily become human shields, more bodies to pile between him and the horror awaiting if things went out of control.

It was an ugly, soul-curdling thought, and he felt unclean even having it. But that didn't change its essential truth.

And Syd felt a fierce sense of duty, a territorial protectiveness that spread like an umbrella to encompass all of them. This place was *his:* everyone who came to this place was *his* charge, so long as they were there.

Good night, he waved. *Don't die* is what he meant.

Then he was walking Jane to the driver's side, scanning the perimeter as she unlocked the door. The rain blinded and deafened him to all but the most obvious sensory triggers, literally dragged down and earth-bound the air molecules that carried scent, replacing them with a pungent rain-smell all its own. Syd had the sinking feeling that, if and when she came, he would have very little warning. A couple of seconds. Not enough.

Jane shut the door behind her, locked it. He went around the front as she cranked the engine and flipped on the headlights. He realized he couldn't see Jane's face through the windshield, and a black hole of panic opened up in his chest.

Then the windshield wipers started, and he saw her: leaning over to unlock his door as he reached it, climbed inside. He slammed the door behind him, locked it up at once. Jane jogged it into reverse and wheeled quickly around, heading for the road. As they were backing up he thought he caught a glimpse of something moving in the tree line. He looked again, saw nothing but rain.

There was a little caravan filing out of the lot; she honked her horn in farewell, faintly received their answering calls. It felt weirdly comforting to be part of a group: almost like a pack, or a tribe. He wondered if any of them knew how lucky they were, or how ugly things could have gotten.

Then they were heading off and away from the others, in the opposite direction down the Mt. Haversford Road. Once again separated from the rest of humanity.

Hurtling headlong into the night.

THEY RODE IN silence, wending from Mt. Haversford to the Old Pitcairn Road, then into Brundle Hollow on their way up the final rise. The silence was tense but not divisive: not aimed at each other, but simply withheld. Her hand stayed tight in his, leaving only to shift, then finding it again. Her hand was his anchor point, keeping his dread from setting him adrift. Jane squeezed it and drove, watching the road. Alert. Lost in thought.

Syd, for his part, was trying hard *not* to think. He was

trusting his instincts. They told him to shut up. Pay attention. Stay alive.

Rain lashed at the window glass, beat a deafening
drumroll on the canvas top, and ran in flooded runnels
down the road to either side. The shotgun sat stiffly between his legs, strangely unassuring. Visibility continued
to be ghastly—between the blinding downpour and the
Jeep's pitiful blowers, they could barely see the white lines
on the pavement ahead—and periodically they would hit a
flooded patch and lurch into a split-second free-fall before
gripping the road again.

Jane cursed and shifted again, her features underlit by
the dashboard lights. It was harsh, subtly unflattering, yet
he had a difficult time finding lines that didn't agree with
him. There was strength in those lines, but they hadn't
gone hard. Character without bitterness. Determination
without malice. Try as he might, he could find *not one feature* that he didn't like a million times more than Nora's.

The Jeep rounded a swooping curve. Syd glanced up.

There was something large and wet and dead in the
middle of the road.

"SHIT!" they yelled, almost in unison, Jane swerving
to avoid the carcass as Syd grabbed the panic bar, held on.
She clipped it, a dull *thwump* that rocked them as she desperately countersteered. The Jeep skidded at thirty-five
miles per hour, sliding toward the narrow, rutted shoulder,
almost flipped as she whipped it back. The whiplash snap
as she regained control whacked his forehead sharply a-
gainst the window to his right. The shotgun fell to the
floor with a dull thump.

Syd let out a yelp and looked back at the dead thing:
a red lump in her taillights' glow, rapidly receding in the
fog-choked distance as she swung back onto the road. The
sense of dread that it gave him was beyond *déjà vu;* more
like a bad omen.

Or a calling card . . .

"What the hell was that?" he asked her.

"I don't know," she said, squinting into the rearview
mirror. "But I think its head was gone."

Syd swallowed hard. He hadn't missed the tremor in her voice. *Abandon hope, all ye who enter here* ... read the banners fluttering across his mind. He could feel the fear flicker like heat lightning inside him. It crawled up his heartbeat, adrenalized his soul even as the force of his vibe flooded the vehicle's cab.

The sight of the thing brought him horribly full circle, to the wolf in the woods where it all began. The power-lessness he'd felt—puny tire iron in hand—was nothing compared to the way he felt now. At least then he'd only had himself to worry about.

This was worse. A million times worse.

"Jane," he began. "There's something I gotta tell you—"

"I know," she interrupted. "And I hate to do it like this, but we're almost out of time. There's a couple of things I've gotta tell you, too. While we still have the chance."

He looked at her, startled, as Jane shrugged her way out of her sodden jean jacket, let it flop onto the seat behind her. Her T-shirt was plastered to her skin. Her skin was goosefleshed, her nipples stiffly erect. "What are you talking about—"

"Hang on," she said.

They burst into the curve that led to her private drive. Jane downshifted and cut across the road, barely slowing as she hit the incline. The headlights burrowed into the blackness before them. Her features jiggled in the dash-board light as smooth pavement deserted them, once and for all.

The deeply-rutted drive was dark and muddy and ut-terly deserted, the woods to either side ominous and thick, tree limbs gleaming like wet bones in the twin beams of light. The smell of plant life hung heavy in the air, incred-ibly oppressive, claustrophobic. Syd shivered. Ambush country.

"Jane ..." he began.

"I wanted to do this before," she resumed, "but it just didn't seem like you were ready ... *shit!*" She veered to avoid a broken-off tree branch jutting into the path. "*Shit*, Syd! You're *still* not ready! But this kinda forces the issue."

The road hooked up sharply to the right. The four-wheel drive dug in: mud and gravel spraying out behind it, floodwater sluicing in its tracks. Syd waited, while the blackness snaked down his spine. She downshifted and gunned it: the Jeep lurched and shot forward, up the last hump of the rise. Her features seemed to crawl in the dashboard light.

"Fact is," Jane said, tearing up the jagged waterslide home, "I understand a lot more than you think I do . . ."

"Oh god." Beginning, finally, to understand.

". . . and I've been watching you for a long time . . ."

They passed the PRIVATE PROPERTY sign. The path went wide, leveled into the clearing. The mist had thinned. He found that he was seeing clearly. Far too clearly, as a matter of fact.

The road smoothed. Her features continued moving.

". . . and I love you, Syd. I always will. But if you want to live, you'd better stay out of our way. . . ."

Up ahead, a light appeared through the trees. The porch light, softly illuminating the figure that hunkered beneath it now. Old and bent, stark in the light from the open front door. Crouching semi-upright and wailing in terror.

Wailing with a voice that bore no trace of humanity.

There was another form, too, coming around the side of the house. Coming toward them now at an incredible speed. The clearing was just over a hundred yards long. There was very little time. Jane slammed to a halt, threw on the brake, and dove out of the door. The thing kept coming. The thing kept coming. It was slowed by the mud and the rain. But not much. Not much at all.

Syd stared through the metronomic windshield-wiper streaks at the monster framed by the headlights' glare. It came on all fours, but virtually nothing looked right: the front limbs too gangly, the haunches too high. And its long tapered snout held a great leering mouth too huge, too huge for comprehension.

There was a tearing sound, and Syd turned to see Jane doubling over, ripping through the thin fabric of her T-shirt, the skimpy little denim skirt. She lowered her head and took a great sucking breath: the sound that came out resonated to the heart of his spiraling DNA. It was deep, wild, feral.

It was the song of the Change.

Jane was metamorphosing rapidly, expanding and mutating so fast he could barely lock on a feature before it rippled and twisted, shimmered and shifted, making the torturous, crazed transition from woman to were-thing to wolf and more in the handful of seconds it took for her assailant to cover ten of its last thirty yards.

Her torso stretched and contorted, hips dislocating into haunches as arms elongated into legs; her spine crackled, evolved a thrashing tail on the one end as her head triangulated at the other; the skull-plates shifting, as her face pushed outward, becoming a naked leering canine countenance. Ears sprouted and pinned back; lush fur bloomed as razored fangs grew and bared, prepared for attack.

"Oh god," he gasped, the last pieces clicking impossibly into place. *"Oh my fucking god . . ."*

Syd stared, numb with shock, as the wolf—that magnificent, mysterious beast from the woods—rose before him. It paused, turning its fearsome head toward him, its eyes filled with love.

Then she snarled and wheeled, launching her counterassault.

As Syd could not move, could not speak, could only watch in paralyzed terror as the two creatures hurtled forward on a killing collision course. They were inverse manifestations of the same primal power: one grotesque, the other divine. It was the very same power that raged inside him.

He watched, sickly wondering which side was the stronger.

In the very last moments before Nora was upon them . . .

•   •   •

. . . AND SHE WOULD *pay, yes she would pay, the bitch who'd snuck in and torpedoed her plans, laid waste to her hopes and left her with nothing but bloodthirsty Vic on her tail. She would pay, and then* he *would pay, for abandoning her when she needed him most. These meat-visions burned in her hindbrain, already telegraphing the taste to her tongue and her teeth . . .*

. . . and then there was only the blood and momentum, the moment of collision, the tangle of limbs. Then there was only that deathrush sensation of wading in, face-first, muzzle lunging for flesh. Nora used the sharp claws of her malformed paws to tear holes in the wolf-bitch's back as they snarled and snapped and rolled. She smelled blood, felt soft pelt and dermis tear.

The next blood she smelled was her own.

NO! *A gushing divot, torn raw from her breast. Nora yowled, lashed out, took flesh in kind. They rolled again, locked on each other: jaws snapping as they slashed bloody ribbons from each other's flailing limbs.*

And there was no thought, no time for thought, no percentage in thought at all. Just the purity of instinct and unmitigated rage. The deafening bloodthunder and the roaring in her ears. The enormous satisfaction of inflicting mortal damage. The excruciating payback of her own flesh, giving way. They rolled, and Nora felt herself under, then over. She lashed out at Jane's throat, missed, went under again.

And the bitch was strong, there was no doubt about it, the bitch was much stronger than Nora'd believed. But the truth of that didn't entirely come home until she felt those jaws lock on the flesh of her cheek. She howled, tissue shredding, the meat peeling back, muscles slicing like cheese as fangs raked over bone, sending hot grinding sparks of anguish to brightly ignite in her horrified brain.

NO! *screamed the dim voice of her human side,* NOT MY FACE! NOT MY FACE! *But before she could stop it, her left eye was gone: impaled and then squeezed till it squirted vitreous fluid and gore.*

And then Nora went utterly, terminally mad; hind legs

coming up beneath Jane's unprotected belly, razored claws tearing at the vulnerable flesh. She felt the abdominal walls give way, felt the agonizing tremors wrack the core of her rival. She didn't stop until the bitch was hitting the high notes and the stink of open bowels was everywhere.

Then she rolled again, over, ignoring the pain, wanting only to feast on the vitals she'd bared. Her adversary writhed in the red mud beneath her, thrashing and flailing.

Nora's half-face showed teeth all the way to the roots, the ragged lips pulled back in a sneer. She lunged for Jane's windpipe and almost nailed it, opening a bone-deep gash that ran the length of the jaw.

It was, in retrospect, a very stupid move.

But by the time she understood, it was already too late.

The pain didn't come for a full second, clearly separating itself from the rest of all creation. It came with a blast of hot breath on the hole where a very large piece of her throat used to be. Nora let out an agonized shriek, full of odd harmonics that whistled and sprayed. She screamed again, and the full pressure of the wolf's jaws came to bear on her trachea, punching down hard.

And then the world was shaking, shaking, a blur of motion and growling sound that burbled and roared and overwhelmed her, battered to silence the thoughts in her head as the killing jaws clamped down on her neckbone: sawing it back and forth, snapping the nerves running up through its core, bursting the arteries and veins that supplied the brain with blood and drainage.

And she knew she could have won, but then the thought just went away; gone, along with all the pretty pictures she'd been saving for just this occasion. There was no cosmic film projector, replaying her personal highlights and lowlights. No award ceremony. No burning hell. No godly affirmation of glory or shame. No Syd, no Michael, no Vic, no Nora. No pups of her own, and no childhood memories.

She'd always believed that, at the end of your life, God owed you a chance at understanding.

That chance disappeared, with her last dying brain cell.

And then, just like that, she was gone. . . .

36

THE TRAUMA WARD at Huntington Memorial Hospital was a state-of-the-art high-octane offshoot of Emergency Services, where pandemonium was the rule rather than the exception, and battle lines between life and death were drawn in deepest red.

Weeknights were slow, the vast bulk of public mayhem saving itself for the weekends, when a Friday or Saturday night would routinely see the carnage from upward of a half-dozen shootings, stabbings, drug overdoses, and D.U.I. traffic victims side by side with asthma attacks, burn victims, and the periodic full cardiac arrest as some hapless senior's bum ticker gave out.

Still, experience had taught that even on the deadest nights things could go from zero to one hundred in the time it took for the big glass doors to hiss open, the next gurney full of mangled humanity to roll in. And the men and women who staffed the ward—from the techs to the nurses, the interns and resident surgeons to the battery of on-call specialists—were battle-hardened adrenaline junkies, accustomed to fighting 'round the clock for their patients' lives.

They had seen a thousand forms of damage, faced death head-on hundreds of times.

But they had never seen anything like this.

She's not dead yet, was the thought that kept echoing through Tanya Martin's head, quickly changing to *I can't believe she's not dead yet.*

It was two thirty-seven when they brought the Jane Doe in. Tanya was the head ER nurse on the night shift, an attractive and intelligent five-year veteran of the Trauma team. She was twenty-nine, with a ready, easy smile and strong youthful features offset by a cascade of copper-colored hair and the clearest gray eyes. Only her eyes belied her age, bore witness to how much suffering she'd seen.

Tanya was by the front desk when the panicked, staggering man came stumbling through the door. He was soaking wet, semicoherent and frantic, bearing a muddy, blood-soaked bundle in his arms. Tanya raced to him and grabbed ahold of the bundle, eased it down. She peeled back the folds of cloth, bit back a gasp.

It was a woman, or used to be. She was nude, semiconscious, and she looked like she'd been through a threshing machine. Tanya reacted instantly, calling a code yellow full alert and scrambling the team, then tried to keep her cool as she sussed out her condition.

It was beyond severe: a half-dozen lacerations of the face and torso, any one of which should have killed her outright. A deep cut along her chin, that hooked down and missed the carotid artery by millimeters. The jawbone gleamed, visible through a frothing sheen of bloody saliva. An eight-inch gash across her lower abdomen had eviscerated the bowel. Pink intestine looped and bulged from the hole. The blood loss could only be described as massive.

Strangest of all were the deep puncture wounds that spanned her arms and legs and back. They were huge, ugly, brutal. Tanya recognized them instantly, though she had never seen anything this bad before. *Bite marks.* All over her body. *Animal bite marks.* Like a dog, but bigger.

Much bigger.

There was no time to waste. Diaphoretic shock had already set in: sweating tremors, heartbeat racing, body temperature and blood pressure perilously low. They got her onto a gurney and barreled down the hall, got her triaged before they even got her name, tagged her Jane Doe 114. They took X rays and abdomen film and started IVs running even as they drew blood and sent it to the lab for blood-gas analysis, typing, and tox screens. The team worked frantically, creating a blood-spattered hornet's nest of activity around the dying woman. Heart monitors were set up, beeping out the ragged tempo of life; catheters and nasal-gastric tubes were run, draining off blood and waste fluid.

Trauma transformed into a hive-mind, a single cacophonous interlocking organism in blue scrubs and surgical gowns. Their mission was to get her stable: stop the bleeding, keep her breathing, suture the smaller lacerations, and pack the bigger stuff until they got her into surgery. There was blood in her mouth, fluid in her lungs. They suctioned and inobated her, running tubes down her throat to clear the passage.

And that was when she went altered.

And started to fight.

Jane rolled her eyes, slipping in and out of oblivion.

Fear raced through her, tearing her mind in two. There was light and noise and yelling voices. There were hands all over her, doing things. Her human side dimly sensed that they were friendly, that they were only trying to help. But the other side of her was animal, and it was wounded. It wanted them to stop.

It would hurt them if they didn't.

Jane gasped, tried to warn them. Her mouth wouldn't work right. Something was in her mouth. The room fragmented, went black, came back again, bringing with it pain. So much pain. Molten agony blossomed in her belly, spread through her limbs and reverberated back, telegraphing torment. There were tubes in her mouth, tubes in her arms, tubes in her groin.

The smell of her blood was everywhere. It made her

animal side crazy. Voices filled her head, strange frantic
buzzings tortured her ears. Blood glued her skin to the
sheet, dripped from the tips of her fingers and the corners
of her mouth. Blood was leaking out of her at an alarming
rate. She took another ragged gasp, tasted Nora on her
breath.

"Look out!"

Tanya ducked as Jane's right arm came up, a wild
roundhouse slash at the tubes anchored to her left elbow.
It missed her head by inches, caught the rigging leading to
the IV stand instead. The needle ripped out; the resulting
tangle sent saline bags and stainless steel crashing to the
floor. Her arm continued on its arc, as her hand grabbed
the inobation tube and pulled it out. Brinks, the intern surgeon, looked up from packing the abdominal laceration.

"Goddammit, keep her down!"

Simmons, the surgical resident, gestured to Tanya. "Hit
her up! Secs-and-Pav, two hundred ceecees!"

Tanya nodded. Seconal choline and Pavulon, enough to
paralyze a pissed-off rhino for a good thirty minutes. She
ran to the cabinet, pulled out a hypo, tore the bag open.

Back on the table, all hell broke loose as Jane stiffened, back arching off the table and slamming down hard,
her legs kicking and spasming. Four more orderlies came
barreling in, grabbed on to her limbs, tried to pin her
down.

"Jesus *Christ,* she's strong!"

"Is she fucking dusted, or what?"

"What does the tox screen say? *Parker!!*"

Parker, the lab tech, came running in. "Blood tox says
negative, she's clean," he reported, "but that's not the bad
news." He waved a chart in their direction. "We can't
match her type."

"*What?!*"

"Just what I said, the lab can't match it! Her blood
type is weird; I've never seen values like this!"

"*Fuck,*" hissed Simmons. "How's her bleeding?"

"Bad," Brinks said. "We're gonna need more units in
here."

"Put her on the infuser, recycle her blood, and keep running saline until we get her matched." Jane's left leg kicked, catching the orderly square in the chest and knocking him back three feet. "And get some goddam restraints in here!" Simmons ordered, then shook his head. "She keeps thrashing like this, her guts are gonna be all over the floor!"

The orderlies grabbed the leather cuffs, began strapping her arms and legs to the operating table. Jane writhed in their grasp, and a low growling sound issued from deep inside her chest.

"What the fuck is that?"

"WHERE'S THAT GODDAMNED HYPO?"

"ON ITS WAY!" Tanya came back, swabbing the space below Jane's collarbone. The needle punched home, deep into the subclavian artery. The drugs took effect almost instantly: Jane's limbs went limp, slacked off. Her head dropped and lolled to the side. The orderlies finished strapping her and looked up, out of breath.

"Okay, she's down."

"Get her on oxygen," Brinks told Tanya, "and talk to her. She's gonna be freaked."

Tanya grabbed the oxygen mask and positioned it over Jane's face. As she did, she checked her eyes. Jane's pupils were completely dilated, her gaze erratic, unable to lock. *Fight-or-flight syndrome;* Tanya sympathized. Secs-and-Pav was scary stuff; nonnarcotic and incredibly potent, it paralyzed the body but left the mind completely conscious. It allowed them to work undisturbed, but for the patient the feeling was rather like being imprisoned inside his or her own skin.

"I know you can hear me," Tanya said softly but urgently, directly to Jane's ear. "We're trying to help you. You're gonna be okay, but you've gotta stop fighting us."

Jane's eyes spun, made momentary, fleeting contact. Tanya's words seemed to register, but the terror there was immeasurable. Tanya grabbed a sponge, gently dabbed Jane's forehead. All around her, the team labored madly.

The X rays came back from the lab; Brinks took one

look and flipped. "These can't be right," he said, pointing
to the shadowy mass on the film. "Look at the shape of
her heart."

Simmons looked up, scanned them. "Jesus," he said.
"What the fuck is that?"

"I don't know, some kind of growth or something."

"What are her vital signs?" he asked.

Hines, the pulmonary tech, looked up from the charts.
"Pulse one-fifty, blood pressure ninety-five over palp, oxygen saturation eighty-five," he replied. "She's slipping."

"Body temperature ninety-two and falling," Hillary,
the OR nurse, reported. She looked at Jane. "Shit, she's
going dusky."

This was seriously bad news. In the space of a second
Jane's skin changed color, drained from a pallid chalky-
white to slate-blue as her circulation turned sluggish, unable to oxygenate.

The electrocardiogram started flipping out: the signal
turning muffled, arrhythmic, unsteady. The waveform on
the screen was a ragged, asymmetrical horizon line.

"We're getting preventricular beats," Hines warned.
"She's losing compression."

"Dammit!" Simmons hissed. "She's hemorrhaging. Do
a pericardialcentesis. Drain her off."

The team switched gears. A large-bore needle was in-
serted into the chest cavity to drain the heart, restore compression. It didn't work. Jane's blood pressure kept
dropping even as her heart sped up, desperately pumping.
Lividity from stagnating blood mottled her flesh. Her
breath was forced, irregular. The monitor continued to
broadcast disaster.

Jane's neck veins began to bulge ominously.

"The bleeding's entered the heart sac," Hines said.
"Must have lacerated the aorta."

"Shit!!" Simmons cursed. "All right, prep for direct
cardiac massage. We gotta crack her chest."

"With an eviscerated bowel?" Brinks said incredulously. "It'll kill her!"

"She'll drown in her own blood if we don't," Simmons countered, gesturing to the monitor. "It's my call. Do it!"

The rest of the team obeyed, shifting positions as suddenly extraneous members fell back and a tray of instruments was wheeled forth and readied. Cardiac massage was exactly that: a last-ditch effort to save a life. Open the chest, reach in, and manually grasp the heart. Squeeze until the blood emptied from the sac. Release, let fill, squeeze again. Repeat until the heart took over or they pulled a sheet over the patient's head.

Tanya loaded another syringe, injected ten milligrams of morphine into the IV feed. Jane's eyes fluttered, rolled back in her head. Her left arm was unstrapped, pulled up over her head to expose the rib cage. "Bag her," Brinks told Tanya. "Regulate her breathing."

Tanya nodded, took hold of the bubblelike attachment beneath the face mask. She began counting and squeezing, forcing air into the lungs as Hillary moved in, swabbed the incision area with Betadine solution.

Simmons stepped over, took a scalpel in one hand, and with one fluid motion made a ten-inch-long incision between the fourth and fifth ribs, just beneath her left breast. Epidermis, membrane, and muscle tissue yawned wide, exposing the glistening slats of bone.

"Suction," he said. Suction was applied, sluicing away more blood. Simmons picked up the rib spreader, a device resembling a large stainless-steel set of salad tongs with the tines pointing out. Working quickly, he hooked them into the space between the ribs and applied pressure, forcing them apart.

There was a hideous cracking noise as the ribs snapped and separated completely, creating a red, raw, fist-sized gap. The surgeon took a deep breath, then began working his hand into the breach—first his fingers to the knuckles, then the knuckles themselves. His hand disappeared to the wrist, blindly pressing into the cavity. Pushing the lung aside.

Reaching for the heart.

Deep in the darkness, Jane stirred, fought her way up

*from drug-induced oblivion. Something was moving inside
her, violating her own healing process, weakening her grip
on the animal.*

*Jane focused, piecing together the scattered remnants
of awareness. Feeling returned, a billion needles thrusting
through her deadened nerve endings. She hovered in the
blackness, hesitating. To fully awaken was to fully experience the pain, and the pain was astonishing: a white-hot
veil on the border of consciousness, like an aurora bore-
alis of agony.*

*Jane was afraid. Her heart felt distant, leaden, slow-
ing. Her thoughts skittered, refused to gel. Her bestial core
howled in her head: maddened, writhing, tormented. If
they didn't stop it would break free and kill them, kill all
of them and herself in the bargain, like a dog with its leg
caught in a steel trap biting the hand of its master. And
there wouldn't be a thing she could do about it.*

*She had to break through and warn them, make them
go away, make them stop, or they were all dead.*

She had to cross over the line. . . .

"Dammit! I can't find her fucking heart!"

"What??"

"Nothing's where it's supposed to be!" Simmons was
mid-forearm deep, straining. "Lemme see those damned
X rays!" He stopped. "No, wait! I got it!"

He took the muscle in his hand, squeezed it. Her heart
squeezed *back*.

And Jane opened her eyes.

Tanya stared down, aghast. Jane looked right through
her, her eyes fixed on some inner distance. Tears welled in
her eyes, rolled down her cheeks. "SHIT, SHE'S
AWAKE!!" Tanya cried.

Across the room, bedlam. *"WHAT THE FUCK?"*
Brinks yelled. "DAMMIT, KEEP HER UNDER!"

"How?"

"Another ten milligrams of morphine!"

"But . . ."

"DO IT!"

Tanya grabbed another dose, fed it into the loop. Jane

went under again. Just as her eyes closed the cardiac monitor went off: a piercing alarm slicing through the chaos of the room.

"SHE'S FLATLINING!"

The team watched in horror as the sagging peaks dropped off, disappeared entirely. "Mother*fucker*!" Simmons spat, sliding his hand out of the hole. This was insane. "Prep for direct cardiac shock, set it for twenty-five jules."

Nurse Hillary appeared beside him, a pair of surgical steel paddles in her hands. The paddles were cabled to the electroshock machine, a squat gray box on a rolling cart. She set the dial, handed him the paddles. Everyone braced themselves: direct shock was potentially lethal. Too much juice would burn her heart, literally cook the muscle inside her chest.

Simmons grabbed the paddles, quickly slid one inside the chest cavity and positioned it over the heart, then placed the other on her breastbone. Simmons backed off, as everyone held their collective breath.

"CLEAR!!"

There was a sizzling buzz as the current hit home. Jane's body arched and stiffened on the table. The jolt shut off; Jane collapsed back onto the table. A ripple rocked her flesh like an earthquake aftershock, spreading through her extremities.

On the monitor, nothing. The alarm wailed maddeningly.

"Damn!" Simmons yelled. "Increase voltage to thirty jules!"

"You'll fry her!" Brinks argued.

"She's dead anyway! DO IT!!!"

Hillary upped the voltage. Simmons repositioned the paddles. "Ready," he said, standing back.

"CLEAR!!"

Another searing jolt, followed by a faint burning smell. The room went deathly still.

Then, on the monitor, a spike.

A cheer went up as another followed, then another. The peaks grew higher, gaining strength.

Yes.

The team breathed a collective sigh of relief, watching her vital signs climb back onto the charts and then set about the task of holding that hard-won ground. Pulse, respiration, blood pressure: all began, bit by bit, to normalize. Her blue color faded, was restored to its previous deathly pallor.

But as they worked, Tanya was struck by the palpable silence that had now fallen over the team. This was not a typical reaction to success. Ordinarily, a victory over these kinds of odds would inspire jubilation. But these people seemed troubled; and even more, they seemed *confused.*

It was a reaction she completely understood. She felt exactly the same way. And all you needed was one look around the room to see that the perception was unanimous. The faraway look in Dr. Simmons's eyes suggested he'd switched over to auto-pilot now: wheels were spinning in his head, already groping for plausible theories. Brinks kept furtively glancing at Simmons; he smelled medical history in the making, was hoping that he'd find a way in.

The eye contact between Parker and Hines, the techies, was just a little more naked. *What the hell is going on?* was what they wanted to know. That went double for the orderlies—especially that lip-flapping weasel Mancini, who kept sneaking little inquisitory looks around the room.

What the hell is going on? It was an excellent question. And she had little doubt that, once it hit the rumor mill, it would take Huntington Memorial by storm. She could practically smell the buzz already, and it hadn't even left the room.

Because *nobody* could have survived all that damage, much less the procedures it had taken to bring her through. Not to mention the weird blood, the improbable X rays, the skewed location of the heart. In the heat of the moment, there'd been too much going on to stop and hold a discussion group; but she knew that everybody here was quietly keeping score. This wasn't good luck and a strong constitution. This was *Ripley's Believe It or Not*.

Already, Jane Doe's readings were pegging up and holding, coming on strong. *You should be dead*, Tanya found herself thinking again.

And as they prepared to take her up to surgery, Tanya wondered gravely about the ordeal this woman faced. Simmons would want answers, that much was for certain. And then everybody would want their piece of the pie. It was no fun being a medical anomaly; there would be tests— lots and lots of tests—plus endless, exhaustive monitoring. If they thought they had a live one here, her little odyssey through the American health care system had only just begun.

Poor girl, she thought, as they wheeled the woman out. Recovery would be the least of her worries. *I don't envy you this part one bit.*

Then the elevator came, and it was out of her hands.

37

I HAVE TO ask you something, he said, and she told him she would tell him what she could. He nodded and buried his shovel in the mud once again.

He said: *you have to tell me what I am.*

The old woman was silent for a time. Her pain was palpable, as was her anger. He waited, while the rain continued to fall. He was knee-deep now. It would soon be dawn.

He tossed up a shovelful of mud, sank the blade deep again. At last, she spoke.

We are what we are, she said, *because we* know *we* are.

Another shovelful, another pause. *And me?* he asked.

What you are, she told him, remains to be seen.

He kept digging. The ground kept bleeding back into the hole, mud and runoff from the infinite rain. The woods hissed and rustled around them. His arms were numb. His back was numb. He continued to dig, tried not to blame himself for thinking so slowly. He had to keep reminding himself that he was still in shock.

I'm sorry, he said. *I don't understand.*

We're creatures of imagination and will, as much as of flesh and blood, she explained. *The power to Change sleeps in everyone.*

But not everyone is a wolf, he said.

No, she said. *Not everyone.*

He threw another shovelful, forced himself to ask the next question: *so what was she?*

She, the old woman replied, *was out of control.*

The hole grew deeper. On the ground beside him, Nora's corpse lay sprawled across a piece of tarpaulin. A solitary Coleman lantern hissed and glowed, the only illumination for miles around. It cast harsh shadows on the body, the pulsing light making the shadows dance. The body had changed much in the last several hours: discolored and bloated, swollen from the rain. She was almost human. But not quite.

He found it very hard to look at her.

How do we die? was what he finally asked.

The old woman shivered, a gaunt silhouette. *It's not mysterious,* she told him. *We're still mortal. When you cut us, we bleed. We live long, and heal quickly. But we die in the end, just like everything else.*

And we can be killed.

The inference hung heavy in the air. Syd said nothing, kept digging the hole.

How did Jane's parents die? he asked.

She shivered again, went on to explain. Mae's daughter Clarisse and her husband, Corey. Gunned down in the mountains, by poachers. It was pretty much just like Jane had said, only she'd neglected to mention that they were actually wolves at the time.

So they didn't need silver bullets, he said. Gramma Mae looked away, shaking her head.

Don't believe everything you see in the movies, she told him. No full moon. No gypsy curses. The Change was not a curse; she couldn't stress that enough. Not unless they caught you, or you lost control. The Change was a blessing.

Albeit a blessing in disguise . . .

Syd threw another shovelful of mud clear of the hole. He was having a hard time seeing it that way. He kept thinking about Jane, with her belly slashed and shredded. Kept thinking about Jane, and the wolf in the woods.

Kept thinking about Nora, and the function of the hole that he was digging.

It was cold. Soon, the old woman would have to go inside. Her face was streaked. Tears, rain. It was impossible to tell. She had suffered, too, in many ways more than him. She had certainly suffered longer.

There were a few more things he needed to hear.

Has she always known what she was?

All her life, came the answer. The power came with maturity, she explained, like the ability to conceive. But she has always known.

The shovel came up, went down again. *Why didn't she tell me?*

She didn't know you, she said flatly. *And she didn't know if you could be trusted.* She looked away, into the shadows.

Already, you're dangerous.

He flinched at the brutal truth of it. The earth was bleeding back into itself, trying to fill the hole. He had to keep digging. He was almost done.

It shouldn't have happened this way, she said.

And he told her, *I'm sorry.*

The hole deepened. He struggled against exhaustion, wondered if there was anything else he needed to ask her. But it was she who posed the next and most important question: *do you love her?*

The digging stopped.

And at first, he thought she meant Nora, and he was horrified by the thought of having to confront his feelings: not right now; not right here; not in front of Gramma Mae.

But, no, that wasn't what she'd meant at all. The question she asked was far easier to answer.

And far more important, in the final analysis.

Yes, he said. *Yes, I do.*

She watched him a moment, then nodded. There was

nothing more that needed to be said. Gramma Mae turned, started back toward the house. He watched her stooped gray form recede, went back to his digging. Just before she melded into the shadows she stopped, turned to him.

Your heart is the key, she said.

Guard it well.

And then she was gone, and he was alone: in the dark, in the rain, in a muddy bleeding hole that he diligently carved from out of the mountainside, while Nora's body slowly decayed beside him. Now that he was alone again, he felt the presence of that body more than ever.

Look at it, said a voice in his head.

No, he answered, out loud, digging in harder. Digging in deeper. Mud flew from his shovel and trickled back in. The war against nature was a losing battle. And yet he had no choice.

Look at it. The voice was adamant.

He shook his head, dug in. The voice was intimate and knowing. *You want to know what you are? You want to know WHO you are?*

He shook his head. Digging and digging and digging.

Take a good hard look at who you are.

Digging it nice and deep.

Do you still love her? That question again, unblunted by mercy. The shovel came down, came up again. The earth's blood ran.

Do you?

The voice was cold, incredibly cruel. He stared down at the hole. It was up to his hips. It was starting to flood. He paused to wipe his face. Tears, rain. It was impossible to tell.

DO YOU???

And it was hard, oh yes it was, to bring himself to look. But every second he waited, it just got harder. Such was the nature of fear. He had always known that. He knew it now, more than ever.

He took a halting breath, braced himself.

And looked at last.

He most clearly saw the undamaged side of her face.

It retained little of its beauty in death: the one remaining
eye gone milky and dull, the features distorted with rage
and rain and pain. The other side of her face mercifully
blended into the night, like the raw bloody gap where her
throat used to be. Her body was the color of chalk, caked
with mud and bits of leaves. Her breasts sagged to either
side, loosened by lacerations, purple with settling blood.

Rows of teats extended down along the torn and sav-
aged abdomen. Her haunches were still caught in that nowhere land between lupus and homo erectus. Neither the
tail nor the fur had completely receded. The feet had elongated into shanks, stiff limbs clawing the air; the toes were
large and padded, each tipped with hooklike talons, and
matted with mud and gore.

He forced himself to look. Forced himself to see it all.
And as he did he flashed back to that lost weekend, as the
fog blew off his memory under the shadow of the storm.
For the first time, he could recall the experience without
blinders against the pain. She had shown him something
then. She was showing him something now.

Syd looked at Nora and saw *himself:* half-human, half-
monster; both devourer and devoured. He looked at her
and saw the naked face of his purest bilateral soul, the
truth of what he was. A creature of great beauty. A horror
unbounded.

Now you know.

The hole was ready. The hole was deep enough. He
leaned on the shovel like a crutch, as the last of his tears
spilled free. They came out hard, were quickly spent. He
climbed out of the grave.

The insects had already begun to explore her. Syd's
human side was appalled, and he wanted them to stop. The
animal side felt no such need. This was the next natural
stage in the journey: meat drawn in as sustenance, spirit
departing to greener fields, the husk returning to soil and
seed.

Her backside had flattened, in livid conformity with
the terrain. Rigor mortis had already begun to set in; it
made her harder to move, but only a little. There were no

words, no tears, no good-bye kiss. Nora slid over the edge and into the pit. Syd picked up the shovel, threw the first faceful in.

By dawn's first light, he had laid her to rest.

Then he went back to the house, to collapse.

And await the inevitable.

PART THREE

Vic

38

SYD GROANED AND opened his eyes. For one all-too-brief moment, he lost all sense of self: didn't know who or where or even what he was. Then the world spun again, re-formed around him. He moaned, brought a hand up to massage his throbbing temples.

The hand was caked with dried mud.

"Oh, fuck," he mumbled, and it all came thundering back.

He was folded in half on the too-small living room couch, curled into an uncomfortable fetal crunch. He clothes were encrusted, stuck to his body. The dampness had settled deep into his bones. Someone had mercifully removed his boots, which sat neatly by the cooling fireplace embers. She'd thrown an old blanket on top of him, too.

Thank you, he mused, looking around the room. A crocheted comforter was piled in the armchair across from him. Evidently, he'd had company while he slept. The shotgun was within instant arm's reach. He recalled his paralysis at the moment of truth, felt a black rush of shame overtake him.

Syd tried to sit up, was immediately greeted by a monstrous backache. His neck and shoulders creaked, one solid slab of tension; the base of his skull ached horribly. The temptation to settle back and lie there forever was overwhelming.

Then he heard Mae's voice, coming from the kitchen. She was talking on the phone. "Oh, shit," he hissed and pulled himself upright, legs wobbling as he stood. He took a few halting paces toward the kitchen, feeling his innards shift and shudder inside him. Gramma Mae was sitting at the table, speaking in clipped, anxious tones. He hovered in the doorway, listening. From her end of the conversation, he could piece together the gist.

First and foremost: Jane was still alive. *Thank God,* Syd thought, felt a knot loosen and unwind in his chest. If anything else had happened, he didn't know what he would have done. In the same breath, he caught that her condition had been upgraded overnight from critical to guarded; and that she had regained consciousness sometime this morning, but refused to answer any questions.

And that was where it grew tense. Apparently, some prick named Simmons was getting nosy: asking very personal questions about the family, wanting to know about Jane's medical history, her extraordinary metabolism, anything and everything he could get his hands on. Syd grimaced; bastard was probably sniffing for his Nobel Prize, though Syd suspected the story was more apt to wind up in the *Enquirer.* He could see the ghastly headlines now. SEXY WEREWOLF'S HEALING SECRETS! LASCIVIOUS LYCANTHROPE'S DEATHBED DECLARATION: "RAVAGE ME IF YOU CAN!"

Mae deflected him adroitly: playing the distraught-but-feisty old mountain girl to the hilt. But for all her diplomacy, her ingrained piss and vinegar, Syd could tell that she was deeply rattled inside.

He retreated from the door, still keeping an ear cocked to the conversation. And as he padded around eavesdropping, he noticed for the first time the fresh scratches all over the hardwood floors, the clawmarks scarring the windows and doors. It wasn't hard to put the picture together.

She must have flipped out as Nora started prowling around outside: running from window to window to window like an old yapping house dog with a rabid stray in the yard.

He felt so bad for her; how terrified she must have been. Thank God, too, that nothing had happened to her. *Unless, of course, you count helplessly watching your only granddaughter get ambushed and almost killed,* he added. *Some folks might regard that as slightly traumatic.*

There was certainly nothing she could have done; of that much, he was certain. He tried to tell himself it wasn't any of their faults, that there was nothing *any* of them could have done. But the anguish underpinning her voice gnawed at his soul, told him that even if this were true, it would be no comfort to her now.

And that was when he understood the simple, ugly truth.

Like exactly whose fault it was.

Syd stood in the middle of the living room, was once again struck by its beauty. This was their *home*. They had lived here for years, without anyone ever having a clue about their true natures.

Until *he* came along.

And that was when it hit him, the responsibility implicit in his role. Syd understood what he would have to do: for their sake, even more than his own.

He didn't know *how* he would do it; quite frankly, he didn't have a clue. It almost didn't matter.

His duty was clear.

39

B Y NOON, A plan of sorts had taken shape.

Syd had slipped out of the back door quietly, pausing only to rinse himself with the hose outside. He wanted to put as much distance as possible between himself and the mountain; and the sooner he did it, the better. Gramma Mae watched him from the kitchen window; she didn't raise an eyebrow as he hopped into Jane's Jeep and drove off.

A quick stop by his room allowed him to grab a change of clothes and the gun he'd almost used on Vaughn Restal, one night a million years ago. Just down the street at Hoeffner's Sporting Goods he scored fifty rounds of hollow points, plus a small can of lighter fluid and a box of shotgun shells.

The ammo jiggled on the seat beside him. It was only marginally comforting, for a variety of reasons. It might not even *work,* for one thing; he somehow doubted Nora could have been stopped by anything short of a bazooka blast last night. To further complicate matters, Treat Her Right was supposed to be playing tonight, and the potential innocent-bystander bodycount a Friday night firefight could generate was genuinely appalling. And the idea of stopping Vic only to end up indicted for manslaughter struck him as a real losing strategy, even if he could make a case for self-defense.

No; in the end, Syd decided that gunplay was a desperate last resort, one he dearly hoped he would not have to employ.

Besides, he knew, if he did this right, he wouldn't need to.

The parking lot floods were still on when Syd pulled up. Another good sign. It meant that Randy hadn't been in, and if he wasn't in by noon he probably wouldn't be until four. All of which suited Syd just fine. He needed the time, and the privacy. He screeched to a halt directly in front of the entrance, grabbed the ammo, and climbed out.

The ground was almost dry beneath his feet as he crossed the lot; a few stray puddles shimmered in the distance, all quickly diminishing under the force of the sun. The rain had hopefully washed away Nora's trail, and the sunshine was eliminating the leftover rain. All of which meant the parking lot was clean, as well as the road leading up to it.

Which left Chameleon's: his first and only line of defense. Common sense and the out-of-state plates on Nora's stolen car told him there were doubtless thousands of other haunts across the country she could just as easily have hightailed it to. All Syd had to do was steer Vic off the trail, send him packing for parts unknown, secure in the knowledge that wherever Nora was, she'd never been here.

In other words, he had to lie like a bastard. And he had to do it so thoroughly that Vic couldn't *help* but believe him.

Syd unlocked the front door, stepped inside. Daylight sliced the dim interior, dust motes wafting in the stale air. He shuddered, an involuntary tremor. It was a little like walking into a tomb.

A lot like entering his own.

He stashed his stuff behind the bar, then went into the kitchen and broke out a bucket and mop. There was a big

five-gallon jug of industrial-grade pine-scented disinfectant
under the dishwasher's station. He poured some into the
bucket, then shoved it under the taps, filled it with steaming water. On the way out he scooped up a sponge and a
pair of rubber gloves from the drainboard.

Syd returned to the main room, surveyed the job before him. It was a massive undertaking. He worked like a
maniac, racing the clock as he swabbed and sloshed and
scrubbed and mopped every square inch of the room.

By three the rest of the crew started filtering in. Bruno,
the night cook, was the first to arrive. He was a big, burly
man with a bristly crop of short white hair and a face like
a basset hound. He took one look around and started to
gag, asked Syd if he'd lost his fucking mind. Syd told him
to mind his fucking business. Bruno walked to the kitchen,
shaking his head.

Bonnie was next through the door. She'd already heard
about Jane. She asked Syd if he was okay; when he nodded wordlessly and kept right on working, she backed off.
The look in her eyes told him everything he needed to
know.

That's right, he thought. *Chalk it up to distress. The
less you know, the better.*

It was four by the time he finished. Syd stashed the
mop and bucket, then grabbed his clothes and the paper
bag, went into the office to change. He shut the door and
quickly stripped, slipping into clean jeans and sneakers,
plus an oversized chambray work shirt. His arms and legs,
already wracked from digging Nora's grave, were in blistering agony; his head wanged from the fumes. He broke
open the box of hollow points, loaded the clip, and stuffed
the gun inside the waistband of his jeans. The shirt he left
untucked; its tail covered the bulge, rendering it all but invisible. Then he bundled the clothes into the bag, stepped
out of the office, and ducked out the back door at the end
of the hall.

The sun was beginning its descent. The dumpster was
just outside the door to his left. As Syd walked toward it

he took the can of lighter fluid and doused the wadded-up bundle, flipped open the dumpster's lid, lit the bag, and tossed it in. As the flames sputtered to life, Syd pulled out a cigarette and lit that, too. He smoked as it burned, thinking *this will work. It has to.*

Randy was standing in the hall when he came back in. He asked if Syd was okay. Syd nodded. Randy asked him if he'd rather take the night off. Syd shook his head, said thanks, but he'd rather work. He needed to keep his mind off of it.

It was four-thirty. Chameleon's had never looked so good or smelled so bad. A sweet chemical stink permeated the air, like the world's largest dashboard deodorizer. Syd returned to the bar, began setting up his station. Word spread quickly, in hushed whispers and raised eyebrows, as the rest of the crew came on for the night. A few of them had heard the news by the time they got there; most hadn't. But everyone knew within minutes of their arrival, as their furtive glances revealed.

Syd pointedly ignored them, throwing a wall up. He could neither accept nor afford their concern. The same policy applied as the first of the evening's customers started to trickle in. Syd manned his station and kept his mouth shut, taking orders and making drinks without a trace of his customary openness. Keeping an eye on the door, even when his back was turned. Glancing at the sinister silhouette of the shotgun, tucked discreetly under the lip of the bar.

It made him think of Jules, starting a pang of long-buried anguish burning in his heart. Dredging up old ghosts helped supplant the fresher ones. Syd allowed himself to think back to that night. The memory was raw, the pain it carried very real. That was the last time he saw Nora, at least the Nora he loved. As long as he could keep himself focused and did not panic, he could say that much with complete authority, and know in his heart that it was true.

Syd kept it up as the front door opened and closed, as

more and more bodies piled in. Kept it up as happy hour waxed and waned and the band arrived, began to set up. Kept it up long after the light outside had faded from white to gold to deepest twilight blue.

And the long night descended upon them all.

40

THE STICKER ON the pickup's bumper read HUNTERS DO IT WITH A BANG! Vic didn't know if he agreed, but judging from the look on its ex-owner's face, he'd certainly gone out with one.

It had been a wearying journey. Covering the remaining hundred or so miles on foot was frankly exhausting, even if he did do it on all fours. The gunshot wound on his left hindquarter didn't help matters. Fucking cop. Even though it was just a graze, really, the pain had slowed his progress. It had forced him to stop and lick the wound every few hours or so, and to seriously debate whether it was worth the risk to Change back, continue the trek in human form.

But the complications of that were many, from the continuing problem of evading the authorities to the knowledge that his face was all over the tube to the simple fact that the fleeting glimpse of a fleeing animal was less likely to draw fire than the sight of a naked, bleeding fugitive from justice humping through the rain-soaked Allegheny outback. Maybe they'd think they were dreaming.

Hell, maybe they'd think he was Bigfoot. And, besides, he healed slower as a biped.

That had pretty much settled it, at least until he reached a tiny burg with the unfortunate name of Droop, West Virginia. It was a little after six in the evening, and it was damp and gloomy out, the storm having let up only an hour or so before. Vic emerged limping and panting from the trees lining Route 219, found himself staring at the rear entrance of a Buster's Army/Navy Surplus Store just as no less than Buster himself emerged from the back door, intent on packing it in for the night. The expression he bore as Vic tore into him indicated that Buster had always figured his great-white-hunter status would keep him safe from the pay-end of the food chain.

Once inside, Vic ate his fill, then pulled down a sleeping bag off the wall and curled up to rest. He slept and dreamt of sweet revenge, awoke in human form, sometime near three the following morning.

The hole in his thigh was not entirely gone, but it had scarred over nicely, forming into a pinkish-red welt just beneath his butt. His left leg was stiff, but not too bad. Vic looked around the store, realized he really couldn't have asked for a better opportunity. Buster's postmortem generosity had proven bountiful indeed, providing Vic with everything he needed: new duds, some much-needed cash, plus the use of Buster's '79 Chevy short-bed pickup, complete with CB radio, police scanner and a Cobra radar detector on the visor. When he came upon a length of heavy-duty steel chain coiled on the truck bed, complete with a tow hook on the end, Vic just smiled.

Oh, yeah.

By three-fifteen Vic was on his way, clad in the height of badass shitkicker fashion in stonewashed Levi's, a black T-shirt with a Harley logo on it, and a pair of honest-to-god black steel-toed Dingo cowboy boots. He missed his duster, but he managed to find a new leather biker jacket that fit.

Life was almost good again.

By three-thirty Vic was on the move, keeping to the back roads as he made his way north, heading for the state line. The going was slow and cautious, but the CB proved invaluable for monitoring the movements of ol' John Law, and the Cobra kept him from running afoul of any more speed traps. And though Buster's musical tastes leaned a little too heavy toward Randy Travis and Patsy Cline for his liking—he still had an *eight-track* tucked under the dash, for chrissakes—a little rummaging under the seat turned up not only a copy of Little Feat's "Let It Roll," but a fresh fifth of Wild Turkey as well. Vic grinned as he broke the seal, wished Buster happy trails. He popped the tape in and cranked it up, bopping along to the strains of "Changin' Luck."

Vic wondered how his was holding up. So far, so-so. The cops were still searching west for the most part, which was good. The miserable weather had finally broken, but not before erasing every last trace of Nora's trail, which was not so good. For the first time in as long as he could remember, he was flying blind. He kept going anyway, relying on instinct to drive him forward.

The miles rolled by. The day wore on. The bottle didn't last long; sometime around two he stopped, got another to keep him company. All the while, Vic thought about Nora, and what she had done, and what he should do once he found her. The past forty-eight hours had given him plenty of time to reflect, and for that Vic was very glad. If he'd caught up to her quickly, he very likely would have killed her on the spot.

But forty-eight hours in animal mode had simplified things, clarified his thoughts. And coming out of it, he had to admit there was something unsettling about the whole turn his life had taken. He still couldn't accept the idea that she was actually gone. As long as he was running, he was fine: hurtling through underbrush and over mountaintops, racing with the wind in his fur and death in his heart. But when he closed his eyes . . .

Every time he closed his eyes he saw Tristana: dancing

John Skipp & Craig Spector

and strutting, inciting the crowd to madness. He saw Tristana, naked and fearless, a snarl on her lips as she bucked beneath him. He saw Tristana, fighting for her life, betrayal burning in her gaze in the seconds before the killing crunch. . . .

Vic winced, gripped the wheel tight enough to break it off. His emotions roiled, barely contained beneath the surface of his skin. God *damn* Nora to hell. How could she do such a thing? How could she . . .

And then it hit him, so clear he couldn't believe he hadn't seen it before. For the first time, he understood how bad he must have made her feel all this time. He hadn't been giving her what she needed. He saw that now. Of *course* she'd run away, just like he had. Of *course* she'd go looking for it somewhere else. Of *course* she'd flip out when he did the same. In the end, he had to admit he'd been wrong. He fucked up. He was big enough to cop to that. She should be, too.

Besides, he realized, only Nora could've spiked him like that. Only Nora could have stuck it in so deep and twisted it so hard. It had been a cold, vicious, brutally calculated thing to do.

Vic couldn't help but admire her for it.

That was the old Nora at work. Vic sighed as the spark rekindled deep in his heart. *That* was the Nora he loved, the Nora he'd mated with for life. Sure she was a bitch. And sure, he wanted to bite her fucking head off sometimes. But wasn't that what relationships were all about?

Such was his state of mind as he crossed the state line. It was world-class denial, but it blotted out his pain, honed his anger to a fine, razored edge. He would find her. He might even give her a scar, to remind her.

And then life would go on.

It was just past twilight when the little glowing sign appeared on the horizon. Vic drove quietly, psyching himself for their reunion. The fact that her scent was still absent bothered him a little, made him wonder *what if I'm wrong? What if she's gone for good this time, and I never fucking see her again?*

Vic shook his head. She was there. She *had* to be. He'd go in, talk to her, tell her how he felt. They'd settle the score.

And then they'd be on their way.

41

BY EIGHT O'CLOCK things had gotten busy; early as it was, the bar was lined three-deep, and more were coming in all the time. If the current crowd-flow was any indication, tonight was gonna be packed.

Red was at his post by the door. On the jukebox, Jimi Hendrix bemoaned that manic depression that was crushing his soul. Bonnie and Katy were hustling butt, working the tables and bringing orders to the bar. Trent was handling table duty, cutting Syd a little slack.

But even running just the bar was immensely distracting.

Especially while keeping one eye on the door.

Syd dropped his guard when a slew of rowdy fratboys ordered a fresh round of pitchers and Seven-and-Sevens. Midway into the order, the Bud keg ran dry, and Syd had to duck down to change the taps.

Suddenly, flesh was prickling on the back of his neck. *Oh fuck,* he thought, standing, scanning the queue at the door. There was a shadow at the back of the line. A familiar shadow. Patiently waiting its turn.

Fuck! Syd braced himself, automatically trading the

drinks for cash. He turned to the register, and his thoughts turned to Jules: how his friend must have felt, the night Vic first walked in. He glanced into the mirror, looking over his shoulder. The hair was longer, but otherwise nothing had changed.

Syd punched the keys and steeled himself, stunned once again by how much sheer *power* the motherfucker exuded. He could feel it with his back turned, from all the way across the room. But even more unsettling was the realization that something felt *off,* somehow. Unstable. Diseased. This only scared him a hundred times more.

Vic was moving through the crowd, obviously favoring one leg. He'd been hurt, evidently. This was not bad news. Syd counted out the change, hoping he hadn't already tipped his hand. He could smell the intimidation, the mounting, thinly veiled menace.

Jules. Please, he prayed. *If you're out there, man, give me strength.*

Then he turned back around. And Vic was there.

"Welllllll ..." Vic began, a big smile on his face. "Long time no—"

"Hang on," Syd interrupted, holding one finger up politely. He went over to the college boys and started counting change. "That's thirteen, fourteen, fifteen, and five makes *twenty*. Have a good one." They thanked him, took off with their drinks. He swabbed the bar down as they did.

That finished, Syd returned to Vic.

"So," he said. "What can I do for ya?"

Vic was confused. Not ten seconds ago, the little fuck had blanched with mortal terror; now he was staring him square in the eye. Without even flinching. Vic wondered if that car wreck hadn't maybe done some damage, joggled his brain out of its socket.

"Remember me?" It was the first time in his life he could recall having to ask that particular question.

"Yeah, I remember you. So what do you want?"

Vic stood there a moment, not believing his ears.

"Well, let's see," he said. "You can start by telling me where Nora is. . . ."

"Can't help ya there." He shrugged. "But how 'bout a drink?" Syd reached below the bar, came up with a can of beer, plunked it down. Vic looked.

Coors Light. The Silver Bullet.

Syd smiled.

"Funny," Vic murmured, blood starting to pound in his head. This boy was beginning to piss him off. Syd kept smiling, except for his eyes; his eyes held another emotion entirely. There was a wall in there, and something was flickering behind it. The little bastard was hiding something, but Vic was damned if he could suss it out.

"So, let me get this straight. You haven't seen Nora . . ."

"Nope."

". . . and you have no idea where she is. . . ."

"Yep."

"Well, then maybe I'll just sniff around a bit. See what turns up."

"Suit yourself."

This idea didn't sit very well with Syd, and it showed. He tried to cover his discomfort, much to Vic's delight.

"Don't mind if I do."

"Though you can see for yourself that Nora's not here," he said, thinking *shut up now, just shut up.* "I mean, I think you'd know it if she was."

Syd paused, waiting for a reaction. The lack of one told him exactly what he needed to know. *Vic couldn't smell her;* he was just blowing smoke, trying to make Syd crack.

The bad news was, it was working. The silence gave Syd's thoughts room to roam, started him thinking about how many ways this could blow up in his face. He wondered whether he should just pull the gun, empty the clip into Vic's head, and hope for the best.

"Look," he said, fighting his panic. "Nora hasn't been back. But if she *did,* you're right, she'd probably come here first. She always liked the tunes."

He looked at Vic; Vic nodded suspiciously. A small crowd was forming: thirsty people, psychic vultures.

"I mean, if you don't believe me, why don't you just stick around and see for yourself?" He spread his arms in mock-welcome. "Hang out as long as you like. Crowd's good, the band is smokin' . . . hell, the drinks are on the house—"

Vic smiled—a very evil smile—and Syd knew at once he'd gone too far. *Why why why did I fucking SAY that?* It was like making a fatal move in chess, except in chess your opponent usually didn't eat your queen if you lost. But one look at Vic told him there would be no retracting the offer.

"So, let me see if I got this straight." Vic absently fingered his scar as he spoke. Syd stood his ground, revealing nothing. "You want me to hang out here, *all night* if I want? And I can drink for *free?*" He shook his head in ersatz-admiration. "I guess you just must be *one hell of a guy!*"

"I guess I am," Syd said flatly. "What'll ya have?"

Just then, a pack of newcomers pushed through the door, a cute young redhead among their number. She looked vaguely familiar to Syd, though he couldn't quite place her face.

Vic followed Syd's line of sight, and his expression changed to one of sly bemusement. He tracked the red-head's descent down the steps and into the room. The red-head saw him, smiled. Vic nodded appreciatively, then turned back to Syd.

"Now that ya mention it, I guess I *will* hang out a while. Seein' as how you offered.

"A little tequila, if you please."

"You got it." Plunking a shot glass down on the bar, skipping over the Cuervo in favor of the overproofed brand. All the while thinking *great! NOW what do I do?*

He came back, set Vic up with a double. Vic picked up the glass, held it up to the light. Then he kicked it back, set it back down again, and tapped his finger expectantly on the rim. His eyes were bright with mirth.

Syd dutifully poured him another. "Anything else?" he
said. Meaning *fuck you, too, pal.*

"Not at the moment," Vic replied. "But if I think of
anything, I'll be sure to let you know."

And with that, Vic ambled over in the redhead's direction. She brightened visibly as he approached. Vic cocked
his head, said something witty. Within seconds, they were
engaged in meaningful social discourse. A minute later,
they had peeled away from her pack of friends and were
making their way toward a booth in the back.

Where had he seen her before? Syd couldn't recall. He
could only watch in horror as Vic's hand snaked out,
lightly made contact with the small of her back. As they
reached the booth, Vic ushered her in, then slid in across
from her. Careful to take the seat facing the door. And the
bar.

Then he fired a little smile at Syd.

The waiting game had begun.

42

THE NEXT HOUR was complete madness. The bar kept filling up. The band came on. The atmosphere grew loud and hot and heavy: down-and-dirty blues goosing the crowd to a good-natured mania, as close to two hundred crazed sweaty people drank and laughed and danced their collective cares away.

By contrast, on the far end of the fun spectrum, there was Syd.

Syd was definitely not having a good time. Between trying to keep an eye on Vic and servicing the ever-increasing stream of customers, his dance card was punched. To complicate matters, he quickly found that he could not so much as step away from the bar or duck into the bathroom to take a leak, without Vic's watchful eye upon him. The motherfucker seemed able to anticipate Syd's every move almost before he thought of it; Syd would no sooner turn to slip away when Vic would be there, waiting. A big malicious grin plastered across his face. An empty glass in his hand.

In fact, the only thing Syd *could* do was keep the drinks flowing. And flow they did: it came as no surprise

that Vic was a quantity user. What was surprising was exactly what quantities he was capable of. By nine-thirty Syd
had already sent Trent to the stockroom to score a fresh
bottle of tequila to replace the one he'd already poured
into Vic's bottomless glass.

And therein lay his only hope.

Because by all appearances, Vic was having a marvel-
ous time. All of his immediate creature comforts were being catered to, and then some. The redhead was
responding to his overtures and generally keeping his li-
bido stoked. The effects of the tequila were slowly beginning to show. If he could keep Vic drunk and happy and
distracted enough, sooner or later the time would come.
And Syd would get his chance.

Halfway through the second bottle Syd noticed that the
grin was getting bigger, if no less menacing. The gleam in
his eye, that much more unfocused. Vic was spending less
and less time eyeballing Syd, more and more time eyeballing the redhead.

Syd motioned Bonnie over, handed her a fresh round
of drinks, nodded toward the couple in the back booth, and
told her to put it on his personal tab. She looked at him
like he was crazy; he told her just do it, please, thank you
very much.

Bonnie shrugged and placed the drinks on her tray,
trundled them off to their appointed destination. Syd
watched. Vic looked up as the waitress arrived, thanked
her graciously, and gave her a nice fat tip for her trouble.

He never once looked back at the bar.

Now, Syd thought. *It's now or never . . .*

. . . and then he was moving, sliding past Trent, who
looked up from busily hefting a double handful of Bud
Light longnecks out of the cold chest. "Back in a flash,"
he said. "Gotta hit the john."

Before Trent could register a reply Syd was ducking
under the swinging counter at the far end of the bar and
heading across the dance floor toward the back hall. In
seconds he was gone, lost in the throbbing mass of humanity clogging the floor.

The door to Randy's office was at the end of the hall, just past the bathrooms and right before the rear exit. Syd paused at the men's room door, waiting to see if he was being followed. When no Vic appeared, he went down the hall to the office, slipped his key into the lock, and quickly ducked inside.

His heart was hammering as the door shut behind him. So far, so good. Syd flicked on the light. He half-expected to see Vic, kicking back in Randy's big leather chair, his mouth splitting into a grin full of teeth that just grew and grew and grew. . . .

Enough, he told himself. He was definitely losing it. Syd moved to the desk, grabbed the phone, dialed information, got the number. His fingers were trembling as he punched it in.

The phone rang once, twice. Three times.

"C'mon, c'mon," Syd hissed. He looked at his watch. Nine thirty-five. Shit. On the fourth ring, a female voice picked up.

"Huntington Memorial Hospital, where can I direct your call?"

"Intensive Care, please."

"I'm sorry, sir," the voice intoned. "ICU closes at nine. You can try tomorrow at—"

"Please," he interrupted, trying to remain calm. "It's an emergency. . . ."

VIC HAD TO admit it: he was having a fine old time. The booth was nice and dimly lit, very cozy. He had a first-class buzz going, his senses swimming in a sea of pleasant sensation. The music was great, the crowd was lively, he certainly couldn't complain about the service. All around him was vibrant sound and color, and the rich ripe smells of excitement and seduction and fun. And underlying and permeating it all, the intoxicating aroma of *lust.*

The scent of fresh meat worked in tandem with the liquor, soothing the nagging feelings that had driven him here, bringing his attention firmly back to the matter at hand. Namely, the sweet young thing sitting across the table from him.

She didn't have Tristana's tough carnality, or Nora's killer looks, but she was quite pleasant to behold, nonetheless. Her hair was wonderful: a burnished, flowing copper, the color of a new penny. Her face was youthful, girlish even, yet there was a strength there that Vic found quite appealing.

It was something in the eyes, he decided. Her eyes were clear and gray, and had definitely *seen* more than most. Life. Death. Pain. Suffering. Triumph. He could read it all in their shining depths, the tiny lines that crinkled around them when she smiled.

She was smiling now. Maybe it was because his hand was on her thigh. Or maybe it was the fact that the two of them were higher than a pair of kites. Maybe both. Vic smiled back, tried to think of her name. She'd told him twice already; three times might tend to put a damper on the proceedings. He thought about it as he leaned forward, insinuating his index finger into the soft crevice between her legs. She shifted in her seat, parted her thighs a little to assist the process.

And then, just like that, it came to him.

"Tanya," he said, drawing it out luxuriously. She paused in mid-margarita and her eyes lit up, radiating inebriated heat and hunger. Vic saw her nipples stiffen under the fabric of her shirt, got a very clear sense of what it would be like to pop them in his mouth, like little flesh gumdrops. It made him reconsider the urgency of his hunt, at least for one more night.

"You're a very interesting woman," he said playfully, feeling the whole rest of the room evaporate, leaving them in a warm little universe for two. "Why do you suppose that is?"

"Guess I must lead an interesting life," Tanya replied, setting down her glass. She was drunk, getting drunker by the minute.

"Ah," Vic said. His hand slipped up under the hem of

her skirt. "And what is it that's so interesting about your life?"

His fingers started tracing artful patterns near the seam of her panties; Tanya shifted again, giving out a dirty little laugh, followed by a low purring sound. "Welllll . . ." she began. "Let's see. I have a very interesting job. . . ."

"Really," Vic said, not caring in the slightest. "What's so interesting about it?" It was a game now, a very enjoyable game, the object of which was to see if he could find the spot that would short-circuit her powers of speech.

Tanya was good; she continued to talk under pressure. "Well, I work at a local hospital, and . . ." She had to stop for a moment, as Vic scored a point. ". . . and, um, it's very . . . exciting. . . ."

"Hmmm," Vic murmured thoughtfully. His grin grew wider and wider. "So what's the most exciting thing that ever happened there . . . ?"

Tanya thought about it for a moment, against overwhelming distraction. Then her eyes went wide, as she remembered. It happened just the other night, she told him. The Jane Doe with the jacked-up metabolism, the one whose blood couldn't be matched. The one who should have died five times over, but miraculously pulled through.

The one with the savage bite marks, all over her body.

Tanya told him all about it, in fabulous forensic detail. By the time she finished, Vic wasn't smiling anymore.

And the game was definitely over.

"What's wrong?" she asked, feeling his hand suddenly withdraw from its warm hiding place. "Are you okay?" Watching him slump back in his seat, his color gone ashen.

"I'm sorry . . ." she began, feeling suddenly very stupid for going too far. Most people had a low threshold for blood, she knew from experience; the macho studly types, doubly so. It was Tanya's curse, to forever be attracted to guys who could bench-press their own body weight but couldn't put a Band-Aid on a paper cut. Most of the time, a look like this spelled an end to the evening's festivities. Tanya sat up, ready to fumble her apologies.

And then, miraculously, he recovered. The smile came back, albeit a little dimmed. And though his color remained chalky, the sparkle in his eyes was pure sincerity. "I'm okay," he said, taking her hand and kissing it gently. "It's just that hospitals make me kinda nervous."

"And nurses?"

"Naw." Once again grinning. "I like nurses just fine."

There was another beat of silence, in which he glanced at their empty glasses. His color was returning, in tandem with her sexual confidence. "Looks like that waitress has gone and forgotten all about us," he said, all at once mock-woeful. He looked back to her. "Darlin', how's about you go and get us a couple o' drinks?"

Tanya smiled. "Sure," she said. "Why not."

He still had her hand as she slid out of the booth; and as she stood he pulled her over, gave her a little kiss on the neck. *"Don't be long,"* he murmured, and nipped her, sharp teeth grazing soft skin. She shivered, smiled again.

"Be back in a flash," she told him, and he said he'd be here waiting.

But of course, when she got back, he wasn't.

43

JANE HEARD THE dying sound at exactly ten oh-three. It separated itself from the rest of the agony by coming so abruptly, and by taking place in the corridor just outside Intensive Care.

It came unexpectedly, yanking her from her twilight haze.

And then, just as suddenly, stopped.

Apprehension settled over her as the near-silence resumed. The half-dozen other inhabitants of the ward stirred uneasily as the sound penetrated through the veil of drugs and destruction, impacted directly on subconscious survival circuits. Instinctively attuned to the subtle frequencies of suffering, they had learned to sift through the minutiae, unconsciously read the many layers of pain.

But this was not the sound of lingering illness.

This was the sound of sudden death.

Jane tensed, shooting fresh agony through her stitched and bandaged torso. The heavy leather restraints on her arms and legs bound her firmly to the bed frame, gave her only a couple of inches of play. The bondage was her reward for resisting the Demerol intravenous they'd forced upon her this afternoon. The drugs left her dazed and groggy, made the arduous task of healing that much more difficult.

Jane fought her way back to the surface; her lidded eyes swam wildly in a head too heavy, too heavy to lift from the pillow. Through the opaqued curtains that ringed her bed she saw only dim light and blurry silhouettes, making a muddled wash of the world.

Then the door opened onto ICU, a bright misshapen rectangle at the far end of the room, and Jane's awareness tweaked up a notch. The drugs and the darkness left her vision blurry and diffuse; she could make out nothing of substance in the dim shadow-world of the ward.

But her hearing was fine; and it was the clack of boot heels that really caught and held her attention. The sound was entirely out of place here, dragging little spurs of dread down her spine as it moved purposefully across the length of the room.

Out in the hall, the phone began ringing at the nurses' station.

The footsteps grew closer. The phone in the hall kept right on ringing. The footsteps were heading directly toward her.

"Syd?" she murmured, barely audible.

Then the smell of him cut through the antiseptic atmosphere; and it was not Syd at all, not by a long shot. And though she had no idea who he was, she knew exactly *what* he was. That was more than enough. The memory of last night's ambush flooded her with panic, made all the worse by her utter helplessness.

"Oh, god," she whimpered, looking desperately for something she could use as a weapon. There was nothing. Not even herself.

The phone stopped ringing. The dark figure came into view: a shadow-shape, looming huge and then halting, strangely hesitant. There was a moment's sheer confusion.

And then the shadow whispered *that name;* and in that one microsecond of perfect horror, Jane understood everything . . .

• • •

... AND SUDDENLY, VIC understood as well. Understood all *too* well. He hovered, heart gripped by the coldest certainty he'd ever known. There was a woman in there, yes, but it was not Nora.

And yet pieces of Nora were there.

"No," he said, though he didn't know why. No was utterly irrelevant when the answer was yes. He reached out for the curtain flap, then staggered back as if struck.

"No." And then again: "No." Like rosary beads he dragged out one at a time. "No no no ..." Accelerating now, as if it were a prayer that could erase what was true. He stood, mouth moving in denial of the dawning horror, until he could stand it no longer.

The woman made a tragic trapped-animal sound as he stepped through the curtain. Her pupils were huge, with fear. She tried to lift her head, tried to lift her hand. Vic growled and showed his teeth. She froze and, despite herself, began to cry. It gave them one more thing in common.

There were tears in his eyes as well.

Because they had scrubbed her down for surgery, yes; but there was so much that they'd missed—the little details that, in the end, meant everything. He smelled Nora under her fingernails. He smelled Nora in her hair. He smelled Nora's blood and meat and sweat.

Most of all, he smelled her death.

Vic reeled as the loss struck him fully, floored him with its finality. His heart went nova in his chest, sent a bloodred haze flooding into his skull as he realized that it was over, all of it, there would never again be a Nora, there would be no forgiveness and no second chances and no going back ...

... and suddenly it was hot, too hot in the room, the walls and floor and ceiling too close, the thick milky curtains closing in to smother him as the murderous urge roared up and up. Vic moaned, low and menacing, felt the sound dip down to become a growl ...

• • •

. . . AND JANE FLINCHED, unable to escape the onslaught as
he began systematically destroying everything around her.
The curtains shredded and tore clear from their hooks as
his hand raked out, smashing into the monitor stand that
stood beside the bed. The screens flatlined an instant before he destroyed them, previews of coming attractions.
Jane winced and mewled as he moved toward the IV
stand, shrieked as he wrenched it away and sent it flying,
ripping the tubes from her arms and her groin in the process. Plasma and catheter bags splattered against the walls,
drenching the floor beneath the bed.

Vic hovered over her like an angel of death, a horrible
rictus spreading across his features.

His features, which began to ripple, and Change . . .

. . . AND THEN HE stopped: his rage barely tethered, caught
in a crossfire of conflicting emotion. Vic was seething
with grief and incalculable pain, burning for vengeance.
But there was another urge, beneath it. Something equally
powerful in its allure.

He wanted to know *why*.

Vic brought his breathing under control, calming himself as best he could. As he moved closer he caught a
whiff of something else on her, and the final piece of the
puzzle clicked impossibly into place. *Oh, no.* The realization instantly reversed itself. *Oh, yes.*

"Of course," he muttered. "Of course."

Vic started to laugh, then; a coarse and guttural
chuckle that bubbled up from the depths of his madness. It
was too perfect. It really was. And he had to admit, as
much as he wanted to taste her blood, as much as he
longed to hear her dying screams as he opened her up and
sprayed her across the room, he was in awe of her as well.
She had taken down Nora, after all. That feat alone commanded his respect.

And now there was no more Nora. . . .

Slowly, Vic peeled the sheet back from her body. Jane
writhed before him, straining against her bonds, as he
plucked at an abdominal suture, took stock of her damage.

There was nothing fatal. Nothing that wouldn't heal, in time. She was young. She was strong. She was already one of them.

And best of all, she was *his*.

And that was the beauty of it. He could smell Syd's mark all over this bitch. It made him crazy to even think of it, filled him with boundless, malevolent glee. At that moment Vic wasn't sure whether he should kill her, or fuck her, or both. And in what order. He drew near, getting very very close in her face before he spoke.

"So here's my situation," he growled. "At the moment, I don't know exactly *what* I'm gonna do with *you*." He smelled the fear on her, loved it. "But I'll tell you what I *am* gonna do.

"First, I'm gonna go and take care of your little chickenshit boyfriend: the one who lets you do all his dirty work for him.

"And then—I swear to you, sweetheart—I'll be back for you."

He smiled then, his eyes alight with dreadful purpose. Vic leaned forward, close enough to graze her cheek. Jane shut her eyes. Trying, in vain, to shut him out.

Vic nuzzled her menacingly, and as he did he brought one taloned finger up to lightly slice its way along the inside of her thigh.

"I'll be back," he assured her.

And then, as quickly as he had appeared, he was gone.

JANE LAY SHIVERING for several minutes afterward: afraid to move, afraid to even breathe. The ward grew deathly quiet again. When she dared open her eyes she saw that a bright track of blood graced her thigh from knee to groin, dripping with malign promise.

There was no measuring the depths of her terror, or the magnitude of her need. Any second now, the room would explode again: with nurses, with doctors, with frantic, screaming people. With police . . . and police . . . and police . . .

She closed her eyes, saw men with needles. Men with guns.

I have to get out of here, she told herself, struggling in her bed. *I have to get out.*

But her every move was agony.

And she had so far to go. . . .

44

I T WASN'T UNTIL the redhead came up to the bar that
Syd realized he was a dead man.

Coming back from Randy's office had been bad
enough. After an eternity of desperate wheedling, the miserable woman at the hospital switchboard had finally relented. But when she'd put him through to ICU, no one
had answered.

As he returned, the crowd was so thick and rowdy that
Vic's table was utterly lost from view. *If I can't see him,
maybe he can't see me,* he hoped. It was an ostrich's
prayer, at best; but that didn't mean that it might not be
true.

And indeed, once safely behind the bar, it was like
he'd never left. Vic didn't come up, demand to know
where he'd been. In fact, Vic didn't come up at all. Fifteen
million *other* people did; and they managed to keep him
running.

But no Vic.

No Vic whatsoever.

So Syd was already feeling nervous by the time the
redhead came up to the bar. "Excuse me," she said, as he

came within range. He nodded, giving her his full attention, and it suddenly dawned on him where he had seen her before.

At the bar, there were people who'd been waiting. They made faces Syd ignored. There was only one face he could see: the one that had greeted him as he'd staggered into the Emergency Room, the bloody bundle in his arms.

"Listen," she said, in the here and now. "Have you seen that guy I was with . . . ?"

Syd's breath sucked in sharply. "He's not with *you*?" Already, he was looking over her shoulder to the empty booth.

"No," she said. "I came up here for drinks, and when I got back, he was gone. . . ."

"How long ago?" Syd was looking all over the bar now, scanning the sea of bobbing heads; but the intensity in his voice commanded her complete attention.

Her eyes startled wide. "It's been almost forty minutes now. . . ."

"Fuck!" He banged the bar with his fist, already moving away from Tanya, racing down the length of the bar. "TRENT!" he hollered, catching his cohort's attention, waiting till they got close enough before going on.

"Got a medical emergency, man. Jane needs me at the hospital."

"Oh, *shit* . . ."

"I know." Acknowledging the madness. "But I gotta go."

Trent looked miserable, and Syd was sorry, but there wasn't a damn thing he could do about it, so he turned away before Trent had a chance to debate it, then slipped through the bartender's exit to the floor. The side door exit was closest, had the fewest crowds to fight through.

As he neared the bathrooms, the lines piled up and gridlocked, clogging the narrow hallway. Syd tried to gently push his way through, then fell back, caught himself on the iron ladder that led to the attic.

"MOVE YOUR ASS!"

The crowd parted reluctantly, let him squeeze through.

Syd broke free to the other side, quickly covered the remaining distance. He slammed down on the push-bar.

The door wouldn't open.

He pushed again, more deliberately this time. The door gave just a little, locked up tight. He peered through the crack, saw a glimmer of steel. It took a second to register.

Someone had chained shut the door.

"Okay," he said, trying to remain calm. "Okay." Backing up, thinking three moves ahead. The next closest exit was the one leading out of the kitchen. He could duck through there.

If it wasn't too late ...

... and before he could even start to rationally examine that thought, he was blowing past the bathroom lines and ramming through the kitchen doors.

The kitchen was deathly still. A horrible burning smell filled the air. Syd coughed and gagged as he rounded the corner, into the first stage of the slaughter.

It was Bruno. Just Bruno. But that was more than enough.

There was Bruno on the walls and floor and ceiling. Bruno on the fridges and the cabinets and drawers. The vast bulk of Bruno sizzled facedown on the grill; his entrails snaked out from under his apron, strung like garlands all the way to the service door, where they wrapped around and around the push-bar. The stench of death was everywhere, red mist still floating through the smoky air, a red sea parting as Syd bolted to the exit.

He had to duck under Bruno's guts, then slide them out of the way, in order to lean on the slickened bar and push. Syd dry-heaved and tried not to look at the intricate veins, the glistening sheen of human tubing never meant to be exposed. But there was no getting around the smell.

The door opened three inches and stopped. More chain was visible, red and silver gleaming.

"SHIT!" he hollered. *"SHIT!"* There was only one other way out. Red was guarding it, which was good. But probably not so good for Red. Syd started back, hurtling

toward the kitchen doors. Behind him, the grease from
Bruno's face popped and spattered on the fire.

Back in the club, Treat Her Right owned the dance
floor. They had the crowd in the palm of their hand. The
music was sinuous, sexual, snaky. It pounded into him the
second he opened the door. *I saw a picture of the future,
and you're not in it. . . .* Syd boggled at the inadvertent
truth behind the lyrics.

There were easily two hundred happy, oblivious people,
movin' to that swamp-rock groove. Faces he recognized:
Tommy, Bonnie, Budd, and Holly. Coworkers. Customers.
Friends. Even Marc Pankowski, doing his weasel dance in
4/4 time, didn't deserve to wind up like Bruno.

And that was when he started to move, pushing out of
the doorway and gathering steam, pumping himself up for
what was coming, coming all too soon. He thought about
the gun tucked into his waistband. He thought about the
tire iron, and the wolf in the woods. *That was different,* he
tried to tell himself, muscling his way through the crowd.
But was it? Syd searched for the magical monster within,
the glorious wolf in his soul, and came back with nothing
but a frightened man who had a peashooter stuck near the
crack of his ass.

And that was when he saw the naked shape slide
through the doorway. The naked shape held a thick steel
chain. Red vaulted off his stool, raised up a hand. The
chain whickered out. It was like watching lightning strike.
One second, Red had a forehead; the next, he did not. The
chain came back with Red's brains all over it.

Vic turned and began wrapping the chain around the
handle, while Red tumbled earthward, the sound of his impact lost in the din. There were several hundred people in
the club. Maybe a dozen of them saw it happen. Syd
pushed desperately forward through the dozens in his path,
pulling the gun, praying Vic would keep his back turned
long enough.

If only there was time . . .

There was a big industrial-strength hook hanging off
one end of the chain. Vic reached for it, as Syd raced to

close the distance. There were still too many people in the
line of fire. Syd cursed and pushed harder as Vic brought
the hook around, fastened it tight.

Syd reached the end of the bar.

Vic whirled, with a smile that grew and grew.

Syd froze in his tracks, transfixed by the horror.

And it was too late now: too late for guns, too late for
anything. Vic was growing, by leaps and bounds: tran-
scending his matter, distorting his form. Translucent derma
rippled over hypershifting musclemeat that surged as fur
enclosed it, rank and reeking of death.

And there was no beauty in the thing that blossomed
into monstrousness before him. No mercy in the lines that
traced the sharp teeth's journey down the burgeoning
snout. It was as far from nature as flesh could be: all Vic's
madness and corruption, his selfishness and bitter rage, lit-
eralized themselves in the shape of the abomination he became.

Vic's true nature, revealed at last.

*The thing that reared up on its haunches was fully
seven feet tall. Its physiology was part man, part wolf, part
goblin: gangly limbs terminating in grotesquely splayed,
black-clawed digits, torso elongating as the shoulders disjointed, pushed back from the deep, jutting breastbone. Its
penis stiffened and retracted into a belly-hugging sheath;
a tail emerged from the crackling coccyx at the base of the
spine, began to slowly wag. The nipple ring glinted off one
of its teats; the tattoos of Nora that graced its arms
twisted in the transition, as well: inked features stretching
and distorting into a hideous screaming face as the flesh
that held it shifted in the light.*

*The creature grinned horribly, lupine head hanging
pendulously between the bony shoulder blades; its jaws
gaped wide, saliva-slick and fiercely-fanged. Its ears elongated, pinned back, the little silver skull-earring still dangling from one lobe. Its blue eyes gleamed bright and wild.
The promise of annihilation burned in them.*

*But beyond all its obvious physical grotesqueries was
the air it carried: a foul vapor wafting off its sheeny, viscid*

skin. It was the stench of Vic's diseased id, marking terri-
tory. Claiming Chameleon's, and everyone in it, as his
own.

Starting with you-know-who . . .

Syd instinctively retreated as the were-thing moved off
the steps and into the crowd. He continued to back up, ac-
cidentally slamming into the person behind him. Awareness of the horror spread through the crowd, creating a
chain reaction of jostling and shouting and shoving as people scrambled to escape.

Vic advanced on his hind legs, claws bared and jaws
snapping. A drunken fratboy stumbled into his path, was
torn in half in one swipe. Blood sprayed and gristle spattered. More screams, lost in the music. *"GET OUT OF
THE WAY!!!"* Syd howled. But they couldn't hear.

And even if they could, there was nowhere to go.

Vic waded gleefully into the terrified throngs, tearing
holes in the scattering dance floor hordes. An arm gone
here. A head gone there. A rib cage exposed to the smoky
red air. Syd turned and ran, shoving onlookers to either
side. Trying to get them out of the line of fire. Trying to
get them out of his way. A half-dozen screeching people
tumbled through the kitchen doors, were greeted by a waft
of greasy Bruno smoke and the first flicker of fire.

Vic snarled and carved an all-meat swath, in hot pursuit of his prey. The crowd indeed parted. Just not fast
enough. Vic split the stragglers lengthwise and
everywhichway, hosing the room down with fresheting
gore. People slipped on the blood-slickened floor, fell, and
were trampled in the rush to escape. All at once, the band
stopped playing.

And then *all* hell broke loose.

Syd glanced back in time to see Tommy closing in behind Vic, a hardwood bar stool raised high overhead. It
was solid, no Hollywood breakaway prop, and it came
down with all the muscle in big Tommy's powerful frame.
It slammed into Vic's skull with a hideous cracking sound.
Vic staggered and howled.

"NO!!!" Syd screamed as Vic whirled and slashed and

his friend's belly opened, gray intestines tumbling out through the hole. The monster cracked open Tommy's chest and dug out his still-pumping heart. It was amazing how much blood it contained, how far it spewed in the very short time it took to reach Vic's mouth and then disappear forever.

Tommy dropped. Vic turned and snarled . . .

. . . but Syd was already to the back hallway. He saw the chained-up emergency exit. Dead end. At the last second he thought of the ladder, and the attic. Syd fought his way back, started climbing as fast as he could.

Halfway up, he heard the roar of a shotgun blast. He saw Trent, falling back behind the bar; the Vic-thing was crouching on top of it, gun barrel still smoking in one misshapen hand. There were several dead people littering the bar area. Syd saw half a skull draped with flowing red hair.

Then Trent, too, was gone, head bluntly staved in. Vic spun the gun around, pumped another round in. He grinned at Syd. Took aim.

"FUCK!" Syd roared, clambering up the ladder, teeth clenched in anticipation of the coming blast. When it came, he flinched—anticipating death—instead got chips blown in his face from the fresh buckshot crater in the wall to his left. He kept climbing, kept climbing. Vic fired again. This time it was wide. Vic was a terrible shot.

Syd hit the trapdoor and shoved his way through. There were more screams, from directly below: he looked down and saw other people behind him, frantically following his lead. Seconds later, something huge hit the ladder, rocking it loose from the wall. Vic tore the stragglers off, flung them wide, started to climb.

The trapdoor was small for Vic's bulk, but somehow Syd didn't think that would stop him. Syd's eyes cast around for a means of escape. There was one skinny little window at the far end of the attic, past the cobwebbed rafters and crates of debris. He bolted for it. Behind him, the trapdoor blew apart.

There was a two-by-four with some nails sticking out, jutting from a box to the window's right. He used it to smash out the window, clear the jagged glass teeth jutting out of the frame. Then he slid out feet-first and belly-up to the sill, just as Vic tore the first massive chunk from the floorboards.

Syd pulled himself out the rest of the way.

Vic stared at him, howled.

Syd let go of the sill.

And then he was falling, he was falling, plummeting fifteen feet straight down to land on unforgiving gravel. Syd hit and rolled, his feet and ankles spiking white with pain. He came up staggering: weaving through the sea of cars, endorphins masking the agony even as the adrenaline pulsed and pushed him forward.

As he ran, he smelled smoke, glanced back in time to see the first tongues of flame lick the windows. A chorus of screams rose up, piercing the cacophony. Syd hesitated a moment, torn between the impulse to smash down the door and the urge to flee. But there were no heroes now; all the heroes were hamburger, cut down in the terrible wake of the monster's onslaught. He forced himself forward, tried to keep his mind clear.

The screams were still ringing in his ears as he made it to the Jeep, leapt into the driver's seat, and jammed the key into the ignition. As he fired it up, he heard the wrenching crack of splintering wood that told him Vic was in the attic now, heading for the window. He looked up in time to see the too-huge shadow filling the tiny window frame.

Syd gunned the engine, threw the Jeep into reverse. *You can't just LEAVE them,* his conscience cried. He started to back out. A second later, the beast's snout appeared, snarling madly as it began to rip chunks from the window frame, enlarging the hole.

Syd pumped the gas, revving in place. To his left, the road beckoned, offering escape. Directly before him stood the front door. The attic window was widening by the sec-

ond. His own survival margin could be measured in micro-
seconds.

While inside, people were trapped and dying.

"Fuck!" Syd cursed, blinking back tears. "FUCK!"

He wrenched the gearshift from reverse to first and
popped the clutch. The Renegade screeched and spun,
lurching forward. The engine whined, picking up speed.
The front door loomed in the headlights. Syd held his
breath, leaned on the horn and at the last second hit the
brakes.

There was a crash and a groan as the plow blade made
contact, and the big door buckled and folded inward. The
impact blew it clear off its frame; it crumpled and fell inside with a deafening clatter. Smoke began to pour out the
top of the mangled transom.

"C'MON!" he screamed, revving the engine and grinding the gears. Inside, he could make out dozens of figures
stumbling and staggering toward the fractured portal.
Some, at least, would survive. Maybe most. It was the best
he could do.

There was another crash, and Syd flinched as a piece
of cinder block the size of his head slammed down onto
the hood of the Jeep, missing him by inches. Syd looked
up, horrified.

Vic was coming out of the hole.

Syd screamed, desperately gnashing the gears into reverse. The transmission ground and locked; the Renegade
groaned, backed out of the wreckage. The plow blade
hung crookedly from the mangled front bumper as Syd
cleared the entrance, wrenched the wheel in the direction
of the road.

By now, the survivors were pouring out the door. Syd
looked back and saw Marc Pankowski fighting for the
lead. A woman tripped before him; he stomped on her
neck, kicked her out of his way. His face was filled with
a strange elation.

Then the Vic-thing landed on his head.

Syd floored it, half a heartbeat before the massive
beast rose. The tires smoked and spun, gripped and caught.

The Jeep took off, just as something flew through the air to slam against the back of the passenger seat. Syd glanced back, saw blond hair on the floor of the seat well.

Then Syd was gone gone gone, out of the parking lot and onto the highway. The Renegade took the turn badly, almost flipped altogether as he whipped it into the turn. The plow blade struck and sparked as Syd rocked the wheel back and forth, felt the high center of gravity tip perilously before leveling out, making solid contact with the road.

The Jeep sped toward the hospital and Jane and escape. The rescue attempt had done some damage: one of the headlights was gone, giving the road a skewed, lopsided quality; and there was a bad-sounding rattle coming from under the hood. A thought kept circling in his head, halfway between hope and prayer, going *don't break down, don't break down, don't break down.* . . .

Syd kept checking the rearview mirror as he drove, half-expecting Vic to appear magically behind him and snatch him by the neck. But the Chameleon's sign rapidly disappeared in the distance, and no light emerged from the lot behind him. It was a moment of victory.

It lasted for roughly another two seconds.

Then the truck's headlights appeared behind him. It was a white Chevy pickup, and it was all over the road: weaving wildly from lane to lane as it bore down hard, hauling ass and gaining fast. Its hide was white, glowing ghostly in the dark; its headlights glared like angry eyes.

Syd jammed on the gas as they reached the foothills, began snaking into the first turns of the upgrade. The rattle under the hood grew louder, howling out its damage as the engine cannibalized itself on the climb. There was a tractor-trailer directly in front of him, gnashing through its gears as it crawled up the hill. The lines on the road went from dotted-white to double-yellow. Syd cursed; he couldn't afford to get pinned here, but didn't know if he had the power to avoid it.

Downshifting and flooring it again, Syd crossed into the

oncoming lane, began inching his way past the rig. The Jeep jerked and whined reluctantly. The speedometer fluttered sluggishly, read fifty-five, fifty-six, fifty-seven . . .

He limped past and kept going, trying to keep up the speed. The Jeep was hurtin' bad now, a low, shuddering rumble joining with the ever-louder rattle beneath the hood. The tractor-trailer receded into the distance as he fought his way forward.

Two hundred yards back, the ghost truck swerved around the sluggish rig, then cut it off. The driver of the big rig blasted his horn and flipped his hi-beams in anger.

Then Syd was 'round the bend, heading into the high-lands. The trees closed in as the road wrapped tight around the mountain; the shoulder to his right grew narrower, then disappeared entirely, leaving only the thin ribbon of guard-rail between him and a very long drop. The Renegade's engine continued to falter as the upgrade grew steeper, the curves more demanding.

The Chevy suffered no such setback. With every new bend, it closed the distance between them. Syd straight-armed the wheel, trying to *will* the Jeep to move faster. As he did so, he pressed himself back in the seat, felt the gun dig into the small of his back. He cursed and yanked its useless bulk free, tossed it on the passenger seat.

The crest of the first rise was dead ahead. The pickup kept coming. One hundred yards and closing. He could hear it now, his pursuer's motor screaming death and power even as his own cried out for mercy. A naked rage flooded him suddenly: fury at the cruel, insane injustice. Syd focused the feeling, trying to shake the terror, desper-ately assessing his strengths.

He knew the road; that much was true. He knew it like the back of his hand. And this time, he knew what he was up against, which diminished the shock, if not the trauma. He was hard-wired on adrenaline but otherwise straight, whereas Vic was clearly blasted out of his mind. And judging from the ghost truck's veering, being a werewolf was no great strategic advantage behind the wheel of a car.

Syd rounded the bend before the last rise that marked
the beginning of the downgrade. The blackness beyond the
edge of the road yawned to his right. Such a long way
down.

And that was when it hit him.

He had a chance: a crazed and fatal one, with a snowball's odds in hell of succeeding. But a chance, nonetheless.

It was the only one he'd get.

The truck lurched around the curve, not more than sixty
yards behind. Syd gripped the wheel and stomped on the
gas. The Jeep surged forward, cresting the ridge. His speed
instantly increased as he tipped into the downgrade, began
the twisting, treacherous descent. The NO PASSING, DANGER-
OUS CURVES AHEAD sign flashed by, was swallowed by the
darkness. The needle arced up to sixty-five, climbing. It was
a fleeting advantage, one that allowed him to gain some
ground and ready himself. Syd grabbed the gun, flipped the
safety, jacked a round in . . .

. . . and then the Chevy was there, roaring around the
corner and over the rise, stealing back the ground it had
briefly lost. Syd watched the rearview as it took the turn
way too wide, clipping the NO PASSING sign and shearing it off at ground level. The sign slid up and smashed
into the truck's windshield before sliding off into the slipstream. Vic just punched out the remaining glass and kept
right on coming, unfazed by the impact—seeming, in fact,
to enjoy it. He howled and pounded the dash, bloodlust
singing through the battered cab of the truck.

The pickup accelerated, closed the remaining distance.
It smacked into the back of the Jeep, just hard enough to
send Syd a message. Marc Pankowski's head pinballed
around in the back. The road ahead hooked to the left. Syd
screeched through the turn, gravity conspiring to push him
to seventy. The Jeep was not built for road-hugging antics:
it oversteered horribly, Syd fighting to hold on. God help
him if Vic got him broadside.

To the left, the concrete retaining wall whipped by, inviting catastrophe. To his right, the guardrail ribbon, then blackness. They were fast coming up on the point where Syd had spun out, so many moons ago. Now Vic was vying for a repeat performance. The Chevy kissed Syd's back bumper again, hard enough to crunch metal and play crack-the-whip with Syd's spine.

The Jeep skittered and fishtailed across the macadam. One more like that and he'd roll the damned thing. Syd swerved into the oncoming lane. As he did, Vic cut right and pulled alongside, then veered to crunch into Syd's passenger side. Syd turned his head, saw the hideous countenance hunched over the steering wheel, cackling, long tongue flapping in the breeze. Vic yanked the wheel, pushing Syd out of the lane, perilously close to the retaining wall.

Just up ahead the road hooked left, then doubled back and swooped to the right, forming a huge, sweeping S-curve that clung to the side of the mountain. The tree Syd had once wrapped his Mustang around was still there; the scar of the wreck still visible upon it. Vic was steering him straight for the spot, like a giant YOU ARE HERE sign beckoning him.

"Not again," Syd hissed. *"Not this time."*

Wheel gripped tight in his left hand, fighting the impossible physics of the situation, Syd brought the gun up and aimed with his right. Vic just looked at him and laughed.

Until he realized what Syd was aiming *at* . . .

. . . and then Vic was screaming, as eight nine-millimeter hollow-point slugs tore through the thin steel skin of the ghost truck's hood. They exploded inside the engine compartment, and then there was an ear-shattering bang: black oil spraying like heartblood as the Chevy's eight-cylinder seized up at sixty, instantly reducing itself to junk and smoking shrapnel. A stray chunk of cylinder head smashed through the firewall to pierce the left front tire, which promptly blew out and chewed itself to smoking bits.

Syd dropped the gun and jammed on the brakes.

Vic snarled and whipsawed the steering wheel, trying to control his now-careening vehicle. The Chevy lurched and screamed like a dying animal as the denuded rim ground and gouged the road. As the back end of the pickup rocketed past him, Syd jacked the wheel to the right, gave it a neat little boot in the ass.

And that was all it took.

The Jeep's bumper whacked the rear wheel well, as the dangling plow blade made contact with the pickup's right rear tire. The spinning wheel ripped the blade right off the bumper; on its way out, the blade caught the sidewall of the tire, violently peeling it apart and sending long corkscrew loops of steel-belted radial flapping in its wake.

Syd braked and veered left as the truck skidded, flipped and rolled: over and over and over, a somersaulting symphony of destruction, building to a deafening crescendo as it headed for the edge of the road. Beyond the guardrail was a rocky ravine, jagged with boulders and thick with trees. The truck hit the rail at close to fifty miles an hour, shearing through it like a worn rubber band. Vic, the truck, and a ten-foot section of rail went sailing into space.

And gravity did the rest.

Syd never saw the impact, busy as he was trying not to crash and die himself. But there was a beat of free-fall silence as he regained control, followed by the tumultuous crash of wood and stone and metal and glass, all colliding and compacting at once. A mute but thunderous *whump* sounded: the death knell of the ghost truck, forever and ever. Syd peered into the rearview mirror in time to see the brilliant red-orange fireball mushroom behind him, cindering the trees as it billowed skyward into the night.

But did that mean that Vic was dead? Syd had no way of knowing. He'd be good and goddamned if he was going to check; he'd seen enough monster movies to know how *that* went. Might as well strip to his underwear and say *who's out there . . . ?* The Evil Dead, lady. Who the fuck do you think?

He couldn't afford to find out. The Jeep's engine was laboring hard; there were no guarantees that he'd even make it.

He had to get to Jane. He had to do it now.

He just prayed that it wasn't too late.

45

It was twenty minutes later when the big Peterbilt
steered into the downgrade, heading for home.

Rusty Myers sighed as he flipped on the Jake brake
and leaned back in his seat; it had been a long damn day.
The Jake brake hissed and killed the engine, releasing
compression to the cylinders and letting inertia do the job
of walking the rig down the mountain. The hulking 450
CAT under the hood groaned as the gears wound down,
immediately began to slow. It was a fail-safe system, designed to safeguard against brake burnout, and it beat the
shit out of double-clutching it all the way home.

Rusty wasn't about to argue. His legs and butt and
shoulders ached to the point of numbness from eleven
hours on the road, and he was bone-tired from lugging a
total of seventy-two tons of Budweiser from Morgantown
to McKeesport to Pittsburgh and back again. Three round-
trips in this one shift, some six thousand pallets in all. He
wondered where people put it all.

Rusty stretched his long legs, pushed his Steelers cap
back on his head, and thought about the wife and daughter
he had not gotten more than a fleeting glimpse of in the

last three weeks. At any rate, he was over the hump and into the homestretch now. Another hour, he figured, till he got back to the yard; another three till he could kick back with his family. If he was lucky.

Then he rounded the curve, saw the sheared-off sign-post lying in the middle of the road.

"God *damn*!" Rusty yelled, as the truck thundered over it, mashing sheet metal to macadam. "What the fuck . . ."

The sign had still been standing when he came over the mountain, not three hours ago. Someone had knocked it off in the meantime, and violently, by the looks of it. The dickheads who had passed him on the way up came screaming to mind. It wouldn't surprise him a bit. Rusty dealt with automotive idiots all day long: cutting him off on the highway, trusting him to somehow defy physics and magically stop short of ramming eighty thousand pounds of jackknifing freight up their butts.

The guys that passed him on the upgrade were no ex-ception. They were either drunk or stupid or both, and Rusty wouldn't have minded slapping the shit out of either one of them, if only to teach them some manners.

But he didn't want them to *die* for it.

So when he came upon the skid marks and saw the yawning gap in the guardrail, his heart sank like a stone. There was no question of what had happened. Rusty couldn't see the wreck, but it didn't take a rocket scientist to figure out that somebody'd played bump-cars and lost, big-time. There was debris all over both lanes and deep gouges heading all the way up to the gaping hole. The fire glowing at the base of the ravine filled in the rest of the picture, and as he rolled down his window he caught a noxious whiff of burning gasoline, plastic, rubber, and hair.

"Jesus." He slowed to a stop some thirty yards short of the breach, reached over to the rocker panel, and flipped on the four-ways. There was a cellular phone in the cab, in addition to the CB. He picked it up, dialed 911, waited for the operator to come on. Interference was formidable

in the highlands, but he managed to get enough of the
message through to count.

He reached under the seat and grabbed the box of
emergency marker flares, then climbed down out of the
cab. The Staters would be there soon enough; in the meantime, he did what any good trucker would do: shut down
the lane, laid out the flares, and waited for help. Taking
care of endangered motorists—no matter how stupid or de-
serving of their fate—was an ongoing responsibility, and
sometimes inconvenient as hell. But he couldn't forget that
it might be him one day, or his mom, or his wife and
child. It was more than the right thing to do.

It was the code of the road.

Rusty hiked over to the edge of the rail, peered into the
abyss. There was no way in hell he could get down there.
The pickup truck was a crumpled inferno, belly-up at the
bottom of a fifty-foot drop. Whoever it was, he was flame-
broiled by now. Rusty swallowed hard and began back-
tracking up the road, striking flares and positioning them
at ten-, hundred-, and five-hundred-foot intervals behind
his rig. The road in either direction was desolate, pitch-
black but for the strobing glow of the flashers, the hissing
glare of the flares. They bathed everything in shades and
grades of red, cast eerie shadows across the rocks and
trees.

An unsettling quiet fell over the tableau. The fire below had banked, settled into a slow, steady burn. The road
curved off behind him, rimming the flickering chasm. His
rig sat blinking, partially obscured by the trees. Rusty
stood just beyond the curve: flare in hand, ready to wave
off the unwary motorist coming 'round the bend.

Down in the ravine, something popped and shifted,
sending up a spray of glowing sparks. Rusty looked back
and cocked his ear, listening to the shifting of dead weight,
the scorching heat. The sparks fluttered and died, like a
miniature fireworks display. The trees rustled, as a breeze
picked up. The breeze shifted toward him, bringing with it
that awful, nauseating smell. The gasoline taint had burned

away, but he could still make out the unmistakable odor of smoldering rubber, blistered paint, melting plastic . . .

. . . and underneath it all, the pungent fetor of charred flesh.

And that was the worst of it, the part that made his skin crawl and his stomach turn. He fought back the nausea, shifting his weight from foot to foot. "C'mon, man," he muttered, cursing the police. "Don't make me wait out here all fuckin' night."

The wind changed direction, blew back toward the truck. It took a moment longer for the big man to realize that the smell was still with him. It was strong, almost overpowering. Something cracked off to the side of the road. Rusty turned, as the smoking shadow rose behind him.

And there was no time to react; not really. There was just a snarl and a flurry of violent motion, and the flare went skittering off down the road, along with the hand that had held it.

And for Rusty, the long day was over.

46

THE ELEVATOR DOORS opened onto a scene of madness. Frightened patients stared from darkened doorways as shocked doctors talked to stricken nurses, their faces as pale and green as the sterile halls in which they huddled. There were police: many, many of them. Wandering the corridors. Crawling all over the ward. Outside, another half-dozen shined lights behind bushes and into parked cars, slowly patrolling the perimeter. They were searching for perpetrators, searching for suspects.

They were searching for Jane.

Syd dreaded it from the moment he first limped the Jeep up to the entrance, caught his first glimpse of flashing red light. *Oh god,* he thought, shutting off the trashed and battered motor. *Oh please no.* Tucking the gun into his belt clip, pulling his shirt over the bulge. The whole way up he prayed, thinking *please please let her be okay. . . .*

Then the doors opened. He smelled the blood.

And knew that she was not.

Neon-yellow CRIME SCENE tape cordoned off the entrance to Intensive Care. A huge crimson smear pooled and spread just downstream from the nurses' station. A pair of rumpled detectives were huddled around the prone form, conversing in low tones. One of them moved, and Syd caught a flash of skull where a face used to be.

He turned away then, his senses awash in fear and panic. He didn't have to see the bed to know that Jane was no longer there. He could smell the death and the terror, the endorphin-laced vapor trail that hung in her wake. Syd followed it, all the way to the other end of the hall. There was a door there, a sign glowing over the transom.

EXIT.

There was a tiny spot of red on the threshold, near the corner of the doorjamb. It was fresh, as yet unnoticed in the chaos surrounding him. Syd knelt, touched a finger to it.

"Jane," he murmured. He peered through the little vertical window, saw another tiny droplet down on the stairs, glistening against the poured-concrete floor. Syd pushed the door open, stepped through. As it closed he glanced back and saw one of the cops looking his way, gesturing to his partner . . .

. . . and then Syd was moving, down and down and down, taking the stairs two and three at a time. He was already to the second-floor landing by the time he heard the door upstairs chunk open, the first angry voices following in his wake.

Syd hit the exit to the street before they even got to the third floor. He took a deep breath, stepped calmly into the night, hiked quickly over to the battered Jeep. He opened the door, was just starting to climb inside when he heard the sudden, nerve-jolting whoop of a siren.

A police cruiser roared up, screeched to a halt. A spotlight pinned Syd as a pair of deputies hopped out, flanking him.

"FREEZE, ASSHOLE!" one of them cried.

Syd froze.

A gaunt figure emerged from the cruiser, ambled over. Syd groaned as he recognized Chief Hoser, a squawking walkie-talkie clutched in one bony hand. As the deputies moved in, Hoser's cadaverous face expanded into an exuberant grin. He thumbed the talk button, brought the box to his lips.

"Roger that," he said. "Yeah, we got yer boy right here."

Syd wheeled around, just as two more of Hoser's deputies pulled up behind him, completely boxing him in. They piled out: one leveling his gun at Syd's chest as the other pulled his flashlight, started nosing around the Jeep.

"Syd," Hoser said, addressing him with utterly contemptuous camaraderie. "Seems like bad news just follows you wherever you go, boy. Now what the hell can you tell us about this mess?"

Syd opened his mouth, tried to think of a suitable lie. But before he could even formulate a reply, the cop with the flashlight, a man named Hardy, spotted something on the floor behind the passenger seat.

"Chief!" he gasped. "I think you better see this."

"What is it?" Hoser snapped. *Oh, shit,* thought Syd. Hoser stepped over, peered into the seat well.

There followed a moment of silence.

The next thing Syd knew, he was grabbed and spun, spread-eagled across the hood of the squad car. One of the deputies, a lantern-jawed man named Gardner, held him by the neck, began rudely patting him down.

"Jesus fucking Christ!" Hoser ran one hand over his close-cropped skull, stared at the severed head. "Any idea who it is?"

"Hard to tell," Hardy replied, squinting. "Kinda looks like Marc Pankowski."

"Pankowski?" Gardner blurted. "God, I fucking *hate* that guy!" His hand moved across the bulge under Syd's shirt, felt it. "Okay, hold the phone. This boy's got a gun," Gardner called out as he flipped up Syd's shirt, yanked the pistol from its hiding place.

"Please," Syd said. "I can explain . . ."

"Shut up," Hoser hissed with disgust. "You sick little prick." The cops all looked at each other, then back to Syd with a sort of queasy fascination, like they'd just stumbled upon their very own homegrown Jeffrey Dahmer.

"You're under arrest, son," he continued. "Get ready for a world of shit." Hoser motioned to Gardner. "Cuff him. And make sure you read him his goddam rights."

"Please, don't . . ." Thinking *please don't make me do this.* He could feel the Change inside, fighting for release.

"Hold still, dammit!" Gardner ordered, then to Hardy, "Gimme a hand with this asshole!"

"I can't let you do this," Syd reiterated, as his right arm was wrenched rudely back. The cuff snicked shut. The sound went right through him. His left arm came next: forced back so hard he thought it would break.

The second cuff snapped shut.

And then Syd snapped, too.

"NO!" he roared, suddenly twisting, too wild to handle. Gardner pressed down on him, felt the sudden surge of strength that lifted his prisoner clear off the hood.

"Shit!" Gardner barked. "He's getting loose!"

"GODDAMMIT!" Hoser bellowed at his other men, furious. "KEEP HIM DOWN!"

The deputies scrambled, trying to restrain him.

"NO!" Syd screamed, control slipping away . . .

. . . and that's when they heard the crunching explosion of metal on metal on metal, the grinding whine of impending doom. Chief Hoser and the other officers looked up to see thirty tons of pissed-off Peterbilt hurdle the divider: smashing through concrete and steel, tossing cars like Matchbox toys as it roared across the parking lot.

Gardner momentarily lost his grip. It was all Syd needed. He broke free, whirled around in time to see the still-smoking apparition behind the wheel . . .

. . . *AND IT WAS worth it, it was worth it, just the look on their faces as he gnashed the gears and smashed his way toward them. Vic howled, half-mad with pain and exhilaration, wreaking havoc as he weaved the huge truck back and forth, playing kick-the-can with a dozen more shiny cars along the way.*

Vic laughed and rasped for breath, smelled his own scorched hide, and laughed some more. The little men in

*blue pulled their popguns, pissed their pants, as Vic rolled
up and over their blinking kiddie-cars, then rolled up and
over the little men themselves. He leaned on the horn
exultantly, drowning out their cries as he mashed them
roadkill-flat.*

*A bullet hit starred the windshield; another whistled
inches past his skull, pinged off the stinking interior. Vic
didn't care. Injury was beyond him now; survival completely beside the point.*

It was blood he wanted. One man's blood.

The man who was running, even now . . .

. . . RUNNING AWAY FROM the carnage, even as the massive
rig plowed through Jane's Jeep and Chief Hoser's two
cruisers, tossing them to the side. Syd glanced back only
once, just long enough to see the old man take his valiant
last stand: six-gun blazing like a righteous David to Vic's
eighteen-wheel Goliath.

Only this time Goliath won, bowling over the chief
with a sickening thud that left pieces of him stuck to the
grill like bugs on a windshield. Syd felt a pang of pure human remorse, and then even that was gone as he rounded
the corner, hurtling toward the Emergency Room entrance
just as fast as his legs could carry him. There was a Taurus
station wagon parked in the pickup zone, its front doors
hanging wide. A yuppie man loaded his yuppie wife into
the passenger seat, her arm freshly set in a bulky white
cast. They stood transfixed, identically frozen as they
stared in the direction of the fearsome noise, the manacled
wild-man coming around the corner.

"GET IN!" Syd yelled, knocking the guy aside even as
he shoved his wife onto the seat. She yipped and slid
away, her eyes bulging with terror.

"HEY!!" The guy stood threateningly, but one look
and Syd knew his heart wasn't in it. Maybe it was the
light in Syd's eyes. Or the fact that Syd was starting to get
in *with* her.

Or perhaps it was the twelve-ton monster that howled
around the corner, snapping at his heels.

It veered savagely, the trailer almost tipping as it took the turn. Vic countersteered and took out a Volkswagen Jetta on the backhand, swatting it out of its spot and up onto the sidewalk.

The man stood in shock, ballpeened by the spectacle.

"GET IN THE GODDAMN CAR!!!" Syd screamed.

The man snapped out of it, vaulted over the hood on his way to the driver's side. The guy's wife was already making doomed whimpering sounds as Syd hopped into the car.

The truck loomed behind them, less than a hundred yards away.

"DRIVE!!" Syd bellowed.

He did.

47

SYD'S RIDE ENDED at the foot of Jane's mountain. They had lost Vic on the back roads, the endless winding upgrades; but Syd knew his lead was fleeting, ticking away fast. He apologized again to the hijacked couple as he stepped out of their car, watched the wagon peel out and take off madly down the road. They couldn't get away fast enough. He didn't blame them a bit.

After they had gone, Syd hunkered down on the side of the road: bringing his shackled hands down and under his feet, then stepping through until the cuffs were in the front. A small but necessary improvement. He stood and took off up the mountain, eschewing the winding drive for the most direct overland route.

Forty yards into the woods, he picked up her trail.

At first, he thought he might have been confused, his senses registering leftover traces of last night's carnage. But it wasn't true. This blood was fresh, and bore the hospital's taint. With a little concentration, he found, he could track it. It led up from the woods, coming out of the south. She had run all this way.

She had lost a lot of blood.

The forest was dark and quiet as he climbed the rocky slope, the trees above filtering out all but the most tenacious tendrils of earthbound lunar light. As he ran, his heart raced in tandem with his thoughts; he'd never known that the darkness could be so rich, invested with so many textures and scents.

And beneath it all, such *clarity*. His terror and his purpose had aligned somehow, come together in perfect and potent counterbalance. The moist scent of evergreen and loam, of damp fur and warm blood—the pulse of a billion forms of interactive life—all touched him deep beneath his skin. He felt inextricably *connected* to the whole of creation, instinctively locking into the rhythm of his soul; as he did, his whole life spread before him, like a preview of the flashing-before-his-eyes that death would doubtless bring.

And death was imminent; of this, he was certain. He could literally feel it in the air, its chill pall like the sweat that clung to his skin. And the acceptance of that fact had freed him somehow, allowed him to see how things had all been perfectly, precisely designed to bring him to this point, this moment. This *choice*.

The lights of the cabin came into view as he crested the hill, headed into the clearing. Syd picked up his speed on the level ground, taking long clean strides, abandoning himself to his senses.

As he bounded up onto the porch, he heard the dead bolt slip. Then the door swung open, and he stepped inside.

"How is she?" was the first thing he asked, and the grim set of Mae's face told him almost more than he wanted to know. She looked at the handcuffs, she looked in his eyes, and a terrible sadness crossed her features. But she did not utter a word.

Mae locked the door behind him as he followed Jane's trail. It didn't go up the stairs, as he might have expected, but down the hallway toward the kitchen. There was another flight of stairs there, leading to the basement.

Gramma Mae appeared behind him, placed a hand on his shoulder.

"When this is over," she said, "you'll have to go away. You're not safe here anymore."

"I know." Breathing deep, averting his eyes. "What about you?"

"I'm too old to run," she replied. "And this is my home."

"Mae . . ." Voice cracking. Thinking of all he had undone.

"You didn't know." Cutting him off. "Just take care of her."

He nodded, tears welling in his eyes. There were tears in her eyes as well. Syd turned, then, and stepped through the door.

Descending into darkness.

The basement was musty and cluttered, with a packed earthen floor. The air was close, heavy with the aroma of dried herbs. He found Jane huddled in a dim corner, lying on a makeshift bed of pillows and quilts. She was panting heavily. She was entirely transformed. Gramma Mae had dressed the wound with a healing poultice; the bandage was nearly soaked through, and he could tell from the way she shivered just how terribly damaged she was.

Syd approached her, at once horrified and amazed. Such a beautiful creature. So unlike Vic and Nora. So literal an embodiment of the beauty at her core. He remembered the first time he looked into those soulful eyes, bore witness to the keen understanding there.

Now there was pain, as well. Incredible pain.

"I won't let him hurt you," he said, reaching out to her. Jane made a mournful sound as he touched her head, stroking the coarse, luxuriant fur. *"I won't let* anyone *hurt you."* She whimpered, and a shudder ran through her powerful form.

Upstairs, the basement door clicked shut. Syd heard the tumblers of a lock slide home, then the sound of Mae's footsteps, moving slowly down the darkened stairs. She reached the bottom and rounded the corner, moving anxiously toward them.

"He's here," she said.

HE HAD FOUND Nora's grave; and from the moment he began to dig, the last shreds of Vic's sanity peeled back once and for all. It was like his mind was the hole being carved now from the living earth, and his soul was the wet, rotting treasure that he sought to exhume. There was no hope in the quest. That didn't matter at all.

Just the digging, and the digging, and the digging.

The carnage at Chameleon's had filled him to overflowing, his nervous system humming like an overloaded transformer with the life-energy of dozens of slaughtered souls. The rush was sublime, a godlike buzz that countermanded the physical damage even as it broiled his brain, jacked his metabolism clear into the kill zone.

He was over the line now, and he might never go back. To revert to human form would be to invite incalculable suffering, more than even he could bear. Aside from the thousand little cuts and contusions, his flesh had been toasted to a blistering crisp—mostly first- and second-degree burns, all the way down to third in a couple of spots—and every little movement sent him slivers of purest agony. He only thanked whatever stars still cared for the lack of broken bones and ruptured organs.

Up above, the moon shone cold, no longer his lover at all. She hated him, clearly, as did all of Creation. He doubted, now, that she'd ever really loved him; no doubt, she'd been lying all this time. She could join the fucking club. And he could be its president.

And that was the big fat joke life had played on him, now, wasn't it? The ridiculous notion that he had ever been loved. As he tore into the soft, packed earth, he laughed and growled and cried, simultaneously tortured and amused and destroyed. He had been lusted after and hungered for, sacrificed and died for a thousand times over.

But had he ever been loved?

And therein lay the bitter irony: that he'd had so many chances, and somehow blown them all. In the course of all that fucking and killing, killing and fucking, he had somehow missed the boat. And now the boat had pulled out of the harbor forever.

It didn't take long to reach the body. The grave was shallow; and once he hit that pocket of muddy soup, he knew he had arrived. Nora had changed substantially in the short time since returning to seed. Her supernature worked against her in death, accelerating the decomposition process. She was like a floater now: soft and rancid, bloated with scavengers and gas. She was barely recognizable as a woman *at all,* much less the woman he loved.

When he took her in his embrace, her flesh sloughed off in spongy, liquefying slabs; the fatty tissues beneath hung loose as well, muscles already going adipocerous, like candle wax made of lye and tallow. Her once-beautiful hair came out in knotted clumps, dragged down by its own sodden weight, leaving naked skull behind. Vic whined and hugged her fiercely to his charred and blackened breast, marking himself with her stench. Carrying her essence with him into battle.

But when he tried to touch what little remained of her face, it came away like wet tissue paper in his hands. Vic stared at the maggot-slick deathmask beneath it.

It could have belonged to anyone.

AND THERE WAS something in the howl that rose up now—something haunting and heart-rending in its expression of irreversible loss—that Syd could not help but identify with. It spoke to his love of the women here with him. It spoke to the deepest part of himself.

It meant that he and Vic had something in common, after all.

His clothes, all at once, had become too constricting, and every fiber of his flesh felt like bursting into flame. At last, the time had come. He stood and wordlessly began to disrobe. Any residual embarrassment at stripping in front of Gramma Mae burned off in the urgency. There was nothing she hadn't already seen.

Besides, she was disrobing too.

While they undressed, he stared at Jane. Her eyes, in the dim light, were luminous pools, unwavering in their focus upon him.

"You know what you have to do," Mae said. She dropped her clothing to the floor. As she stood, he saw that her weathered flesh was covered with scars: the raised welts of long-healed bites and slashes, each one marking the ghosts of battles past.

Syd nodded, peeling off the last of his clothing. He stood naked before her. Mae came to him, a small cloth pouch in her hands. She reached inside, pulled out a small stoppered vial. The vial was strangely familiar; Syd thought of Nora and shuddered.

"Remember," she said, "in the end, it's not so much a matter of finding it as it is of letting it *come to you.*"

She uncapped the vial, then tipped a quantity onto the crown of his head. The oil was sharply bitter, sweetly pungent, wild-smelling. It burned his skin as it soaked in.

"Just let it out," she told him, began daubing oil at his chakra points: the center of his forehead, his throat, the center of his chest, then down to his belly and on, all the way to his root chakra. Syd tensed up as she neared his crotch.

"Relax," she said, reaching between his legs. "Don't forget to breathe. . . ."

As the front door exploded, directly above their heads . . .

. . . AND VIC DIDN'T understand why they bothered, it made no sense at all, it barely even slowed him down. Just as the pain meant nothing to him. Just another ridiculous makeshift matchstick obstacle.

Like anything in the world could stop him now.

He moved straight past the shattered storm door, great wolf-goblin body surreal against the quaint Americana he now so pointedly destroyed, lashing out to smash all the accoutrements of domestication he passed: rustic antiques decked with pewter and chintz, all the homey little touches that really made a cage a cage.

Laying waste to this worthless crap collection was one thing. But as Vic moved deeper into the house and caught a whiff of the old woman, he started going really crazy. The drying flora hanging from the eaves were enough to give her away, along with the wheat braidings and corn dollies and assorted other bits of funky pagan *kitsch*.

But more than that, Vic could smell her *power*. The reek of it made his hackles rise and his flesh writhe. She was trying to help them, that bitch, and for that he would make her pay. Vic would split her open and floss with her withered fallopian tubes.

Just as soon as I find you . . .

SYD CLOSED HIS eyes, began taking deep measured breaths. The biting aroma filled his head. He asked what was in it, and she explained. Herbs. Roots. Blood from each of the women.

All, in their own way, centering him.

Facilitating the Change.

Mae continued to anoint him, her movements quick but unhurried, all the while murmuring softly to herself. Her method was in marked contrast to Nora's; it was controlled and deliberate, with a quiet, intensely focused sense of *purpose*. By comparison, he and Nora had been like a pair of preteens with a Ouija board: dilettantes and dabblers in an art they barely grasped.

Still, he couldn't help wishing she would hurry things up a little.

Upstairs in the living room, something crashed and shattered. "Here," she said, handing him a small piece of root. "Chew this."

Syd took it, sniffed. It smelled horrible.

"Just do it," Mae urged. "We don't have much time."

The root tasted as bad as it smelled. As he chewed, his mouth flooded with bitter saliva. He looked down at his naked body; it seemed to *glitch* momentarily, as if slipping in and out of focus.

"What is this?" he asked. The words came out slurred, like he was talking through a mouthful of Novocain.

"Kava kava. Very mild. Just loosens you up a little."

"Is this what makes it happen?"

"No." Mae shook her head. "*You* make it happen. Now close your eyes. Empty your thoughts."

Syd did so: closing his eyes, letting his mind go blank and still. The destruction moved down the hall, searching. Gramma Mae scooped up a handful of earth from the floor, began rubbing it on his arms and legs and chest.

"There are lines of power that link your spirit to the earth," she told him. "Find them. Trace them to your core."

And as Syd reached inside, fire began to light up and down his spine: spreading through his arms and down his legs, coming out the soles of his feet, reaching into the soil upon which he stood. A greater power waited there, swelling just under the surface: a vast and swirling sea of energy, to which he was connected, and which connected him to all things.

Syd tapped into it, instantly felt his limbs go loose and wobbly, as if suddenly buoyed by some powerful inner current. His head filled with stars, went vertiginous, whirling. Mae appeared alongside him, helped to lower him to the floor. She was much stronger than she looked. Her gnarled hands were calloused, her fingertips smooth and pebbled as a dog's paw.

His own hands and feet were tingling, the nerves itching as if awakening from a long and deadening sleep. Syd brought his fingers up, stared in amazement as the whorls and peaks merged and receded, like ripples on the surface of a pond.

Then disappeared before his disbelieving eyes.

Taking his identity with them.

Upstairs, Vic had found his way to the kitchen. The sounds of destruction paced him, sliding under the basement door. From her pallet, Jane whimpered, high and faint.

"Just remember," Mae said. "Your heart is the key."

Then the basement door blew open . . .

. . . AND AS HE came down the steps, then rounded the corner, he saw the two bitches huddled at the cellar's far end: one young and familiar, one very, very old, neither of them looking too happy to see him.

And, hoo *doggies!* it was tough to rightly assess just how bad that made him feel.

He would fuck them both, he decided right then. He would do it just for the hell of it: gobble their life-spark even as he made them spread that one final time, before death took them over the last plateau.

But first, he would make them watch what happened to their boy.

Which raised the very important question: where *was* their boy? Had he snuck out the back? If he had any brains, then yes, he probably had, though Syd hadn't exactly struck him as the brainy type. He guessed he'd just have to crack that skull and see for himself . . .

. . . and suddenly there was a dark form rising from the corner; but instead of stopping where it should have stopped, it just kept getting larger and larger.

Until its proportions were utterly wrong.

Until it was nearly as huge as himself . . .

. . . AND IT WAS SO easy, so easy to do. Like falling off a bicycle, once you understood the secret. There was your true nature—your irreducible essence—and then there were just all the obstacles you threw in your own path. Like fear of the unknown. Like thinking too much. Like blindly doing what you're told.

Like joining the herd in turning its back on the powerful truth of its animal heart.

But those days were gone forever.

Syd felt the fires of Change roar through him; and for the very first time, he stayed out of their way. Letting them liberate his spirit, burn down the walls of imprisoning flesh. His new body rose from those glorious flames, reinventing itself in a matter of seconds, seizing the reins of his destiny.

He looked down at the handcuffs still binding him. Flexed. The shackles fractured and burst, fell away.

Syd stepped from the shadows, and into full view.

Like Vic, he was fearsome, fangs bared in his massive, capacious jaws; but that was where all physical similarities ended. His form, like Jane's, was sleekly lupine, his pelt jet-black, silver-threaded; his features, like Jane's, were more wolf than monster. It was such a different manifestation of the Change that it took even Syd by surprise. Vic, on the other hand, looked like he'd been lightly napalmed: mangy fur singed to blackness, polka-dotted with sores.

Vic squared off, at Syd's advance; and then suddenly, he smiled. It was a nasty grin, meant to destabilize Syd, but it was also completely sincere. Syd could see, in that moment, that Vic *loved* this shit. He lived for the kill. He was in it for the mayhem.

That was fine, to Syd's way of thinking. Right now, he was living for this shit, too. He threw the smile right back at Vic.

From there, it all happened with terrifying speed.

There was no hesitation, no snapping, no baiting. There was no one and nothing to hold them back. Vic dropped to all fours and launched himself forward. Syd matched him and met him halfway.

First blood was drawn in the very first second: Vic's jaws, clamping down on Syd's hunched shoulder blade. Syd smelled his own blood, and the pain was galvanizing. He went for Vic's throat.

Then Vic bit him again.

And this time was worse: at the base of the neck, the fangs sinking in deeper before tearing loose. Syd felt ganglia shred and moist fascia wrench free. The pain and terror were blinding. He yipped and lashed out, caught Vic's ear and removed it. Vic howled.

And then he bit him again.

And then he bit him again. And again. And again. Until Syd was streaming from a half-dozen holes, strength and confidence spurting red from the chinks in his armor. He had never fought as a wolf before; he didn't know dick, and it showed. Vic, on the other hand, was a consummate pro . . .

. . . and then suddenly, the old wolf appeared: strategically worrying Vic's flanks from behind, despite its age and smaller size. Vic turned on her, roaring and Syd seized the opportunity to tear a sputtering chunk his from neck.

And then Vic went wild, abandoning all caution, shaking her off and plowing face-first into Syd. Syd rolled onto his back, frantically brought up his legs to defend his exposed underbelly. His claws raked tracks across blistered tissue. Vic yowled and lurched forward, moving in for the kill.

There was a blur of motion, then: a gray streak, aimed right at Vic's throat. Mae came within an inch before he seized her by her open jaws: wrenching them wide, cracking them like a walnut. Gramma Mae shrieked as her skull bisected. Death was instantaneous.

But momentum lingered on.

And as Vic fell back, propelled by Mae's hurtling corpse, Syd threw himself desperately forward. Catching Vic's charbroiled belly momentarily exposed.

And burrowing deep inside it . . .

. . . and there was no death more intimate, no murder more complete, than devouring from within. To gnaw through the bowels of another—to feel oneself being eaten alive—was the essence of the dance at its most fundamental.

Syd buried his face in Vic's belly, ripping into the weakened flesh. Claws tore at his back. It didn't matter a bit. His razored fangs hacksawed straight up the abdominal cavity, slicing through innards and soft belly-sausage, until they found what they were looking for . . .

. . . until they locked on Vic's thundering heart . . .

. . . and it was hard to remove, to tear loose from its moorings. The muscle was strong. It held on. It fought back. Syd bit down and shook, ignoring his own pain, ignoring the great howl that welled up within . . .

. . . and this time, the black heart wrenched free, collapsing within his crushing jaws. Syd pulled it out, felt the hot gushing muscle deflate. The nature of Vic's tremors dramatically shifted, from desperate resistance to anticipation of death.

Syd withdrew his gore-drenched maw abruptly, the better to look Vic in the eye.

Then he spat out the heart, like the poison it was.

Vic stared at the heart, at the sputtering hole. Then his eyes rolled back, empty. He teetered. And fell. He was dead long before he stopped twitching, the soul outlasted by involuntary muscle response.

Syd remained standing, just long enough to make sure.

And then he was falling as well. . . .

48

THE WORLD WENT black, phased out, bled back again. Syd felt his physiology shift rearranging itself even as the bloodlust receded, like a red tide returning to the sea. The tide pulled at him, beckoning. Inviting him to join it, and sink into its peaceful, thoughtless depths.

A sound like distant thunder rumbled across its surface; a storm on the far horizon. Beneath it, all was black and still. Syd closed his eyes, panting, soaked in blood and sweat.

Dimly, he heard his name being called. When he next opened his eyes, he saw a flickering mirage with Jane's face on it. She was human, too, or nearly so. Or maybe he was dreaming.

He heard his name again, realized, no, this was real. He shook his head. When he looked again, he saw Jane: her features now clearly human, pale and trembling. She was crying, and trying to sit up.

Trying to get to him.

Syd moaned, pulled himself upright. As he did he saw Gramma Mae's body, lying on the floor. She had not reverted. Her back was to him, the pelt ragged and bloody.

A wave of sadness and regret washed over him. *I would like to have known you better.*

She died to save them, he knew. To save him and . . .

"Jane," he murmured, crawling through a haze of pain. She cried out in response. The old woman's words came back to haunt him.

Do you love her?

Yes, he knew. Yes. Unquestioningly. If he lived, he wanted to be with her. If he was to die, he would do it by her side. They were the most complex equations of which he was capable, just at the moment. Maybe later he could think of something else.

The last few feet were the hardest of all. He could see Jane's eyes now, though they swam in a fog of pain. He kept thinking about secrets, and trails left behind.

He closed his eyes, saw men with guns.

It could not be allowed.

As Syd made it to where Jane lay, he realized that the police would come eventually; the police always do. But when he thought of the toolshed out back, the little kerosene lamp and the big can that fed it, he knew that the firefighters would never make it here in time. And that even if they did, their trucks would never make it up that damned hill.

It guaranteed that the inferno on the mountain would be complete. That, once alight, the cabin would gladly take its mysteries with it.

That the secrets would remain secret.

It was a comforting thought, as he gazed into her eyes. There was a whole world out there that they could disappear into. In a little while, they'd rise, and do what they had to do.

But for the moment, at least, it was enough to reunite with his lover.

Holding each other, as best they could.

And licking each other's wounds.

ABOUT THE AUTHORS

Since 1986, best-selling authors JOHN SKIPP and CRAIG SPECTOR have seen over two million copies of their books in print, including six novels and two anthologies, with reprints in six languages worldwide. They've written four screenplays, including *A Nightmare on Elm Street 5: The Dream Child* and the screen play for *Animals*. They also wrote, performed and produced the soundtrack album for their 1991 ecological thriller, *The Bridge*.

Upcoming projects include a new novel, two new anthologies, several film and comics projects, and gigging and recording with their psychedelic r&b band, Blood Brothers. *Animals* is their ninth book.

They reside in Los Angeles.

A terrifying debut novel of life after the fall,
desire and Hunger after death,
and death in the wake of the Afterlife...

AFTERAGE
by
Yvonne Navarro

A plague of vampirism has swept the country, reducing once-thriving cities to ghost towns. In Chicago, a few scattered survivors hide behind the fortified walls of office buildings and museums, raiding deserted stores for dwindling supplies of food and clothing. Meanwhile, a hungry vampire population also struggles for survival as their prey grows scarce, forcing them to capture alive the last remaining humans as breeding stock for the blood farm that will ensure their future.

Now a small band of humans make a desperate last stand against their vampire masters, fighting back with the only weapon that can kill the dead....

JOHN SAUL

John Saul has produced one bestseller after another: masterful tales of terror and psychological suspense. Each of his works is as shocking, as intense and as stunningly real as those that preceded it.